"WHY DID YOU BLACKMAIL ME INTO MARRYING YOU?"

Frank sat absolutely still. Then he leaned back in his chair. "Because I wanted you. And I've learned to take what I want."

"No. You wouldn't have done that."

"You called me friend for three years and then accused me of being without principles. Now after a fortnight you think I have them?"

"Let's say I've learned to see ambiguities. Did you think you could protect me from my father, was that it?"

He stared at her for a moment. "Oh, God." He pushed himself to his feet. "Charlotte, don't. Don't turn me into a hero. Not now."

Before she realized she had made any sort of decision, she stood and crossed the carpet between them and put her hand on his shoulder.

A shock went through her. The next instant, Frank's arms were around her and his lips were against her hair. His mouth was soft, gentle, feather-light. She closed her eyes and choked back a sob. Surely she could surrender but still hang on to some core of herself without being swept free of the moorings of reason. She hesitated, hovering on the brink between need and fear, desire and the knowledge of what desire could bring.

Frank started to draw back. She put her hand behind his neck and pulled his head down to her own. . . .

HIGH PRAISE FOR TRACY GRANT'S PREVIOUS NOVELS

SHORES OF DESIRE

"A BEAUTIFUL, EVOCATIVE LOVE STORY with the sweeping power of an epic, told in the grand tradition of a Diana Gabaldon tale."
—Penelope Williamson, author of *The Outsider*

"FABULOUS . . . fast-paced and intriguing . . . *Shores of Desire* freshens up the genre with elements of suspense and a unique lead protagonist . . . all the characters add something special to this wonderful tale."
—*Affaire de Coeur*

"INGENIOUS . . . Tracy Grant couldn't have found a more exciting setting for her story, the period of Napoleon's imprisonment and escape. Passion simmers, but is held in check by loyalty, intrigue, and honor."
—*Rendezvous*

"RIVETING."
—*Publishers Weekly*

"Tracy Grant continues to rise to the top of the historical genre . . . [she] writes some of the best romance books around today . . . filled with intrigue, romance, and suspense."
—Harriet Klausner, *Painted Rock Reviews*

SHADOWS OF THE HEART

"WELL-WRITTEN AND FASCINATING,
Shadows of the Heart is compelling reading. From
page one you'll be hooked. This is the first of what
readers will hope is a long string of first-rate
historical novels from a new talent on the horizon."
—Kathe Robin, *Romantic Times*

"A STORY YOU WILL NEVER FORGET . . .
a moving portrayal of the redemptive,
healing power of love."
—Penelope Williamson

"A BRILLIANT HISTORICAL ROMANCE."
—Harriet Klausner, *Affaire de Coeur*

"Adding sexual tension to the fast-paced suspense
is Grant's skillful depiction of the growing
attraction between Sophie Rutledge and Paul
Lescaut."
—*Publishers Weekly*

Dell Books by Tracy Grant

Shadows of the Heart
Shores of Desire
Rightfully His

Tracy Grant

Rightfully His

A DELL BOOK

*This book is dedicated to four people who helped in
the creating of it:
For Doug, for the railways,
For Jim, for the political intrigue,
For Monica, for the "sting,"
And for Penny, for all the double crosses and for the
dark side of Frank's character.*

ACKNOWLEDGMENTS

In addition to the four people named in the dedication, a profound thank you to Christine Zika, for taking this book under her wing and showing me how to improve it, to Laura Cifelli, for first believing in the book, and to Angela Catalano, for nurturing it along the way. To Maggie Crawford, for the title. To Ruth Cohen, for always supporting me. To Madeleine Mills, for reading countless chapters, offering insightful feedback, and sharing research tidbits. And finally, thank you to Devlin Sevy, for being such a perfect model for Juliet Storbridge, and to Gemma and both Lescauts, for inspiring Millamant and Knightly.

Prologue

Edinburgh
September, 1817

The chill northern air seeped into the parlor and cut through the heat of the fire burning in the grate with the sharpness of an icicle. Despite the cold, sweat prickled Frank Storbridge's forehead and dampened his palms. There was an ache in his chest and throat that could only be called longing. Or desire.

He took a turn about the rose-trellis-papered room and stared at the scarred oak panels of the door. He wanted to fling it open and go tearing through the house looking for her. He wanted to pull her to him and say all the things that had been too long unsaid. But though he was light-headed with fear and urgency and lack of sleep, some vestiges of sense and propriety and the rules of a lifetime remained.

He straightened his coat, rumpled from eighteen hours' travel, pushed his tangled hair back from his face, ran his fingers over the stubble on his chin. Perhaps he should have taken the time to find an inn room to bathe and shave. But when he'd arrived in Edinburgh, all that mattered was seeing her as quickly as possible. He'd walked—run—straight to this house where she was staying in Old Fishmarket Close.

The door eased open, slowly, almost reluctantly. The

rose chintz curtains stirred. The girandole candlesticks tinkled in the draft. There was a rustle of fabric, a firm, light step, and she stood before him. Charlotte de Ribard. His employer's daughter, his best friend, the bright, particular star that had always been out of his reach.

"Hullo, Frank."

Her voice was strangely flat. It was only five days since he'd seen her, but she seemed to have aged five years. Her face was pale, the hollows beneath her cheeks deepened, the point of her chin painfully sharp. Her abundant, honey-brown hair, usually a riot of disorder, seemed limp and colorless. Worst of all, the brightness had been wiped from her brown eyes. Curse her father and that bastard who had been her betrothed.

"Charlie." He was at her side in an instant. It took all the willpower he possessed not to pull her into his arms. Instead, he seized both her hands, as he often had in the past.

She snatched her hands away and sprang back as though he had struck her. "What do you want, Frank?" Her voice was as cold as the wind that whipped through Edinburgh.

"I came as soon as I heard." He tried to warm her with his voice, since she wouldn't accept his touch. "I'm so sorry."

"Sorry for what? That my father and Ned are monsters without a scrap of decency or conscience? That Ned is dead? It's no more than he deserved. If justice had been done, *Papa* would be dead as well."

She moved to a faded tapestry settee and sat, back straight, hands folded tightly in her lap. She was wearing a plain, dark green gown that someone must have lent her. The skirt looked as if it had been hastily tacked up, and the bodice pulled across her chest. He forced his gaze away, but not before he had noticed the fullness beneath the fabric. He drew a steadying breath. "I'm sorry Ned Rutledge is dead, because it means I can't give him the thrashing he deserves. I never thought he was good enough for you."

She laughed, a dry, cracking sound, like the breaking of dead wood. "A blackguard for a blackguard's daughter. What match could be more appropriate?"

Her voice was as tight and pinched as her expression. He searched her face, seeking some way back to the girl he loved. The image of their first meeting was etched in his mind as clearly as the engraving of Paris that hung on the wall across from him. He had been in her father's study, being interviewed for the position of secretary. Fresh from Oxford, he'd had only one thought in his head—to secure the employment that was the key to all his future ambitions.

Then Charlotte had stepped into the dark, formal room, bringing lightness and sunshine. She had worn an apricot-colored dress and a smile that was just as warm. Frank had never considered himself a romantic, but her smile had pierced his heart. There was no other way to describe it. At that moment Daniel de Ribard could have been an humble country squire and Frank would have gone to work for him just to be near her.

Now her mouth was folded into a tight line, the corners turned down as though to suppress any spurt of feeling. He was used to seeing her mouth curved with laughter. Once he had felt it warm and pliant beneath his own. The memory of their single kiss was so vivid he could still feel the texture of her lips and taste the sweet heat of her response.

But that kiss was not to be spoken of, for at the time it happened her hand and heart had been promised to Ned Rutledge. Perhaps that was the problem now. Though they had both scrupulously avoided mentioning the kiss, it had cast a shadow over the ease of their friendship. "Rutledge didn't deserve you," Frank said, keeping his voice even, "but I know how much you loved him."

Charlotte stared down at her hands. "I thought I knew him."

Those five words contained a world of pain. Frank had cause to know the world was not a pretty place, but she was too young, at one-and-twenty, to have the veils ripped from her eyes. "I never liked Rutledge," he said. "But even I never guessed what he was capable of." Nor had the people of Lancaster, where Ned owned a cotton mill and the Rutledge family had been powerful for two generations. Five days ago rumors had swept the city that Ned Rutledge and Daniel de Ribard had been up to their necks in lies and swindles and attempted murder. The news had been like tinder to the Lancaster millworkers already suffering economic privation. The city had been engulfed by rioting.

"I was there," Charlotte said, as though her thoughts were following a similar path. "I'd gone into Lancaster to get Ned to tell me the truth. I was in his house when the mob broke in."

She must have seen him killed. She must have seen her betrothed's fair head bashed in with a club. And while she had gone through that hell, Frank had been miles away. Self-reproach twisted his guts, but he kept his voice gentle. "Charlie—"

"Paul Lescaut saved me," Charlotte went on. "He got me and my cousin Sophie out of Ned's house and out of Lancaster and brought us here to his family in Edinburgh."

"Thank God for it," Frank said. Paul Lescaut was Charlotte's half-brother, her father's bastard son. Frank liked and admired Lescaut, but he was aware of a distinct wish that he himself could have played a part in the rescuing. "How is your cousin?" he asked.

"Remarkably well, considering *Papa* and Ned did their best to have her murdered." Charlotte's fingers clenched, the nails pressing into her palms. "*Papa*'s own niece. His ward. He always treated Sophie like one of his daughters."

Frank kept his hands clamped at his sides to suppress the urge to touch her. "I'm sure he—"

"Sure he what?" Charlotte's voice cut like glass. The words spilled out as though she were lashing herself with the truth. "The facts are plain enough. *Papa* stole Sophie's inheritance and used it to build his own fortune. Then, when Sophie grew up and started asking questions, he decided it wasn't safe to let her live. He inveigled Ned into helping him. After all, Ned was going to marry me. He had an interest in preserving the Ribard fortune. He and *Papa* plotted Sophie's murder as cold-bloodedly as any fox hunt. Only a fox is at least given a sporting chance."

Frank moved to a straight-backed chair covered in sturdy black fabric. "How long do you and Sophie plan to stay with the Lescauts?"

For a moment Charlotte's face lightened. "Sophie's going to stay permanently. She's to marry Paul."

Frank sat back in his chair. On the surface it was odd to think of Charlotte's elegant, worldly cousin Sophie married to the radical journalist Paul Lescaut. But Lescaut had saved Sophie from the machinations of Daniel de Ribard and Ned Rutledge. Danger must have drawn them together. "I'm glad," he said. "Sophie deserves all the happiness she can find. Lescaut seems a very decent sort despite the abrasive exterior."

Charlotte gave a half smile that held an echo of the girl she used to be. "I always wanted a brother." Her eyes darkened. "And *Papa* always wanted a son. But that didn't stop him from trying to kill Paul too. I suppose he would have been as quick to get rid of me if I'd been in his way."

"No." Frank again remembered the first time he'd seen Charlotte. Daniel de Ribard had looked up at his daughter, and for a moment his cool, controlled face had been transformed. "Ribard loves you, Charlie. I'd stake my life on it. I think you're the one person he does love."

"I doubt he's capable of loving anyone."

Frank leaned forward. His fingers ached to smooth the lines from around her eyes and mouth. "He's planning to pay a visit to his plantation in Jamaica. He admits nothing."

"Of course. It would take more than scandal to bring *Papa* down. He can occupy himself with his foreign investments for years." Charlotte adjusted the folds of her gown, as though she regretted having spoken so freely and was armoring herself to hold back further revelations.

Frank crossed his legs, aware that this next would not be easy. He stared down at the travel-stained toes of his Hessians. "Ribard wants to make some provision for you before he leaves the country," he said at last.

Her head jerked up. Her eyes were as ice cold as her father's could be. "So he did send you after me. I thought as much."

Frank returned her gaze without flinching. "He asked me to see you, yes. If he hadn't, I'd have come anyway. I'm leaving his employ."

"I don't want his money."

"Ribard thought as much. He isn't offering you money. He wants to sign Chelmsford over to you."

He could tell from her face that this took her by surprise. Chelmsford, in Lancashire, was one of her father's smaller estates. Frank had accompanied Ribard and Charlotte on visits there more than once. He had vivid memories of riding out with Charlotte to visit the tenants, most of whom she had known by name since childhood. "I'm sure the tenants would prefer for you to have the property than to be left to the mercies of Ribard's man of business," he said.

Charlotte's fingers twisted in the dark green fabric of her skirt. "You mean I can justify taking largesse from a murderer in the name of protecting others?"

"You can't expiate Ribard's sins by denying yourself, Charlie."

"Nothing can expiate his sins."

The silence in the room was thick and painful, like the coal smoke that hung over one of Daniel de Ribard's factories. "Will you go back to stay with your mother when Ribard leaves the country?" Frank asked.

"No." Charlotte's voice was firm. "*Maman* must know what *Papa*'s done, but she'll insist on putting a good face on it for the sake of appearances. I can't bear that."

"You'll stay with Sophie and Lescaut then?" It was too early to speak of the future, but his mind had been racing ahead from the moment he knew Charlotte was free.

"They've asked me to, though I'm sure they're longing to be alone together."

He could see it in her eyes now. The numbing pain and the cold, bitter anger cracked like a sheet of ice, revealing stark need. The need that came from being alone, cut off from the father she had adored and the man she had thought she would marry. The need that would have brought Frank to Edinburgh, regardless of Daniel de Ribard's instructions.

He was on his feet in an instant. The words tumbled from his lips without thought or planning. "Marry me, Charlie."

Her eyes went wide. For a moment she sat absolutely still, gripping the folds of her gown so tightly her knuckles turned white.

The blood pounded in Frank's head. His pulse was racing, but it hurt to draw a breath. He stood immobile, held by her gaze, locked in unbearable uncertainty.

"Marry you?" Charlotte pushed herself to her feet, slicing through the stillness in one swift motion. "Have you gone mad, Frank?"

She was only an arm's length away. He could reach out and pull her into his arms, as he had once before. She had responded to him then, for all she'd been betrothed to Ned Rutledge. He looked down into her dark eyes, seeking some spark of what had been between them. "It's too soon, I know. But I'd care for you, Charlie. You wouldn't be alone."

She moved down the length of the small room, her skirt whipping about her legs. "I'm not going to marry, Frank. Not now. Not ever."

"It's natural for you to feel that way, but in time—"

"No." She turned to face him, standing in front of the parlor windows. The cool sunlight brightened her hair but left her face in shadow. "What is it, Frank? Do you think because I kissed you once I'm ready to tumble into your arms?"

She had broken the barrier. She'd referred to the embrace they had both scrupulously avoided mentioning in the month since it happened. The memory pulsated in the air between them, redolent with unspoken words and unexpressed longings. For a moment they weren't in this unfamiliar parlor in Edinburgh; they were on a winding path on the grounds of her father's estate. The sun was warm, the air thick with the scent of roses, a thrush called from the beech coppice. He had relived every moment of it so often in memory. The way Charlotte had stumbled, the way he'd steadied her, the way he'd bent his head and taken her mouth, reason overwhelmed by need. The way her lips had parted with an urgency beyond all expectation.

"After what you've been through no one could expect you to want anything but a safe harbor." His voice was hoarse and strained, which wasn't surprising because he'd quite lost control of his breathing. He pushed his fingers into his hair. "Hell, I've made a thorough mull of this. Look, Charlie, when I asked you to marry me, I didn't mean . . . We could go on being friends, just as we've always been. There wouldn't have to be anything more. Not until you were ready."

She stared at him, the bones of her face sharpened by the shadows. "What makes you think I'll ever be ready? You shouldn't read too much into a kiss, Frank."

Her voice was cold, but the memory of the kiss was too warm and alive to be denied. He could smell the scent of her skin, vanilla and almond oil, pure and sweet and somehow potently erotic. He chose his words with care. "I'm not reading anything into it. It was a beautiful day and you looked beautiful and we both lost our heads. Such things happen. But you can't deny that there was something between us, if only a potential."

She drew a breath. For a moment he thought he'd got through to her. Her pulse quickened above the high braided collar of her gown. Her face flushed with color. Then she turned her head with deliberation, breaking eye contact. "I told you, I'm not going to marry. And even if I did . . . do you imagine I'd marry you?"

She might as well have pummeled him with her fists. He sucked in his breath. He had been prepared to find her hurt, angry, even bitter. But he had never thought to hear scorn in her voice. She had always been free of the family pride that was so marked in both her parents. "Turn me down if you must, Charlie," he said, "but you can find a better excuse than that. I know you've never cared a rush for such distinctions."

She stared straight into his eyes. "You were his secretary, Frank. You kept his accounts, you answered his correspondence. You knew his business better than any of us. How could you not have known what he was doing?"

"Christ." Shock made his voice rough and his language violent. "Do you think I'd have stayed in that house an hour if I'd had any glimmering of the truth? Do you think I'd have kept silent?"

"I don't know." Her voice was cold and even, deadened to feeling. "I don't trust my judgment of anyone anymore."

"You *know* me, Charlie. Whatever else we've been, we've been friends—"

"Less than three years. I've known *Papa* all my life. I'd known Ned since we were children."

"On my word of honor, Charlie—"

"Honor?" She gave a laugh that was like the grating of a knife on a rock. "Honor is a sugar syrup that makes lies go down more easily."

He dragged his fingers through his hair. He wanted to shake her, to break through this wall of cynicism. "Damn it, Charlotte—"

"You've always been ambitious, Frank. You've made no secret of it. You told me often enough that you disagreed with *Papa*'s politics, yet you continued to work for him. It sickened you to write to the plantation in Jamaica, but you did it just the same. A penniless clergyman's son needs powerful friends if he's to have a hope of standing for Parliament. Isn't that how you put it?"

He drew a breath. "Near enough. But it's a long way from ambition to criminality."

"Not so very far." The accusation in her gaze held him

rooted to the spot. "Can you honestly claim you knew nothing?"

The denial should have been automatic. Instead, the words turned to ash in his mouth. Had he known Daniel de Ribard plotted murder? No. Had he seen anything in writing that even hinted at his employer's schemes? Certainly not. But had there been clues to the truth that he'd ignored, moments when he'd glanced the other way because it suited him to do so? "If I'd had any proof—"

"But you had suspicions. And you overlooked them."

He swallowed. There was a rank taste in his throat. "If I did, I'll regret it for the rest of my life."

"I doubt it. I expect you'll soon find another powerful man to work for. You'll be in Parliament yet." She regarded him for a moment. "I've known it from the first, you see. I used to admire you for it."

"Known what?"

"That you and *Papa* are cut from the same cloth."

Her words slashed deep, laying bare a part of him he didn't want to look at. Something inside him turned as dry and cold as the look in Charlotte's eyes. "I see." His fingers had gone numb, but his hands were strangely steady as he reached inside his coat and drew out a sheaf of papers. "The Chelmsford documents. I think you'll find they're self-explanatory, but if you have any questions you can contact Ribard's solicitors." He picked up his hat from the sofa table. "I'll see myself out."

Mercifully the narrow entrance hall was empty. He went down the stairs two at a time and strode out into the bustle of Old Fishmarket Close. Hawkers' cries and snatches of argument and the clop of horse hooves split the air, but it was Charlotte's words that echoed in his ears, bombarding him with his folly. She was right. It was ambition that had driven him to seek employment with

Daniel de Ribard. There was no hope of accomplishing any good in the world without power. He had learned that watching his own father struggle to aid his parishioners.

He had known his purpose that first morning in Daniel de Ribard's study. Then Charlotte had stepped into the room, and laughing brown eyes and a lopsided smile had made him yearn for something more.

The northerly wind whipped up, cold and biting, propelling him down the street. He turned up the collar of his coat. He had been mad to come here, mad to follow the impulses of his heart. But he would not make such a mistake again.

Charlotte had pointed him back in the right direction. She had accused him of caring for nothing but his own ambitions. Very well. He would show her exactly how right she was.

Chapter 1

London
December, 1822

Céline, Viscountess Silverton, swung her feet from the blue velvet chaise longue to the gold and cream Savonnerie carpet with a firm thud. "You can't go on like this, Charlotte. You're going to turn into an old maid."

"I'm six-and-twenty, Céline. I've been an old maid for years." Charlotte set down the scissors and studied the paperboard figure she'd just finished cutting out. "Shall I give Roger the knight on the black horse, or do you think Charles would like it better?"

"I haven't the least idea." There was a rustle of silk as Céline twitched the skirt of her peignoir into place. "It's not funny, Charlie. You go about mothering everyone else's children, including mine, when you ought to be raising some of your own."

Charlotte picked up another figure of a knight, this one on a cream-colored mount. "I was going to give the one with the black horse to Roger, because you know how he likes villains, but this other one has the most wonderfully fierce-looking face—"

"Bother the horses."

Charlotte looked up at her sister.

"Yes, yes, I know." Céline waved a hand, catching the cool afternoon light with her sapphire ring. "They're my children and you think I'm a hopeless mother and you're probably right, but honestly, Charlie, at the moment I'm more concerned about you. Now that *Maman*'s gone—"

Charlotte's back stiffened. "*Maman* being dead doesn't change anything. She gave up on me ages ago. I'd seen her only a half dozen times in the last years."

"Well, someone has to take an interest in your future." Céline pushed herself to her feet and crossed the boudoir, her turquoise silk skirts and golden hair swinging with her determination. "I thought I could rely on Sophie to do it, but she's lost all sense of proportion since she married that disreputable journalist and went to live in Edinburgh. In Old Fishmarket Close, for God's sake."

"Paul's our brother, Céline. He may have been born on the wrong side of the blanket, but that doesn't change the biology."

"Oh, heavens, one meets bastards in the first circles every day. But Paul's not—"

"Respectable?"

"I'm as grateful to him as anyone for saving Sophie's life, but she didn't have to go and *marry* him. The last time I saw her she actually had ink on her nails." Céline paused in front of the windows and peered at her own well-groomed hands.

"Actually, Sophie fusses about me just as much as you do." Charlotte put the knight on the cream-colored horse in the box she was preparing for Roger and the one on the black horse in Charles's box. "Though I think perhaps she's finally begun to give up. It's been months since she's had Paul dredge up an unattached man to invite to dinner."

"Good God, I should hope so. I wouldn't want to see you married to a journalist."

"You aren't going to see me married to anyone. There." Charlotte sat back and brushed a stray bit of paper from her bombazine skirt. "These are all ready to give to the boys at Christmas. You won't forget, will you?"

"I'm not as bad as that." Céline glanced over at her. "I do wish you'd stay and spend the holidays with us."

"I'll miss all of you, but Edinburgh's home."

"Oh, Charlie." Céline crossed the room and dropped down on the sofa. "I know how dreadful it's been for you." She put her arms around Charlotte, enveloping her in the scent of tuberose and jasmine. "Ned was a perfect beast, and I'd like to throttle him—that is, I would if he were still alive—but you can't go on like this forever."

Charlotte pulled away from her sister's embrace before Céline could notice she was trembling. She rubbed her hands together. After more than five years the mere mention of Ned's name made her want to get up and wash them.

Céline didn't try to touch her again, but Charlotte could feel her sister's anxious gaze upon her. "It's worse for you, of course, Charlie. But I hated it too. I still can't bear to think of what *Papa* tried to do to Sophie. For years I was convinced people were whispering behind my back whenever I went into company. But the talk's begun to die down. No scandal lasts forever, even in London. Especially in London." She was silent for a moment. "It's odd. There are times when I can't quite picture *Papa's* face."

"I can." Charlotte got to her feet. She saw echoes of her father's face every morning when she looked into her own glass. She moved across the room and adjusted one of the fringed silk curtains. Sometimes, when the past threatened to suffocate her, it helped to keep moving.

Behind her, she heard Céline fluffing the sofa cushions. "I saw Francis Storbridge the other night," Céline said. "At Covent Garden, the evening you stayed home because of Roger's cold. I think Francis is the one person to have done well for himself out of the whole debacle. I doubt he'd have achieved so much if he'd gone on working for *Papa*."

Charlotte ran her fingers down the cold, ice-blue silk of the curtain. "I think Frank would have done well for himself whatever happened."

"You knew him better than I did. I must say it was very clever of him to marry Lord Vaughan's daughter. I can't see *Papa* having given him permission to marry any of us."

Charlotte's nail snagged on the curtain fringe. She jerked her hand back.

"I know his birth was good enough," Céline continued, "but it was nothing exceptional, and his father was a younger son with no fortune. Not the match one would expect for an earl's daughter. Of course, Julia Vaughan gave birth to his daughter seven months after the marriage."

"So I've heard." Charlotte broke off her torn nail. "It happens in the best of families."

"Some people say he set the whole thing up—seduced the daughter, forced the father to consent to the marriage and get him into Parliament." Céline's voice took on its familiar brittle quality as she moved from the painful past to the more comfortable topic of scandal. "Francis Storbridge always was indecently attractive. One can't blame him for making use of his assets."

"I always knew he'd end up in Parliament, one way or another." Charlotte turned from the windows and began to tidy a stack of periodicals on a pier table. It was odd how the thought of Frank still hurt, almost as much as thinking about Ned and her father. More in a way. She never got this lump in her throat when she thought about them.

For a moment a welter of memories clouded her vision. Facing Frank across a chessboard by the mellow light of the library fire. Walking along the stream bank with him, leaves crunching underfoot, sharing confidences. Standing locked in his arms, her mouth parted beneath his, his hands moving over her body.

"They say he hasn't been without a mistress since his wife died," Céline said. "And before that, I shouldn't wonder. The latest *on-dit* is that he's having an affair with Ianthe de Cazes. He was sharing her box at Covent Garden and they left as soon as the curtain came down. And to think only a few months ago Ianthe's name was being linked with my husband's."

Charlotte looked at her sister, wondering if Céline's voice was a little sharper than usual or if she was imagining it. "Céline—"

"Oh, don't look so serious, Charlie. I've hardly been a model of fidelity myself. So long as we don't embarrass each other, Silverton and I rub along very well." Céline stretched her legs out on the sofa with studied unconcern. "But I can't help but wonder if Francis Storbridge went after Ianthe to annoy Silverton. Do you think he's the sort who'd try to steal the mistress of his political rival?"

Charlotte looked down at the periodicals. The greens and yellows of the pelisse on the cover of *La Belle Assemblée* blurred before her eyes. "I can't say what Frank might be capable of doing."

"He's turned into a very interesting man. It's a pity he and Silver are so at odds. I can hardly invite my husband's main foe in the Opposition to dinner. Otherwise, I could pair him off with you. You could do worse, Charlie."

"No." The word burst from Charlotte's lips, echoing off the Chinese wallpaper.

Céline raised her brows. "I was only funning. I don't really want you to marry a Whig. Sophie's brought enough radicalism into the family as it is."

"Céline." The boudoir door burst open. Silverton strode into the room, his riding gloves and crop clutched in one hand, his fair hair plastered to his forehead, his face flushed as if he'd run up the stairs. He cast a quick glance around the room and gave Charlotte a careless nod. "Your maid isn't within earshot, is she, Céline?"

Céline pushed herself up on the sofa. "I think she's taking tea with the housekeeper, but why on earth does it matter?"

"Because we're in the devil of a pickle, and I'd as soon not have the servants gossiping until we've decided how to handle it." He took a turn about the room. "Christ, I still can't believe he's done it."

"Who? Done what?" Céline asked.

"Silverton." Charlotte took her brother-in-law by the arm and drew him to a chair. "What's happened?"

Silverton drew a breath and mopped his brow with his York tan gloves. "I ran into Litchfield in the park. He told me. He saw him last night, so there's no doubt it's true."

"Saw whom?" Céline demanded.

Charlotte put her hand to her abdomen, ill with suspicion.

Silverton looked from Céline to Charlotte, his boyish features set in grim lines. "Your father. He's come back to England."

"Daniel de Ribard is back in England?" Francis Storbridge—whom few people called Frank anymore—pushed himself up against the damask-covered headboard. The languorous aftermath of lovemaking was gone. His pulse quickened in a way that had nothing to do with desire.

"That's what Sally Litchfield told me when she called at an unconscionably early hour this morning." Ianthe reached for a cashmere shawl that was draped over the nightstand and wrapped it about her bare shoulders.

"And you waited until now to tell me?"

"Darling." She touched her fingers to his lips. "We were otherwise engaged."

Her skin smelled of cool lilies and the musky aroma of sex. Frank reached up to caress her hand, but his mind was elsewhere. "Has anyone actually seen Ribard?"

"That's the whole point." There was a slither of silk as Ianthe sank back against the pillows. "Sally saw Ribard leaving Henry's house in St. James when she was driving home from Drury Lane last night. So she rushed over to tell me this morning before I'd even finished my chocolate, let alone had my hair dressed."

Frank swung his head around to look at her. "Ribard was at your brother's house?"

"So Sally insists."

"What was he doing there?"

"How on earth should I know? I make it a point to stay as far away from Henry as possible. His house fairly reeks of commerce."

"He's your brother."

Ianthe made a moue of distaste. "I had to marry a Brazilian count to cleanse myself of the taint of trade. I'd hardly risk reexposure now."

"You must have some idea of what Ribard might want with him."

"No one knows what Ribard wants with anyone." Ianthe twirled a strand of sable-colored hair around her finger. "That's what makes it so interesting."

"After five years." Frank stared up at the tented canopy as though he could see the workings of Daniel de Ribard's brain in the violet and white stripes. "Why now?"

"Francis." Ianthe sat up. The cashmere shawl slipped down, revealing one bare breast. "It's a delicious piece of gossip, but I didn't expect you to take it so seriously. It's not as if he's the first man to come back to England after being exiled by scandal."

"Ribard did more than run off with someone's wife or kill someone in a duel." Frank picked his shirt up from the floor where he'd dropped it, shrugged it on, and began to pace around the room. "I know Daniel de Ribard. He's—" He stopped before a tasteful landscape by Turner and sought words to describe his former employer. *Evil? Conscienceless? Amoral?* All of those, and yet the words seemed at once too melodramatic and too easy. "If he's come back it's because he thinks he can reestablish himself."

"That's plain enough." Ianthe lounged on the bed, half-covered by the shawl, watching him. "Ribard was never legally charged with a crime. Scandal dies down eventually."

"Especially when one has money. Ribard still has a fortune." Frank realized his hands had curled into fists. He forced himself to relax them.

"His wife died last year, didn't she? Perhaps he means to marry again."

"Christ."

Ianthe raised her elegantly arched brows. "Disagreeable for the girl in question, perhaps, but hardly your problem. You were his secretary, not his son. Or his accomplice."

Was there the faintest lilt of question in her voice, or were his own demons making him imagine it? Frank stared at a patch of sunlight streaming through the gauzy subcurtains. "I didn't know what he was doing, but I should have. I should have guessed."

"Regrets?" There was surprise and a tinge of amusement in Ianthe's voice. "I thought you didn't believe in them."

An image rose up before Frank's eyes. Sun-kissed, tousled brown hair, vivid brown eyes, a warm, generous mouth. And then another image of the same face, wiped of life and color. He leaned against the mantel, forcing himself into a deliberate pose of unconcern. "Daniel de Ribard has a way of making people act against their natural instincts."

"I'm getting more and more curious to meet him." Ianthe gave a catlike stretch. "He sounds much more interesting than the typical English gentleman."

"He's neither a gentleman nor English."

"That's right." She made a lazy circle with her foot. "He's a Frenchman, isn't he? He came to England after the Revolution?"

Frank sometimes forgot that though his mistress had been a widow for over a year, she was only twenty-three. Seven years younger than himself. Three years younger than Charlotte. Ianthe had still been in the schoolroom at the time of the scandal. And then she had spent the last four years in Brazil, until her husband's death sent her home a wealthy widow.

"Ribard came to England during the Reign of Terror," he said. "He was involved in a plot to assassinate Robespierre. But he struck a deal with the government and betrayed his confederates. Two of them were guillotined. The third committed suicide. He was Ribard's own brother-in-law."

"Not one to let scruples stand in his way, is he?"

"That's putting it mildly. Ribard pocketed his brother-in-law's fortune and made it look as if it had been confiscated by the French government. It worked very tidily until the war ended and communication opened up with France. His niece started making uncomfortable inquiries about her inheritance. Ribard tried to have her killed and very nearly succeeded."

"He should have realized she'd grow up one day and make things difficult. If he'd been really clever, he'd have got rid of her when she was a child."

She sounded as if she were discussing the plot of the latest novel. Frank studied her, stretched out on the rumpled counterpane, wearing nothing but the shawl and a pair of emerald earrings. It occurred to him that though they had been lovers for nearly a month, he didn't really know her. At least not in any but the carnal sense.

Ianthe brushed her hair back from her shoulder. "It's bound to be awkward for Silverton. He can't very well cut his own father-in-law. Poor boy."

There was more mischief in her smile than sympathy. "Are you this cavalier about all your former lovers?" Frank asked.

Ianthe laughed, a smooth, rippling sound like the touch of her fingers. "*I* most certainly don't believe in regrets. Silverton was amusing enough, but nothing compared to you."

"I'd be flattered, if I didn't think you'd be speaking of me in precisely the same way three months from now."

"Oh, my dear." Her eyes gleamed like fine jade. "You should allow us six months at least." She shifted her position on the bed. "I would think you'd be glad of anything that made problems for Silverton. If you speak on slavery in the new session, the government's bound to choose him to oppose you."

"I don't need Daniel de Ribard to defeat Silverton."

"Of course not. I believe you could do anything if you put your mind to it." She stretched out her hand. "Do come back to bed. I was growing intrigued with Daniel de Ribard, but I shall be thoroughly cross if you let him spoil the afternoon."

Frank crossed the room, seized her hand, and brought

it to his lips. The image of a bright smile tugged at the recesses of his mind. He collapsed on the bed, pressing Ianthe's body beneath his own.

"Such ardor." Ianthe pulled back from his kiss, at once laughing and breathless. "Anyone who says you're cold obviously hasn't been to bed with you, Francis."

Frank buried his face in her hair and set his fingers to work disentangling the shawl. "Last I checked, that still applied to at least half of London."

"The Marquis de Ribard was one of a party in Henry Sunderland's box at Drury Lane last night. Ribard may not have achieved acceptance among the haut ton, *but in Sunderland's case, money apparently speaks to money."* Céline flung her copy of the *Morning Post* down amid the celadon-green breakfast dishes. "He's been out every night since he arrived in London. At Vauxhall, at Covent Garden, even at the Harrowgates' rout. It's only a matter of time before we run into him."

"When he wants to see us, he'll make sure he does." Charlotte took a sip of coffee. Strong and bitter. It suited her mood.

Céline shot her a quick, speculative look. "He'll want to see you. You were always his favorite."

Charlotte set down the cup and looked at her sister. "Did you mind?"

"Not most of the time. Not at all, really." Céline wrinkled her straight nose. "Not if being his favorite meant learning about investments and estate improvements and tenant problems." She toyed with a piece of toast and marmalade. "Do you mind?"

"That I was his favorite?" Charlotte stared at the steaming dark liquid in her cup. "Yes."

"That it didn't turn out as we expected. It was all going to be yours. Oh, I know he provided for the rest of us, but you were to have the estates and the investments. I wonder what he'll do with them now."

"I couldn't care less." Charlotte picked up her cup and pressed it against her forehead, wishing the heat could drive out the thought of her father. Sometimes she hated herself for having taken even a penny from him. But if she hadn't, she would be wholly dependent on Sophie and Paul. Chelmsford assured her of an independent income.

"Oh, good." Céline glanced up as the breakfast parlor door opened to admit Michael, the second footman. "I'm famished for another pot of chocolate."

The footman coughed and glanced from side to side. Charlotte came to his rescue. "It's Michael, not Stephen. Stephen was waiting at table this morning. Michael's on duty in the hall. What is it, Michael? Has someone called?"

"Ah . . . yes, Miss Charlotte." Michael hesitated. His face was pale against the dark blue of his livery.

Charlotte's insides twisted, exactly as they had the afternoon Silverton burst into Céline's boudoir. She knew. She had been expecting this moment for four days. "He's here," she told Céline.

"He? Who?" Céline set down her toast. "Oh, merciful heavens."

Michael cleared his throat. "The Marquis de Ribard is in the hall, my lady. Are you at home?"

"Yes. No. Oh, poison." Céline threw her napkin on the table.

"Show him up, Michael," Charlotte said.

"Are you mad, Charlie?" Céline said when the footman had withdrawn.

"If we have to face him, we'd best get it over with." Charlotte forced a sip of coffee down her tight throat. "Would you rather receive him now or confront him in public, where you'd be afraid to speak your mind?"

Céline slumped back in her chair. "You're right as usual." She straightened up, patted her loosely dressed hair, and glanced about the room. "I really should have had him shown into one of the salons."

"No." Charlotte looked with satisfaction at the toast crumbs and bits of congealed egg. "This is just the place to receive him." She could feel her hair slipping down her neck. She was tempted to tuck it into place, but she'd be damned if she'd make any concessions to his arrival. The blood was pounding in her head, and her stomach was tangled into knots.

The door opened. Michael stepped back into the room. "The Marquis de Ribard."

Charlotte straightened her back and pressed her hands together under the table, where he wouldn't be able to see if they trembled.

His footsteps were the same, firm and measured. The sound smashed through the defenses she'd built in the past five years. There was a roaring in her ears. Her throat was choked with an emotion that might have been rage or fear or loathing. Or loss.

All of a sudden he was in the room. The moment she had dreaded for five years went from nightmare to reality. He seemed to fill the doorway, his presence invading the airy, white-painted breakfast parlor. His skin had darkened, as if he'd spent most of the past five years in the sun. There was more gray in his chestnut hair than she remembered. But his dark, deep-set eyes were the same. She knew that, because they were the twin of her own.

The door clicked quietly as Michael withdrew. Daniel

de Ribard looked from Céline to Charlotte, his gaze cool and appraising. "You're looking well, both of you. Thank you for agreeing to see me."

Céline lifted her chin. "Did you think we wouldn't?"

He smiled, a disarming, loathsome smile. "I had my doubts. May I?" He drew out a chair and seated himself without waiting for a reply.

Céline glanced from her father to the breakfast things, as if unsure how far the rules of civility applied. "Would you like anything? Coffee?"

"Thank you."

Céline filled a cup and handed it to him, her movements unusually jerky. Beneath the table, Charlotte's nails dug into her palms.

Daniel sipped the coffee, as easy and unruffled as she remembered. "I trust Silverton is well. And the children."

"If your sources of information are anything like they used to be, you already know everything there is to know about us," Charlotte said.

"Sharp as ever, Charlie." He met her gaze for a moment. She wouldn't let herself look away. "I was sorry to hear about your mother."

"Spare us," Charlotte said.

"And your sisters? Are they well?"

Céline picked up her empty cup of chocolate, then set it down. "Georgine's in the country, and Marie-Louise and her husband are at the Hague. He's attached to the British Embassy."

"And Sophie is in Edinburgh with Paul," Charlotte said.

"Yes, so I heard." Daniel settled back in his chair. "An unlikely pairing, but apparently it's working."

"They have a second child. You're a grandfather again."

"I'm glad to hear it."

He sounded as if he meant it. Charlotte wanted to hit him. "What do you want with us, Daniel?"

He raised his brows. "When did I become 'Daniel'?"

She looked him straight in the eye. "When you stopped being my father."

"I see. Well, I've been called worse." He set his cup down with a firm click. "If we're going to be blunt, I'll come to the point. I'd like to speak to you alone, Charlotte. If you'll excuse us, Céline."

Céline looked at Charlotte. "Can you name one reason why I should agree?" Charlotte demanded.

He smiled. "None."

She wanted to refuse. She wanted to dash hot coffee in his face and wipe away that self-assured expression. But even more she wanted to know why he had come back to England. "It's all right, Céline," she said. "I'm sure you have more important things to do."

Céline hesitated a moment, then got to her feet, looking at once relieved to escape and curious about what was to follow. "I'll be in my sitting room if you need me, Charlie." She glanced at Daniel. "Good day—" She stopped abruptly, his name dangling in the air.

Daniel moved to open the door for her. "You'd best call me Daniel as well. We're none of us hypocrites. My regards to Silverton, Céline. And to the children."

Céline paused on the threshold for a moment, uncertainty flickering in her eyes. Then she left the room, her vandyked sarcenet skirts rustling with her haste.

Charlotte remained where she was, willing her breathing to be steady. Her palms smarted where her nails had broken the skin.

Daniel moved back to the table and seated himself with leisurely grace. They'd often shared breakfast like this, just the two of them, while her mother and sisters were sleeping late. It had been one of her favorite times of the day.

Her stomach cramped. For a moment she thought she was going to vomit. She stared at him, blocking off the past. "I'll give you five minutes. What are you doing in England, Daniel?"

Chapter 2

Daniel leaned back in his chair and crossed one leg over the other. "You've grown up, Charlie."

"It's been five years."

"So it has." He added fresh coffee to his cup and blew on the steam, as though he were dispersing a cloud of memory. "Would you believe me if I said I missed you?"

"I wouldn't believe anything you said to me."

"Ah. Fair enough." He added milk to the coffee and stirred it with careful precision. "How much longer are you staying in London?"

"Until Wednesday."

"You're going straight to Edinburgh?"

"I'm stopping at Chelmsford for a few days first." Charlotte continued to watch him. She remembered his eyes being warmer. A trick of memory? Or was she only now seeing him as he had always appeared to others?

Daniel sipped his coffee. "You still make your home with Sophie and Paul?"

"They're my family." She made the words as clear and sharp as rifle shots.

Her attack made no discernible dent in his armor. "How much time do you spend at Chelmsford?" he asked.

"I visit several times a year. Sophie and Paul bring the

children in the summers. It's not being neglected," she added, and then wished she hadn't. She didn't need to justify herself to him.

"I didn't mean to imply that it was."

The ormolu clock on the mantel chimed the quarter hour. His five minutes had passed, and she was no closer to having an answer to her question. The uncertainty about where the interview was headed drew her nerves taut as a bowstring. Which must have been exactly what Daniel intended.

She forced her spine to stiffen. "Your time is up. What do you want, Daniel?"

"What I lost." The words were light, almost mocking, but the opaque assurance in his gaze wavered. She could have sworn she caught a glimpse of pain. Another trick. He played people like a pianoforte.

"You want to restore your reputation?" She forced a harsh laugh from her lips. "You can hardly expect help from me."

"I don't need help from anyone."

"Then what do you want?"

He set down the coffee cup and spread his hands palm down on the table, as though laying claim to it. "I want Chelmsford, Charlie. Will you sell it to me?"

For a moment she was sure she hadn't heard him aright. "You want what?" She laughed again, with mirthless incredulity. "Do you seriously imagine I'd agree?"

"Why not?" He took a muffin from a silver warming dish and broke it neatly in half. "You've just admitted you spend less than a quarter of the year there. I'd give you a good price for the place. You could invest the money in the funds and get a far better return on it. A handsome inheritance for your children."

"I'm not going to have children."

He raised his brows. "A pity."

"It's my decision."

His eyes softened. "All men aren't like Ned, you know, Charlie. Or like me."

The look in his eyes was as dangerous as it was deceptive. She lashed out to defend herself. "Why would I want to give birth to your grandchildren?"

This time she saw her blow register in his eyes. "A palpable hit. I hadn't realized—But that's neither here nor there at the moment." He picked up the butter knife. "Settle the money on those nieces and nephews you're so fond of, then. Or start a school or endow an orphanage if it eases your conscience."

"There's no burden on my conscience," she said, a shade too quickly.

"I'm glad to hear it." He looked up from spreading butter on the muffin. "Well, Charlie? I'll give you ten thousand for the estate."

She folded her arms across her chest. "If you think money is the only variable, you aren't as clever as I always thought."

"Ah, yes. Your tenants." He bit into the buttered muffin. "But are they really best served by an absentee lady of the manor?"

Charlotte pushed her chair back from the table. "Why do you want Chelmsford? You always complained it was one of your poorer investments. You signed it over to me easily enough five years ago."

Daniel continued to eat the muffin without dropping any crumbs on the immaculate linen of his cravat or the smooth biscuit superfine of his coat.

Charlotte subdued the urge to empty Céline's Sèvres coffeepot over his head. "You've been back in England five days. You want to restore your reputation—a Herculean task, even for you. Chelmsford should be the last thing on your mind."

She got to her feet and paced across the carpet, doing sums in her head. "It'll be ten or twelve years before you can realize any return on ten thousand pounds. If then. That's not like you."

"As quick at figures as ever." His voice held the same note of approval as it had when she showed him her schoolroom slate.

Charlotte continued pacing, piecing together fragments of news gleaned from Céline and Silverton, bits of gossip from the paper. One name, she realized, stood out among those with whom Daniel had been seen since his return to England.

She stopped her pacing and turned to look at him. "The first night you were back in London you dined at Henry Sunderland's. You were in his box at Drury Lane last night."

"Sunderland's an old friend."

"Please, Daniel. I'm no longer twenty. You had business dealings with him, but he was never your friend. He was too much on the fringes of society. What do you hope to get from him? What does he hope to get from you?"

There was no reply. She didn't really expect one. She stared out the window at the linden tree that Roger and Charles loved to climb. She didn't know Henry Sunderland well. He'd made a fortune in drapery, enough to buy him a certain amount of influence but not invitations to the best houses. Still, Céline and Silverton dined with him occasionally. She'd accompanied them once. A dull evening. Sunderland had gone on all through dinner about—

"Railways." Charlotte spun around to look at Daniel. "Henry Sunderland has a passion for railways. He wanted to invest in the Stockton and Darlington, but the other investors kept him out. It's common knowledge that he's looking for another railway to invest in."

"You'd know better than I," Daniel said without looking up. "I've been out of the country, remember?"

"That's it, isn't it?" Charlotte crossed back to the table. "That's what you're planning." She rested her hands on the table and leaned toward him. "You want to build a railway in Lancashire. A railway that runs across your land. And Sunderland's. He owns property in Lancashire as well."

"Clever girl, Charlie." Daniel shook out a napkin and wiped the crumbs from his hands with fastidious care.

"And you want Chelmsford because it would give you a nice smooth stretch of land from Lancaster to Liverpool to make a profit from. Well, it will be a cold day in hell before you get it."

Daniel looked up and met her gaze. She caught a whiff of his shaving soap, a citrus scent that had once wrapped her in comfort and now made her breakfast rise up in her throat. "Why so vehement? Surely you wouldn't stand in the way of progress?"

"No, but I'm not about to let you dispossess my tenants."

He raised his brows. "Harsh words. Proximity to a successful railway could only benefit your tenants."

"Yes, they'd benefit immeasurably from the fact that coal could be transported from Lancaster right past them to Liverpool with greater ease. Meanwhile, streams would be diverted and woods cut down and half their land would be swallowed up by the railway company as a right-of-way. I've heard the stories."

"If you refuse to cooperate, Parliament can authorize compulsory purchase of the land, you know."

"Which would make it much more difficult to pass the railway bill in the first place. If you thought that was a solution, you wouldn't be trying to buy the land from me yourself at a handsome price." Satisfaction surged through her, as warm as the sun, as strong as the coffee. "Give it up, Daniel. You're mad if you think I'd cooperate in any scheme that could reestablish your power."

"Perhaps." He sat back and watched her for a moment. "It depends on how much you care for Céline and her children."

A chill prickled her spine. Unwarranted. Daniel couldn't hurt any of them anymore. "What does Céline have to do with this?"

"Nothing directly." He folded the napkin and laid it beside his plate. "But she is Silverton's wife."

Disquiet began to coil in her stomach. She drew back, not taking her eyes from Daniel. "And what does Silverton have to do with it?"

Daniel sat back in his chair. "He's done well for himself, hasn't he? I always thought him an idle fribble, but Sunderland tells me Silverton's seen as a rising power in the Tory party now. His friend Canning just became Foreign Secretary, and suddenly Silverton finds himself a junior minister. Céline must like that."

He was toying with her, like a cat with a mouse. *A master chess player,* Paul had once called their father. Charlotte began to realize that she had been sickeningly outplayed. "Out with it, damn you. What are you threatening?"

Daniel smiled, not triumphant or menacing, just supremely confident. "Silverton sits on the committee that makes recommendations on railways."

"He does. But if you expect him to support you—"

"There's a lot of money at stake in these new railways," Daniel went on. "Money for those who build them, money for those whose land they cross. There are surveyors who recommend the best locations, of course. A man might have a lot to gain from influencing those reports. Or even making a report disappear entirely."

"Is that what you did?" Charlotte wouldn't take her gaze from him. She felt as if he were a snake that might bite her the moment she looked away.

"Oh, no." Daniel twisted his signet ring around his finger. "My property is ideally suited to the Lancaster and Liverpool railway. So is yours. Sunderland isn't so fortunate."

"Henry Sunderland falsified a surveyor's report?"

"Not personally. He wasn't in a position to do so. He paid Silverton to do it for him."

Checkmate. A cloud of fury blotted her vision. She willed the blackness to clear. "What makes you think you can prove that? Your word against Silverton's? People will laugh in your face."

In one fluid motion Daniel reached inside his coat and withdrew a folded paper. "Read," he said, offering it to her across the table. "I have the original safely locked away. It's far less neat. He scrawled it on the back of a bill from his bootmaker."

Charlotte stared at the innocuous cream paper as though it were poison. "Did you keep something on all of us? Even me?"

He shook his head. "I never thought I needed a hold on you, Charlie."

She snatched the paper from his hand, jerked it open, and scanned the contents.

Sunderland,

Your terms are acceptable.

It was signed *Sn.*, the way Silverton always signed notes.

Charlotte folded the paper and looked at her father. "Even if you're telling the truth, this note hardly proves anything. They could be talking about a wager at Newmarket."

"It may not prove anything in and of itself. But if it prompted an investigation into the report, Silverton's crime would come to light soon enough."

"If there is a crime. If there is an original of this note. You could have made the whole thing up."

"So I could." He sipped his coffee. "You can always take a chance that I'm bluffing. Or you can sell me Chelmsford and I'll give you the original of the note to do with as you please."

Charlotte fixed her gaze on the pristine white folds of his cravat. She could hear her sister's voice. *Silver had got so tightfisted about the accounts. He was threatening not to let me serve champagne at our receptions. Can you imagine? Thank heaven he had a run of luck at the gaming tables in September. He's been a perfect lamb ever since.*

"And if I don't sell you Chelmsford? You'll send the letter to the newspapers along with a story of what you claim Silverton did?"

"Oh, no, I have a much better use for it." A smile crossed Daniel's face. "Your old friend, Francis Storbridge. The great hope of the Whigs now, I understand. And something of a rival of Silverton's. Storbridge has turned into a fine orator, they say. I'm sure he could make quite a speech in the Commons based on the contents of that letter. Isn't Silverton opposing a bill Storbridge is sponsoring?"

"You know damn well he is." Charlotte balled up the copy of the note and threw it on the table.

Daniel's eyes hardened, closing in on the kill. "I do. I also know that Storbridge sits on the railway committee too."

The full extent of his strategy fell into place in her head. "You'd sell Frank the letter in exchange for his support of your railway?"

"I could. Or I could sell it to you in exchange for Chelmsford." He watched her as though he were a detached observer, idly curious about the outcome of the scene. "The choice is entirely yours, Charlie."

Charlotte stared out the grimy glass of the hackney window. Gaslight fell across the stiff spikes of the area railing, the cool, uncompromising stone of the steps, the formal, Ionic columns of the portico.

Frank Storbridge's house. The house he had married into. It was a far cry from the childhood he had described as the son of a genteel but impoverished clergyman ministering to the poor in Spitalfields. Why had he ever been mad enough to propose to her? She couldn't have given him anything half so fine.

The hackney creaked as the driver climbed down from the box. Another thirty seconds and he'd be handing her from the carriage. But at a word he would turn around and drive her home. Frank need never know she'd been here.

"Miss?" The driver opened the door and offered her his hand. Cold, bracing air blew in her face. She knew what she had to do. She'd convinced herself there was no alternative.

She gathered up the velvet folds of her evening cloak, climbed down from the carriage and up the steps of the house, and rang the bell.

"I've come to see Mr. Storbridge," she told the footman who answered the door. She gave him her card, as if it were perfectly ordinary to pay social calls at a quarter to midnight. After all, much as she might try to forget it, she was a Ribard. She knew how to damp pretensions with the simple lift of an eyebrow.

The footman's eyes widened. He quickly composed his features. "If you'll wait in the hall, Miss Ribard, I'll inquire if Mr. Storbridge is at home."

The hall was circular, columned, and stately. A chill rose up from the Italian marble floor and seeped beneath the folds of her gown. Too tightly wound to sit, she occupied herself with calculating the number of acanthus leaves in the frieze. Her eye was caught by the portrait that hung over the huge fireplace. A titian-haired girl wearing a white dress and a string of amber beads. She was looking over her shoulder and she seemed to be laughing at the portrait painter. It must be Julia Vaughan. Frank's wife. The girl he was said to have seduced. The girl whose father had helped him to a seat in Parliament. She was pretty. More than pretty. Striking. Beautiful.

Charlotte started at the sound of footsteps. It was only the footman, of course. Frank wouldn't come out into the hall himself. He might even refuse to see her.

"Mr. Storbridge said I was to show you into the study, miss."

So. There was to be no turning back. Charlotte realized that part of her—the cowardly part—had been hoping he would refuse the interview. She followed the footman. Her hands had grown clammy beneath her long white gloves.

The footman opened a door off the corridor that he had led her down. She saw an oblong of yellow lamplight, caught a whiff of fresh ink, heard the scrape of a chair. "Miss Ribard," the footman said and stepped aside. Charlotte lifted her head and walked into the room.

Frank was standing behind his desk. Except for one brief glimpse of him in the park and another at a reception, she hadn't seen him in over five years. He was taller than she remembered. Perhaps it was something to do with the set of his shoulders. His face was leaner. The lines of his mouth seemed firmer, the bones of his face at once more finely chiseled and more unyielding. His coal-dark hair was brushed back from his forehead instead of falling carelessly across it. He'd always had a hard edge, but now he seemed stripped of all boyishness.

The door closed. His gaze moved over her face, but his eyes gave nothing away. Like Daniel's. "What can I do for you, Miss Ribard?"

His tone was courteous, but the words were almost a mockery. He never used to call her anything but "Charlie" when they were alone. She felt an unexpected pang in her throat. "You can give me a few minutes of your time."

"Of course." He waved her to a leather-covered armchair.

She seated herself, unclasped her cloak, and let it fall over the chair back. The room felt close and warm, but she immediately regretted her decision. Her fawn-colored gown had full sleeves and a modest neckline—*puritanical*, Céline called it—but the light silk was meager armor. She had kissed only two men in her life. One had been killed before her eyes. She was alone in this small room with the other. Though his gaze was veiled and impersonal, she could feel its pressure on her bare skin. "I'm sorry to call so late. I thought it would be best if we could talk alone."

"I didn't ask for an explanation." There was a stir of movement by the desk. A small black-and-white spaniel emerged, stretching its legs. "Stay, Millamant," Frank said.

The dog lay down. Frank glanced at the half-full glass of whisky that stood amid the papers on his desk. "Can I get you anything? A glass of sherry? Or I could ring for tea."

She started to refuse, then realized she was in need of fortification. "Whisky."

She thought perhaps he smiled, but it was quickly gone. He moved to a table of decanters and filled a glass. The dog lifted her head and regarded Charlotte out of large brown eyes. Charlotte was tempted to hold out her hand to the animal. But to play with Frank's dog would be to cross an unspoken boundary.

She glanced about the room. It was less lavish than she would have expected, without the gilding of Silverton's study or the rich woodwork she remembered in Daniel's own. Nearly everything in the room spoke of unvarnished business. There were parliamentary registers on the bookshelves, papers and sheaves of foolscap piled high on the desk. The only incongruous note was a small framed picture that hung beside the desk. Not a picture at all really, just a crude, childish wash of pastels.

Frank followed the direction of her gaze. "My daughter's."

Of course. She knew he had a daughter. A daughter whose mother was the woman in the hall portrait. She wondered if the little girl had inherited her mother's glorious titian hair or if she was dark like Frank. With two such parents, she could hardly fail to be lovely. "How old is she?" she found herself asking, though she had intended to avoid all personal topics.

"Two last month."

A two-year-old and a dog. Frank had always liked dogs. But that Frank seemed like a different person. Francis Storbridge, the man pouring whisky with deft precision, his eyes as cold as the crystal of the decanter, looked as if he should have a wolfhound, not this friendly spaniel with soulful eyes and floppy ears.

Frank held a glass of whisky out to her. She tried to take it without touching him, but somehow her hand brushed against his own. The warmth of his skin shot through the thin kid of her gloves. Damn her shaking fingers. Unless he was the one who had deliberately touched her. She glanced up at him, but his eyes gave nothing away. "Your sister and Silverton—do they know you're here?" he said.

She tightened her fingers around the glass. "I left them at Lady Sheriton's rout. I told them I had a headache and was going home. It seemed prudent."

"An understatement if I ever heard one." This time he definitely smiled.

His smile was disconcertingly the same as it had been in the old days when they were friends. She'd forgotten the way his eyes lit when he smiled, so that the steely gray actually became warm. She felt her own mouth curve in response, then quickly schooled her features.

Instead of returning to his chair, he pushed aside some papers and perched on the edge of his desk. He was in evening dress, but it looked as if he'd hastily shrugged on his coat when she came into the room. His neckcloth was loosened and his shirt collar fell open. Yet for all that, there was an elegance about him. The cut and fabric of the black coat and cream-colored breeches were far finer than anything he had worn as Daniel's secretary. "You still haven't told me why you came," he said.

She took a sip of whisky and set down the glass. "I need your help."

His brows snapped together. "What's Ribard done?"

Frank was quick, she'd give him that. "He wants to build a railway from Lancaster to Liverpool."

"Of course. I should have guessed. Ribard always had an eye for where power and money would move."

"He wants me to sell him Chelmsford. It's in the path of the railway."

"And you refused."

"Of course."

"What's he threatening you with?"

She picked up her glass and took another sip, more to

stall for time than anything. Once she told him, there would be no taking the words back. But if he refused to help her he would learn the truth from Daniel soon enough. And if she didn't tell him, she couldn't ask for his help at all. She set down the glass, folded her hands, and told him what Silverton had done and what Daniel was threatening to do if she refused to sell him Chelmsford.

Frank listened in silence. His eyes were like hard, polished pewter. The lamplight seemed to bounce off them, leaving his thoughts hidden deep inside. "I'm a little confused," he said when she finished. "Last time we met, you accused me of having no integrity. Now you're asking me to conceal a crime."

"I'm asking you not to stab a fellow politician in the back with illicit information." Her voice was sharp because she knew he had a point.

"You think Silverton would do the same if our situations were reversed?"

"I think he would if he behaved with honor."

"Honor. *A sugar syrup that makes lies go down more easily.* Wasn't that your definition?" He leaned back and rested his weight on his hands, mockery in the lines of his body. "Five years ago you made it clear you didn't trust me. Why turn to me now? Why expect me to help?"

His gaze bored into her, warning her she could hide nothing from him. The book-lined walls of the room seemed to shrink closer. She subdued an impulse to pull her cloak about her shoulders. "Because I couldn't think of anything else to do."

He gave a brief laugh. "Honest as ever. So you're desperate enough to turn to a man you think is no better than your father?"

Unaccountably, her face grew warm. "I never said—"

"*Cut from the same cloth* were the words, as I recall."

He picked up his glass and turned it in his hands. "How can you be sure the incriminating note really exists?"

"I can't. But I know Silver was short of funds this autumn. I said something to him tonight about Sunderland wanting a railway in Lancashire. His face turned green. He's never been a very good liar."

"He manages well enough in parliamentary debates." Frank took a sip of whisky and looked at her over the rim of the glass. There was something in his gaze that made her skin go tight. "What will you do if I refuse?"

Dread coiled in her stomach like fingers of ice. "I don't know."

He stared at her for a moment as though probing for a deeper truth. "You take such responsibility for your brother-in-law?"

"It's not just Silverton." The words burst from her lips with the passion she was trying to control. "If he's involved in a scandal it will hurt Céline and the children. I don't want to put them through—"

"What *you* went through."

She could feel the pulse pounding in her head. "At least I was grown up. Lydia is not yet fourteen. The boys are scarcely out of the nursery."

"Would you be so determined to protect him if he'd done what your father had?"

"Of course not. But Silverton's not a monster. He's just . . . weak."

"What does that make me?" Frank's voice was smooth and lethal.

She swallowed, her mouth dry. The blond lace at the neck of her gown stirred against her skin with her quickened breathing. "I know I haven't any right to ask for favors—"

"But you are."

"Yes."

He watched her, saying nothing.

She could stand the waiting no longer. "Well? What's your answer?"

He was silent for so long she thought she was going to scream. "You could trust me to do the right thing, but you've made it clear enough you don't trust anyone," he said at last. "If you really want to ensure my cooperation, I'll make a bargain with you. That's how most deals are consummated in Westminster."

She tensed, wary of a trap. "What sort of bargain?"

He was silent again. His eyes glittered like the diamond in his cravat. "I'll get the letter for you—if you marry me."

Chapter 3

Charlotte's fingers closed on the carved arms of her chair. "You're mad."

"So your brother-in-law and the other Tories are always saying, particularly when it comes to reform or the Spanish situation." Frank watched her, his gaze unwavering. "But mad or not, I'm quite in earnest."

"Blackmail." Her voice shook with disbelief. "You're as bad as Daniel."

He tilted his head back, his eyes hard with mockery. "Isn't that what you've always claimed?"

"In God's name, why do you want me?"

There was a brief silence. His gaze moved over her skin as though it could cut through the silk of her gown and any other defenses she possessed. "You're not a child anymore, Charlotte. Surely you only have to look into your glass to realize why a man would want you."

There was nothing cold about his eyes now. They glinted with a dark, compelling promise that reverberated through untouched places deep inside her. Something within her shivered and cracked, like a sheet of ice breaking to let loose the churning waters beneath.

She drew a ragged breath. Desire was an animal response, intruding when one least expected, clouding one's judgment, overwhelming reason. But if baser impulses could not be banished, at least they could be controlled. "Don't be silly, Frank." Her voice was ash-cold to quench the heat in his eyes and in her own body. "Rumor has it you could have any woman in London. So why me?" She studied his face, searching for some clue to what lay behind his outrageous demand. Whatever else Frank might be, he wasn't crazed by lust, certainly not for a twenty-six-year-old spinster. "Don't tell me *you* want to build a railway in Lancashire."

He gave a shout of laughter. "I have no such ambitions. Should you agree to my terms, you have my word that Chelmsford will always be yours to do with as you see fit."

"Kind of you."

"I may be a great many things, but I'm not overbearing."

She released the chair arms and folded her hands in her lap. "If this is your idea of revenge—"

"Revenge is a corrosive luxury. I haven't time for it." His leg swung idly against the desk. "A politician needs a wife. Or so my friends are always telling me."

"There are dozens of women you could marry. Why not Ianthe de Cazes? I understand you're halfway there already."

His eyes lit with sudden humor. "Ianthe would say what we have is a world away from marriage. That's the charm of it."

"Then why the devil would you want—"

"My daughter has never known a mother. My late father-in-law left me guardian of his four children, including two unmarried girls—"

"Who I'm sure are very capably looked after by a governess."

"Their governess got married and moved to Hertford-

shire last month. Their aunt has been serving as chaperone, but she'll be leaving shortly. I've been in the devil of
a fix as to what to do."

Charlotte stared at him. "You expect me to believe you
want to marry me so you'll have a chaperone for your
wards?"

He shrugged his elegantly disheveled shoulders. "As
my wife you could hardly give me two weeks' notice."

"Your wife." She pushed herself to her feet. "Good
God, can you know me so little that you believe I would
even consider such an arrangement?"

He stood and faced her, little more than an arm's length
away. She caught a whiff of cedar and felt the warmth of
his breath on her skin. "The last time we met I realized I
didn't know you at all," he said. "Who can say to what
lengths any of us will go in pursuit of a goal?"

"I'd never sell myself. I'm not a whore."

"Or a politician." He smiled, though there was no humor in his eyes. "Life's all about compromise, Charlotte.
What we want and how far we'll go to get it. If you play
the game your hands are going to get dirty."

His mouth was drawn into a hard line. She had a sudden memory of how that mouth had felt, once, moving
over her lips. "This isn't a game, Frank. But I was a fool
to think you'd understand." She snatched her cloak from
the chair back, flung it over her shoulders, and walked to
the door.

"As you wish." His voice was impassive. "If it's any
comfort, I agree Silverton's not worth the sacrifice."

Her hand closed on the polished brass of the doorknob.
The mahogany panels wavered before her eyes. Images
chased themselves across her mind. Daniel flicking crumbs
from his coat as he threatened to destroy Céline's family.
Lydia perched on the bed, watching her get ready to go

out this evening. Roger and Charles sprawled on the nursery carpet, playing with their lead soldiers, when she went in to kiss them good night.

She swallowed. She could still taste the peaty fire of the whisky. It reminded her of home. Edinburgh. Sophie and Paul, who had been her family for the last five years. Neither of them was given to preaching, but they had proven their creed by example time and time again. Determination. The courage of one's convictions. The willingness to do what was necessary to protect those one loved. God knew they had protected her often enough through the years. So had Céline in her way. Even Silverton had stood by her when political expedience dictated he put as much distance as possible between himself and the Ribard family.

Her fingers loosed on the doorknob. She looked back over her shoulder at Frank. "It would have to be a marriage of convenience." She turned to face him. "I mean, a marriage in name only."

Something flickered in his eyes. Surprise? Calculation? Triumph? "Is that an acquiescence?"

"It's a counteroffer. If I'm going to be blackmailed, at least it will be on my own terms."

"An interesting concept. Your logic used to be more straightforward."

"Frank."

"Yes?"

"I made my offer. I'm waiting for a reply."

He was silent for a long moment. The heat of the fire scalded her. The air in the small room was thick and choking.

"Charlie—" He took a step forward, his hand extended.

She backed against the door, wary of being touched, even more wary of his use of her name. "Don't dawdle, Frank.

It's a wonder you can ever agree on legislation if it takes you this long to come to terms."

He let his hand fall to his side. "I've never had difficulty keeping my bed warm."

"Meaning?"

"Meaning provided you entertain my colleagues and give maternal attention to my daughter and my wards, you may keep your bedchamber inviolate."

She leaned against the door panels, grateful for their firmness. "We're in agreement then?"

"It seems we are." He gave a strange, twisted smile. "I'd go down on one knee, but it would only embarrass us both. Shall we drink to it instead?" He picked up the whisky glasses. "To our future, Miss Ribard?"

She moved away from the door and took her glass from him. She was tempted to dash the contents in his face. But she had made her bargain. She had better start learning to live with it. She touched her glass briefly to his. "To defeating Daniel de Ribard, Mr. Storbridge."

"Yes, let's not forget the higher purpose." He tossed off the last of his whisky. "It goes without saying that our *betrothal* had best remain secret until Ribard's given up the incriminating letter. How long did he give you to make a decision about Chelmsford?"

"Two days. He said he'd come to me."

Frank nodded. "Refuse him. Enjoy it. Leave the rest to me. I'll let you know when I have the letter."

His eyes shone with the light of the chase. "You're looking forward to this," she said.

"You have to admit Ribard's a more interesting opponent than most of our government ministers."

"How do you know I won't back out of our agreement once I have the letter?"

He smiled. "Because I know you, Charlotte. You may

think honor is a sugar syrup, but you're honorable to the core."

His gaze was warm again and soft in a way it hadn't been before. She wanted more than anything to look away from his eyes. She wouldn't let herself do so. She lifted her glass to her lips, forcing her fingers to be steady, and drained the contents.

The door swung open behind her. "Francis—oh, I didn't know you had company."

Charlotte turned around. A girl stood in the doorway, curly, red-blond hair spilling over the shoulders of a pale green dressing gown.

"Hullo, brat," Frank said. "What are you doing up?"

"It's only half-past twelve." The girl bent down to pet the dog, who had padded over to her. "Diana and Bertram won't be home for ages. I don't see why I should have to go to bed hours earlier when I'm nearly eleven and a half."

Frank turned to Charlotte. "My sister-in-law, Lady Serena Vaughan. Miss Charlotte de Ribard."

Serena's gaze swept over Charlotte, as though taking her measure. "Hullo." She held out her hand.

Charlotte shook the hand of the girl who was to be her sister-in-law. A ready-made family. But she wasn't entirely averse to the idea.

Frank moved to the door. "I'll see you out myself. Is your carriage waiting?"

"I came in a hackney. It seemed prudent. I asked the driver to wait."

He considered a moment, as though debating the wisdom of offering one of his carriages. Then he nodded. "Sensible as usual." He held open the door.

Charlotte moved past him into the hall. The satin-piped folds of her gown brushed unavoidably against his legs. She didn't allow her stride to falter. They walked down the corridor in silence, Serena and the dog trailing behind. Frank accompanied her down the front steps, but did not attempt to take her arm. He did take her hand to help her into the carriage, the light, impersonal touch any gentleman would have offered to a lady. But he climbed up the carriage steps and maintained hold of her hand as she seated herself. And then he lifted her hand and pressed it to his lips.

It was a courtly, old-fashioned gesture, but there was nothing courtly or old-fashioned about the way he did it. The heat of his lips shot through her chilled body. She sat absolutely still, afraid that to move or even to breathe would be to betray herself.

He looked at her for a long moment. His gaze held a challenge and something else she couldn't name. "A safe drive home, Miss Ribard."

He closed the door. The hackney jerked forward, throwing her back against the squabs. She realized she was trembling. She stared at the empty seat opposite her. *God in heaven, what have I done?*

Frank returned to the hall to find Serena perched on a red velvet bench with Millamant beside her. Serena sprang to her feet. "That was Daniel de Ribard's daughter, wasn't it?"

Frank pushed the double doors shut. "It was."

"Why did she come to see you? Does she know why her father's come back to England?"

"No one seems to know why Ribard's come back to England." Frank moved to the baize-covered door to the servants' quarters. "If you're not going to sleep, do you want a midnight snack?"

Millamant jumped down from the bench with a hopeful bark. Serena grinned. "I thought you'd never ask."

She was quiet as she followed him down the servants'

stairs, but it was too much to hope he'd silenced her questions. "Are we going to be seeing a lot more of this Miss Ribard?" she asked when they'd reached the warmth and quiet of the stone-floored kitchen.

"You may see her again." Frank opened the cooler and took out a bottle of milk. No matter how many servants he now had at his disposal, the lessons he'd learned as the motherless son of an impoverished clergyman remained with him.

Serena hitched herself up on the pine worktable. "She's not in your usual style, is she?"

Frank went to the pantry and found a bar of chocolate. "I wasn't aware that I had a style, usual or otherwise."

"You know what I mean." Serena leaned forward and hooked her hands around her knees. "What's happened to Ianthe de Cazes?"

"Nothing as far as I know." He reached for one of the gleaming copper pans that hung from the wall.

Serena rubbed Millamant's stomach with her foot. "You've never brought your mistresses to the house before."

Frank poured milk into the pan and set it on the range. "Serena, you know I'm not given to confidences, but I can assure you that Charlotte de Ribard is not and never will be my mistress." He bent down to coax the coals into a blaze.

"I didn't think she was, actually." Serena was silent for nearly half a minute. "Are you going to marry her?"

"Ianthe de Cazes?" He began to scrape chocolate into the milk.

"Charlotte de Ribard."

He took a white metal sugar tin from the shelf above the range and added a spoonful to the chocolate. "I've been married."

"For less than a year. Add more sugar. You never make it sweet enough."

He put another pinch of sugar into the chocolate. "At this rate you'll never learn to appreciate good dry wine."

"At this rate no one will ever admit I'm old enough to try." Serena swung her foot against the table leg. "You really ought to have a hostess, you know. Now that you're getting so important in the party, you'll have to entertain more. I don't care about having a chaperone, but Diana does and I suppose Juliet will someday. Besides, I expect Juliet would like to have a mother." She twisted a red-blond ringlet around her finger.

He paused in stirring the chocolate. "Would you?"

"Well . . ." Serena let the ringlet go. "I'm very nearly grown up now. But I suppose sometimes it would be nice. . . ."

Frank turned back to the stove. Serena was going to like having Charlotte in the house. Christ. He stared down at the pan of chocolate. Charlotte had agreed to marry him. No, he'd coerced her into it. The words had been out of his mouth before he knew what he was saying, a sort of challenge, a test to see how far she'd go in her determination to save Silverton's worthless hide. When she accepted, he'd very nearly told her not to be a fool.

But he hadn't. He told himself Ribard would continue to try to manipulate her. He told himself that as her husband he could protect her. He told himself it would be good for Juliet and Serena and Diana and even Bertram and Val. He knew none of the reasons was sufficient explanation.

The truth was he wanted her. He had never stopped wanting her. Not in the manner of gothic romances or simple lust. He wanted something from her that went far beyond the carnal. Something he hadn't a prayer of getting, even were she ten times more willing to become his wife. Yet when he realized that she had agreed to be his, he had been unable to let her go. Unwilling rather. He'd never claimed to be a saint. To listen to Charlotte, he wasn't even a man of honor.

The chocolate bubbled up with a sudden *whoosh*, spilling over and hissing on the range. Frank made a grab for the pan. The hot metal seared his hand.

"Are you all right?" Serena asked.

"Only slightly singed. I'll survive." Frank reached for two cups. "I always do."

"Catch, Aunt Charlie." Charles drew back his arm and loosed a snowball.

Charlotte ducked. The hard-packed snow knocked her hat from her head and the pins from her hair. She bent as if to retrieve the hat, but instead snatched up a handful of snow and hurled it at her nine-year-old nephew.

The snowball caught Charles in the chest. He staggered backward. Beside Charlotte, Roger, almost five, jumped up and down. "A hit! We win!"

"Not so fast." Lydia pulled her hand from under the blue velvet folds of her cloak and threw a snowball at her youngest brother. Fair hair spilling over her shoulders, cheeks flushed with exertion, she looked more a little girl than a young lady of almost fourteen.

Roger grabbed more snow and threw it at his sister. Charlotte made the mistake of glancing at them. A well-aimed snowball sent her over backward into one of the snow drifts that covered Hyde Park. Charles gave a crow of delight, then landed in the snow with a sudden *thud*, thanks to a missile from Roger. Lydia felled Roger, lost her balance, and sprawled on the ground herself.

Shouts of laughter cut the cold, still, early-morning air. Charlotte reached for her hat. Boots crunched on the snow.

"Such energy before noon. I find myself quite envious."

The warmth of exertion and laughter fled. Charlotte picked up her beaver hat, jammed it on her head, and stood to face Daniel.

He was standing just beyond a line of plane trees, lean and dramatic in a sweeping black greatcoat. Charlotte heard Lydia and the boys scramble to their feet. She wanted to fling her arms around them and shepherd them away from him, but she knew it would be fruitless.

Lydia took a step toward Charlotte. *"Grandpère?"*

"Lydie. You've grown, *ma chère*. You're getting to look very much like your mother."

"Are you our grandfather?" Charles was staring at Daniel.

"I am." Daniel smiled at his grandson with hideous frankness. "I'm not surprised you don't remember me. Though you've changed more than I have since we last met. You've turned into quite a young man."

Roger walked up to Daniel. "We aren't allowed to talk about you."

"Regrettable, but understandable." Daniel stooped and held out his hand. "Roger, I take it? You're five?"

Roger shook the proffered hand. "I will be in March."

Daniel reached beneath his greatcoat and drew out a red-and-white-striped bag. "When I was five I had a fondness for peppermints. I thought perhaps you would too."

Roger gripped the bag, eyes shining. Lydia cast a questioning look at Charlotte. Charlotte moved forward, suppressing an impulse to snatch the peppermints from Roger's hand and throw them in the Serpentine. "Go on with the game for a few minutes," she told the children. "Your—Daniel and I need to talk."

She moved to a bench that stood a few feet back from the curving waters of the Serpentine, glittering coldly in the morning sunlight. Daniel had set the situation to his advantage—like a commander choosing terrain for battle. She would at least shift the ground a little. She seated herself, back straight. The bench was hard and stiff. Her fingers closed on the mulberry wool of her pelisse, drawing strength from the softness.

"Do you have a bribe for every occasion?" she asked.

"Surely a man may give a simple gift to his grandchildren without being accused of bribery." Daniel walked to the bench, but did not sit. He rested his hand on the back of the bench, standing over her.

"Nothing you do is ever simple, Daniel." She was tempted to rise and face him, but to move again would be a sign of weakness. "I take it you've come for your answer."

He looked down into her eyes. "I have."

She held her own gaze steady despite the merciless glare of the sun against the snow. "Did you really flatter yourself into thinking I might give in?"

There was a slight flicker in Daniel's eyes. As close as he ever came to showing surprise. "Do I take it that is a refusal?"

"It is." She enunciated the words with care.

"I see." Daniel sank down on the bench, one arm stretched along its back, almost touching her shoulder. She wanted to draw back but wouldn't let herself. "You haven't deluded yourself into thinking I don't mean what I say, have you?" he asked.

A gust of wind stirred the barren, leafless trees overhead. "Where you are concerned, I was stripped of my delusions long ago," Charlotte said.

"Then the answer is no?" Daniel's voice was smooth and even, unroughened by wind and cold.

Roger gave a shout of glee. Out of the corner of her eye, Charlotte caught a glimpse of his red coat, Lydia's blue cloak, Charles's green scarf. She swallowed, savoring the delight. "The answer is no."

His eyes narrowed. "Very well." He got to his feet. "You know the consequences."

She stood and faced him. "You made them clear enough."

He regarded her a moment longer. He might pretend that he would benefit either way, but she could read the subtle tension in the set of his mouth and jaw. He had wanted Chelmsford, and she had denied it to him.

At length he gave a brief nod. "Good day, Charlie. For the moment we've said all there is to say."

He turned on his heel and walked away.

Charlotte watched him go. She had won. Chelmsford would remain hers. Silverton and Céline and the children would be safe. She had checkmated her father more effectively than she ever had done across a chessboard. The taste of victory lingered on her tongue, sweeter than the freshest strawberries.

"Aunt Charlie." Roger's voice came from the bank of the Serpentine, sharp with indignation. "Charles pushed me."

Charlotte walked down the bank. Roger had unwittingly restored her to reality. She had won, yes. But she had also burned her bridges. In denying Daniel, she had closed off all her options.

She had no choice now but to marry Frank.

Chapter 4

"Caught you." Ianthe seized Frank's arm as he passed beneath the archway. "Tiresome man, what's the good of a yuletide party if you won't walk beneath the mistletoe?"

She twined her arms around his neck and pulled his head down to hers in a kiss that made no attempt to disguise their relationship. None of the guests crowding Lady Granby's rooms appeared to take particular notice. Talk and behavior had grown increasingly boisterous as the party wore on.

Frank wrapped his left arm around Ianthe and held his punch cup steady with his right hand. Her mouth tasted of cinnamon and cloves. Her gloved fingers moved over his back. Her velvet-gowned body molded against his. But even as one part of his mind was stirred by her proximity, another part—a part he had scarcely known existed—was left untouched.

He drew back and forced a smile to his lips. Christ, a week into his farce of a betrothal and he was turning into a bloody puritan. "You seem to have been enjoying yourself well enough."

Ianthe's eyes gleamed. "Oh, my darling, it would be a shame to let all this holiday cheer go to waste." She took his arm and drew him into the corridor, just in time to avoid a trio of gentlemen staggering out of the crimson saloon, the smell of spiced wine wafting before them.

He and Ianthe threaded their way between black-coated gentlemen, ladies in velvets and silks and satins too scant for the cool evening, and footmen in powdered wigs and heavy coats of blue and buff. The corridor was thick with the punch-tinged chatter of the guests and the scent of the pine garlands strung from the walnut-paneled walls.

"Storbridge," Henry Brougham called. "Come and set Wilson straight on emancipation."

"Not now, Henry." Ianthe stopped to tap Brougham on the arm with her burgundy silk fan. "I haven't had him to myself all evening."

"Lucky dog." Brougham grinned at Frank. "Some of us have to make do with politics as the attraction of the evening."

Ianthe pulled Frank into a niche boasting a statue of Aphrodite emerging from a seashell. "Wretched man." She looked up, her face inches from his own. The candle-light from the wall sconces warmed her cool, lily-scented skin. "I haven't seen you in a week." She reached up, her lips against his cheek. "I've slept alone for seven nights."

Once Frank would have seized the opportunity to kiss her. Now he took her by the shoulders and held her away from him. "My dear, don't tell me you've spent a night alone since you left the schoolroom unless you've chosen to do so."

"You know me too well." Ianthe stroked her fingers against his cheek. "Perhaps that's why I can't put you out of my head."

"My sweet, you've spent the evening flirting shamelessly."

"Merely staying abreast of the latest news." Ianthe fingered the ivory sticks of her fan. "Everyone's talking about Canning and whether he'll prove Castlereagh's equal."

"He would seem to be the man of the hour." George Canning had recently been appointed Foreign Secretary following Lord Castlereagh's unexpected suicide. Canning was an intelligent man, far less reactionary than Castlereagh and the majority of the government. Frank searched his mistress's face. "I'm surprised you haven't set your sights on him."

"He's disgustingly devoted to his wife. Besides, his mother was an actress and his stepfather was in trade." Ianthe's rouged lips curled with distaste. "There's enough of that in my own background as it is. But don't think you can divert me." Her gaze fixed on his own, hard and steady as the cut glass of Lady Granby's punch bowl. "*I* didn't desert *your* bed. Who's taken my place, Francis?"

Frank looked down at the face he knew intimately, though the mind behind it remained a mystery to him. What could he say? *I've become secretly betrothed, and I feel myself bound to remain faithful to my fiancée though she refuses my smallest touch.* Ianthe would laugh in his face. Besides, he could not break off with her yet. He could not do anything that would seem in the least out of the ordinary until he had gained possession of Silverton's incriminating note.

He put his lips against her ear and framed a clever lie, surprised at the prickle of distaste he felt. "No woman could take your place, Ianthe. You're a fool or woefully disingenuous to suggest it."

"Doing it much too brown, Francis." Her gaze was knife-sharp. "We've always known this wasn't permanent. But—"

"Storbridge. The very man I've been looking for. I trust I'm not interrupting anything."

Frank had never thought to find himself grateful for

Daniel de Ribard's appearance. Life was full of surprises these days. He released Ianthe and turned to his former employer. "If you think that, you're losing your touch, Ribard."

Ribard's gaze skimmed over Ianthe. "I trust whatever I'm interrupting can be continued more profitably in private. You'll forgive me, madame?"

"Never, save that I've been longing to meet you since I learned of your arrival in England." Ianthe held out a shapely, white-gloved arm. "The Marquis de Ribard, I take it?"

"The *Condesa* de Cazes." Frank completed the introduction as Ribard bowed over Ianthe's hand.

Ianthe let her fingers linger in Ribard's own. "I suppose it's too much to hope you interrupted us on my account rather than Francis's."

"Were it simply a matter of inclination . . ." Ribard smiled. "But I fear I need to discuss politics, and Storbridge has a tiresome tenacity for details."

"Sometimes to the exclusion of the more piquant aspects of life." Ianthe blew Frank a kiss, gave Ribard a smile that was nearly as seductive, and moved off with a stir of burgundy velvet, dark ringlets, and lily scent.

Ribard glanced after her, then raised an eyebrow at Frank. "My compliments. Your taste has improved."

"My circumstances have given me more scope to exercise it." Frank took a sip of his now lukewarm punch. "I trust you didn't send my mistress off to sample other men's charms simply so we could reminisce over old times?"

"Were I interested in idle conversation I would have disposed of you rather than Madame de Cazes." Ribard inclined his head toward a gilded door across the corridor. "Perhaps we could speak in private?"

Frank was conscious of a few raised brows and a

sharp look from Brougham as they made their way across the corridor. He was going to have to answer some questions about his tête-à-tête with the Marquis de Ribard. No matter. His years in Parliament had taught him to deflect unwanted questions as easily as he had learned to deflect the point of a rapier in boyhood fencing lessons.

The gilded door gave onto a small, circular anteroom hung with cherry-colored silk. The remnants of a fire smoldered in the grate, and a brace of candles burned on the mantel. The flames flickered at the opening of the door.

Frank moved to the fireplace, set his punch cup on the mantel, and poked up the fire. Laying claim to the room. With an opponent such as Ribard, no tactical nuance could be overlooked.

Ribard's voice sounded from behind him. "I always knew you were ambitious, but I confess you've out-stripped even my expectations."

"I studied under a master." Frank coaxed the coals and fragments of pine into a brisk blaze. "I knew you weren't beaten. I've expected to see you in London these two years and more." He straightened to face Ribard, still gripping the poker. "But I'm a bit surprised to find you at Granby House. Aren't you afraid you'll be tainted by contact with so many Whigs?"

Ribard moved to a chair of satinwood and cherry damask, the most commodious in the room. "I've always made it a point to have friends in both camps. I see other Tories here tonight. Including the new Foreign Secretary."

"Canning's hardly a true Tory to hear some of his fellow Cabinet ministers tell it."

"Yes. His sheer brilliance forced them to give him a Cabinet seat, but they're terrified of which way he'll jump. Castlereagh may have been humorless, but at least he understood the risks inherent in any sort of political reform. It's a pity about his breakdown."

"I'm as sorry as anyone for Castlereagh's death, but you'll forgive me if I don't share your nostalgia for his politics." Frank stared at the leaping flames, his back to Ribard. "You had something you wanted to say to me?"

The chair creaked as Ribard settled himself. "I have a proposition for you."

Frank returned the poker to the stand of andirons. "I don't need your help anymore."

Ribard's eyes glinted like polished onyx. "I think we can be of use to each other."

Frank rested his arm along the mantel. To sit would be to dignify the conversation as too important. "I can see how I could be of use to you. I take it you mean to enlighten me as to how you might be of use to me."

Ribard reached inside his black cassimere coat and drew out a folded paper with his kid-gloved hand. "If you don't see the profit in this, you're not the man I take you for."

Frank was compelled to walk forward to take the paper. He carried it back to the fireplace and held it up to the candlelight. On one side was a bill of sale for a pair of top boots. On the other was a quick black scrawl in Silverton's handwriting. "You'll have to do better than this if you want to interest me, Ribard. So Silverton and Sunderland were agreeing to terms about something. It sounds like a private bet between gentlemen."

Ribard gave a slow smile. "Not a bet. A bribe." He went on to describe the compromise Charlotte had so unstintingly recounted.

Frank listened with a carefully calculated expression of surprise. "I take it you have your reasons for showing your son-in-law's dirty linen to his rival?"

"You can be of more use to me than Silverton."

Frank folded the paper. "What do you want, Ribard?"

Ribard sat back in his chair. "Your support for the Lancaster and Liverpool Railway."

Frank widened his eyes slightly. "I haven't heard of the Lancaster and Liverpool Railway."

"You will in the next session."

"With you as the chief investor?"

Ribard's mouth curved. "I'd never be fool enough to make myself chief investor in anything."

Frank tapped his fingers against the marble mantel. "And that's all you ask?"

"All? You underrate yourself, my boy. With your support the railway will easily sail through the committee."

The fire had begun to crackle. Frank glanced down at the red-orange flames. He didn't want to betray undue suspicion, but neither did he want to appear unnaturally guileless. "And?" he asked.

"And what?" Ribard's gaze was bland as butter.

"With you there's always an 'and,' Ribard."

"If so that's my affair. This is all you need concern yourself with." Ribard tented his fingers into a sharp steeple. "Of course, if you don't want the letter I can always offer it to your friend Brougham or one of the other Radicals. I don't take kindly to waiting for an answer."

"You never did." Frank stowed the paper inside his coat. "You were right, Ribard. We can be of use to each other."

Ribard rose. "Then I can count on your support?" He extended his hand, but Frank knew he was quite capable of trying to take the letter back by force if he thought it necessary. Frank could not say which of them would prevail in such a contest.

He gripped the hand of the man who was to be his father-in-law. "When I use this against Silverton, you can assume you have my support."

* * *

The footman, the same footman who had admitted Charlotte the first night she called on Frank, showed her into the study and slipped from the room. His face was expressionless, but he must be growing curious about her visits to his master—the first indecently late at night, this one unconscionably early in the morning. Charlotte realized it didn't matter what he thought. The next time he saw her she would be openly betrothed to Frank.

Frank was at his desk, but he rose and came forward at her entrance. Though it was not yet ten o'clock he wore a pale gray coat that fit without a crease and a cravat tied with a simplicity it would take most men half the morning to master. His dark hair was combed smoothly back from his forehead. The perfect facade. Just like Daniel.

His gaze was level and controlled, but she didn't trust the cool surface. She'd seen the fires banked beneath. She stood by the door as he approached her. For a moment she thought he meant to walk right up to her and take her hands or even put his arm around her, claiming the liberty of a betrothed. Instead, he stopped a few feet off. "You came promptly," he said.

"Your letter wasn't specific. Have you—"

He held out a folded paper. She snatched it from him and spread it open. Silverton's black scrawl jumped from the creased paper.

Something shriveled inside her at the sight of the familiar handwriting. Not so much because she now had no choice but to marry Frank as because there was now no doubt of her brother-in-law's culpability.

She looked up at Frank. "Did Daniel suspect anything?"

"I don't think so. But then Ribard's always been a difficult man to read."

She clenched the paper, so light and insubstantial, yet heavy with Silverton's sins. "Frank. You won't . . . that is, you can see to it . . . The falsified survey won't affect the ultimate decision about the railway, will it?"

His mouth curled. "Still determined to tie everything up in a neat package? You can't have it both ways. You can't cover up a crime and rectify it all at once."

She looked straight at him, the paper twisted between her fingers. "I'm not proud of any of this. Would it be better if I turned a blind eye to the harm Silverton may have done?"

"You could argue it would be better if you let him take the consequences of his own actions."

"You could."

He looked at her in silence for a moment. Some of the hardness left his face. "If the railway succeeds, it won't be for lack of opposition on my part, Charlotte. I don't want Sunderland to profit from his bribe any more than I want Ribard to reestablish a base of power."

"Thank you." She moved to the fireplace and dropped down on the worn cream and brown of the hearthrug. She tugged off her gloves and tucked them in her reticule so she wouldn't get ash on the lemon-colored kid. She looked once more at the note, forcing herself to absorb Silverton's perfidy. Then she held the paper out to the fire.

She gripped the note and watched the flames curl around the crumpled edges, afraid that if she let go she could not be certain it would be destroyed.

"Charlotte." Frank knocked the paper from her hand an instant before the flames would have reached her fingers. She drew her hand back, but even now she could not look away from the fire. Frank knelt beside her as the remnants of paper turned to ash. Then, without speaking, he handed her the poker.

She ground up the ashes and pushed them into the coals. Daniel's careful schemes turned to dust in the space of a few minutes. He could not hurt Silverton now, nor Céline, nor the children. Triumph surged through her like an illicit sip of champagne at a party when she was a girl. She looked at Frank and felt a smile break across her face.

He echoed the smile easily, as he might have in the past. She lifted her hand to seize his own. Then she looked into his eyes, no longer the bright eyes of the friend of her girlhood but the shadowed eyes of the man who had forced her into an unspeakable bargain. The burning eyes of the man who had stirred feelings she strove to keep decently buried. Intoxication gave way to cold reality.

"So." She straightened her back and folded her hands in her lap. "That's finished. You needn't think I'll renege on my part of the bargain."

He sat back on his heels. "There's nothing to hold you to it."

"Nothing but my word. If I went back on that, I'd be no better than him."

"You'll never be like him, Charlie. You couldn't if you tried." He stood and held out his hand.

She ignored his hand and clambered to her feet, catching her heel in the merino folds of her skirt.

Snow was drifting beyond the windowpanes. Frost glimmered on leafless branches in the garden. White and shimmering. Pure. Chaste. She wondered what color she would wear at their wedding.

"When we announce our betrothal Daniel will know we've tricked him. He doesn't take kindly to losing," she said.

"It will be too late for him to do anything about it."

"Too late to do anything about Silverton's letter.

Daniel makes it a point never to let a defeat go without retaliation."

"So he does." Frank's eyes darkened. "Are you saying you want to postpone the announcement of our betrothal?"

"No. It would only delay the inevitable. Besides . . ."

"Yes?" he asked.

"I want him to know he's beaten."

"Even if it means sacrificing yourself." He regarded her, his head tilted to one side. "That's either commendably noble or lamentably bloodthirsty." He turned to his desk and picked something up. "Since we're to be publicly betrothed, perhaps you'll consent to wear this publicly."

He held out a black velvet jewelry box from Asprey's. She stared at it, her brain thick with surprise. Such a token seemed to have little place in the devil's bargain they had struck.

He flicked open the lid of the box. A square-cut citrine set in wrought yellow gold glowed against the black velvet. The band was engraved with roses, the stone brilliant as it caught the light of the fire.

"Yellow was your favorite color, as I recall," Frank said.

She looked up and sucked in her breath. There was an intensity in his eyes that shook her even more than the unexpected gift of the ring or the fact that after all these years he remembered her favorite color. "It was. It is." She swallowed. "My favorite color, that is. Thank you."

"It's a customary betrothal gift."

Damnation. He had her thanking him for the ring that sealed the betrothal he'd blackmailed her into. The man was lethal. "But under the circumstances it was hardly necessary," she said.

"On the contrary. We must observe the forms." He lifted her left hand and slid the ring onto her third finger.

"And for the sake of the forms, shall we seal the betrothal in a time-honored manner?" Before she quite realized what was happening, he bent his head and covered her mouth with his own.

At first, shock held her immobile. She was aware of things in isolation—the texture of his lips, the heat of his mouth, the feel of his fingers on the nape of her neck. His mouth moved over her own with sure, skillful, deliberate provocation. As though he were testing her. With some part of her brain she realized that to make any response, even a struggle, would be to cede victory to him. So she held herself still beneath his onslaught.

Then all at once his mouth softened and his arms went tight around her. There was a desperate edge to his kiss now. All her senses quickened, as though they'd been touched by fire. Something buried deep inside her broke free of restraint. Her lips parted. She felt herself falling into a dark vortex.

She wrenched herself out of his arms and took a step backward. "That didn't seal our bargain. It violated it."

Frank's gaze was level, though his breathing was as uneven as her own. "As I recall, we agreed not to share each other's bed. I don't remember anything about kisses."

"One has been known to lead to the other."

He lifted his brows. "My dear girl. At ten o'clock in the morning surrounded by parliamentary registers? You're quite safe from me, I assure you."

There had been nothing safe about the kiss, but she wasn't about to say so. She looked down at her betrothal ring. It felt cold and heavy. The citrine shone against her skin, where a diamond would have made her look sallow. Yet that ravishing circle of yellow and gold was a brand of her fate. She spoke the first words that came into her head. "I want to be married in Edinburgh."

"From Sophie and Paul's house. I assumed as much."

"I mean, I don't want a fashionable wedding at St. George's Hanover Square."

"That would be a bit difficult if you mean to be married in Edinburgh." He seemed to have his breathing under control by now, which was more than she could say for herself. "The wedding can take place between the Christmas holidays and the opening of Parliament."

"With only family and close friends in attendance."

He inclined his head. "As you wish. I believe such decisions are generally left to the bride."

"Damn you, Frank." Her voice shook. "The *bride* hasn't decided any of this."

"On the contrary." He moved past her to the door. "I merely proposed the bargain. The final decision was yours, as I recall." He opened the door. "If you'll grant me another quarter hour, I think it's time you met your new family."

She could not protest. In truth she was curious to meet the rest of the Vaughans. And she didn't think she could take another moment alone with the man who was about to become her husband. She followed him into the hall, past the portrait of his first wife, and up the main staircase.

At the head of the stairs Frank threw open a pair of carved double doors. A female voice drowned out the sound of the doors opening. "There. Is that straight?"

A young woman with titian ringlets and cinnamon-and-cream-striped skirts stood on a step stool before the fireplace, fastening a cedar garland to the overmantel.

"It would look better if we added some red ribbon." Serena Vaughan was perched on an ottoman, her back to the door, the dog Millamant beside her.

"True beauty is in the wild and dramatic, Rena." The girl on the step stool added another tack to the garland.

"In Mr. Wordsworth's poetry maybe. Not in Christmas decorations. What do you think, Bertram? Bertram?"

A young man's tousled red-blond head appeared above the back of the sofa. "It looks fine." He subsided back on the sofa.

Frank moved into the room. "*Fine* is a tepid word, Bertram. It never satisfies a lady."

The girl in the cinnamon-striped skirt turned around. "Francis, thank goodness, someone with taste."

The young man on the sofa straightened up and shook his head, as though trying to clear it. Serena sprang to her feet. She held a dark-haired little girl of about two in her arms. The child wriggled to be put down and toddled over to Frank.

"Is the garland straight?" the girl in the cinnamon skirt asked.

"With just enough wildness to lend it rustic charm." Frank bent down to pick up the toddler, who had thrown her arms around his knees. "Gather round, infants, there's someone I want you to meet." He held out his free hand to Charlotte. She moved to his side but did not take his hand.

The young woman in the cinnamon skirt jumped down from the step stool and smoothed her gown. The young man stood and pushed his hair back from his face, moving with the care of someone suffering from the aftereffects of a drink. Serena cast a sharp look at Frank. Millamant pricked up her ears. Only the dark-haired toddler, now settled in Frank's arms, continued to smile with simple delight.

Frank turned to Charlotte. "You've met Serena already. Her sister, Lady Diana, and her brother, Bertram. Lord Vaughan."

The toddler tugged at his sleeve. "I was saving best for last," Frank said. "My daughter, Juliet." He looked from

Juliet to the three young Vaughans. "Charlotte de Ribard, an old friend of mine. She's just consented to be my wife."

Three pairs of blue-green eyes widened. Three pairs of straight, fair brows rose. Three delicately molded mouths parted in surprise.

"Oh, how lovely. To think your attachment has endured all these years." Diana Vaughan ran across the room and seized Charlotte's hands in both her own. "I'm so very happy for you. Welcome to the family."

Charlotte found herself murmuring, "Thank you." Any lesser response seemed ungenerous. Diana's lovely face shone with sincerity.

Serena glared at Frank. "You might have admitted it last week."

"We weren't ready to make the announcement last week." Frank looked down at the child in his arms. "Do you understand what we're talking about, Ju?"

Juliet looked back at her father with grave blue eyes.

"You're going to have a new mama, darling," Diana said into the silence. "Isn't that splendid?"

Juliet turned her face into Frank's shoulder. "Don't need a mama."

"Of course you don't need a mama." Charlotte suppressed an impulse to touch the little girl. There was nothing worse than imposing oneself on children. "You already had a mama, and a very lovely one. But I hope we'll be friends."

Juliet raised her head and peeked at Charlotte out of one eye, then buried her face in Frank's shoulder again.

"I'm sorry." Serena ran over to Charlotte. "I should have said congratulations. I was too busy being cross with Francis for keeping secrets."

"Storbridge is good at secrets." Bertram Vaughan spoke

up for the first time. He stood alone now by the fireplace. Charlotte had the impression he liked it that way. "Allow me to offer you my felicitations, Miss Ribard, as at least titular head of the Vaughan family."

Frank looked at the younger man. "There's no question that you're head of the Vaughan family, Bertram."

"No. I just don't control the purse strings." Bertram gave Charlotte a crisp nod. "If you'll excuse me, Miss Ribard." He strode from the room.

"Never mind him." Serena took Charlotte's arm. "He likes to pout because Papa left Francis in charge of the money. And a jolly good thing too, or Bertram would have gambled away our doweries by now. Not that I want to get married, at least not for years and years."

"There's no need to tell Miss Ribard all our family history at once, Rena." Diana took Charlotte's other arm. "Though I suppose Francis has told you most of it already. Do sit down, Miss Ribard, and tell us how you and Francis found each other again."

Charlotte looked over her shoulder at Frank as the two girls drew her to the sofa. "The credit for that must all go to Francis."

"On the contrary." Frank gave her a smile of unadulterated sweetness. "It was you who first sought me out, my darling."

Diana plumped up the embroidered sofa cushions. "We don't mean to intrude on private matters."

"Diana doesn't really mean that. She's dying for the details." Serena dropped down on the sofa and tucked her feet up under her. "When are you going to get married?"

Charlotte looked at Frank. His gaze held the same challenge that had been in his kiss. She glanced away. He said such decisions were up to the bride. Very well, she would make the decision. She might be an unwilling wife, but she would not be a passive one. "Three weeks after Christmas. In Edinburgh." She looked at Frank and Juliet, who still had her face hidden, then back at the two girls who were to be her sisters. "We hope you will be there to wish us well."

Chapter 5

"You don't have to do this, Charlie."

Charlotte tied a red velvet ribbon in a neat bow around the handle of a basket and smiled at her brother with determination. "I want to do it, Paul."

Paul Lescaut folded his arms across his chest and rested his shoulders against the pinewood of the parlor mantel. "Gammon. If you expect me to believe—"

"Don't shout, Paul. You'll wake the children." Sophie Lescaut added two oranges and a bag of chocolates to the basket on the floor in front of her.

Paul glared at his wife. "Don't pretend you aren't as upset about this as I am, because I know perfectly well that you are."

"Perhaps." Sophie picked up a length of green ribbon and wound it around the basket handle. "But there's no good to be gained by either of us storming about. Sit down and help us or we'll never have these baskets ready for the party tomorrow."

Paul dropped down on the carpet. "Charlie, you can't seriously expect us to believe that you want to marry Frank Storbridge."

"Why not?" Charlotte nestled a carved wooden horse

in a fold of colored paper in a new basket. "You've been wanting me to get married for years."

"Unworthy prevarication, sister." He began to fill a basket with oranges and candy. "You've always claimed that you don't trust Storbridge. That he knew about Ribard's schemes."

"And you disagreed."

"I said I wasn't sure. I didn't say you should marry the man." Paul's fingers closed around an orange. "What did that bastard threaten you with, Charlie?"

Charlotte carefully tucked a bag of chocolates beneath the wooden horse. "Frank?"

Paul fixed her with a hard stare. "Our father."

Charlotte adjusted the horse so it would stand up amid the delicacies in the basket. "Daniel doesn't have anything to do with this."

"Don't try to bamboozle me. The whole business reeks of Ribard. He returns to England, and a fortnight later you come home and tell us you're going to marry his former secretary. Don't try to make me believe there isn't a connection."

"Paul, I can safely promise you that the last thing Daniel wants is for me to marry Frank."

"And that's why you're doing it?" Paul's gaze was razor-sharp. His eyes were a dark, deep brown, the color of peat or sherry or polished walnut. Her own eyes. Daniel's eyes.

"I long since ceased to care what Daniel de Ribard thought about anything I did," Charlotte said. "I'm marrying Frank because I want to."

"Are you telling me you're in love with him?"

Charlotte let out a whoop of laughter. "Is this my cynical brother talking? There are other reasons for marriage, you know."

"Charlie—" Sophie laid her hand over Charlotte's own. "You're a grown woman. You can make your own decisions. But we want you to be happy."

Charlotte fixed her gaze on the blue-and-cream border of the carpet. "Marrying Frank Storbridge is the best thing for me to do. I've thought about it very carefully."

"Damn it, Charlotte." Paul pushed himself up on his knees and took her by the shoulders. "Tell us what you're afraid of. Tell us what you're trying to accomplish. We'll take care of it, whatever it is. You don't have to do this."

"But I do." Charlotte squeezed her brother's hands. She had been one-and-twenty before she met him, yet she could not be more certain of his love if he had carried her about in his arms since babyhood. "I know what I'm doing, Paul. It's what I want to do." She looked at Sophie. "We're going to be married three weeks after Christmas. I'd like you to attend me."

"Of course, love." Sophie smiled, though her eyes had darkened to cobalt. "I'd be honored."

Charlotte looked back at Paul. "And I'd like you to give me away."

"Charlotte—"

"I won't forgive you if you don't." She got to her feet. "The baskets are almost done. If you'll excuse me, Sophie, I'm awfully tired."

"Of course. You've done yeoman duty as it is."

"Charlie—" Paul stretched out his hand.

"Trust me, Paul," Charlotte said. "I've always trusted you."

Paul Lescaut watched the parlor door shut behind his sister. "You were a fine help," he said to his wife.

Sophie wiped her hand across her eyes, smearing

traces of eyeblacking below her lids. It was a sure sign that she was exhausted. "She's made up her mind. Nothing we can say is going to change it."

"Do you seriously think Charlotte's decided she'll find everlasting happiness with Frank Storbridge?"

Sophie rubbed the muscles in her neck. "I don't think Charlotte's ever expected to find everlasting happiness. Any more than you have."

Paul looked at his wife. There was blacking beneath her eyes, her nut-brown hair was slipping from its usual elegant twist and curls, her fragile blue gown was crumpled from sitting on the floor. Just a glance at her could stop his heart and bring a lump to his throat. "But I found it," he said. "Doesn't Charlotte deserve as much?"

Sophie put out her hand and touched his face. "Don't you think I want Charlotte to be as happy as we are? But she's an adult. We have to let her make her own decisions. It's good practice for when Fenella grows up."

"If you think I'll let our daughter throw her life away any more than I'm going to let Charlotte—"

"Charlie's too intelligent to throw her life away." Sophie pulled the pins from her hair and shook it out over her shoulders. "I always liked Frank Storbridge. He and Charlotte were very close until she got him all wrapped up in her feelings about Uncle Daniel."

Paul inched across the floor. "Don't tell me you think she's been secretly in love with Storbridge all these years." He pushed aside Sophie's lacy collar and began to massage her neck. "Now who's talking like a hopeless romantic?"

"I think Charlotte's reasons for marrying Frank may be more complex than even she realizes." Sophie rested her head against his shoulder. "I'm not pretending I'm overjoyed about this betrothal. I wish Charlotte would be more forthcoming about her reasons. But since she won't, the best we can do is support her decision."

Paul was silent for a moment, staring at the dark water-fall of his wife's hair. "When I met Storbridge five years ago, before all the business with Ribard, it was clear he was in love with Charlie."

Sophie twisted her head around to look at him. "I know they were friends—"

"This was more than friendship. He was besotted with her. And he knew she was as out of reach as the moon." He smiled into Sophie's eyes. "Being in a similar state at the time with regards to you, perhaps I was more inclined to notice."

"And so a part of you is inclined to have sympathy for him now?"

"Yes, I suppose so. It's probably foolish." He pulled Sophie close against him. "Ribard's behind this some-how. I'm sure of it."

"Charlotte wouldn't bow to pressure from Uncle Daniel."

"No. So she's trying to stop him from something. The question is, what?"

Sophie turned her face into his shoulder. "Paul. Are you prepared for the whole business with Uncle Daniel to begin again?"

He tightened his arm around her. "It never really ended."

"No, but at least he was out of sight if not out of mind."

Paul rested his cheek against her soft, rose-scented hair. "He's only admitted to being my father once in his life, and even then he did it obliquely. Believe me, I'm no more troubled by filial scruples than he is by parental ones."

"Oh, but I think he is. To the extent Uncle Daniel has scruples at all. To try to destroy you cost him far more of a pang than to go after me, for all I grew up in his household. It isn't that he didn't like me. He simply didn't think about me much one way or the other. Or Céline or Marie-Louise or Georgine, if the truth be told. But you're his only son, acknowledged or not. And Charlotte—"

"Charlotte's his weakness."

"Yes." There was a troubled note in Sophie's voice. "And I'm very much afraid that he may be hers."

Céline flipped through the morning post on the tray beside her chocolate. There was a letter from Charlotte. She slit it open, expecting the latest news from Edinburgh mixed with radical politics. She scanned the letter, gave a shriek, and jumped out of bed, spattering chocolate over the blue silk coverlet.

She threw open the door to her boudoir, ran across the room, and opened the connecting door to her husband's room without knocking, which was something she hadn't done for years. "Silverton. Charlotte says she's going to marry Francis Storbridge."

Silverton was sitting up in bed drinking coffee. He set the cup down, sloshing coffee into the saucer, and stared at her out of heavy-lidded eyes. "Charlie's in Edinburgh."

"She sent me a letter." Céline marched across the room, perched on the edge of her husband's bed, and dropped the letter in front of him. "Apparently it was all decided before she left London, but she wanted to go home and tell Sophie and Paul before she told us."

Silverton picked up the letter and ran his gaze over it. "Quiet little Charlie. Who would have guessed?"

"I can't think where she even found the time to see him. And I can't imagine what brought them together in the first place."

Silverton folded the letter. "They used to be thick as

thieves when he worked for your father. Always whispering together and going off on rambles about the estate. Even after she became betrothed to Ned Rutledge, I used to wonder—"

"Yes, but that was years ago. She turned her back on Francis Storbridge when she turned her back on Daniel." Céline picked up the letter and tapped it against the coverlet. "The wedding's to be in Edinburgh in January. We really ought to go."

Silverton's fair brows lifted in surprise. "Of course we'll go. It's Charlie. We should take the children."

Céline regarded her husband for a moment. The thick hair, still as brilliant a gold as when she'd first met him; the blue eyes, tinged by shadows now but still able to dazzle; the quick, disarming smile. Her husband of fifteen years, the father of her children, the man she was tied to for the rest of her life, even if the bonds had loosened. There were times when she felt she could read the thoughts behind the charming facade no better than on the day she met him. "Silver . . . don't you mind?"

He took a sip of coffee. "Mind?"

"That she's marrying Francis Storbridge of all people."

"He's not the man I'd have picked for a brother-in-law, but then that's the point, isn't it? I'm not the one who has to marry him."

She fingered the letter. "I've never understood what started it. The rivalry."

His mouth twisted. "To tell the truth, nor have I. We rose to prominence in our respective parties at much the same time. We're often chosen to oppose each other." He grimaced. "If Storbridge speaks on emancipation I may have to answer him. Not a prospect I look forward to."

"Because it will be difficult to do?"

"Because it's a dirty subject." His eyes clouded. For a moment Céline felt as though he wasn't really looking at her. "Storbridge may be aggravating, but I'd never deny his brilliance. And he has rather more integrity than—than a number of others I could name." His hand tightened on the blue velvet of the coverlet. "It's nothing to be sneezed at, integrity."

Céline looked down at his hand and had a sudden memory of his fingers moving against her skin. Strange, for his was hardly the only touch she had known, that it should be the one to leave indelible memories. "Silver . . . is something the matter?"

"The matter?" He gave her a brilliant smile that didn't reach his eyes. "No, save that I drank more than I should have last night. I don't think that the brandy at White's is as good as it used to be. I have the devil of a head."

She wasn't sure she believed him. She didn't want anything to be wrong, but with sudden intensity she wanted him to confide in her. And it was clear that he was not going to do so. Perhaps he'd had a quarrel with his current mistress, whoever that might be. It would be vulgar to tease him.

She got to her feet. "We'll leave for Edinburgh after we spend Christmas with your parents. I do hope Sophie can be trusted to see to the wedding arrangements. If it's left to Charlie she's liable to decide to be married in the print shop."

Daniel settled back in a chair by the window. It had seemed expedient to accept Henry Sunderland's invitation for the holidays, but the charms of the Sunderland circle were rapidly fading. He had taken to lingering in his room rather than joining the others at breakfast, where the talk was of horses and the air smelled of kippered herring and grilled tomatoes.

He had finished with the *Morning Post*. He picked up the *Morning Chronicle*, which Sunderland also took. A Whig paper, but often more lively than the *Post*. He flipped through the pages. A name caught his eye. His own name. The newsprint crackled between his fingers. He pulled it taut.

Mr. Francis Storbridge, M.P. for Howitt, and Miss Charlotte de Ribard will be married in Edinburgh on the fourteenth of January.

Daniel threw back his head and gave a shout of laughter. Very neatly done. They had managed to keep the betrothal quiet until the wedding was less than week away. And then there it was in print, a quiet, dry statement that they had thoroughly outfoxed him.

He'd underestimated Charlotte. She'd played that scene by the Serpentine to perfection. But then he'd always known she took after him. He just hadn't realized how thoroughly. She had evidently learned, as he had long ago, that the secret to getting what one wanted was being willing to go far enough.

Daniel set the newspaper down beside his coffee and muffins. Storbridge had played him well too. Daniel had glimpsed brilliance in his former secretary from the first, but he hadn't realized quite how formidable a man Storbridge had become. A pity he hadn't had a chance to mold Storbridge for longer. He might have become a useful ally.

The laughter left Daniel. He took a sip of strong black coffee. Storbridge was not his ally. Neither was Charlotte. Daniel could acknowledge that he had lost a hand. He could appreciate the cleverness of his opponents. But he had no intention of losing the ultimate contest.

He studied the betrothal announcement for a moment, then rose and went to the bellpull. His valet, Guillaume, answered the summons with his usual promptness. "Yes, *monsieur*?"

Daniel glanced down at the paper in his hand. "Pack my things. We leave for Edinburgh in the morning."

Chapter 6

Juliet tugged at Frank's arm. "Almost there?"

Frank shifted his position on the soft leather upholstery of the Vaughan traveling carriage and settled his daughter more comfortably in his lap. "Just a few minutes more, poppet." He reached down to pet Millamant, who was lying patiently beside him.

Diana pushed the veil back from her bonnet. "The streets are terribly crowded."

"I like it. It's exciting." Serena pressed her face closer to the carriage window.

"We're going to get jolly wet if this rain holds up." Valentine Vaughan, home from Harrow for the holidays, turned to look at Frank. "I say, Storbridge, you didn't tell us this girl you're going to marry lives in a slum."

"Val." Diana's voice was sharp.

"Her brother runs a newspaper, Val." Bertram, sprawled in the corner, pushed his hat back from his face long enough to look at his brother. "You know Storbridge has always had a soft spot for the masses, however finely he dresses."

"Bertram." Diana frowned at her elder brother, then clutched the carriage strap as they rounded a corner. "This is supposed to be a joyous occasion."

"It is?" Bertram cast a sidelong glance at Frank. "You could have fooled me."

Val looked from his brother to Frank, his youthful face mirroring his uncertainty. At fifteen he was still feeling his way, unsure whose lead to follow. Frank recognized the boy's struggle, but he knew if he interfered he would only tip the scales in Bertram's direction.

Bertram subsided in the corner and dropped his hat back over his face. Diana smoothed the creases from her traveling cloak. Serena continued to peer out the window. Rain beat down on the carriage roof with increased intensity.

The carriage came to an abrupt halt, as if the coachman had nearly missed the house. Frank looked out the window for the first time since they'd left their hotel. A jumble of tall buildings rose beyond his line of sight. Rain and gray mist obscured the houses. Like time blurring images of the past. But he would never forget the stone-framed wooden door that he had once approached with the laughable dreams of youth burning in his chest.

Serena and Val scrambled down onto the rain-slick paving stones as soon as the steps were lowered. Diana followed, lifting the velvet folds of her cloak carefully. Bertram pushed his hat into place and swung down with a weary sigh. Frank left the carriage last, Juliet in his arms, Millamant at his heels.

Wind whistled through the narrow street as on his visit five years ago. But Charlotte no longer lived in the house where he had found her then. That house belonged to Paul Lescaut's cousin, Robert. Paul and Sophie had bought the house next door, where Charlotte now made her home. A different house, a different time, a different objective. His hand cupped around Juliet's head, Frank hurried through the wind and the rain to join the others in the doorway.

A maidservant led them upstairs. Frank had sent a note around when they arrived in Edinburgh. They were expected. The Lescaut family were gathered in the parlor, a fire casting warm light on the blue-gray wallpaper, the smell of sherry and tea and hot, buttered scones in the air.

"Frank, how nice." Charlotte came forward, her smile bright and steady. The betrothal ring on her left hand caught the firelight. "We were afraid you might get lost."

Frank smiled directly into her eyes. He had an acute recollection of kissing her and an urgent impulse to do so again. "You forget I've been to Old Fishmarket Close before."

He saw the memory register in her eyes, but her gaze did not waver. "Of course. How silly of me."

She proceeded to introduce the two families with admirable aplomb. Paul Lescaut shook Frank's hand, his grip firm, his gaze hard with challenge. Sophie Lescaut gave Frank a smile that was lovely and cool and every bit as challenging as her husband's. Her children, a girl of five and a boy who must be close to Juliet's age, clung to her skirts and peered at the new arrivals. Paul and Sophie's wards—Dugal, a wiry, dark-haired boy of about seventeen and Amy, a pretty, forthright young woman with hair the color of a copper skillet—echoed the guarded reception.

"You'll meet the rest of the family this evening," Sophie said. "We're to dine with Paul's cousin Robert and his wife, Emma. They have the house next door." She moved to the Pembroke table where the refreshments were set out and smiled at the Vaughans and Juliet with a warmth that was unalloyed. "Do sit down and have something to eat. I know how tiring the journey from London can be."

Charlotte pulled Frank to a blue velvet settee. "The

wedding is set for ten-thirty, the day after tomorrow."
She seated herself and drew him down beside her. She
kept her hand tucked beneath his arm. It was the first
time in five years that Frank could remember her initiat-
ing physical contact between them. He noted the measur-
ing looks of Paul and Sophie and realized Charlotte
was trying to prove something to them. He would have
been encouraged, save for the cool rigidity of her fingers
against his arm. There was no hint of the pliant warmth
he had felt, briefly, when he kissed her to seal the betrothal. Yet even Charlotte could not deny that it had
been there.

Serena slathered a scone with strawberry preserves.
"Are Diana and I still going to be bridesmaids?"

"Rena." Diana set down her teacup with a clatter.

"I just wanted to know. Shouldn't we practice or
something?"

"Yes, of course you are to be bridesmaids. We'll practice tomorrow." Charlotte smiled at the girls. "Amy's going to be a bridesmaid as well, along with Robert and
Emma's daughter Kirsty."

Serena and Diana exchanged looks with Amy, as
though the three were debating whether or not they would
prove to be friends.

"And you're to be a bridesmaid too, Juliet." Charlotte
turned to Juliet, who was sitting on Frank's lap. "Do you
know what that is?"

Juliet leaned back against Frank's arm, putting maximum distance between herself and Charlotte. "I throw
rose petals."

"Exactly." Charlotte lifted her hand as though to reach
out to Juliet, then let it fall in her lap.

Frank glanced from his daughter, wary of her new
mother, to his future wife, equally wary of her new hus-

band. "Juliet's been practicing with dried flowers in the drawing room all through the holidays," he said. "You'll have to let her give you a demonstration."

He detached his arm from Charlotte's grip and clasped her hand in his own—partly because he wanted to make up for Juliet's lack of response, and partly, he admitted, because he wanted to see what Charlotte would do. He felt the tremor that ran through her, but she made no attempt to pull away. She wouldn't in front of her family. She would not turn to them to help her out of the bargain she had made. Quite the reverse, it seemed. Her determination to stand by her word was extraordinary.

"I've always wanted to visit Scotland." Diana stepped into the conversational void. "I adore Sir Walter Scott. I must confess I was disappointed not to see any tartans or hear any bagpipes when we arrived."

Dugal paused in the act of reaching for a scone. "Tartans and bagpipes are Highland. They dinna ha' them i' the Lowlands." He still spoke with a trace of a Highland accent, which Frank suspected he was exaggerating for effect. "That's a lot o' twaddle cooked up by Sir Walter Scott."

"Like all the 'Scots' fashions you see in Ackermann's. They're so"—Amy broke off as if she had just become aware of the tartan ribbons on Diana's bonnet—"pretty."

Silence fell over the parlor. Sophie broke it by asking who needed more tea.

Bertram waved aside tea and looked up from his sherry with an innocence that didn't deceive Frank for a moment. "Are your sisters coming to the wedding, Miss Ribard?"

"Not all of them, I'm afraid. Georgine is expecting a baby, and Marie-Louise is at the Hague. But Céline and Silverton and the children are coming." She gave Frank's hand a warning squeeze. "We expect them tomorrow."

"Silverton's no' so bad for a Tory," Dugal said. "We even dine wi' him."

"Well, well." Bertram settled back into the sofa. "This should be interesting."

Frank said nothing, because there was nothing to say. Charlotte's fingers were motionless in his own.

"We're sorry our eldest sister couldn't be here for the wedding," Diana said. "She and her husband went abroad for the Congress of Verona last summer. They stayed to travel in Italy."

"Her husband's the Duke of Howitt." Serena slipped a piece of scone to Millamant, who was lying at her feet. "Diana isn't saying so because it sounds pretentious to toss about titles, only I don't suppose you're impressed by titles because you don't believe in them anyway."

An appreciative gleam lit Paul Lescaut's eyes. "That's an admirably succinct way of putting it . . . Lady Serena."

"Howitt and Francis are the greatest of friends," Diana said.

"Yes." Bertram crossed his legs. "Storbridge sits in Howitt's pocket. I mean his pocket borough. Nice to keep these things in the family."

"More scones?" Sophie asked.

The awkward scene only continued a short time longer. Charlotte took Diana and Serena up to her bedchamber to look at the bridesmaids' dresses. Sophie, Amy, and the Lescaut children went with them. To Frank's relief, Juliet agreed to accompany them as well, though she clung close to Diana. Frank suspected it was the lure of spending more time with the young Lescaut children that drew her. Juliet didn't often have company her own age.

While the women were leaving the room, Dugal said he had to walk over to the university. He asked if Bertram and Val wanted to go with him. Both agreed—Val eagerly, Bertram with an air that implied it was better than cooling his heels in the parlor.

When the door closed behind the boys, Frank turned to Paul. "Very adroitly done. Did your family rehearse getting everyone out of the room, or do you improvise exceptionally well?"

Paul's mouth relaxed into a reluctant grin, though his eyes remained hard. "I confess I've been wanting to have a talk with you. Shall we go down to the print shop? We can be sure of privacy there."

The print shop occupied the ground floor of the house and of Robert Lescaut's house next door, for the two cousins published the *Edinburgh Leader* together. The walls had been knocked down to form a single long room, with a large, new-looking printing press at one end. Newspaper was everywhere, hung to dry from sheets of clothesline strung across the room, piled high on desks, on counters, on chairs, on the floor. The air smelled of ink and machine oil and wood polish.

"You and your cousin have done well for yourselves," Frank said. "I've heard the *Leader* talked of in Westminster on more than one occasion."

Paul perched on the edge of a well-worn oak desk. "Talked of or cursed?"

Frank dropped down in a ladder-back chair. "A bit of both. Even stalwart Whigs claim you go too far."

"Including you?"

Frank settled back in the chair, avoiding the newspaper that was draped over its back. "Oh, I'm not a Whig, I'm a Radical. Ask any of my colleagues."

Paul's eyes narrowed. "It hasn't stopped you from rising within your party."

Frank shrugged. "There are times to toe the line and times to push the limits. One learns."

"Perhaps that's the difference between us. I've never learned to hold my tongue. But then, I know I'd never make for a politician." Paul thumbed his finger through the newspaper on the desk beside him. "There's talk that you're going to introduce an emancipation bill in the next session."

"Yes. It's long overdue, as your paper has been pointing out for some time. There was an article last spring that I particularly admired. About the way tyranny warps the tyrants as well as the oppressed."

"Sophie wrote that." Paul glanced down at the paper. "The *Leader* isn't just mine and Robert's. Sophie and Emma write as many articles as we do. Charlotte devises a mathematical puzzle every week. It's very popular. She also keeps our accounts."

For a moment Frank could hear the voice of a younger Charlotte, explaining seemingly impossible formulas to calculate the number of flowers in the garden or the number of slates on the roof. "She always had a head for figures."

Paul's head jerked up. "She has a genius for them."

Frank took the other man's measure. "I know."

Paul's fingers clenched. The bones of his right hand had been smashed in battle years ago when he was a soldier, Charlotte had told Frank. The hand was bent and ridged with scars and next to useless. But even one-handed, Paul Lescaut radiated power like a finely honed blade. "I'll be blunt," Paul said. "I don't want Charlotte to marry you. I tried to talk her out of it. But she's even more stubborn than I am. So all I can say is this: If you hurt her, I'll kill you."

His eyes left no doubt that he meant it. Oddly enough, Frank felt a moment of kinship with Charlotte's brother. "I have no intention of hurting Charlotte." It was true, though it depended on one's definition of what he had done to her already.

The pressure of Paul's gaze remained hard as steel. "Charlotte won't tell us why she's marrying you. I'm convinced it's something to do with that bastard who sired the pair of us."

"I'm no ally of Daniel de Ribard's." Frank's voice rang out with a sharpness he hadn't intended.

Paul raised his strong, slanting brows. "I never said you were."

Frank leaned forward. It mattered more than he would admit that Paul believed him. "If Ribard tries to manipulate Charlotte, you have my word I'll do my utmost to defeat him."

"That," said Paul, "is the only reason I'm even tolerating this farce of a marriage." He pushed his untidy, dark gold hair back from his face. "I liked you when we met five years ago, Storbridge. I don't know what to make of you now. But if I don't want to lose my sister, it seems I have no choice but to welcome you to the family."

Frank got to his feet and held out his hand. "I'd be honored to call you friend, Lescaut. But for the time being, it seems I'll have to settle for calling you brother-in-law."

"They're a dashed odd family." Val held his hands out to the fire in the private parlor Frank had engaged at their hotel on Princes Street. "Amy told me straight out that she used to work in a mill, and from what I can make out, Dugal seems to have lived on the streets before the Lescauts adopted him."

Serena untied the ribbons on her slippers and rubbed her feet. "I like them. They're alive." She grinned at Frank, who was sitting beside her on the sofa.

Bertram poured himself a glass of brandy and downed half the contents. "They're certainly different from anyone we visit in London."

Diana peeled off her white gloves. "They may be unconventional, but there's nothing unrefined about them." She smoothed her simple cream-colored skirt. "And Sophie Lescaut does wear the most beautiful clothes."

Bertram refilled his brandy glass. "Her uncle Ribard signed quite a bit of money over to her before he fled the country. And to Charlotte, apparently. You're marrying into a wealthy family, Storbridge."

Frank met the challenge in Bertram's gaze. "For the second time, you mean?"

Bertram glanced down at the brandy, then looked back at Frank. "You said it, I didn't."

Frank got to his feet. "If you choose to believe I married your sister for her money, that's quite your own affair, Bertram, just as it's your affair if you think I'm marrying Charlotte for the same reasons." He moved to the door.

"Francis." Diana's voice stopped him.

He looked back to see her pleading with her eyes. She wanted him to say he loved Charlotte with all his heart, and that he had loved Julia every bit as much. Poor Diana. At twenty, her romantic dreams still burned bright.

Bertram tossed his brandy down in one draught. "You haven't got this one pregnant too, have you?"

The room went absolutely still, save for the crackling of the fire and the patter of rain against the windows. Diana swung her head around to stare at her brother. Serena's hands clenched on her skirt. Val blanched.

Frank looked Bertram directly in the eye. "You can say what you will to me, Bertram. But if you think I will allow you to insult Julia's honor—or Charlotte's—you are very much mistaken." He reached for the door handle. "We have less than forty-eight hours to get through before the wedding. I trust we can all manage to keep a civil tongue in our heads."

He glanced over his shoulder one last time. "By the by, Miss Ribard is not at present expecting my child."

Chapter 7

Charlotte started at the rap on her door. She had fallen into a reverie, staring at the shadow patterns the candlelight made on the apricot silk of her wedding dress, which hung on her wardrobe door.

"Charlie?" Sophie's voice sounded from the corridor. "May I come in?"

"Of course." Charlotte sat up straighter against the pillows and adjusted the shawl she'd wrapped over her nightdress.

Sophie slipped into the room, her red silk dressing gown rustling, her hair a mass of curl papers. She stopped by the wardrobe and adjusted the wedding dress. "It's beautiful. You're going to look lovely."

Charlotte pushed her braided hair back over her shoulder. "Not next to my bridesmaids. Not to mention you."

"Don't sell yourself short, love." The bed creaked as Sophie perched on the edge. "No last-minute doubts?"

Charlotte forced a smile to her lips. "Is that the voice of hope?"

"Concern." Sophie's gaze skimmed over Charlotte's face, as though she were still looking for answers. "All the preparations can have a certain inevitability. You do know you can change your mind up until the last minute, don't you?"

"I'm sure Paul will remind me as he walks me down the aisle."

Sophie smiled. "I expect he will." She fingered a fold of the chintz quilt. "Charlie, is there anything you want to talk about? It's our last chance for a nighttime chat for a while."

Charlotte swallowed. She looked from the familiarity of the primrose-splashed basin and pitcher on her dressing table to her wedding dress and the trunk already packed with her crisp new bride clothes. Back at her old life and forward to her new. Most girls probably felt this way the night before they got married. But in her case the feelings were twisted, like light filtered through a distorted glass. "I'll come to visit often. You can still come to Chelmsford in the summers. And I hope you'll visit me—us—in London."

"Of course. I look forward to it." Sophie drew a breath. The flame of the candle in the little silver candlestick on the bedside table wavered. "But I was wondering . . . that is . . ." She tugged at a loose thread on the quilt. "I know it seems silly when you're all grown up, but here it is the night before your wedding and I'm not sure how much anyone's ever explained to you—"

Charlotte felt the blood rush to her face. "You want to know if I understand the intimacies of the marriage bed."

Sophie looked up, her eyes rueful with self-mockery. "Ridiculous that we find it so difficult to talk about, isn't it?"

Charlotte pulled her shawl tighter about her shoulders. "It's all right, Sophie. I may not know as much about the marriage bed as I do about quadratic equations, but I think I know enough to suffice."

Sophie toyed with her wedding band. "I'm sure you know the general outlines. But there's such a lot of misinformation, and I thought no one might have told you the gory details. Oh, poison." She shook her head. "That's just the point. It needn't be gory at all. In fact, it can be quite splendid."

Charlotte drew up her legs under the bedclothes and clasped her arms about her knees. "I had gathered that much. I've seen the looks you exchange with Paul."

"Thank heaven we've managed to set a good example." Sophie glanced away, then looked back at Charlotte. "The first time doesn't have to hurt, you know, not if the man is considerate. But it can be . . . awkward . . . in the beginning. It helps if you can talk about it with your lover. You shouldn't be afraid to tell him what you find agreeable and what you don't."

Charlotte choked back a desperate laugh. "Frank and I will manage."

Sophie's mouth curled with mischief. "I trust you'll do much better than manage." She tucked a paper-wrapped curl behind her ear. "Dearest, your feelings for Frank are your own affair. But one doesn't have to be madly in love with a man to find pleasure in his bed."

Charlotte's face went from warm to burning hot. "I know. That is, I expect I'll learn. I mean—" She stared at the yellow roses on her quilt. The memory that came to her was not of Ned Rutledge, as she would have expected, but of Frank kissing her the day he gave her her betrothal ring. For a moment the memory was so vivid that she could feel the pressure of his lips on her own and the force of his arms around her. She drew a breath and met her cousin's gaze. "Thank you, Sophie."

"I'm afraid I made rather a mull of it. And to think I pride myself on my sophistication. I shall try to do better with Amy and Fenella." Sophie squeezed Charlotte's hand. "There's nothing you want to ask me?"

Her eyes invited confidences. The pressure of her hand was warm and comforting. Charlotte caught the rose scent she'd sampled on her cousin's dressing table as a child. Words rose up in her throat, a torrent raging to break free. Yet they stuck in her mouth, choking her. She couldn't find a way to break the barrier of five years' silence. Nor could she find the words to confess what she could scarcely admit even in the privacy of her own thoughts.

"Nothing." She swallowed, burying her secret shame deep inside. "Thank you, Sophie, but I think I'm as prepared for this marriage as I'll ever be."

"Your Miss Ribard has a lot of family present, considering she isn't on speaking terms with her father." Bertram spoke softly, his back turned to the wedding guests assembled in Sophie Lescaut's drawing room.

Frank stepped away from the heat of the fire blazing in the fireplace behind them. "We're not exactly underrepresented ourselves."

"All our family's in the wedding party." Val tugged at the dark blue kerseymere of his new coat. His gaze skimmed over the guests settling themselves in the chairs that had been gathered up from all over the Lescaut house and arranged in rows on the green and gold carpet. "I suppose it would have been a bit far for our friends to make the journey from London."

"Yes. Aside from us the only ones to travel up from town are the Silvertons." Bertram glanced at Frank. "Life's full of ironies, isn't it?"

"Quite." Frank looked at the front row of chairs. Céline

Silverton was speaking to Emma Lescaut, her white-gloved hands gesturing with animation, the net and ostrich feathers on her bonnet stirring as she spoke. The Silverton boys were squirming in their chairs, while their elder sister tried to keep them quiet. Silverton leaned over and said something to the children, then looked up and met Frank's gaze. His brows rose in a kind of mocking salute.

The muscles deep in Frank's gut clenched. Irony was too light a word. Next to Daniel de Ribard, Silverton was the last person Frank wanted at his wedding.

"The bridal party is practically as large as the number of guests." Bertram flicked a bit of lint from his coat. "It's almost as though the bride wanted to armor herself with her family."

"I like weddings in houses," Val said. "This is a jolly sight less stuffy than when you married Julia, Francis."

Frank gave his younger brother-in-law a smile, aware of the gleam of hostility in Bertram's eyes at the mention of the earlier wedding. Nearly three years ago Frank and the Vaughan brothers had stood at the altar in St. George's Hanover Square, Bertram as hostile as he was today, Val more distant and nearly half a head shorter. Otherwise, the two settings could not be more different. Frank could still recall the early-spring sunshine and the close air, heavy with the fragrance of the candles and the scent worn by the throng of fashionable, politically influential guests. He had felt suffocated by the hot, sweet air. Or perhaps by the awareness of what he was getting himself into.

Today the air carried the clean scent of the pine sprays set about the room in vases tied with apricot ribbon. The heat of the fire could not entirely ward off the chill of January in Edinburgh. The crowd was smaller and more diverse. Children ran about at the back of the room. The boys who distributed copies of the *Edinburgh Leader* were present, as was the man who supplied ink, and several persons who, according to Charlotte, contributed stories to the paper. They plainly did not move in Edinburgh's first circles.

But most of all, there was something less forced, less artificial, more *real* about today.

Frank shook his head at this fancy. The minister, who had been speaking to Robert Lescaut, joined Frank and the Vaughans, smiling as if the wedding were an occasion of simple joy. Emma Lescaut moved to the piano. Frank realized that he was actually about to marry Charlotte de Ribard. He felt a moment of sheer, dizzying exhilaration, followed by a bitter, numbing chill.

The crowd grew quiet. Emma began to play a Bach saraband. The door at the opposite end of the room opened. Three little girls stepped into the room, dressed in peach-colored frocks with lace collars. Juliet toddled in the middle between Fenella Lescaut and Robert and Emma's daughter Alison, who were both five. The three girls strewed dried rose petals, just as Frank had promised.

Juliet's eyes were bright. The excitement had at least momentarily overcome her qualms about the marriage. She looked up at her father, her mouth widening in a smile. Frank echoed the smile and felt some of the tension leave his body.

The older bridesmaids came next. Diana looked as though she was determined to find joy and solemnity in the occasion if no one else did. Serena winked at him. Amy and Kirsty were smiling but reserved, as if they still hadn't made up their minds if they were supposed to be welcoming him to the family or protecting Charlotte from him.

Sophie followed the bridesmaids, a vision of peach silk and nut-brown ringlets. As she reached the end of the room, she met Frank's gaze for a moment. The message was clear, the same words her husband had spoken to him. *If you hurt her, I'll kill you.*

The girls arranged themselves on either side of the makeshift altar. Then Charlotte came through the doorway on her brother's arm. She stepped into the clear purity of the wintry sunlight streaming through the windows at the back of the room, and the breath stopped in Frank's throat.

She wore a dress of palest apricot. Her hair was arranged in ringlets and adorned with roses of apricot silk, though nothing could make the unruly mass appear entirely tame. No doubt she didn't remember that she had worn an apricot dress that first day he had seen her in her father's study. Perhaps she didn't remember that day at all. But he did. For a moment he was lost in the dreams of his youth. Charlotte was walking down the aisle toward him, and she was going to be his.

Charlotte and Paul moved closer, and Frank saw the pale set of his bride's face, the steely determination in her eyes, the taut line of her mouth. The dreams turned to bitter ash in his mouth. Whatever Diana persisted in thinking, this wedding was as artificial as the silk flowers in Charlotte's hair, as lacking in true feeling as the flowers were in scent.

They took their places before the minister. Frank was aware of Paul's and Sophie's gazes stabbing into him on either side. When the minister asked Paul to give his sister's hand in marriage, there was a pause, brief but weighted with tension. Charlotte turned her head slightly toward her brother. Paul gave his assent, his voice even but harsher than usual.

When it came to the vows, Charlotte gave Frank her hand without hesitation, but her fingers were cold and stiff.

"Do you, Francis, take this woman Charlotte to be your wedded wife . . ."

Frank stared down at their clasped hands. He could feel the tension running through Charlotte. He wondered if they had ever been farther apart than they were at this moment.

Christ, he'd been mad to propose this bargain, and despicable to hold her to it. He should end it here and now.

". . . until God shall separate you by death?"

Charlotte lifted her head and met his gaze. She looked like a duelist who has just heard the order to turn and fire.

Frank took her up on the challenge. "I do."

"Charlotte looked beautiful." Emma Lescaut took a sip of champagne and regarded Paul over the gilded rim of the glass. "It can't be easy, giving your sister in marriage."

Paul downed the contents of his own glass. Céline and Silverton had brought four cases of champagne as a wedding present. He wished it were whisky. "Nothing about this wedding was easy."

He looked across the drawing room. Charlotte and Storbridge were standing in front of the fireplace, accepting the congratulations of some of Emma's cousins who had come in from the country for the wedding. The newlyweds weren't actually touching, but if one didn't look closely they could pass for a conventionally happy bride and groom. Paul recalled the shadowed look in Charlotte's eyes as he gave her his arm to lead her down the aisle. He clenched the fragile stem of the champagne glass. If he didn't know how Sophie prized it, he'd snap the bloody thing in two.

Emma followed the direction of his gaze. "She means a great deal to him."

Paul swung his head around to look at his cousin's wife. "What the devil makes you think that?"

Emma regarded him from beneath level, unplucked brows. "He couldn't take his gaze off her as she came down the aisle. His eyes were burning."

Paul tugged at his carefully tied cravat. Christ, was the whole family going mad? He looked into Emma's gray-green eyes, as earthy and uncompromising as the Scottish countryside. "Don't you start too, Em. I never took you for a romantic."

Emma pushed a loose auburn ringlet behind her ear. "No, but you've always said I'm observant."

Paul groaned. "Damn it, Emma—"

"Well, all things considered, we're getting through this remarkably well." Sophie joined them, Céline at her side. "Thank you for your restraint, my sweet." Sophie slipped her hand through Paul's arm. "If one were blind and deaf one might almost imagine you were in charity with the whole event."

"You and Silverton both." Céline adjusted a diamond bracelet. "I don't see why you object to the match, Paul. I would have thought Francis Storbridge was enough of a Radical to suit even you."

"No one could be radical enough for Paul and still get elected." Sophie squeezed Paul's arm. It felt like a gesture of warning as much as affection.

Céline accepted a glass of champagne from one of the footmen Sophie had engaged for the wedding. "I must confess I'm glad to see Charlie married, even if it is to a member of the Opposition."

Paul looked at the velvet-gowned, golden-haired woman who, according to sheer biology, was as much his sister as Charlotte. He didn't really understand Céline, any more than she understood him, but over the years he had come to feel a certain rude affection for her, if only because they both called Charlotte sister. "There's more to marriage than politics, Céline," he said.

Céline raised her pale, perfectly arched brows. "When you've been married to a politician as long as I have, it's difficult to believe so." Her voice was playfully arch, but there was an undercurrent that carried a sting.

Emma stepped into the difficult moment. "Poor Mr. Storbridge doesn't have much luck with his brothers-in-law from either marriage. Bertram Vaughan was looking daggers at him all during the ceremony."

"Oh, it's no secret that Bertram resents Francis." Céline took a sip of champagne. "Bertram was past his majority when his father died, but old Lord Vaughan made Francis guardian of the younger children and gave him control of the Vaughan fortune and estates until Bertram turns twenty-five."

"I see." Emma glanced at Bertram, who had sought refuge in a corner and was refilling his glass from a spare champagne bottle. "Not an arrangement calculated to ensure domestic tranquillity."

Paul looked from the callow young Lord Vaughan to his sister and Storbridge. "Not the household I'd have wished on Charlotte."

"Never mind." Sophie pressed his arm. "Charlotte's equal to anything. She's your sister."

Serena drew her satin-slippered feet up beneath her silk skirt and lacy petticoats onto the green-striped damask of the drawing-room window seat. If she craned her head she could glimpse Francis's profile and the silk flowers that adorned Charlotte's hair. They were still standing together. That must be a good sign. Of course, Francis and Julia had stood side by side for most of their wedding breakfast, though Serena could scarcely recall more than a half dozen occasions when she'd seen them together afterward.

There was a sudden *thunk* as someone plunked down on the window seat beside her. "Oh." It was Kirsty, Emma Lescaut's daughter, who had also been a bridesmaid. "I didn't realize anyone was here."

"Sorry." Serena straightened up, feeling like an interloper. "I'll leave."

"No." Kirsty settled the folds of her skirt. Her peach dress was identical to Serena's, but it fit her differently, clinging to curves Serena did not yet posses. "I don't blame you for wanting a bit of peace and quiet."

Kirsty looked at Serena. Serena looked back. She had the feeling they resembled two cats circling each other, debating whether or not to touch noses. "It's always chaotic when you put two families together," Kirsty said. "Some of my relatives didn't like my stepfather, Robert, when he married Mama, but look at them now." She gestured, indicating the various members of her mother's family crowding the drawing room. "They think of the Lescauts like blood kin."

Serena twisted her fingers in the folds of her skirt. "I like Charlotte."

"So do I." Kirsty's gray-green eyes were serious and a little challenging. "Charlie's splendid. She's had a beastly time of it with everything that happened with her father. But she's always ready to listen to my problems, even silly ones like scraped knees. She deserves to be happy."

"So does Francis." Serena didn't understand the undercurrents that had been running through the Lescaut family since their arrival in Edinburgh, but she did know that Francis wasn't properly appreciated by the Lescauts and perhaps not even by Charlotte. "Francis has taken care of all of us since Papa died. Even before that, he wrote Papa's speeches for him and looked after the accounts and saw to just about everything."

Kirsty twisted a long auburn curl around her finger. Her hair was dressed in an effortlessly grown-up style Serena at once envied and scorned. "Did Mr. Storbridge love your sister very much?" Kirsty asked.

Serena opened her mouth, then closed it. To say no seemed to be an insult, both to Francis and to Julia, yet to say yes would be dishonest. And somehow unfair to Charlotte. "They weren't married very long. Julia died when Juliet was born. Francis was busy standing for Parliament, and Julia was ill during her confinement."

"She must have loved him. I mean, he couldn't have been considered a brilliant catch in those days."

"I'm sure she loved him. Because whatever anyone says, Francis would be too honorable to do anything like that unless the woman encouraged him."

There was a brief pause. "Like what?" Kirsty asked.

Serena swallowed. She hadn't realized Kirsty hadn't heard the rumors. But if she hadn't already, she soon would. "Juliet was born seven months after Francis and Julia were married."

"I see." Kirsty's eyes narrowed. "And people say Mr. Storbridge seduced her so she'd have to marry him?"

"But Francis wouldn't. Besides, I don't think he'd have had to *seduce* her. I mean, I'm not really old enough to notice things like that, but even I can see Francis is very—"

Kirsty grinned. "Yes, he is. Very."

"I say, Rena—oh." Val stopped beside the window seat, taking in the sight of Kirsty sitting next to Serena.

"Kirsty—" Dugal came up at nearly the same time and likewise was brought up short.

"Sorry," said Val, his manner as stiff as his posture. "You want to talk to your cousin. Serena and I'll go elsewhere."

"Nay." Dugal was less stiff than Val, but equally on his dignity. "You're the guests. Come on, Kirsty."

It suddenly occurred to Serena that the sight of the two boys facing off against each other was silly, just as the way she and Kirsty had been picking around each other was silly. She looked at Kirsty and saw the same realization in the older girl's eyes. They both burst into giggles.

Val and Dugal stopped staring at each other and stared at the girls instead.

"Look here." Kirsty leaned forward and looked from Serena to the two boys. "I don't quite understand what's going on between Charlotte and Mr. Storbridge, not to mention Uncle Paul and Aunt Sophie and my parents. But there's no reason that should be a problem between us. Especially since one way or another we're all related now."

Val opened his mouth, then closed it, as though realizing he couldn't very well argue with a girl, at least not when she was his hostess rather than his sister.

Dugal's brows drew together. Then he gave an unexpected grin. "Curse it, if you aren't right as usual, Kirsty." He held out his hand. "Truce, Vaughan?"

Val hesitated a fraction of a second. Then he grasped Dugal's proffered hand. "Truce."

"I never saw such a crowd. One of the Lescauts just introduced me to a fellow who writes for the *Leader*. As best I could make out, the man's a former thief. Though I wouldn't swear to 'former.' " Bertram dropped down on a settee beside Diana. "What's the matter? Lost in romantic reveries?"

"Just ignoring your complaints from force of habit. And keeping an eye on Juliet." Diana indicated their niece, who was sitting on the carpet nearby playing with the young Lescauts and the smallest Silverton boy. "She likes to have one of us within view." She rested her head against the back of the settee and turned to look at her brother, daring him to mock her. "But there is something very romantic about a wedding, especially one like this, with no stuffy trappings."

Bertram snorted. "Next you'll be saying you'd choose such a wedding yourself."

"Yes, I would. A simple ceremony reduced to pure emotion. The only thing more romantic would be to elope."

Bertram straightened up. "Good God."

"Oh, don't play the high-handed brother, Ber. You needn't worry. It's difficult finding men who are tolerable enough to endure for a dance, let alone a lifetime."

"It would be, with your impossibly high standards." Bertram changed tactics in that odious way brothers did. "There's nothing romantic about withering away *waiting* for a grand passion, Di."

Diana folded her arms across her chest. "I'll meet the right man at the right time."

"Perhaps you've met him already."

"No." She shook her head, dislodging a ringlet. "When I meet him, I'll know."

"Lady Diana, Lord Vaughan. I hope the children haven't cornered you." Amy came up to the settee, accompanied by Robert Lescaut's son David, a handsome, dark-haired young man. Both were smiling, but they were the smiles of those doing their duty as hosts.

David offered Diana a glass of champagne. Bertram gave Amy his place on the settee. "Tell me," Diana said, determined to pursue friendship with her new relations, "how did Francis and Charlotte find each other again after so many years? We still haven't heard the whole story."

There was a brief silence. Amy and David exchanged glances. "Find each other?" Amy asked.

"Yes, I understand there was a deep attachment between them when they were younger."

"He was her father's secretary." David seemed to choose his words with care.

"That didn't stop him with our sister," Bertram said.

Diana shot her brother a look of warning. "Have they corresponded much through the years?"

Amy and David looked at each other again. "Mr. Storbridge came to see Charlotte once when she first moved to Edinburgh." Amy's eyes were dark, as though she remembered more than she'd admit. "I don't think they saw each other again until recently."

Diana glanced at Francis and Charlotte. "It must have been a very strong attachment to have endured such a separation."

"You'll have to excuse my sister," Bertram said. "She's determined to cast a romantic glow on everything."

Diana looked up at her brother. "I choose to do so, Bertram." She looked at the newlyweds again, feeling a prickle of unease. "It's pleasanter that way."

David followed the direction of her gaze. "I sincerely hope you're right, Lady Diana."

Diana turned to him. "Just Diana. After all, we're all family now."

Charlotte looked at the window seat. Kirsty and Serena were sitting side by side laughing, and wonder of wonders, Dugal and Val appeared to be shaking hands. Diana and Bertram were talking with Amy and David. Juliet was playing with the other children. Perhaps at least the younger generation could form friendships out of all this. It made the situation seem a little less bleak. Or perhaps that was the amount of champagne she'd drunk. But if she couldn't afford to grow a little drunk at her own wedding breakfast, when could she? Besides, when she had a glass in her hand, she didn't have to worry that she should be hanging on to Frank's arm.

"Well?" Frank murmured. They had a brief moment to themselves as the latest in a long line of well-wishers moved off. "Does it feel different being married?"

Charlotte took a sip of champagne. "It feels like being a horse on display at a sale at Tattersall's."

He smiled. "Apt enough. But I don't think we need worry anyone will inspect our teeth." He looked down at her for a moment. His eyes softened in that disconcerting way they sometimes did. "It's difficult, I know. Do you want a moment alone? I could—"

"Charlie." Silverton came up and gave her a light kiss on the cheek. "I hope you'll be very happy."

"Thank you, Silver." Charlotte embraced her brother-in-law, for a moment forgetting that he was the reason behind her mockery of a marriage.

"Storbridge." Silverton turned to Frank and put out his hand. "You don't deserve her. But then, neither would most of my Tory colleagues. She's a remarkable girl."

The practiced smile Frank had worn throughout the morning faded from his eyes. His mouth hardened. Unlike Val, he made no move to return the handshake.

"Frank." Charlotte gripped his arm.

Her touch seemed to recall Frank to his surroundings. He grasped Silverton's hand briefly. "Thank you, Silverton." His voice was as cold as the wind beating against the drawing-room windows. "I'm glad you appreciate Charlotte's qualities."

"I could say the same to you." Silverton cocked an eyebrow at Charlotte, as though in acknowledgment of a difficult situation, and took himself off.

Charlotte stared up at Frank. "What—"

"Not now, Charlotte."

She tightened her grip on his arm. "Francis Storbridge," she said in a lowered voice, "don't you dare talk to me about appearances—"

"Charlie." Sophie appeared beside them. "The report from the kitchen is that they're ready to serve the breakfast. Will you and Frank lead the way in?"

"Of course." Frank's smile was back in place—the easy, confident smile that hid his thoughts and covered all sins.

Charlotte realized she was still holding his arm. She had gripped it out of anger. It was the first time she had touched him unconsciously. Now she became aware of the hardened muscles beneath the fine fabric of his coat and the heat emanating from his body. She suppressed an impulse to pull away and instead let him tuck her arm beneath his own. She could feel the gazes of the company on them as they moved toward the door. No doubt half the guests were still trying to make out the reasons behind the marriage. She choked back a laugh. No matter how long they speculated, she doubted they would ever guess the truth.

The dining-room table had been extended to its greatest length, with all five leaves. The table glittered with all Sophie's crystal and china and most of Emma's and more borrowed from various relatives. The wedding cake rose in splendor from the center, snowy white with icing and sugar roses. It looked as cold as Charlotte felt inside.

Chairs creaked and clothes rustled as the guests took their places around the table and at the additional tables in the adjoining breakfast parlor. Diana brought Juliet over to Frank and Charlotte. Juliet's rosy face went shuttered. Charlotte, who had insisted that Juliet sit between them, began to think she'd done the child a disservice.

At least Frank was distracted, helping Juliet with her napkin. Charlotte unbuttoned her gloves. Her head felt stiff from the unusually elaborate arrangement of her hair. She was afraid if she turned too quickly, the whole mass would come tumbling down.

Footmen poured more champagne. Charlotte realized Paul was going to have to make a toast. She heard him push back his chair and get to his feet. She looked up at him in a silent plea. But Paul was looking beyond her. She glanced over her shoulder. The door from the hall had opened and a footman had come into the room, but he was not carrying a serving tray. He was the one who'd been assigned to admit guests to the house, she realized. But surely everyone was already present. She glanced around, wondering which of the invited guests had missed the wedding.

The footman cleared his throat, as though preparing to make an announcement. The room fell silent. Frank straightened up from Juliet and cast a quick look from the footman to Charlotte.

The footman coughed and swallowed and announced the new arrival in a clear, carrying voice.

"The Marquis de Ribard."

Chapter 8

The blood rushed from Charlotte's head. Her glass tilted in her fingers, spilling drops of fine champagne on Sophie's Irish linen tablecloth. She set the glass down. Her fingers rattled against the crystal, echoing in the suddenly still room.

Daniel was standing in the dining-room doorway, eyes gleaming like the silver buttons on his coat, face as calm and unruffled as the pristine folds of his cravat.

Frank pushed his chair back and looked at Charlotte, a question in his eyes. Paul was looking at her as well. He probably would have lunged at Daniel by now, but Sophie had him by the wrist. Robert, too, was standing. They'd all be glad to throw Daniel from the house, but they were leaving the decision up to her.

She cast a quick glance around the room, taking in Céline's pale face, Serena's wide eyes, Juliet's innocent bewilderment. Then she looked at Daniel. He expected her to have him thrown out. His gaze told her as much.

Always do the unexpected. Daniel had taught her that. She got to her feet and walked toward the man she had once called father. It was the first time she had seen him since she'd bested him. She looked him directly in the eye, not having to pretend fear as she had by the Serpentine. Triumph coursed through her like a rush of fresh, exhilarating air. "Daniel, we didn't expect you. But perhaps we should have."

"I wouldn't have forgiven myself if I'd missed my own daughter's wedding. However unexpected." He leaned forward and touched his lips lightly to her cheek.

For a moment she was enveloped by warmth, the scent of citrus, the touch of familiar hands. Her impulse was to hit him, but that would be to play the game his way.

"My lord marquis." Her attention on Daniel, Charlotte had not been aware that Frank had come up beside them. "We're most . . . impressed . . . that you made such a long journey for our sake."

She felt the pressure of Frank's arm around her waist. Its solid warmth was like an anchor.

"I wanted to deliver Charlie's wedding present in person." Daniel reached inside his coat and drew out an oblong box. From Asprey's, like her betrothal ring. He opened the lid to display a bracelet of burnished gold, each link shaped like a primrose. It was exquisite and obviously expensive, and she would die before she'd wear it.

"Thank you." She took the box and closed it, taking satisfaction from the sharp snap of the lid. It was the only outlet she allowed her anger. Daniel had come to disrupt the wedding, but between them she and Frank would transform him into just another guest.

"Do sit down, Daniel," she said. "You're just in time for the cake."

Frank was aware of Daniel de Ribard throughout the wedding breakfast. He wouldn't dignify the other man by glancing in his direction, but Ribard's presence was a palpable force in the room, like the ominous damp in the air that warns of a coming storm.

Sophie had had a seat placed for Ribard between herself and Emma Lescaut. Sophie had as much reason to hate her uncle as any of them, but she spoke to him as politely as to any of her guests. After all, she had grown up in the first circles. She knew about keeping up appearances. But Frank noted that Emma did her best to keep Ribard occupied.

Ribard drank champagne and ate wedding cake and spoke in a quiet voice that somehow managed to carry through the murmur of general conversation. Paul kept a wary eye on his father, like a duelist anticipating a surprise attack. The muscles in his shoulders were knotted beneath the finely twilled black cloth of his coat. Frank felt the same tension running through his own body. He met Paul's gaze across the table and for once found himself in perfect accord with his new brother-in-law. Better if they had seized Ribard by the exquisitely tailored lapels of his coat and thrown him down the stairs and out into the street.

But Charlotte hadn't wanted that. Charlotte surveyed the company, her face a smiling mask. Frank could not read the thoughts behind her bright, steady gaze, but she had stood side by side with him to face Ribard and she had not gone still and tense when he put his arm around her. For that, perhaps he owed Daniel de Ribard a debt of gratitude.

At length the meal was done and the company dispersed about the house again. Kirsty and Serena took the younger children up to the nursery. Juliet wanted to go with them, but she wanted Frank to take her. Once there, however, she was soon absorbed in a game. Serena tugged at Frank's sleeve. "You can go back to Charlotte now. You shouldn't be away from her long."

Frank grinned, though he felt the irony in his smile. He

got to his feet, ruffled Serena's hair, and made his way downstairs.

"Storbridge." Ribard's voice stopped him midway down the staircase. "I've been hoping to have a word with you."

Frank descended the rest of the steps, slowed by wariness. "What about?"

"Advice to my son-in-law."

It would be satisfying to spit in Daniel de Ribard's face, but far too obvious. There was much to be learned from parlaying with the enemy. "We'd best go in the parlor." Frank opened the nearest door and walked into the family's private room, which was free from wedding guests.

Ribard's gaze swept over the Brussels carpet, the blue velvet upholstery, the crystal vase on the mantel. "Sophie's created quite an elegant nest." He dropped down in one of the chairs. "Still, Old Fishmarket Close is hardly what either you or I are accustomed to."

"Yes, I find it a great deal more pleasant than most houses in Mayfair." Frank sat opposite Ribard. "I hope this isn't going to become a pattern, Ribard, taking me aside at social events. It could rapidly grow tedious."

Ribard smiled. "The price of marriage, Storbridge. Putting up with one's in-laws." He crossed one leg over the other. "You aren't keeping Charlie in the wilds of Scotland for your wedding journey, are you?"

"No, I'm taking her into the wilds of England."

"Of course. Your late wife's property in Northumberland."

"Yes. St. John's Court."

"I trust you aren't taking all your wards along with you."

"We're taking Serena and Juliet. Bertram and Diana are taking Val back to Harrow. Then they're both going to stay with friends." Frank kept his tone conversational, but the message was clear. *They'll all be well looked after. You won't be able to interfere with them.*

"Not exactly the most romantic interlude with two children along."

"We'll manage. Neither Charlotte nor I are in our first youth."

"No." Ribard regarded Frank for a moment. "There was a time when I'd have horsewhipped you for so much as touching Charlie."

Frank raised his brows. "You mean you don't intend to do so now?"

Ribard laughed. "I must admit it's tempting, but it would be a crude punishment for the man you've become."

"Then I take it you have something else in mind."

Ribard shrugged. "I know when to cut my losses."

"Doing it much too brown, Ribard. I worked for you three years, and I never saw you let anyone get away with besting you."

"I don't recall that you saw me bested at all. I make you my compliments, Storbridge. An alliance with you was one move I didn't foresee Charlie making."

"Perhaps you don't know her as well as you thought."

"Perhaps." Ribard drummed his fingers on the chair arm. "I can see what Charlie gets out of the bargain. I don't see what's in it for you."

Frank returned his father-in-law's stare. "Charlotte."

"A girl whose father has fallen from favor and whose brother is a Jacobin printer from Edinburgh?" Ribard shook his head. "Hardly the most eligible wife for an aspiring politician."

"I already made one eligible marriage."

"And having had the . . . misfortune . . . to lose your wife, you were free to make an even more glittering alliance. I understand you have your pick of women in London, married or unmarried. So why Charlotte?"

"If you have to ask that, you fail to appreciate your daughter, my lord."

Ribard's eyes narrowed. Then he gave a shout of laughter. "A good try, Storbridge, but I know you too well. You'll never convince me you're guided by anything as simple as love or even lust. You're too much like me."

Frank's fingers closed on the arms of his chair. He stared at the man opposite him. Like Frank, Ribard wore a coat of dark blue kerseymere. Frank instantly recognized the cut: Stultz, the tailor he himself had patronized ever since he had been able to afford it. Ribard's shoes sported silver buckles that were almost the twin of Frank's. His neckcloth was tied in the mathematical, the style Frank also favored. Frank swallowed, tasting the bitterness of self-recognition. "Then you can be sure I do nothing without having excellent reasons."

"I make no doubt of it. You're a far more able man than that weakling Charlotte almost married five years ago."

"Ned Rutledge." Frank's lips curled around the name. "Your accomplice."

"My pawn. Ned didn't have the brains to be an accomplice."

"Yet you were ready to give Charlotte to him."

"Charlie wanted him." Ribard smoothed a crease from his sleeve. "She has told you, hasn't she?"

The wind whipped up outside. Frank chose his words with care. He recognized a trap. "Charlotte's earlier betrothal is her own affair. As my first marriage is mine."

"Commendable. But one generally thinks a husband has a right to know."

Frank pushed himself to his feet. The room smelled of lemon oil from the cleaning the house had been given for the wedding, but Ribard's words stirred a rank odor. Frank started for the door. "If there's anything more I need to know, I make no doubt my wife will tell me."

"Perhaps. But it's not the sort of thing women find easy to talk about. I hope you'll be understanding, Storbridge. Some men would lose their temper if they discovered their bride wasn't a virgin on the wedding night."

Frank released the doorknob, strode back across the room, and smashed his fist into Daniel de Ribard's face.

Ribard wiped his hand across his mouth with deliberation. A red mark rose on his cheek. "So. You're not quite as bloodless as you let on." He got to his feet. "A word of advice, Storbridge. Emotion can prove fatal. Don't let it get the better of you."

"What the devil did Ribard want?" Paul Lescaut strode to the parlor window and stared through the mist-filmed panes, as though if he looked hard enough he could find the answer in the garden beyond.

"To see Charlotte." Sophie collapsed into the sofa cushions and gave a catlike stretch. "All things considered, it was a very satisfactory party."

"Yes." Charlotte looked from Paul to Frank. "Thank you for not turning it into a brawl."

Paul gave a grunt of acknowledgment and continued to stare out the window. Frank, who was leaning against the mantel, turned to look at Charlotte. His wife. She was sitting alone in a straight-back chair, the soft folds of her wedding dress and the frivolity of her ringlets belied by her resolute posture and the set of her face. Daniel de Ribard's revelations echoed in Frank's ears. The more he learned about Charlotte, the less he felt he knew her. "If you could bear Ribard's presence it wasn't for any of us to make a scene."

"Much as we might have wanted to." Emma Lescaut smiled.

Robert Lescaut perched on the arm of his wife's chair. "Ribard was spoiling for a fight. I've faced soldiers like that in battle. The worst thing one can do is give in to them."

"But one shouldn't concede the fight." Paul turned from the window. His shattered right hand was clenched white. Frank was reminded that he, too, had once been a soldier.

Sophie held out her hand to her husband. "Blows bounce off Uncle Daniel. We have to be as subtle as he is."

"We were so bloody subtle a detached observer would have missed the point entirely," Paul said. But he moved to Sophie's side and took her hand.

"You never care what detached observers think." Sophie pulled Paul down on the sofa beside her. "What matters is what Uncle Daniel thinks."

Paul draped his arm around his wife. "I don't mind fighting, but it's damned hard without knowing the rules of engagement." He looked at his sister. "For God's sake, Charlie, what did Ribard say to you in London?"

Charlotte looked levelly at her brother. "I've told you."

"Christ, Charlotte." Paul stared at her, then swung his head around to look at Frank. "You gave me your word you'd do your utmost to defeat Ribard. We don't stand a chance against him if all we can do is scrap at each other. I think it's time we laid our cards on the table."

Frank hesitated. The soft, seductive strains of a waltz drifted through the open door to the drawing room, where the younger members of the family were dancing. But the atmosphere in the parlor had gone as taut as the halls of Westminster just before a vote was called. Frank looked at the two Lescaut couples. Paul and Sophie knew Ribard as well as any of them. Robert had once been one of

France's best intelligence agents. Emma, so warm and disarming, had—according to Charlotte—once killed a man to save her husband's life. They were none of them strangers to risk. They could all, in their own way, be formidable allies. Politics had taught Frank that one must take allies where one found them.

"Fair enough," he said.

"Frank." Charlotte jumped from her chair.

"Your brother's right, Charlotte. We're all family now." Frank turned back to the others. "Ribard wants to build a railway from Lancaster to Liverpool. He wants Charlotte to sell him Chelmsford so he can run the railway across the land and make a profit from it. He wants me to use my influence to get parliamentary approval for the railway."

"Which you refused," Emma said.

"Naturally."

There was a brief pause. Paul's eyes narrowed. "But the price was Charlie's hand in marriage." He pushed himself to his feet. "By God, Storbridge—"

"Steady, *mon ami*." Robert looked at Frank. "I don't know you well, Storbridge, but you don't strike me as a man to resort to blackmail."

Self-disgust rose up in Frank's throat.

Charlotte moved to Frank's side, her silk skirts rustling with determination. "None of you knows me if you think I could be manipulated so easily. Frank is my husband. As Paul said, the important thing now is to present a united front against Daniel. He makes it a point of honor never to concede a fight."

"He still wants Chelmsford," Frank said. "It's possible he'll try to get at Charlotte through her family. I'd advise you to be extra cautious in the stories you run in the *Leader*. Ribard may have been out of England for five years, but he still has influence with the authorities."

Robert grinned. "Caution is a death knell to journalism. But we'll keep one eye on the bailie."

"We always do," Emma said. "We're none of us the sort to be intimidated."

A shriek of childish glee rose above the music from the drawing room. Emma swallowed. "Perhaps I spoke too soon. You don't think—"

"That Ribard would harm the children?" Paul tightened his arm around Sophie. "We know he's capable of it."

"Then we'll be sure the children are never left unaccompanied." Sophie spoke as calmly as if she were discussing plans for a picnic.

"I'm sorry." Charlotte's control cracked on a note of anguish. "I didn't realize . . . I knew he was dangerous, but I was too wrapped up in myself to think how far it might go. I never wanted any of you to be involved in this."

"We were all involved the moment Ribard returned to England, Charlie." Paul's voice and eyes softened.

"And even if we weren't, you couldn't expect us to stand by and let you carry on the fight alone," Emma said. "Families must stick together."

Paul looked from Charlotte to Frank. "We can handle anything Ribard tries in Edinburgh. You look after yourselves."

Sophie reached for Paul's hand. Their fingers seemed to twine together effortlessly. Robert leaned closer to Emma. His chestnut hair brushed her auburn curls. His leg, draped over the chair arm, was tangled in the moss-green folds of her skirt. Intimacy was written in the posture of both couples. Charlotte was standing only a few inches from Frank, but those inches seemed a vast gulf, a gulf that could not be bridged by anything as simple as a marriage ceremony.

"We should warn Céline and Silver as well," Sophie said. "Uncle Daniel must know how close you are to the children."

Frank felt Charlotte stiffen and heard the quick intake of her breath, but he doubted the others could read the signs. "I'll see to it," she said.

Paul looked at Frank. "For your sake I hope you don't have any skeletons in your closet, Storbridge. Ribard makes it his business to know everyone's secrets."

Frank smiled. "I don't have any more secrets than the average politician."

Paul raised his brows. "That bad?"

"Francis, Charlotte." Diana ran through the doorway from the drawing room, face flushed with exertion, ringlets slipping free about her face. "You must dance at your own wedding."

"Of course." Frank took Charlotte's arm. "We were just waiting for the chaos to die down."

Charlotte made no protest. Perhaps the discussion in the parlor had been painful enough that even dancing with him was a relief.

Diana clapped her hands for silence when they stepped into the drawing room. "A waltz for the lovers."

Anne Lescaut, Robert's mother, was at the piano. She launched into a waltz. The others remained still, waiting for the bridal couple. Charlotte stepped toward Frank. Frank clasped her hand, put his arm lightly around her, and drew her into the dance.

She performed the steps with ease, but the stiffness of her body was in sharp contrast to the pulsing seduction of the music. She kept her gaze fixed firmly on the top button of his waistcoat. The scent of almond and vanilla washed over him. He looked down at the top of her head, apricot silk flowers and honey-brown ringlets beginning to spring loose from their careful coiffure. She went stiff whenever he touched her. Save when he had kissed her. Then, for a moment, he had tasted the heat of response, followed by a welling of panic.

He had thought the panic stemmed from the realization that she was aroused by a man she held in aversion. In light of Ribard's revelations he wondered if it had more to do with the treatment she had received at the hands of Ned Rutledge. He thought of Rutledge's white fingers laying claim to her body, Rutledge's soft mouth moving over her flesh. His hands clenched involuntarily.

She looked up. "What is it?"

He looked into her deep-set dark eyes. "I'm wondering what sort of woman I've married."

She smiled, though her eyes were hard with irony. "Whatever the answer, husband, you have no one to blame but yourself."

Charlotte made a show of smoothing the skirt of her wedding dress, crumpled from the carriage ride to the hotel. She could feel the blue-green eyes of the four Vaughans stabbing into her. Mercifully, Juliet had been taken off to bed by her nurse. It was her own fault the Vaughans were in the parlor. She had insisted they order tea when they arrived at the hotel. A craven way to put off being alone with Frank.

"Actually I don't think I want tea." Diana's voice was high and a bit artificial. "Come on, Rena."

Serena looked up at her sister. "But it's only a quarter past eight. I'm not sleepy—oh." Her eyes went round. "I see."

Charlotte felt herself color like a schoolgirl. Hopefully the Vaughans would put it down to bridal blushes. Frank, damn him, was poking up the fire, which gave him an excellent excuse to avoid looking at anyone.

Serena rose from the sofa. "Good night, Francis. Good night, Charlotte. Have a pleasant—"

Diana gripped her sister's arm. "Good night," she said, shepherding Serena from the room.

Val squirmed in his chair. "I . . . ah . . . suppose I should go up as well. It's been a long day."

"In more ways than one." Bertram pushed himself to his feet. "Storbridge. Miss Ri—Good God, a fatal error tonight of all nights—Mrs. Storbridge. Welcome to the family."

His voice was dry, but not, Charlotte thought, wholly insincere. Or perhaps she was just desperate for sympathy.

The door closed behind the Vaughan brothers. Charlotte resisted the impulse to tug the square neck of her gown higher. She had the unnerving sense that she could feel her pearl-embroidered sleeves slipping off her shoulders.

Frank remained by the fireplace. He seemed to be taking an inordinately long time pushing the coals about in the grate. At length he turned. His gaze went not to her, but to the neglected tea tray. "Shall we ring for something stronger?"

She stared at him, hands clenched in her lap. "I have no intention of getting drunk."

He rested his shoulders against the mantel. "If I were going to try to seduce you, I wouldn't resort to alcohol, believe me. But if we want to preserve the illusion of our wedding night, we should give my wards time to settle themselves before we retire."

He dropped into a chair with the easy grace of a panther. Charlotte watched him. The loose-limbed, elegant body, the ever-changing gray eyes, the fine-boned, undeniably handsome face. Her *husband*. She forced herself to frame the word. There was no turning back now. And their private bargain had no legal standing. A husband could do what he willed with his wife, take what he willed from her. She knew just how powerless the married state rendered a woman before the law. Emma had written a cogent article comparing marriage to slavery only last summer.

"It will get easier after the honeymoon," he said. "People will stop expecting us to retire to bed at inconvenient times of the day."

The heat in her face spread to her temples, where her hair was coming loose from Sophie's careful pinning. "I suppose your wards would be shocked at the thought of you sleeping alone on your wedding night."

He smiled, a lazy, disarming smile that was as calculated as a deliberate caress. "Who says I'm going to sleep alone?"

Her stomach gave an unexpected lurch. "Of course. Silly of me. I do hope you had someone point out the best brothels in Edinburgh."

He lifted his brows. "My dear Charlotte. I've never paid for a woman's favors in my life. I don't intend to start on my wedding night."

"You have a former mistress in the city?" She matched his mocking tone. "Or you found someone at the wedding breakfast? Dear me, that was quick work."

"I'm rarely without resources." He watched her for a moment. "Though I'd be quite prepared to reconsider the terms of our agreement, if you were."

His gaze promised all they might do if their wedding night was a true one. A shiver ran along her skin, sharp as glass. She drew a breath, focusing her mind to control the betraying impulses of her body. Frank could batter her defenses like no other man. No other man save Ned.

She forced herself to look steadily at him. "A bargain is a bargain, Frank."

"And the one who set the terms is the only one who can change them. I wasn't suggesting otherwise." He glanced toward the fire, blazing briskly now, then looked back at her. "You go up first." There was a different note in his voice, a sympathy that in its own way was far more dangerous than deliberate charm. The corner of his mouth lifted. "They'll think I'm waiting for you to disrobe."

She stood. Her legs felt wobbly, but she managed not to sway. "And to think Sophie insisted on presenting me with a trunk full of new nightdresses. What a waste."

He moved to the door and held it open for her. She walked forward, not letting her steps falter. She was going to have to learn to cope with his physical nearness.

"Charlotte," he said as she moved past him.

She turned to look at him, armoring herself against what she might see in his gaze.

The firelight flickered over the sharp bones of his face and danced in the unreadable depths of his eyes. He lifted his hand, hesitated, then brushed his fingers against her cheek, as though she were something that might break.

She swallowed. Of all the weapons he possessed, she hadn't realized that tenderness was the most devastating. She walked quickly through the doorway. "Good night, Frank."

"Sleep well," he said. "Wife."

Chapter 9

Serena pressed her face to the mullioned window and peered down into the inn yard. "If the horses aren't ready yet, I daresay they soon will be. Francis is good at getting people to do what he wants."

Charlotte set down her teacup on the linen-covered table. "So I've noticed."

Serena turned from the window. "You'll like St. John's Court." She moved to the table. "Julia used to complain that it was dreary, but it's not really, just isolated. The hills are beautiful and there's a capital stream and you can see the sea."

"You've spent a lot of time there?"

Serena dropped into a ladder-back chair and cut a slice of Stilton from the wedge left on the table. "Francis goes at least four times a year. More now that he has the factory."

"Factory?" Charlotte paused in the midst of reaching for her cup.

"On the estate." Serena licked the Stilton crumbs from her fingers. "He started it last year."

Charlotte took a sip of tea. She had been married to Frank for two days, and she knew less about him than she did about many of her casual acquaintances. "What sort of a factory?"

"They make rails. You know, the things that railways go on."

Rain spattered against the windows. Shouts and the neighing of horses came from the yard below. The ostlers scurrying around in response to Frank's orders, no doubt. Charlotte pushed a loose curl behind her ear. Railways. The bloody things seemed to be following her everywhere.

"He calls it a demonstration project," Serena said. "To make jobs for people who lost their farm jobs because of the railways. I think it's splendid of him. But then Francis is a very splendid sort of person, isn't he?"

Charlotte looked into Serena's earnest blue-green eyes and summoned up her brightest smile. "Francis is an extraordinary man."

Footsteps sounded in the corridor. The oak door swung open. Millamant bounded into the room and plopped down in front of the fire. Frank stood in the doorway, beaver hat in hand, rain dripping from his greatcoat. "I have the ostlers' solemn promise that the carriage will be ready in five minutes."

Serena jumped up from the table. "What did you say to them?"

"That I have a sister-in-law who throws hysterical fits." He closed the door and looked at Charlotte. "Are you ready?"

She nodded and swallowed the last of her tea. Frank's hair was ruffled by the wind and fell in damp disarray around his face. There was something disturbingly intimate about the break in his polished facade. "Where's Juliet?" she asked, hoping conversation would still the uneasy feeling in the pit of her stomach.

"In the stable with Nancy, making friends with the horses."

Charlotte got to her feet and glanced out the windows. "It's awfully wet."

Serena ran to the windows. "You sound like a mother already."

Charlotte avoided Frank's gaze. "I'm only being prudent."

"She's thoroughly bundled up, and the stable is as dry as the inn. Drier. The innkeeper has more care for his cattle than for his guests." Frank lifted Charlotte's cloak from the settle before the fire and held it out to her.

She hesitated a moment, then walked forward, aware of Serena's gaze. Frank's hands skimmed over her shoulders as he set the cloak about her. It was the most he'd touched her since he brushed his fingers against her cheek on their wedding night.

Charlotte stepped away from her husband and knotted the ties of her cloak firmly under her chin.

"I see the carriage." Serena snatched up her own cloak and ran to the door.

"Don't knock anyone over," Frank called after her. He held the door open for Charlotte. "I hope she hasn't been talking your head off."

"On the contrary. She's been very informative." Charlotte moved past him into the corridor. "She's been telling me about your factory."

"I see." Frank waited for Millamant to follow them from the room, then closed the door. "And you're wondering whether the fact that my factory rolls rails has anything to do with my determination to marry you."

"Well, yes. That is, I was wondering. But then you'd hardly have agreed to a marriage settlement that gives me control of Chelmsford, would you?"

"You left me little choice."

"Doing it much too brown, *Francis*. You'd never have given in half so easily if you hadn't been willing to concede

Chelmsford to me from the first." She started down the corridor.

"So I'm acquitted of that at least?" He fell into step beside her.

"For the present." She looked sideways at him. "Why didn't you tell me about the factory?"

"Oh, there are any number of things I didn't tell you about. Just as I assume there are a good many things you didn't confide to me."

She swallowed. There were a number of things she should rightly have confided to her husband. But theirs was no ordinary marriage. There was no reason Frank should ever know her secrets. "Serena told me the factory is a demonstration project for finding jobs for displaced farm workers. She added something about you being splendid."

They had reached the stairs. He stepped aside to let her precede him. "I trust you've learned to take Serena's words with a grain of salt."

Charlotte lifted her skirt and started down the narrow staircase. "Not half so much as I do yours."

It was folly to care what she thought of St. John's Court. She'd made it abundantly clear she had little use for him. Why the devil should he care what she thought of a house that was his only because of the fortunes of marriage? But he did care. Frank's fingers dug into the buttery leather of the carriage seat.

He forced his hand to relax and glanced down at Juliet, who was curled against him. Her face was buried in his greatcoat, but from her even breathing he thought she was asleep. Across the carriage, Serena and Juliet's nurse, Nancy—who was little more than a child herself—were playing cat's cradle with a length of bright red Christmas ribbon.

Charlotte was looking out the window. It was difficult to read her expression beneath the deep brim of her bonnet. Frank glanced out the window himself. He caught a glimpse of the gnarled old oak with the forked branches and knew they were nearly there. A moment later they turned down the drive. Millamant, who was lying beside Juliet, lifted her head and sniffed the air.

"Oh, good." Serena looked at Charlotte, holding the cat's cradle ribbon steady with her fingers. "It doesn't take forever to get to the house, not like at Vaughan Hall. It's too bad you can't see the factory from the drive, but I'm sure Francis will take us there soon."

Charlotte glanced at Frank, brows raised in a sort of challenge. "Of course," Frank said.

Serena looked out the window. "There aren't follies and grottoes and things like there are in modern gardens, but there's a walnut grove and a strip of beach where we have picnics and you can bathe in the summer."

Charlotte's gaze was fixed out the window. Frank tried to see the estate as she must be seeing it. Undulating hills and a tangle of sodden trees, washed gray by the steady fall of rain. He wished he could have brought her here in the spring when there were wildflowers and a chance of blue sky and the countryside was at its best.

He caught a whiff of salt in the air seeping into the carriage. He looked back at Charlotte, seeking clues in her expression. Curiosity, disdain, wonder. *Fool.* St. John's Court would never fill her senses and quicken her blood as it did his. It meant something to him it could never mean to her. It was his.

Charlotte turned from the window, as though aware of the pressure of his gaze. Her eyes widened, and he knew the intensity of his expression had betrayed him.

Gravel crunched beneath the wheels as they rounded a bend. "There's the house," Serena said.

Charlotte rubbed at the condensation on the glass. Frank settled back against the squabs, but his gaze remained on his wife. The house before her was nothing compared to Rossmere, her father's Palladian estate in the Lake District. Nothing even compared to Chelmsford. St. John's Court was little more than a glorified Tudor farmhouse of pale, ivy-covered brick. Two towers at the back lent it a sort of dignity. Or gave it pretensions above its station.

Charlotte gave a small exclamation of surprise. "It's charming." The words seemed to escape her lips unbidden. She turned from the window, but tugged at the brim of her bonnet as though to shield her face from his view.

The carriage came to a stop. Juliet sat up and pushed her hair out of her eyes. "Home?"

Frank swung her into his arms. "Home."

The coachman hurried the ladies through the rain beneath an umbrella. Frank entered the house to find his wife standing in the midst of the stone-floored hall, shaking raindrops from her cloak. There was a brisk fire burning in the fireplace, casting golden light on the walnut wainscoting and gray stone. That same light seemed to warm Charlotte, softening the shadows around her eyes, making her look more like the girl he remembered.

"Mr. Storbridge." An agitated voice came from the stairs. "We didn't look for you until this evening. You must have flown like the wind."

Frank glanced up the newel staircase. "My wife's doing, Mrs. Cardew. She was eager to see her new home." He moved toward Charlotte. "Mrs. Cardew, my dear. She really runs St. John's Court. I just visit when I can."

"Oh, Mr. Storbridge, you do talk such nonsense." Mrs. Cardew hurried forward with a rustle of well-starched skirts and a waft of lavender scent. Her smile was warm, but Frank did not miss the sharpness of her gaze. She was appraising Charlotte, trying to see if she was good enough for her Mr. Storbridge. Christ, if Mrs. Cardew knew the truth.

"It is such a delight to welcome you to St. John's Court, Mrs. Storbridge," Mrs. Cardew said. "Forgive me for not having the staff assembled to greet you."

"I'm very glad you did not. I would hate to think of them standing around on my account." Charlotte held out her hand to the older woman. "I'm very pleased to meet you, Mrs. Cardew. Serena says you keep everyone in order."

"Oh, that child, she does chatter on." Mrs. Cardew glanced at Serena, now chattering on to Newell, Frank's valet, who had arrived in a second carriage with the luggage. "But do come by the fire, Mrs. Storbridge, you must be chilled. You'll be wanting—Yes, dear, heavens, how you've grown." She stopped to pat Juliet, who was tugging at her skirt. "You'll be wanting to take refreshments. I'll tell Cook—"

"Please don't trouble yourself for my sake." Charlotte pulled off her gloves and held her hands out to the fire. "The children might like something, but I should much rather go up to my room and rest until dinner."

"Oh, dear me, yes, I should have realized. Of course you must be tired from . . . from the journey." Mrs. Cardew cast a quick glance at Frank and tugged her crisp white cap into place. "I've had fires laid in the bedchambers. You go right up. Don't worry about Serena and Juliet. They'll do very well with me."

Frank schooled the ironic smile that was threatening to break across his face. "Thank you, Mrs. Cardew." He turned to Charlotte. "My dear? Shall we?"

He watched the color rise in Charlotte's cheeks as she

realized, later than he and Mrs. Cardew, that there were reasons other than exhaustion why a honeymooning couple might wish to retire to their bedchamber in the middle of the afternoon. But she kept her chin high and her voice steady. "Of course." She smiled at Mrs. Cardew and the children and placed her fingers lightly on Frank's arm.

She kept her hand on his arm as they climbed the stairs. She must have been as aware as he was of the gazes fixed on them from the hall below, but her steps were firm and even.

"An admirable performance," Frank said when they reached the upstairs corridor. He looked at the polished doors across the corridor, beset by images of how they might spend the next hour or so if their marriage was a true one. He drew a breath, inhaling the scent of almond and vanilla and tantalizing possibility. It would only take one movement to pull her into his arms. But the least he owed her was to keep to his side of the bargain as she had kept to hers. He had already violated it once by kissing her.

He nodded toward one of the doors. "Your bedchamber. Adjoining mine, but you can bolt the door if it makes you feel more comfortable."

He felt the frisson that ran through her, but he could not have said whether it was fear or anger or the stirring of desire. She released his arm as though it burned her. "Go to the devil, Frank," she said, and walked into her room without a backward glance.

The footman set the platter of baked haddock on the smooth white tablecloth beside Charlotte's plate. Charlotte stared at the fish. For the first time she noticed the fish-slice lying above her plate. Of course. As the lady of the house she was expected to serve the fish, just as Frank, seated at the bottom of the table, had ladled out the soup. Her fingers curled in a brief moment of rebellion. Then she picked up the fish-slice and began to divide up the haddock, feeling that each slice branded her more irrevocably as Frank's wife. "It looks splendid, Mrs. Cardew. After three days in inns, this is heaven."

Mrs. Cardew made a self-deprecating noise, though her eyes brightened at the compliment. "It's only a simple family dinner. You'll be wanting to order your own dinners now, Mrs. Storbridge."

"I think I can leave that in your very capable hands." Charlotte nodded to the footman to hand around the fish.

"I wish you could have been at the wedding, Car-Car." Serena took a sip of lemonade. "Charlotte looked beautiful. And Francis was very handsome. It was much nicer than when he married Julia."

"Serena." Charlotte realized she was once again sounding like a mother.

Frank set down his wineglass. "You've forgotten the first lesson of dining in polite society, Serena."

Serena wrinkled her nose. "Never say what you're really thinking?"

"Precisely."

"Really, Mr. Storbridge. The ideas you put in that child's head." Mrs. Cardew clicked her tongue, but more in the manner of an indulgent aunt scolding a favorite nephew than with any real disapproval.

"Well, I think that's silly." Serena took a bite of haddock. "It makes for the most boring conversations."

"No one ever accused polite society of being scintillating." Frank grinned. His gaze met Charlotte's down the length of the table. She found herself grinning in response. They had often looked at each other in just such shared amusement across the table at Daniel's house, heavy with silver and crystal and formality.

A gust of wind rattled the dining-room windows. Charlotte caught herself up short. Memory was a seductive trap. It was just that now, his face relaxed with laughter, Frank seemed so very like the boy who had been her best friend.

She glanced down at the simple blue and white delftware of her plate and cut into her haddock with determination.

The dining-room door was flung open. "Frank—oh. I'm terribly sorry. Didn't realize the ladies were still at table."

A man of about Frank's age stood in the doorway, light brown hair plastered to his face with rain, greatcoat and boots sodden.

"Hullo, Jack." Frank pushed back his chair. "You know Serena and Mrs. Cardew. My wife, Charlotte." He looked at Charlotte. "Jack Matthews, my factor. What is it, Jack?"

"Mrs. Storbridge." Matthews nodded at Charlotte, but his gaze at once went back to Frank. "We've had flooding in the rolling mill."

"I'll come at once." Frank got to his feet. "Forgive me, Charlotte, but I fear this can't wait." There was no irony in his voice, merely concern and a genuine apology. He nodded at Mrs. Cardew and Serena and strode from the room. Matthews followed.

Charlotte stared after her husband. The concerned factory owner was as alien to her image of him as the teasing brother-in-law.

"Dear Mr. Storbridge," Mrs. Cardew said, her gaze misty. "So conscientious."

Charlotte picked up her wineglass and took a long sip.

* * *

Charlotte shifted her position on the high-back rose damask settee. The springs creaked, cutting through the monotonous patter of rain against the windows and the steady crackle of the fire. It was unnatural, this silence. Rooms where children were playing were supposed to be filled with laughter and shouts and occasional wails, not stultifying quiet.

She glanced at the hearthrug. Juliet was laying a red block on top of a blue one, her small hands moving with careful concentration, her porcelain-skinned face intent. Serena was sprawled beside her, uncharacteristically sub-dued as she added a tower to the block castle they were building.

Serena looked up, as though aware of Charlotte's gaze. "I hope Francis comes back tonight. The problem at the factory must have been very bad."

Charlotte nodded. Frank had been away all night. He had sent them a brief note to say he was snatching a few hours' sleep at Jack Matthews's house and returning to the factory in the morning.

Juliet tugged at Serena's sleeve, as though resenting the loss of her attention. Serena sent Charlotte a look of apology and returned to the blocks.

Charlotte picked up a white china cup from the low ta-ble in front of the settee and took a sip of lukewarm chocolate. She had ordered it for the girls, but Juliet had taken no interest in the refreshment. Juliet took no inter-est in anything relating to her new stepmother. Charlotte almost found herself missing Frank. At least when he was around, Juliet was happier and Charlotte didn't feel such a miserable failure.

"What's that?" Serena looked toward the window.

Charlotte set down her cup. Then she heard it too. A high, plaintive wail. "It sounds like a cat." She went to the window and looked out across the rain-drenched expanse of lawn. A small gray kitten was huddled beneath a leafless rosebush not five feet away. As Charlotte knelt on the window seat, the kitten's gold eyes looked straight through the mullioned panes at her. It opened its small pink mouth and let out another cry.

"It doesn't look like any of the stable cats." Serena had come to stand behind Charlotte. "They're all black and white. It doesn't sound very happy."

Charlotte unfastened the casement and pushed open the window, letting in a gust of cold, wet wind. The kitten ran straight to the house. Charlotte leaned out the window and reached down, half expecting the animal to run away. Instead, it sprang into her outstretched arms.

It was feather-light, but the force of the jump tipped her forward. For a moment she thought she was going to overbalance. She heard a cry that sounded like Juliet. Then Serena grasped her from behind and she was able to scramble onto the window seat, rainwater dripping from her hair, the kitten clutched to her chest.

The kitten let out a loud purr that vibrated through the poplin of her gown.

"It's only a baby," Serena said.

Charlotte looked down at the tiny bundle of fur in her arms. Sophie and Paul had two cats as well as a dog. "No more than two months, I'd judge." She dried the kitten carefully with a fold of her skirt. There was a small white spot on its chest. Its fur was cashmere soft, but she could feel its bones sharp beneath the skin.

The kitten continued to purr, more loudly than any cat Charlotte had heard before. Serena reached out and scratched it behind the ears. Juliet stood beside the window seat, watching with grave blue eyes. "Do you want to pet the kitten?" Charlotte asked.

Juliet was still for a moment. Then she stepped forward

and ran her hand over the kitten's gray fur. Her fingers brushed against Charlotte's arm. It was the first time she had touched Charlotte of her own volition.

"Do you think it's hungry?" Serena asked.

"I'm sure it is." Charlotte got to her feet, carrying the kitten, and went to the table. There was a jug of milk beside the chocolate pot. She poured some into her saucer and set it on the hearthrug. The kitten lapped it up as though afraid the milk would be pulled away at any moment.

"Is it a boy or a girl?" Serena asked.

Charlotte knelt down and got her first good look at the kitten from behind. "A boy. Definitely."

Serena followed the direction of her gaze. "Oh, yes, I see. Most definitely."

Juliet tugged at Charlotte's sleeve. "We keep kitten here?"

Charlotte looked at the kitten that had offered her instant trust. Then she looked at Juliet and realized that for the first time her stepdaughter had included her in the word *we.* "Absolutely," she said.

Charlotte stroked the kitten behind the ears. He had a name now. *Knightly.* Knightly gave one of his loud purrs and continued kneading her, his paws pushing against her chest. His claws cut through the lawn of her nightdress, but it seemed a small enough price to pay. There was something miraculous about the feel of a warm baby animal. But this was more. In scarcely half a day this small animal had carved a special place in her heart. He was hers.

She leaned back against the bolsters, beneath the old-fashioned flat canopy in the room she had been given at

St. John's Court. The room that had once belonged to
Julia Vaughan. Julia Storbridge. Her own trunks piled
beside the wardrobe and her brush and comb laid out on
the chest of drawers were a meager badge of ownership.
She could hardly say that anyone in her new family—if the
term even applied—belonged to her, any more than this
room did.

She no more doubted that Sophie and Paul loved
her than that she loved them. And their children. Not to
mention Céline and Silverton and Robert and Emma and
their children. She was lucky to have so many people
who loved her. Yet she had never let herself lay claim to
any of them. Or even to the animals who thronged the
house in Old Fishmarket Close. She hadn't had anyone,
human or animal, who was hers exclusively. Not since
her father.

She sucked in her breath. Knightly gave a protesting
cry. She stroked him and willed the tension from her
shoulders. A bark sounded from next door, as though in
answer to the kitten's cry. Millamant. Frank had come
home late in the evening. Charlotte had heard the thud
of his boots dropping to the floor, the creak of his wardrobe door, the murmur of his voice talking to the dog. He
hadn't knocked on her door or sent her a note. Not that
she wanted him to. But she was a bit curious to know
what had happened at the factory.

She wondered what Frank would make of the change
in Juliet's attitude toward her. She and Serena had eaten
dinner in the nursery with Juliet. Except for a few minutes when she was actually persuaded to swallow food,
Juliet had spent most of her time playing with Knightly.
But the palpable tension that had radiated from the child
from the moment Frank had introduced her to Charlotte
was gone.

A knock echoed through the room. Knightly tensed

and jumped from Charlotte's lap. Charlotte tensed as well, thinking it was Frank. Then she realized the knock had come from the door to the corridor, not Frank's room. She climbed off the bed and went to the door.

Serena stood outside, eyes wide with an alarm that was out of character. "I need to talk," she said.

Chapter 10

"Of course, come in." Charlotte stepped aside to let Serena enter the room.

Serena took an awkward, halting step. Her candle tilted in her fingers, spattering wax on the dark floorboards.

Charlotte took the candle and put a hand on Serena's shoulder. "What's the matter? Are you unwell?"

Serena looked up at her. "Yes. No. Sort of. I'm bleeding."

"Bleed—oh. I see." Charlotte set the candle down on a table by the door, taking care not to spill more wax. "For the first time?"

Serena looked at the floor. "Yes."

"You poor love. Have you done anything for it?"

"I stuck rags between my legs. I wasn't sure how to fasten them. I think Diana pins them, but she never showed me how."

"Right. First things first. Come over to the washstand." Charlotte poured water—mercifully still warm—from the blue-flowered pitcher into the matching basin. While Serena sponged herself, Charlotte went to one of her trunks. Thank goodness she always packed a supply of cloths and pins. She contrived a pad and showed Serena how to pin it into place. There was blood on Serena's nightdress. Charlotte sponged it, bundled the soiled garment into the laundry basket, and helped Serena into one of her own nightdresses.

"There," she said, as Serena rolled up the long frilled sleeves. "It's a bit disconcerting at first, but believe me, you get used to it."

"I didn't think it would happen so soon. Diana was thirteen. I think Marianne and Julia were older."

"I was twelve." Charlotte could still vividly remember the day. Sophie and Céline had taken charge and explained matters to her. She hadn't even told her governess, let alone her mother.

Serena plucked at the embroidered lawn of the borrowed nightdress. "It's a very strange sort of thing."

Charlotte put her arm around the younger girl and drew her toward the white silk chaise longue that stood beneath the window—an incongruously modern touch in the Jacobean room, but a good place for a chat. "It doesn't change anything, you know." She remembered her own fear that the changes in her body would propel her from childhood too soon. "You're still the same person."

Serena looked up at her in the warm light from the brace of candles on the bedside table. "It means I could have a baby."

Charlotte drew a deep breath, inhaling the scent of wax tapers and lemon oil. "Well, yes. Technically it does."

"Not that I'd do anything so silly." Serena plunked down on the chaise longue. "Not for a long, long time. If ever."

Charlotte sat beside her. "Very prudent for the present. Wait ten years or so and see if you change your mind."

"I'm not sure I want to. Change my mind." Serena picked up a silk cushion and hugged it to her chest. "Mama died when I was born. And Julia died when Juliet was born."

Charlotte touched Serena's hand. "I'm sorry. It must have been beastly for you."

Serena shrugged, her gaze fixed on the fringe on the cushion. "I don't remember Mama at all, so I can't really miss her. And I didn't know Julia that well. She always seemed bored by anything to do with the nursery. Sometimes I wonder how she'd feel about Juliet if she were still alive."

Charlotte had an image of the titian-haired girl in the portrait in the hall at Vaughan House. Julia had been Frank's wife for less than a year, but she had given birth to his child—the only legitimate child he was ever like to have. She had known him in a way Charlotte never would. For some reason Charlotte's insides twisted at the thought. "Some women have a disgustingly easy time of childbirth," she said. "Sophie had Fenella in a Highland croft. Paul delivered her."

"Kirsty told me. I might not mind having a baby if I could have those kind of adventures along with it."

Charlotte tucked the folds of her nightdress about her legs. "Serena . . . what I said was a bit misleading. I mean, starting your courses doesn't make you a different person, but you are starting to grow up, and you may find yourself . . . having . . . having feelings you haven't had before." She looked at Serena. The girl seemed at once younger and older than usual, dressed in one of the nightdresses Sophie had insisted on presenting to Charlotte for her honeymoon. Sheer lawn, lavish with lace, cut low at the neck and gathered with a simple primrose ribbon that seemed to invite a gentleman to tug it loose and send the fabric slipping over one's shoulders. Why couldn't Sophie be here now? She'd do this so much better. "That is, you may find yourself looking at boys differently."

Serena regarded her, level brows drawn together. "You mean I'll want them to kiss me?"

"Perhaps," Charlotte said. "I was thinking more that you'd find yourself wanting to kiss *them*."

"Oh." Serena pondered this for a moment, staring at her bare feet. "I asked Marianne about it once. She said I'd understand when I got married."

Serena's elder sister had a lot to answer for. Married for seven years, she could have managed this talk much better than Charlotte. Though perhaps this particular aspect was something Charlotte was uniquely qualified to discuss. "That's not strictly true," she said. "That is, one can have such feelings regardless of one's married state."

They're healthy and natural. That's what Sophie would say. *They're a trap,* Charlotte wanted to scream. *They can blind you to truth and reason.* But that wouldn't be fair. She held Serena's fragile view of her emerging womanhood in her hands. The wrong words could leave an indelible scar. "Such feelings are perfectly natural," she said, dutifully quoting Sophie. "But they can cloud one's judgment." *And unleash the baser side of your own nature.* Charlotte folded her arms across her chest. Memory tightened her body and warmed her flesh. Hands and lips coaxing a response, inchoate desires brought to blazing life, heat pulsing through her body. Ned. Frank.

Serena frowned. "You mean I might want to kiss the wrong boy?"

Charlotte's nails dug into her arms. "Exactly."

There was a stir of movement followed by a sudden *whoosh*. Serena screamed and sprang to her feet. Knightly raced toward the bed in a streak of gray. The door to Frank's room was flung open. "Charlotte." Frank's voice was sharp. "What happened?"

He stood in the doorway, carelessly wrapped in a burgundy dressing gown, hair disordered, eyes unfocused.

"It's all right, Francis, it was me." Serena moved toward him. "The kitten jumped in my lap."

Frank pushed his hand through his hair. "Serena. I didn't realize—What kitten?"

"We found him this afternoon." Charlotte got to her feet, smoothing her nightdress, conscious of the ridigity of her limbs. "We aren't sure where he came from, but he was hungry, so we're looking after him."

She could hear the defiance in her own voice. Frank merely nodded. "Splendid." He dug his fingers into his hair again. "I heard the scream . . . I thought . . . I'm sorry I disturbed you."

"It's all right." Serena sidled toward the door. "I should go back to bed. I—" She glanced at the door. "Charlotte can tell you about it." She looked at Charlotte. "Thank you."

Charlotte went to the younger girl and put her arms around her. "Do you think you can sleep?"

Serena hugged her back. "Yes. I'm glad you're my sister. Good night, Francis."

She slipped from the room. Charlotte watched her leave, then turned to Frank. She was suddenly aware that she hadn't even thrown a shawl over her nightdress. The thin lawn felt light and insubstantial against her cold, stiff body. The light from the candle by the door must be shining right through the fabric. She stepped sideways and subdued the impulse to cross her arms over her chest.

To her surprise, Frank avoided her gaze. "I'm sorry," he said again. He turned to go into his room, then stopped and looked back at her. "*Is* Serena all right?"

"She's fine."

He looked at her for a moment and nodded, as though he would accept her clipped words though he didn't believe them.

"No wait." Charlotte took a half step forward, then checked herself, fingers clenched on her nightdress.

"What is it?" Frank's brows drew together. "Don't tell me she had a bad dream. She outgrew them years ago."

"No, it wasn't a dream." Charlotte drew a deep breath and looked straight into the eyes of the man who had been her friend and was now her husband, but whom she neither knew nor trusted. "Serena's courses started."

"Her—oh. I see." Frank gave a smile that was faint and yet somehow piercingly genuine. "It seems I brought another woman into the family just in time."

"Barely." Charlotte found herself smiling in response. "A clever man like you should have been able to find an easier way to do it."

"When it came to you, there was no easy way. You made that clear enough." He pulled his dressing gown closed at the neck. She realized he wore no nightshirt beneath it. Even in the shadows of the doorway she could see dark hair curling against the burgundy cloth. "How's Serena taken it?" he asked.

"Quite well." Charlotte forced the words from her suddenly dry mouth. "She pointed out to me that she's now able to have a baby, but she also assured me that she won't even consider doing so for years and years."

"Very like Serena." He looked at her for a moment. "Thank you."

There was a softness in his eyes, which unsettled her more than his bare chest or her scant apparel. "I did no more than anyone else would have done."

"You did considerably more than I could have managed." He regarded her a moment longer. She wanted to step backward into the protection of the shadows, but she wouldn't let herself move.

It was Frank who broke eye contact. He glanced about the room. "Where's this kitten of yours?"

"Under the bed." Charlotte hesitated. Something in

her balked at the thought of sharing Knightly even this much. But to refuse seemed childish. In her war with Frank, she would not stoop to the childish. She bent down and lifted the embroidered coverlet. The space under the bed was swept meticulously free of dust, as one would expect in any house run by Mrs. Cardew, but there was no sign of Knightly. She straightened up. "He must have run somewhere else." She stood and glanced around the room.

"Charlotte." Frank was looking through the doorway into his own room. "I think you should see this."

She moved to the doorway. She had to stand close to Frank to be able to see through, so close that she could feel the heat of his body and the stirring of his breath.

"He must have slipped past me," Frank said. "He seems a bit confused. He looks old enough to be weaned, but he seems to have reverted to infancy."

Her kitten was lying on Frank's bed. Millamant was beside him, obligingly rolled onto her side. Knightly was pushing industriously against Millamant's chest and suckling at her teats.

"Nearly starving made him want the security of his mother." Charlotte felt an unexpected pang in her throat. Knightly had been looking for his mother when he kneaded her, but she hadn't been nearly as effective a substitute. "He looks happy. I suppose—" She swallowed. "Do you mind if he sleeps with you?"

"No. But—" Frank gave her a sidelong glance. "I have a better idea." He walked over to the bed. Millamant looked up at him, but continued to let Knightly nurse. "Here, little fellow." Frank stroked Knightly with one finger. Knightly stopped nursing and rolled over on his back, feet curled in the air. Frank grasped Knightly by the scruff of his neck and scooped him up. The kitten almost fit into the palm of his hand. He looked across the room at Charlotte. "He purrs loudly enough, doesn't he?"

"Yes." She swallowed her disappointment that Knightly purred for Frank as much as for her.

"Come on, Millamant." Frank jerked his head at the dog and started for the door. Millamant jumped off the bed and padded after him.

Frank brushed past Charlotte, carried Knightly to the bed, and set him down on the coverlet. Millamant crouched at his feet and looked up at him. Frank patted the space beside Knightly. Millamant jumped up and curled up beside the kitten. "Good girl." Frank scratched her behind the ears, then looked at Charlotte. "Satisfied?"

"Yes." She stared at him, not sure how he could have understood her feelings so well, yet unable to see how he would have acted as he had if he did not. "Thank you, Frank."

He gave a twisted smile. "Watch out for Millamant. If you move too quickly she gets startled and nips your feet." He moved to the door. "Pleasant dreams, wife."

"There." Serena pointed out the carriage window. "You can see the smoke from the blast furnace."

Charlotte glanced out the window. A plume of gray curled above the fir and Irish yew trees in the distance. The carriage turned, jolting over a road still rutted from the storm. Juliet pushed herself up on her knees to peer out the window. They had given Nancy the afternoon off, so it was just the four of them in the carriage—the two girls, Frank, and Charlotte herself, a disconcertingly domestic arrangement.

They had left Knightly at home, and Millamant as well to keep him company. Juliet had protested, but at least she had been brought to carry on a discussion with Charlotte and to accept Charlotte's say in the matter.

Frank, sitting beside Juliet, was silent, as he had been when they arrived at St. John's Court five days ago. Yet Charlotte sensed he was watching her as he had that day. He was leaning back in a corner of the carriage, seemingly relaxed, but she had the odd feeling he was trying to read her thoughts. She was at a loss to understand why he should be interested in the workings of her mind as they approached his factory, but the very fact that he cared was enough to raise her defenses.

For herself, her attention was all on the factory. She had the strange feeling that it held the key to understanding Frank.

Granite walls, slate roofs, and white-painted window frames flashed by. "The cottages for the factory workers," Serena said. "The school's over there."

Juliet turned her head around to look at her father. "Go to school?"

"Not just yet, sweetheart." Frank put a steadying hand on her shoulder. "Charlotte wants to see the factory."

Charlotte looked at Frank. "You have a school for the factory workers' children?"

His eyes glinted. "You might try sounding a little less shocked, my darling. Did you expect me to have them laboring from the moment they could toddle?"

Charlotte had an image of the children who worked in Daniel's factories—children like Amy, who was now Sophie and Paul's ward. Amy had begun working in a cotton mill at the age of five. "Many people do," she said.

"But I'm not everyone. As you've often pointed out."

She turned from the window to look him full in the face. The factory interested her, but his reasons for building it interested her more. "Why rails?"

He shrugged, ruffling the capes on his greatcoat. "A lot of the collieries hereabouts have railways, so there's a demand for rails. And it's a fair bet the demand will increase tenfold in the future. I may not have Ribard's knack for shrewd investment, but he taught me something about spotting promising industries."

Charlotte fingered the silver chain on her reticule. "So if Daniel builds his railway, your profits will increase."

Frank regarded her for a moment. "True enough. I'd have everything to gain from Ribard building his railway. If profit was my motive."

The carriage turned off the road and pulled up in a wide, cleared area. The smell of burning coke washed over her as the coachman handed her from the carriage. For a moment she was Serena's age and the man beside her wasn't Frank but Daniel, taking her to visit an iron foundry he had just purchased in Yorkshire. The memory brought a bite to her throat more acrid than the smell of the smoke.

Serena came to stand beside her, half boots squelching through the mud. She had been complaining of cramps this morning, but Charlotte had made her some chamomile tea and now she seemed back to her usual self.

"That's the blast furnace." Serena gestured to the taller of the two long, warehouselike buildings that dominated the yard. "When they first built it I used to pretend it was a dragon."

The furnace's chimney towered a hundred feet in the air, belching gray smoke against the paler gray of the sky. Though she had seen blast furnaces before, Charlotte still found the sheer mass and barely contained power of the thing overwhelming.

Jack Matthews came hurrying from a smaller, slate-roofed building that seemed to be an office, tugging at his brown coat as though he had hastily donned it. "Frank. Mrs. Storbridge. I'm so glad you're here. Serena. You too, moppet." He ruffled Juliet's hair as she sat in Frank's arms. "The men were excited to hear you were coming," he said to Frank. "Though truth be told, I think they're really eager to get a glimpse of Mrs. Storbridge."

He led them across the yard to the furnace. Charlotte walked beside him, while Frank followed behind with the girls. "We smelt the iron ore in here," Matthews explained to Charlotte, his pale blue eyes lit by enthusiasm. "Then we take the pig iron to the rolling mill"—he gestured to the other building—"where we roll it into rails."

He opened the double doors of the furnace building. A shock of heat greeted them. "You'll want to take your cloak off," he warned her.

Charlotte untied her cloak and folded it over her arm. Even so, the warmth from the furnace brought an instant prickling of perspiration to her forehead and made her long for muslin rather than the twilled cashmere of her gown.

Two men in their shirt-sleeves, sweat glistening on their bare arms, were loading iron ore, coke, and limestone into the cart that would trundle up a skip incline to the mouth of the furnace. Two more men were shoveling coal into the stove, which powered the furnace. Still others were gathered around the hearth where, as Charlotte remembered, the pig iron flowed into sand molds.

The work stopped at their entrance. The men nodded at Frank, but without the snapping to attention Charlotte remembered when Daniel entered any of his factories. Frank nodded back with easy familiarity. "It's good to see everything back in working order. My wife wouldn't wait another day before she saw the most important part of the estate. My dear." He turned to Charlotte with one of his unsettling smiles and introduced each of the factory workers by name.

The men offered her their best wishes with cheerful sincerity. "We're all very glad to see Mr. Storbridge married, if you'll permit us to say so, ma'am," said a broad-shouldered man with graying hair. "Why, only last summer at my own daughter's wedding I was telling Mr. Storbridge he worked too hard. No sense in building all this if there's no one to share it with."

"And you know I always listen to your advice, Will." Frank glanced over at Charlotte, eyes gleaming. "You see, my love, if it wasn't for Will we wouldn't be here now."

Charlotte returned his gaze. "If it wasn't for a number of circumstances we wouldn't be here now. Remarkable how circumstances can conspire."

Will nodded. "Fate, you could almost call it."

"It wasn't fate, Will, it was Mr. Storbridge." A younger man with red hair and a friendly grin spoke up. "We all know there's no stopping him when he makes up his mind he wants something. I'm sure he was the same when it came to Mrs. Storbridge."

Charlotte felt Frank's gaze upon her. She avoided looking at him. "You could put it that way," she said.

The men laughed in appreciation. "Oh, you've done well, Mr. Storbridge," Will said, wiping his eyes. "You've done very well indeed."

"Thank you," said Frank. "I'm well aware of it. Wasn't there something you wanted to show me about the slag notch?"

The men clustered about Frank, asking questions. Juliet dragged Serena off to look at the skip incline. Charlotte remained beside Matthews. Her face was warm, but she hoped Matthews would put that down to the heat of the nearby blowing furnace or perhaps to bridal modesty. That last was very nearly true, though not in the way he would think. "Frank said you supply rails to many of the local collieries," she said.

"Yes." Matthews smiled, as though pleased by her interest. "That's how the idea of the factory was born. Frank got to know George Stephenson, who's been experimenting with locomotives in the colliery at Killingworth. Stephenson's designed a new sort of rail with half-lap joints that make for a much smoother and more economical ride. Our rails conform to his design."

Charlotte glanced at Frank. He had stripped off his greatcoat and coat and looked little different than the shirt-sleeved factory workers clustered about him. Save that none of them were built quite like Frank. "The men seem very at ease with him."

"I hope you don't mind their teasing. They all consider Frank a friend. And, of course, in a sense it's their factory as much as his."

Charlotte looked up at him. "Their factory?"

"Didn't he tell you?" Matthews tugged his neckcloth loose against the heat. "The workers all own a share of the factory. Frank planned that before he even decided what the factory would produce."

Charlotte stared at him, wondering if the whir of the blowing engine had distorted his words. "Frank wanted to start a factory owned by the workers?"

"Yes." Matthews gave a rueful smile. "He hasn't told you much, has he? It's like Frank not to want to boast. Look, I know your brother publishes the *Edinburgh Leader*. Frank says you've contributed to it yourself. There was a fine exposé of conditions in the textile factories in Glasgow in the *Leader* only last month."

Charlotte nodded. "Paul spent a week there interviewing the workers. We all knew conditions were bad, but it's worse hearing it firsthand."

"Quite. Yet there's no going back. Your brother pointed that out in his piece. More and more people are going to be employed in factories in the coming years."

"Especially if railways develop as some think they will."

"Precisely. Frank wanted to show that a factory could be run along humane lines and still be profitable. That ultimately it could be even *more* profitable if the workers had a stake in what they were doing and weren't worked to death."

Charlotte looked at her husband again. He had rolled up the sleeves of his shirt and was gesturing toward the furnace hearth to make a point. The light from the coal-oil lamps on the walls picked out the lines of muscle in his bare arm. His eyes shone, not with mockery but with excitement. The impeccable facade of the politician had been stripped away with his outer garments. "Quite a vision."

"Yes. But Frank's always had a broad vision."

Charlotte looked back at Matthews. His open, guileless blue eyes were so different from Frank's impenetrable gray ones. "Have you known him long?"

Matthews pushed his sweat-dampened hair back from his forehead. "Since we were boys. I was a student at the school his father ran in his parish in Spitalfields. Mr. Storbridge helped me get a scholarship to Oxford. Frank would like to do the same for the children in his school— only on a larger scale."

Charlotte thought back to stories Frank had told her about his father in the old days. "I never met Mr. Storbridge. He must have been a remarkable man."

"He was a saint. Always thinking about others—except

possibly about Frank. I think he thought the rest of humanity needed him more than his own son did."

Charlotte frowned. But before she could frame a question there was a sudden whistling sound. Someone screamed. She felt a flash of blinding heat and heard a tearing explosion. Then something struck her in the forehead and all went black.

Chapter 11

"Charlie."

The voice seemed to come from a long way off. Charlotte burrowed away from the intrusive sound and pressed herself deeper into the comforting blackness.

"Charlie."

The voice sounded again, more insistent. Something brushed her forehead, warm, firm, making her skin prickle with a sensation that was unfamiliar but not unpleasant.

"Charlie, can you hear me?"

There was a note in the voice she could not understand, but it broke through her cocoon. She opened her eyes and saw a fold of drab green fabric and a sinewy arm. Pale skin, stiff black hairs, a rolled-up white sleeve. The smell of sweat and soot. And something else. Cedar. Cedar oil. Frank's shaving soap. Frank's skin. Frank's arm. The drab green was Frank's greatcoat. She was wrapped in Frank's greatcoat and Frank's arm was around her. No, Frank was holding her cradled against his chest.

She turned her head to look up at him. His breath shuddered through him. He pulled her tight against him, and she felt the pressure against her forehead again. Frank's lips, moving over her temples, brushing her hair.

Sensations tugged at her memory. The sound of the explosion, the force knocking her backward, the impact of something striking her forehead, the rush of blood-chilling terror before she lost consciousness. She had thought she was going to die. The sweet reality of her escape washed over her. She shifted her head so that instead of brushing her forehead, Frank's lips met her own.

Life-giving heat spread through her. His mouth tasted of fear and relief. The pressure of his lips and the strength in his arms anchored her to the present. She was alive and breathing and in Frank's arms. Frank, her husband. The man who—

She jerked away from him and half fell off his lap onto the sofa on which they were sitting. Pain stabbed her in the temples. Frank grasped her shoulders. "Careful. You got a bad crack on the head. The explosion knocked you to the ground, and I think a fragment of metal struck you in the head. Do you remember?"

"Yes. No. I'm all right." She drew back into the cool leather of the sofa.

"My goodness, you gave us a fright." Serena ran across the room and dropped to the floor beside the sofa.

Charlotte looked down into her young sister-in-law's face. Good God, she had been kissing Frank like a wanton in front of the children.

"You remember who you are and who we are and what country we're in and everything, don't you?" Serena said.

Charlotte nodded, then winced at the pain in her head. "My cousin Sophie lost her memory once, but I think it takes a worse injury than I received."

"Yours was bad enough." Frank's gaze was sharp and appraising. But in that instant before she kissed him, there'd been a strange fierceness in his eyes that she had never seen before. It had been so fleetingly glimpsed she could not now be sure she hadn't imagined it.

She glanced about the room. They must be in the factory office. There was a desk against the opposite wall piled with papers and ledgers and sheaves of foolscap. A coal fire burned in a small fireplace. Juliet sat on the rug before it, watching with wide eyes. "Are you all right, love?" Charlotte held out her hand to the little girl. "You didn't get hurt?"

"We were on the other side of the building." It was Serena who answered, but to Charlotte's surprise, Juliet got to her feet and crossed the room with firm, determined steps. Her eyes held an anxious inquiry.

"All better now?" Juliet asked.

"All better now," Charlotte said, though she was careful not to move her head.

Juliet took another step, then stopped and looked up at Charlotte. Her dark brows drew together. "Not go away?"

"No, poppet." Frank scooped Juliet up and set her on the sofa between him and Charlotte. "She won't go away. Not like your other mama."

Charlotte expected Juliet to make a demur at the word *mama*. Instead, a smile broke across her face.

Frank pushed himself to his feet. There were soot smudges on his face and shirt, Charlotte realized, and shards of debris tangled in his hair. "I'll see if Jack's learned anything," he said. He ruffled Juliet's hair and strode from the room.

Charlotte watched the door close behind her husband. She shifted her position on the sofa, drew a breath, and looked from Serena to the solemn Juliet. "Quite an adventure we're having, isn't it? Thank you for helping look after me."

Juliet smiled again. Serena got to her feet and dropped down in Frank's place on the sofa. "I've never seen Francis in such a state. He was whiter than the best table linens."

"Was the damage to the factory very bad?"

"The blast furnace won't be working again for a time. But it wasn't the factory Francis was upset about." Serena looked at Charlotte as though she were being very slow. "He screamed your name when the explosion happened." She paused for a moment. "I've never heard him call you Charlie before."

Charlotte rubbed her arms. "He used to call me that when we were younger."

Serena tucked her feet up under her. "Then he wrapped you in his coat and picked you up and carried you in here. Diana would be green with envy. It was just like a scene from one of those novels she's always reading."

Charlotte smoothed her satin-banded cuffs down over her wrists. "I can assure her the reality isn't nearly so romantic."

"Explosion noisy." Juliet wriggled closer to Charlotte and climbed onto her lap. Charlotte put her arms around her stepdaughter. She felt a catch in her breathing as Juliet settled back against her.

Serena's brows drew together. "You are feeling all right, aren't you? Francis said we had to keep you warm."

"I'm fine." If anything she was too warm. But the heat came from within, not from the coal fire or Frank's greatcoat.

The door opened and Frank stepped back into the room. "We have a charcoal brazier in the carriage. Do you feel able to travel?"

"Of course." Charlotte stood, holding Juliet in her arms. Her head swam, but she maintained her balance. "Do you know what caused the explosion?"

"Not yet. Jack will come to the house when he has something to report." Frank moved to her side and took Juliet from her arms. Their eyes met for a moment. Charlotte drew back, seeing the knowledge in his gaze. She could not deny that she had blatantly initiated that kiss. No matter that she had been disoriented; he had felt the shameful, wanton heat that swept through her. He knew the extent of her weakness. It gave him one more weapon in the war between them.

She stepped toward the door. "Serena, do you know what happened to my cloak?"

"And then Francis lifted Charlotte right up in his arms and carried her into the office. She was completely unconscious, just like Juliet—Shakespeare's Juliet, I mean, when she's in the tomb, only before she stabs herself, of course." Serena paused to take another bite of curried fowl.

"Merciful heavens." Mrs. Cardew cast an anxious look in Charlotte's direction. "My dear Mrs. Storbridge, are you quite certain you feel equal to dining at table?"

Charlotte gave a controlled smile. "You must know how Serena exaggerates, Mrs. Cardew. I was little more than momentarily stunned."

"It was a singularly long moment." There was a sharper edge to Frank's voice than he intended. Mrs. Cardew darted a glance at him. Serena stared at him with open curiosity. Charlotte's gaze was fixed on her lap, where her new kitten lay curled up. Her head was bent slightly forward as she stroked the kitten's fur. The light from the beeswax tapers in Mrs. Cardew's lovingly polished silver candlesticks caught the red mark on her forehead. By morning that mark would be a bruise to rival anything he had received or been dealt at school.

His fingers closed around the fluted stem of his wineglass. "We're fortunate the accident wasn't worse." It was as great an understatement as any he had made in the course of political maneuvering.

Serena pushed bits of Brussels sprout to the edge of her plate. "Well, it was bad enough as it was. Francis just sat on the sofa holding Charlotte for what seemed like the longest time. It *was* the longest time, only then she finally did wake up and she—"

"I think we can spare Mrs. Cardew the boring details." Frank sent Serena a meaningful look.

Serena went on describing the scene in the factory office, but avoided any mention of the kiss. Charlotte took a sip of wine. She had scarcely met his gaze since they returned to the house. Frank studied her. The curve of her neck. The pulse beating above her collarbone. The glowing purity of the pearls resting about her throat. The shimmering peach ribbon threaded through the fabric at the neck of her gown. Normally the mark on her forehead would have been hidden behind the hair escaping about her face. But tonight she had scraped her hair back, baring her forehead, allowing no stray tendril to fall loose. It must have taken every hairpin in her possession to achieve such order.

He knew, as plainly as if she had told him, just what had driven her to pin back her hair so ruthlessly. It had been in the heat of her mouth and the quickening of her breath and the haste with which she pulled out of his arms.

He twisted the stem of his glass between his fingers. He'd scarcely touched his claret, but his head swam as if he had downed a bottle. The passion in that kiss had been far stronger than her fleeting response the day he gave her her betrothal ring. Whatever else she felt for him, he now knew for a certainty that she was not indifferent.

He stared down into the rich, red depths of the claret. Knowledge is power. Daniel de Ribard had said that to him. Like so many lessons he had learned from his former employer, it had proved disgustingly apt.

The door swung open, cutting through Serena's chatter

and Frank's thoughts. Jack Matthews strode into the room, hair windblown, cravat askew. "I'm sorry. I seem to be forever interrupting you at dinner." He made a hasty bow in Charlotte's direction. "Your pardon, Mrs. Storbridge. It's good to see you looking so well recovered."

"Thank you." Charlotte smiled, a genuine, uncontrolled smile, a small crack in her facade, which made jealousy coil in Frank's gut. "Won't you sit down?" she said.

"Ah . . . no. That is—" Jack glanced at Frank. "We should talk."

"Don't be beastly, Jack." Serena was staring at him with saucer-round eyes. "We all want to know what caused the explosion."

"A problem with the blowing engine."

Serena leaned back in her chair. "That doesn't tell us anything."

Frank pushed his chair back. "We can talk in the study, Jack. Don't worry, brat, I'll give you a full report when I understand it myself."

As he got to his feet, there was the sound of another chair being scraped back. "I'd like to come too," Charlotte said.

Frank looked down the length of the table at his wife. She stood facing him. Her gaze was steady, a little challenging. "Of course," he said.

Serena folded her arms across her chest. "It isn't fair."

"Life—"

"—isn't fair. I know."

Frank gave Serena a grin and went to hold the door open for Charlotte. When they had traversed the corridors and he was holding open the door of the study, he realized that though their betrothal had begun in his study in London, this was the first time she had been in the apartment at St. John's Court. He watched her sweep over the threshold into the room that was most uniquely his.

She settled herself in an armchair where he often sat to read, the kitten in her lap. His schoolboy collection of Shakespeare was on the shelf at her back. A factory ledger he had been reviewing lay on the table at her elbow. There was a stain on the carpet at her feet where he had spilled a bottle of ink last August.

Charlotte seemed unaware that she had entered his inner sanctum. She was looking at Jack, her attention all on the factory. As his own should be. He swung the chair around from his desk and dropped into it. "Well, Jack? What caused the problem with the blowing engine?"

Jack leaned forward in his chair, his brows drawn together with unaccustomed intensity. "The pressure in the blast pipes rose too high."

"Not an accident?" Frank said.

Jack shook his head. "No. Not possibly. I wasn't sure about the flooding, but this was deliberate. The controls had been tampered with."

"Damnation." An image of Charlotte lying on the factory floor rose before Frank's eyes. "I didn't think they'd go this far. Not against us. I didn't think we were important enough."

"Who?" Charlotte's voice was sharp.

"Canal interests worried about railways ruining their business. Landowners afraid their fox hunting will be spoiled. Farmers trying to protect their livelihood. There's no shortage of antirailway interests. There've been a number of acts of sabotage against railways themselves. But I didn't think they'd turn on us."

Charlotte stared across the room, as though she could see something through the burgundy curtains. "I don't think they have."

"It was sabotage, Mrs. Storbridge." Jack's voice was gentle. "There's no question."

"I don't doubt it." Charlotte's betrothal ring glowed

golden as she stroked the kitten methodically. "But I don't think it was antirailway interests."

"Who then?" Frank asked, though he already knew her answer.

She looked him full in the face. "Daniel."

There was a brief silence. A log thudded against the grate. "Daniel?" Jack said.

"Daniel de Ribard." Charlotte turned to him. "My father, Mr. Matthews. He didn't want Frank and me to marry. You could say we outwitted him by doing so. Daniel makes it a point of pride not to let himself be outwitted."

"I see." Jack's unblinking gaze betrayed neither curiosity nor surprise. "And in your opinion, if Ribard is behind the sabotage, will he now consider the matter closed?"

"No," said Charlotte and Frank almost as one.

"He wants my support for the railway he's trying to get through Parliament," Frank added. "He may see this as leverage. If he's behind it."

"He is," Charlotte said.

"Regardless," Frank said, "we'd better put a twenty-four-hour guard on the factory."

"Right." Jack nodded. "I've already arranged one for tonight. I'll start getting estimates on repairing the damage tomorrow." He paused for a moment. "Even with the best of luck we're going to be shut down for a fair time. We'll have to alert the collieries. We'll try to have things up and running as soon as possible, but—"

"It's going to take a large outlay of capital. I know," Frank said. "It can't be helped. I'll return to London directly and speak to my banker." He looked at Charlotte. "I'm afraid we're going to have to cut short our visit."

"Of course," Charlotte said at once. But then, she would have no particular reason for wishing to remain at

St. John's Court. She was probably eager to return to the wider world, where she would have more of a buffer against his company.

She said little more as they rejoined Serena and Mrs. Cardew. He and Jack gave an edited version of the damage, with vague mentions of the possibility of sabotage and assurances that they didn't think it would go further. "I don't believe a word of it," Serena said when Jack had left. She and Charlotte and Frank were lingering in the great hall. Mrs. Cardew had gone to see about preparations for their departure tomorrow. Serena fixed Frank with a hard stare. "You know who's behind the explosion, don't you?"

Frank bent down to pet Millamant. "If we had any sort of proof of who it was, we'd call in the law."

"Which means you don't know, but you suspect."

Charlotte took a candle from the hall table and gave it to Serena. "Go to bed, love." She kissed Serena on the forehead. "We all have to get up early tomorrow."

Serena scowled, but she did start to climb the staircase, making a great show of dragging her feet. Charlotte went to take a candle herself, but she seemed to be dawdling, as though to linger until Serena was out of earshot. Which was surprising, because normally she was quick to escape his presence. Especially at night.

"Frank." Charlotte stood at the table, her gaze on the candle flame.

His blood quickened as though he were a schoolboy awaiting a signal from his sweetheart. "Yes?"

She gripped the silver candlestick, then released it. "Will you be able to repair the damage?"

The breath rushed from his lungs. "Eventually. It will put us behind schedule, but we'll manage."

She turned her head to look at him. "You must have sunk all your money into the factory."

A smile pulled at his mouth. "Oh, no. I haven't got any money, remember?" He went to the table and took a candle for himself. "I sunk all of Julia's money into it. Or very nearly all."

"I think Julia would be proud of you."

He stared down at the wax taper. His memories of his first wife were scarcely more substantial than the wavering flame. "She'd have been a good deal more cast down by the explosion than you were." He looked at the red mark on Charlotte's creamy skin. He wanted to brush his lips against it. He wanted to sweep her into his arms and carry her upstairs and use the comfort of his body to atone for what she had been through today.

But Charlotte wouldn't accept that sort of solace from him. At least not yet. Today's events had given him hope that their marriage might someday be more than it was now. But he knew enough of seduction to know that surrender had to be given, not taken. He lifted his hand and brushed his fingers against her cheek, as he had on their wedding night. He felt the wary tension in her body, but she gave him a brief smile.

A genuine smile from Charlotte could stir him more than a passionate caress from any other woman. He smiled back into her eyes. Then he stepped aside to allow her to precede him up the stairs, before his good intentions fled altogether.

The carriage rolled over rain-slick paving stones. It had been raining since they changed horses in Enfield, just as it had rained on their journey from Edinburgh to St. John's Court. But this time Charlotte was sitting on the backward-facing seat in the traveling carriage. A small distinction, but it summed up the changes during her short honeymoon. When they got into the carriage at St.

John's Court she had settled on the forward-facing seat
with Serena and Nancy, as on the earlier journey. But before they had even pulled away from the house, Juliet had
climbed off Frank's lap and toddled across the carriage
and tugged at Charlotte's skirt. And so Charlotte was sitting on the backward-facing seat, with Knightly and
Juliet and Millamant. And Frank.

Frank was at the opposite end of the seat. Juliet was
stretched between them, her arm around Millamant, who
lay beside her. Charlotte looked down at Juliet's shiny
black half boots, just touching the chocolate-brown wool
of her own traveling cloak. Juliet's head was in Frank's
lap. Still, even this much trust brought a welling of
warmth to her chest, just as the small weight of Knightly
in her lap did.

Juliet stirred, disarranging the folds of her traveling
cloak. Charlotte straightened the merino, then looked up
to find Frank's gaze upon her. Nothing overt in his behavior had changed since the explosion and the brief, revealing kiss that followed it, but she would swear his eyes
were different when he looked at her. It was as though
she could read in their depths the knowledge she had
given him of herself.

She looked away at the yellow pools the gaslight made
on the rain-black paving stones. With a start she recognized the wrought-iron railing she had glimpsed the night
she called on Frank and entered into their bargain. They
had turned into South Audley Street. The carriage was
slowing. Ionic columns flashed into view. Vaughan House.

Serena, asleep beside Nancy on the opposite seat,
opened her eyes. "Are we home?"

"Bundle up," Charlotte said. "It's raining."

The coachman let down the steps. Two footmen hurried out of the house. They called her Mrs. Storbridge.
They asked which of the bags were hers. Standing in the

circular entrance hall, Knightly cradled against her chest, Charlotte realized she didn't even know which bedroom in the vast house was her own. Just as long as Frank had made it very clear he and his bride occupied separate chambers.

"Mrs. Storbridge." One of the footmen—the one who had admitted her the night she called on Frank—appeared at her elbow. "Shall we tell Cook to arrange a supper?"

"Yes." It was late, but Serena would be hungry. So would Juliet, who was now wide awake, blinking at the world from Frank's arms.

"I'm sorry." Frank moved to her side. "It's not the homecoming a bride should have."

"Perhaps not, but it seems in keeping with the rest of our marriage."

A door was thrown open. Bertram staggered into the hall. He was in his shirt-sleeves, his hair lank, his eyes wild, his face flushed with drink or anger. His gaze swept the hall. "Storbridge." He took a halting step forward. "I didn't expect . . . But perhaps it's as well." He looked into Frank's eyes, his own dark with anguish. "God forgive me. I didn't mean to do it."

Chapter 12

Bertram's words echoed off the still white columns in the hall. Knightly mewed, breaking the stillness. Charlotte stroked him.

Frank took a step forward. "I can't answer for God, Bertram, but for my part I doubt it's as bad as you think. If you'll give me a moment we can talk it over."

Bertram opened his mouth as though to protest, then drew a shuddering breath and nodded. The footmen and Nancy were looking fixedly at the wall sconces or the marble floor tiles. Juliet pressed closer into Frank's arms. Serena was staring at her brother. "What have you done, Bertram?"

"Rena." Bertram seemed to become aware of her presence for the first time. He squared his shoulders in an attempt at big-brotherly bravado, then slumped back against the gilded door jamb. "I'm sorry. You know I never wanted to hurt you."

Serena's brows drew together. "But—"

"Serena." Charlotte walked over to her sister-in-law. "Could you look after Knightly for me? He's going to be confused by the new place. There." She settled the kitten in Serena's arms and was pleased to see self-possession return to Serena's eyes. She turned to one of the footmen. "Alan, isn't it? Could you arrange for a cold supper to be served in the schoolroom? And I think the gentlemen would like coffee. And sandwiches. As soon as possible."

"Charlotte." Frank turned to her. He had just given Juliet into Nancy's care. "I think you should hear whatever Bertram has to say."

Bertram lifted his head.

"A husband and wife have no secrets," Frank said.

Bertram glanced away. "Perhaps it's just as well."

Worse and worse. Brash, angry Bertram was so beaten he could tolerate not only Frank but herself as well. Charlotte squeezed Serena's shoulder, patted Knightly, smiled at Juliet, and followed the men to the study.

"Do you want to wait until you've had some coffee?" Frank asked when they were all seated.

Bertram had fallen to staring at a nick in the cherry-wood arm of his chair. It seemed to be a moment before he heard. Then he raised his head and pushed his hair back from his forehead. His face was pale now rather than flushed, and though his eyes were bloodshot, his gaze was focused. "No. No sense in waiting." But he drew a breath and continued to stare at the chair arm.

Frank leaned back and crossed his legs. "My guess is cards or a woman. Since you didn't object strenuously to Charlotte's presence, I'd guess it's cards."

Bertram nodded. His expression reminded Charlotte of Roger and Charles when she'd caught them filching iced cakes Céline had ordered for a reception. "I went to Brooks's—oh, a week or more ago—just after I returned to London. I was with Rowan, whom I was staying with, and de Verney and a bunch of fellows from university. We met this new chap. Folyat was—is—his name. In the army with de Verney's elder brother. Very amiable and full of capital stories about the army and . . . ah . . . and so on"—women, Charlotte guessed—"so we asked him to have supper with us."

Bertram said this last as though it explained everything. Frank regarded him steadily. "And after supper he took you to a new gaming hell that's all the crack?"

Bertram flushed. "The next night, actually. We asked him along to a play at the Haymarket and then he took us to this new place. Marable's. Very exclusive. You have to be a member to get in. Which none of us were. Except Folyat."

There was another silence. Charlotte looked at Bertram. "Did Folyat introduce himself to you?"

Bertram looked at her as though he'd forgotten she was in the room. "I suppose he did. Came up to de Verney and said he recognized him because he looked so like his brother."

Charlotte glanced at Frank. Frank gave a slight nod, but his gaze warned her against pursuing the matter now. "I've heard of Marable's," he said to Bertram. "I gather play there is unusually deep."

"Well, yes." Bertram fumbled with his crumpled cravat. "That's part of the . . . ah . . ."

"Excitement?"

Bertram flushed again but did not avoid Frank's gaze. "Yes." He pulled his cravat taut with sudden force. "But I did all right that first night—more than all right. Never had such a run of luck." This last was said with a bitterness so sharp Charlotte could taste it.

"And the next night?" Frank asked.

"I lost—and won. Lost more than I won, but I kept thinking—"

He was interrupted by a knock at the door. Charlotte opened it to find Alan bearing a tray with a steaming pot of coffee and a plate stacked with plentiful sandwiches. She took the tray from him and served the refreshments herself. Bertram accepted a cup of coffee gratefully but declined the food. Charlotte found herself saying, "You may not be hungry, but you'll feel better for it," in the tone she would have used with one of her nephews. To her surprise Bertram gave her a sheepish smile and took a triangle of roast beef. He ate the sandwich and downed half a cup of coffee with apparent relief, though whether at the sustenance or the break in the conversation she couldn't have said.

"It went on like that for several visits." Bertram broke the silence. "I'd win and lose, end the evening a bit behind, but be sure my luck was about to turn." He took a long gulp of coffee. "Then two nights ago Folyat and I went to Marable's without the others. Rowan and de Verney had a box at Covent Garden, but I cried off. I was determined to gain back what I'd lost." He stared down into his empty coffee cup.

Charlotte refilled his cup without speaking. Bertram downed half the contents again. "I lost," he said, giving the words a speaking weight. "I . . . I never knew one could lose so much so quickly. Christ." He pressed his hand to his temple. "I had to keep playing, you must see that. I couldn't leave things as they stood. Fortunately fellows were terribly decent about accepting my marker."

"Who?" Frank asked.

Bertram frowned into his coffee cup. "Toby Lawrence. The younger MacIntosh son. Chap called Fortescue. But mostly Folyat. He lent me whatever I needed."

"So I suspected." Frank's voice was quiet but bone-dry. He set down his coffee cup. "How much?"

Bertram shifted in his chair. "It kept adding up. One

scarcely realizes . . . That was when I moved back to Vaughan House. I couldn't face Rowan after I'd been such a fool."

"How much?" Frank said again.

Bertram stared at the crumbs on his plate, then looked his brother-in-law straight in the eye. "Seven thousand pounds."

Charlotte drew in her breath. Even Daniel at his most powerful would have blinked at such a sum.

Frank added milk to his coffee, though Charlotte knew for a fact that he always drank it black. "Obviously the debt will have to be honored. What a lucky thing it is your father was so obscenely wealthy."

Bertram's gaze hardened. "You needn't try to cosset me. I know damn well we don't have that kind of money. Even if I don't control the purse strings."

Frank lifted his cup and took a sip of coffee.

Bertram released his breath. "And I can now see Father was—perhaps—right not to leave them in my hands."

The corner of Frank's mouth lifted in a faint smile. "Then this incident may be said to have had its positive side."

Bertram scowled. "You know bloody well we can't pay the debt."

Frank set his cup down with barely a clink. "Not directly. But there are ways of raising money. We'll manage."

In Bertram's bright eyes Charlotte saw the struggle between the boy who wanted to believe and the man who was too clear-sighted to do so. "It's my problem. I want to pay it myself. But—"

"But as your father was so disobliging as to tie your money up in my hands, you need my help to raise the funds. I have to call on Hawkins tomorrow in any case. I'll see what he has to say."

"I should come with you."

"Let me talk to him alone first. I have to speak to him about St. John's Court as well."

"You'll tell me whatever you learn?"

"Of course." Frank leaned forward. "Go to bed, Bertram. If there's one infallible lesson I've learned from my own scrapes, it's that matters always seem less horrendous in the morning."

Once again, the boy warred with the man in Bertram's countenance. At last he got to his feet. But he paused at the door and looked back at his brother-in-law. "Storbridge? Why didn't you ring a peal over me?"

"What purpose would that have served? You're miserable enough already."

Bertram gave a reluctant grin, nodded at Charlotte, and left the room.

The aroma of coffee drifted through the still air. Rain pattered against the windows. Charlotte wondered if the storm had just picked up again or if it had been raining throughout the scene with Bertram and she had been too absorbed in his story to notice. She took a sip of coffee and looked at Frank. "What's your yearly income?"

Frank leaned back in his chair and crossed his legs at the ankles. He did not prevaricate as she half expected him to do. As many men would have done. "St. John's Court brings in about a thousand a year. My investments add up to another five hundred."

"And the loan you took out to start the factory?"

"Twenty-one thousand."

"At four percent?"

"Four and a half."

"So the interest is nine hundred forty-five pounds a year. And the Vaughan income? No, wait a minute." She walked around behind the desk and reached for a sheet of cream-colored writing paper, plain save for Frank's name, neatly embossed in black at the top. She found a newly mended pen, dipped it in ink, and wrote down the figures he had just recited. "What about the Vaughans?"

Frank turned his chair around so he was facing her across the desk. "The net income from the estates is just over nine thousand pounds. But five hundred a year is set aside for the expenses of each of the younger children, and Bertram's allowance is a thousand pounds. Then there's about eighteen hundred in annuities to various retainers and poor relations."

"So combined with your own net income, that makes a total of 5,250 a year." She dipped the pen in the inkpot and began a new column. "And the expenses?"

Frank moved aside a letter rack and a bronze paperweight and rested his elbows on the desk. "In round figures, fifteen hundred for the staff at Vaughan House and Vaughan Hall. Probably another fifteen hundred for horses and carriages. About twelve hundred for housekeeping and another thousand for repairs and anything else that falls under miscellaneous."

"Adding up to a total of five thousand two hundred. Well, at least your expenses don't outstrip your income."

"Thank you. I was vaguely aware of that fact."

Charlotte nibbled the top of the pen. "I put about half the Chelmsford income back into the estate, but I still have a clear five hundred a year of my own, so—"

"No," he said with sudden force.

She looked up from her notes. "No, what?"

"No, your money doesn't come into this."

She set down the pen, making a black streak across the pristine paper. "I don't see what I'm to spend it on, except for living expenses. I live here."

"Christ, Charlotte." Frank sat back and stared at her. "Listen to what you're saying."

She glanced down at the page of figures. The Vaughan income, Frank's income, and her own added in at the bottom. In good black ink she had joined herself to Frank and his family in a way that seemed far more intimate than their marriage vows. Those had been forced upon her. This she had done of her own free will.

She looked up into the dark, hard gray of Frank's eyes, unwavering in the green-shaded light of the desk lamp. She could see the shadow of a beard on his face, the faint creases around his mouth. The mouth she had felt against her hair and lips. Her blood pounded in her forehead. Tension coiled in the pit of her stomach. "If it weren't for me, none of you would be in this fix," she said. "You know as well as I do Daniel must be behind Bertram's losses."

"He may be." The hardness did not leave Frank's eyes. "I'll send for Diana in the morning. She should be safe enough at the Brandons', but I'd feel better if she was under my own roof."

"Then you do suspect Daniel."

"I'd suspect Ribard if one of us turned an ankle on a loose paving stone. But Bertram had a weakness for gaming long before Ribard returned to England."

"Has he ever before lost seven thousand pounds?"

Frank's silence was response enough.

"I thought not," Charlotte said. "Daniel put Captain Folyat up to it. I'd stake seven thousand pounds on *that*. If my money can help checkmate Daniel you can't expect me to remain on the sidelines."

"Sophistry, Charlotte," Frank said. But he gave a faint smile as he said it.

"I shouldn't quibble if I were you, Frank. You haven't much choice." She looked back at the paper. "We can use my five hundred to service a loan. Even at five percent we can borrow ten thousand. After you pay Bertram's debt there'll be at least three thousand left for the factory repairs. Will it be enough?"

"It should be." He was silent for a moment. "Charlotte?"

When he looked at her like that, she felt as though she were dancing upon a knife edge. She straightened her spine and drew back in the chair. "Yes?"

He smiled again, cutting through her defenses in one clean stroke. "My wards are lucky to have you for a sister."

Josiah Hawkins, senior partner in Hawkins's Bank, drummed his slender, tapered fingers against the tooled green leather of his desktop. "Seven thousand pounds. Young Bertram always was a bit feckless."

Frank met the veiled accusation in Hawkins's cool blue eyes. "And I have perhaps failed the trust Lord Vaughan placed in me when he appointed me guardian. But dwelling on past mistakes will do nothing to remedy present problems."

Hawkins made no comment. Frank drew a breath. The air in the banker's office smelled like it always did, of ink and leather and prosperity. "A loan of ten thousand pounds would take care of Bertram's debt and cover the repairs at St. John's Court. Thanks to my wife"—Frank glanced at Charlotte, who was seated beside him—"we have enough income to cover the interest."

Charlotte gave Frank a brief, achingly sweet smile— God, how necessity could forge alliances—then turned to Hawkins. "I have an estate at Chelmsford, in Lancashire. It gives me a clear five hundred a year. I can provide you with receipts to show as much."

"I don't doubt your word, Mrs. Storbridge." Hawkins

coughed, glanced away, adjusted the letters in a silver fili-gree basket on his desktop. "Ten thousand pounds is a large sum, Mr. Storbridge. The bank has already loaned you twenty-one thousand."

"I haven't forgotten." Frank leaned back into the com-modious claret-colored leather of his chair. "And I have made all the payments when due."

"I didn't say you hadn't." Hawkins realigned his ivory-handled pen and penknife on the blotter. "But the bank has a responsibility to all its clients. To extend over thirty thousand pounds to any one person . . ."

Frank fixed the Vaughan family banker with a hard stare. "What are you saying, Hawkins?"

Hawkins picked up a letter opener with an ornate han-dle and a lethal-looking blade. "I fear the bank cannot loan you any further sums, Mr. Storbridge. We regret the necessity, naturally. But had you not chosen to squander half of Lady Julia's marriage portion—"

"I invested half my late wife's money in my factory."

"Just so." Hawkins tapped the letter opener against the blotter. "I believe I told you at the time that I considered it to be a rash action. To say the least. Half your capital is gone, and the factory is a sinkhole that could suck down the rest before you know what's hit you."

"We have a disagreement there that only time will settle."

"Perhaps." Hawkins flicked the globe that stood beside his desk. He watched it whirl around for a moment, the continents of the world blending into a blur of color. "But under the circumstances . . ."

His voice trailed off, but an ominous tone lingered in the air. "What?" Frank said.

The globe came to rest. Hawkins looked directly at Frank. There was discomfort in his eyes, but also a sort of triumph. "We will not be able to extend your original loan when it falls due in March."

It was a moment before Frank could speak. He drew a breath, bit back an instinctive protest, and moderated his tone if not his temper. "It was always understood that the loan could—would be extended. May I ask what has changed?"

Hawkins folded his hands on the blotter. "A bank must always guard its assets, Mr. Storbridge."

"Hawkins's has guarded the Vaughan family assets for three generations. But I'm not a Vaughan, is that it?"

"If that were the case, he wouldn't have refused the loan to cover Bertram's debt." Charlotte was looking at Hawkins. "Mr. Hawkins, has the bank recently changed ownership?"

Hawkins's papery skin blanched. "Ma'am?"

Charlotte smoothed a wrinkle from her glove. "It's a simple enough question. Surely you know the answer. Has someone recently bought a controlling ownership in the bank?"

Frank looked at Charlotte. Hawkins looked at the desktop, at the floor, at the fire burning in the grate. "Yes, Mrs. Storbridge. I'm surprised you heard of it."

Charlotte continued to hold him with her gaze. "And would the new owner happen to be Daniel de Ribard?"

A silence hung over the office, heavier than the claret-colored leather or the dark paneling or the brass inlay on the desk. Hawkins released his breath. "Yes, Mrs. Storbridge. The new owner is your father."

"I underestimated him. Damn everything to hell, I underestimated him." Charlotte jammed her hands into her beaver muff and glared at a branch of yellow winter jasmine.

"You've said that at least five times since we left Hawkins's," Frank told her. They were sitting on the garden steps, watching a well-bundled-up Serena push an equally well-bundled-up Juliet in the swing that hung from one of the plane trees.

Charlotte turned her head to look at him, dislodging the cashmere scarf about her shoulders. "It rankles more each time."

Frank rested his elbows on the stone of the step behind them. "I underestimated him too."

"But you don't know him like—"

"Like you do? In spite of being cut from the same cloth?"

Good God. She'd forgotten she'd said that to him. She brushed aside a dry leaf that had caught on the mulberry folds of her pelisse. "I don't think two people could be cut from the same cloth as Daniel."

Something lightened in Frank's eyes, as though he had let go of a long-held burden. "As I said to Hawkins, dwelling on past mistakes won't solve present problems."

"No." She glanced at the expanse of flagstones in front of them, where Millamant and Knightly were wrestling. "We have plenty of time to take out another loan before yours falls due in March. We'll have to pay higher interest, but we'll manage." Millamant had Knightly pinned beneath her. Knightly had his paws around Millamant's neck and was kicking her stomach. They looked as if they were having a wonderful time and hadn't a care in the world. "Mr. Hawkins said you disposed of half Julia's marriage portion. There's still capital left?"

"Ten thousand pounds in the funds. Her marriage portion was twenty."

"Lord Vaughan was a generous father."

Frank's mouth curled. "You didn't think I became prosperous on my own account, did you?"

Charlotte folded her hands in her lap. "Don't be self-mocking, Frank, we haven't time for it. You can sell out of the funds and use the ten thousand pounds to cover Bertram's debt and the repairs to the factory. Bertram can pay you back over time. My money can replace the lost income."

"I had thought of that. But it leaves us with no reserves."

"But if we borrow the ten thousand as well, we'll be paying five percent interest or more on it. This will keep our payments lower. Meanwhile, I can raise a few hundred pounds more by selling that bracelet Daniel gave me as a wedding present."

"Charlie—"

"Oh, don't protest that, Frank. Surely you don't imagine I'd ever wear it. If we didn't have a use for the money, I'd give the thing away." She traced a line of ornamental black stitching on the ecru kid of her glove. "Daniel must have known we could go to another bank."

"Undoubtedly." Frank scrunched the gravel below the steps with the toe of his Hessian boot. "But buying Hawkins's was a clever way of showing us the extent of his power. Besides, if he wants to reestablish a financial base in England, he'll find it useful to control a bank. He'd probably have bought into one in any case. We just helped him decide which."

"But he'll know he hasn't beaten us. Which means it isn't over." She hunched her shoulders, fighting off a chill that had nothing to do with the air in the garden.

Frank reached out and tucked her scarf more closely around her shoulders. For a moment she thought he was going to leave his arm around her. For a moment she wanted him to. There was a steady warmth in his touch that drove out the cold. The breeze came up, sending a hail of yellow petals from the jasmine and loosing the sweetness of their scent.

Frank dropped his arm and hooked his hands around his knees. "Diana will be back from the Brandons' tomorrow. Val should be safe enough at Harrow. Safer than if we bring him into the thick of this."

"Yes." Charlotte pulled the velvet collar of her pelisse closed. She felt a strange pang, as though she'd lost something she hadn't realized she wanted.

"Mummy!" Juliet's shout carried across the walled garden. "I swinging."

"I see you, darling," Charlotte called back. Then she realized what Juliet had called her. Her throat went tight. Unexpected tears prickled her eyelids.

Beside her, Frank had gone still. "I know," he murmured, his eyes unusually bright. "But try not to make too much of it."

"I finished, Rena," Juliet told Serena.

Serena lifted Juliet down from the swing. Juliet marched across the garden. Her rosy cheeks were flushed even rosier by the cool air and exertion. With feathery dark curls escaping beneath her snug red bonnet, she looked very like the porcelain doll Charlotte had given Sophie's daughter, Fenella, for Christmas.

Juliet stopped and looked up at her father and Charlotte. "Shall we read a story?" she asked in her lilting voice.

The grown-up phrasing startled Charlotte. With a shock of surprise, she realized Juliet was parroting her own words back at her. She felt a smile break across her face, as though she had received a tremendous compliment. She held out her hand. "What a good idea. Let's go into the library and choose a book, and perhaps Daddy and Serena can find us something to eat."

"All right." Juliet gave a determined nod. Her small, gloved hand closed around Charlotte's own. Charlotte got to her feet, aware of Frank and Serena watching them. As she walked into the house holding her stepdaughter's hand, she wondered if she could manage to feel like Juliet's mother without letting herself feel like Frank's wife.

Chapter 13

Bertram stared into the library fire. "I don't understand. Why would Daniel de Ribard care about my gambling debts?"

Charlotte smoothed the chestnut lustring of her dinner dress. "Daniel's motives are frequently difficult to understand. But the simple answer is that you're Frank's brother-in-law and Frank is married to me."

Bertram turned in his chair to look at her. "But he's your father."

"Precisely."

His eyes widened. Whatever the tensions in the Vaughan family, this was apparently something quite beyond his comprehension.

Frank leaned back into the crimson velvet of the sofa, as if this were no different from an ordinary after-dinner discussion. "The point is, while there's no doubt you were foolish, you were actively abetted in your folly."

Bertram's eyes turned as hot as the coals in the grate. "By God, I should call Folyat to account."

Frank brushed a loose thread from the smooth black of his evening coat. "I wouldn't advise it. While we can cope with your gambling debts, I really don't think the family fortune would extend to packing you off to the

Continent. Not to mention the bribes it would take to hush up a duel."

Bertram pushed himself to his feet and took a turn about the hearthrug. "Damn it, I want to do *something*."

"Very understandable." Frank surveyed him for a moment. "To begin with, you could consider how you can cut back on your expenses. The sooner we can pay off our debts the better."

Bertram's eyes widened. Poor boy, Charlotte thought, this wasn't the sort of heroics he'd had in mind. "Of course." He straightened his shoulders. "I can put my team up for sale at Tattersall's. And my hunters. And I could sell my watch—"

"Thank you, Bertram." Frank inclined his head. "I have no doubt you're prepared to make a grand gesture. But for the moment I think all that is required is a little domestic economy. Tedious perhaps, but in the end far less painful."

Bertram opened his mouth, then closed it. "I see. That is . . . It's a relief it's not worse. Charlotte." He gave her a stiff nod. "If you'll excuse me. I should . . . I should look over my accounts."

Charlotte watched the library door close behind him. "Poor boy." She turned back to Frank. "He's longing for battle, and you sent him off to do sums."

Frank grimaced. "Care to wager on how long it will last?"

"No, thank you. There's been quite enough gambling without me entering into the fray." She watched Frank for a moment. Now that Bertram had left the room, some of his sangfroid had deserted him. She could see tension in the set of his mouth and blue-tinged shadows of strain about his eyes. "All things considered, I think you handled him amazingly well," she said.

"Did I?" He gave a faint, twisted smile. "I can't exchange two words with Bertram without knowing he'd like nothing better than to knock my teeth in."

"That's plain enough. It's also plain that he admires you."

He raised his brows. "*Admires* me? My dear Charlotte, I always thought you were perceptive about people."

"If he didn't admire you he wouldn't be so dreadfully jealous." She folded her hands in her lap. "It must have been difficult from the first. I daresay he resented his father trusting you."

"How do you know Lord Vaughan trusted me?"

"He made you guardian of his children."

"Yes." Frank crossed his legs at the ankles and stared into the fire. "He did do that."

In the silence that followed, it occurred to Charlotte that this was the first time since their wedding night that they had sat alone together in the evening. At St. John's Court they had kept country hours and retired when Serena did. Now they faced each other on the matched velvet sofas like any other couple in Mayfair who happened to be home for the evening. The library was a large room, but aside from a single lamp the only light came from the candelabra on the mantel and from the fire itself. What was it about the warm glow of firelight that seemed so disturbingly intimate?

She pushed herself to her feet with a crisp rustle of her skirts. She felt stiff and awkward, as though her gown was buttoned too tight and her limbs would not quite obey her. "Good night, Frank."

He swung his head around to look at her. "There's no need to run off. I don't have any designs on your virtue." Something of the old mockery was back in his eyes and voice. "At least not any that I mean to act on."

The air in the room suddenly felt close and heavy, like the change in the atmosphere that warns of a thunderstorm. She sat down because the words were a challenge and to leave would be to cede victory to him. "I'm not worried about my virtue."

"No?" His smile broadened.

She looked straight into his eyes. "I didn't mean it that way."

"No, I didn't think you did." If the air felt like the warning of a storm, the lightning was in his eyes. Though she risked being singed, she wouldn't let herself be the one to look away first. At length, when she wasn't sure she could stand it much longer, he broke eye contact and glanced about the room. "We could play chess," he suggested in a bland voice.

She followed his gaze and saw a chess set on a table in the shadows on the opposite side of the room. Her throat went tight with a pang of memory. In the old days, when he was Daniel's secretary, she and Frank had often escaped to the library and spent the evenings playing chess. She wasn't sure she wanted to dredge up those memories. On the other hand, she loved the game and she hadn't played since their wedding. Surely an activity that required as much cool calculation as chess would be safe. "All right," she said.

They moved the chess set to a low table in front of the fire and pulled up chairs. Frank shrugged out of his coat. "Do you mind?" he asked. "The fire's a bit warm."

"Not in the least," she said, studiously ignoring the way the light shot through the fine linen of his shirt. She should be able to stand the sight of a well-made male body with equanimity. Heaven knew she'd seen enough classical statues when Paul and Sophie took her to Italy three years ago. But none of the statues had given her this strange, unsettled feeling, as though she were being pulled two different ways at once.

She turned her attention to the chess board. The pieces were of carved soapstone, black and white equally luminous. She chose black, which made Frank smile. She made her first move in silence, but it had always been Frank's style to talk during a game. He murmured something inocuous as he made his first move. When he made his second he looked up at her and said, "Thank you for what you did for Juliet." His gaze was sincere. This was more than just tactics to distract her during the game.

She picked up a knight. Juliet had called her Mummy again when she went into the nursery to say good night. The sound still echoed sweetly in her memory, but perhaps it was silly to place too much emphasis on what was after all only a word. "She heard Fenella and Gerry calling Sophie Mummy. I think she wanted to try out the name. You know how she loves new words."

He reached for one of his rooks. "I think it's a little more than that."

"Perhaps. I hope so." She shifted a pawn.

He looked down at the board for a long moment, made his move, then looked back at her. His gaze was open and direct, as it seldom was. "Juliet doesn't give her trust easily. But when she does it's absolute."

She paused, her hand hovering over the board. "I'm very fond of her, Frank. I'm fond of the Vaughans too, even Bertram." She reached for her knight. "I won't go back on my responsibilities to them."

"Whatever your private war with me." He moved a pawn.

She looked up at him. "At the moment we're both fighting a war with Daniel." She moved her knight again and captured his rook.

He stared down at the board. "You've been setting that up from your first move, haven't you?"

"Well, I was trying to. I wasn't sure it would work. It all depended on whether you did what I predicted."

He gave a shout of laughter. "Touché, my darling. I've

been called a number of disagreeable things in my life, but none of them as lowering as *predictable*." He bent his attention to the board.

"Trying to redeem your lost honor?" she asked.

He looked up at her, his gaze hard and still in the flickering firelight. "I wouldn't go quite that far. I know my limitations." He moved a bishop. "Check."

She shifted a pawn to protect her king. "You can't get round me that easily."

"I didn't think I could." He rested his elbows on the table and studied the pieces ranged on the black and white squares of the board. It was like stepping into the past. She knew that pose, the way his long-fingered hands were tented beneath his chin, the way his brows were drawn in concentration, the way his eyes were deliberately veiled to avoid giving away his strategy. Even in the old days he'd been good at hiding his thoughts.

A lock of hair had fallen over his forehead. He ignored it. She had an unexpected impulse to smooth it back.

Frank glanced up. She could swear he knew what she'd been thinking. She hoped the heat in her face didn't mean she was blushing. "Dear me," she said, her voice as dry as she could make it, "it does take you a long time to make up your mind."

"I'm weighing the consequences of my next move."

He wasn't looking at the board as he said it. He was looking at her. The heat of the fire felt stifling. And far too revealing, as though the fabric of her gown had suddenly turned to gossamer. She drew a breath. The library door opened.

"Forgive me, Mr. Storbridge." Alan stepped into the room, his powdered wig slightly askew, as though he'd been dozing at his post. "Sir Thomas Brandon is asking for you. He says it's urgent."

She could swear Frank bit back a curse. He turned to Alan. "Is Lady Diana with him?"

"No, sir." Alan's gaze was fixed on a point beyond Frank's shoulder.

Frank's expression hardened. "Send him in."

"Dear God." Charlotte stared at Frank as the door closed behind Alan, her thoughts of a moment before gone. "Something's happened to Diana."

"Possibly, but not necessarily." Frank pulled his coat on.

"Daniel's got to her too."

He settled the coat over his shoulders. "We don't know that."

"You think it's just coincidence that things keep happening to your wards?"

"Charlie—" He reached across the chess board and took her hands in a firm clasp. "I don't know what's happened. I don't know if Ribard is responsible. But I do know that *you* aren't."

She should have been beyond such simple comfort, but his words steadied her nonetheless. Amazing what conviction his voice could carry. Without conscious thought, she returned the clasp of his hands.

The door opened once again. "Sir Thomas Brandon," Alan announced.

"Brandon." Frank released her and walked forward. "I don't believe you've met my wife."

"Mrs. Storbridge." Brandon shook Frank's hand and nodded at Charlotte. He was a short, stout man with the ruddy complexion of a country squire. But there was an ashen cast to his weathered skin, and his dark gaze darted from side to side.

"No sense in formalities." Frank waved Brandon to a chair. "Is Diana ill?"

"No." Brandon lowered himself into the armchair.

"Not ill." He wiped his hand across his forehead. The candlelight glinted off a sheen of sweat on his temples.

"Has there been an accident?" Frank leaned against the library table.

"No." Brandon drew a deep, rasping breath, reached inside his coat, and pulled out two papers, one creased, the other still sealed. "You'd best read these. They speak for themselves."

Frank took the papers and held the creased one to the light of the lamp on the table. Charlotte moved to his side and read over his shoulder. It was a letter from Diana to her friend Edwina Brandon.

> *Dearest Edwina,*
> *By the time you read this I shall be gone from your father's house. When next we meet I shall no longer be Diana Vaughan, but Mrs. Christopher Linton. Please forgive my deception. You know how strongly I believe in being honest in all matters, but Christopher persuaded me that we could not burden anyone else with our plans. I think you know or can guess how deeply I have come to love him. Please believe that we have chosen this course because it is the best way to ensure the future happiness of all concerned.*
> *Pray say nothing of our flight until morning. Please see that Francis gets the enclosed letter.*
> *Your devoted friend always,*
> *Diana Vaughan*

Frank set the letter on the table without speaking. His own name was written across the other paper. He broke the red wax seal with his finger. The handwriting on this letter was uneven and the ink blurred, as though Diana had shed tears as she wrote it.

My dear Francis,

Please forgive me for what I am about to relate. I have found the man with whom I wish to spend the rest of my life. I know you would not readily agree to the match. My dearest Christopher and I could not bear to be separated, so we have decided it will be best if we marry at once. If there is to be any scandal attached to my name, I wish to keep it from the rest of the family.

I can only hope that you can bring yourself to forgive me. Please give my dearest love to Serena and Juliet and Bertram and Val and to your Charlotte. If you and she are half as much in love as Christopher and I, I know I need not fear for your happiness.

Your devoted ward,

Diana

The paper crackled between Frank's fingers. "When did she leave?"

Brandon coughed. "Earlier this evening. Must have been about ten. We keep early hours. Edwina decided it was her duty to inform me at once."

Frank ran his finger along the jagged edge of the broken seal. "I daresay she was piqued that Diana hadn't confided in her."

Charlotte looked at Brandon. "Why is Diana so convinced Frank wouldn't consent to her marriage to Mr. Linton?"

"Ah . . . I'm not quite certain." Brandon sucked in his breath, puffing out his cheeks. "Don't know Linton well."

Frank dropped the second letter beside the first on the table. "He was a guest in your home."

"My nephew brought him down. They met in the Argentine. Or perhaps it was Brazil." Brandon tugged at his neckcloth. "Linton has no fortune to speak of. Perhaps Lady Diana felt—"

Frank lifted his brows. "I'm not a monster, Brandon. Diana has a comfortable fortune of her own. I wouldn't stand in the way of her happiness. But neither would I permit her to fall victim to a fortune hunter."

"Quite so." Brandon breathed deeply. "See here, Storbridge. The girl was under my protection. I'd have gone after her myself, but I wasn't sure—"

Frank crossed his arms over his chest. "That I'd want her back?"

Brandon glanced at the well-polished toes of his shoes, then back at Frank. "Thought you might think it best to put a good face on it. No doubt they've"—he glanced at Charlotte, coughed, looked back at Frank—"no doubt they've stopped at an inn by now. Might be best to let the marriage go forward. Not brilliant, but Linton doesn't seem such a bad fellow—"

"If Linton was a decent fellow he'd have asked me for Diana's hand, not persuaded her to an elopement." Frank moved to the door. "Please forgive my lack of hospitality, Brandon. Too much time has been lost as it is. Charlotte—"

Charlotte was already at his side. "Of course I'm coming with you. Let me get my cloak."

Fog lay thick on the ground, like piles of yellowed cotton wool. The carriage was creeping along at a pace that set Charlotte's teeth on edge. She turned from the bleak sight out the window and fell back against the squabs. "Dear God, how could we have been such fools?"

"A singularly apt question." Frank's face was hidden in the shadows, but she could hear the bitter edge to his voice. "I thought of elaborate revenge schemes he might try. I didn't think of the obvious—that he'd use Bertram's and Diana's own weaknesses against them."

"Daniel to the core." Charlotte pressed her gloved fingers to her temples. "He's not above violence, but he resorts to it only in the most extreme cases. I should have guessed—"

"So should I. I do it myself every time I try to steer a bill through the House. Whose votes need to be changed and where I can find the chink in their armor that will allow for the persuading."

She stared across the dark expanse of the carriage at her husband. His motives remained as shrouded to her as his face now was by the shadows. "Are you telling me you lure fellow politicians into gaming hells and seduce them into elopements?"

"Usually less drastic measures suffice. But it's frequently not pretty. And it's fatal to underestimate one's opponent. As I just did. Three times."

She could hear the self-reproach in his voice. She felt it herself, a bombardment as relentless as the clop of the horse hooves and the rattle of the wheels over the road. "You sent for Diana as soon as you knew about Bertram," she said.

"And in doing so I may well have precipitated the elopement."

"If Daniel is behind the affair, the damage had already been done." She tucked the carriage rug more closely about her legs. The damp, numbing chill of the fog seeped into the carriage. "For all her romanticism, I can't believe Diana would decide to elope so easily. Linton must have persuaded her to it. He must have something to hide."

"Ribard wouldn't have picked someone who didn't have something to hide."

"Frank—" She leaned forward on the carriage seat

and tried to look into his eyes in the darkness. "You can't let Diana marry Linton. Not if he turns out to be unscrupulous."

"I have no intention of doing so."

She sat back, but Brandon's innuendos echoed in her head. "Not even if—"

"If he's compromised her?"

Images flashed across her mind. She gripped the carriage seat, anchoring herself to the present. "There are worse fates. It's so easy to make a mistake when you're young." She drew a breath and realized she was trembling. "I nearly married Ned."

She couldn't see Frank's expression, but she could feel his gaze upon her, feel an understanding that was more than she could bear. "And as I recall, even at one-and-twenty you had considerably more sense than my ward," he said, his voice mild. "Don't worry. I won't sacrifice Diana's happiness on the altar of propriety."

A light flashed feebly into view through the fog. She saw the outline of a swinging inn sign, though she could not make out the picture painted on it. The coachman slowed. As they pulled up before the inn, she made out a carved lion, painted red, projecting from the front of the building.

"Barnet," Frank said. "If I'm right, they'll have stopped here."

"How can you be sure they'll stop? They might change horses and push on through the night."

"They'll stop," Frank said, his voice hard. "Wait in the carriage. I'll let you know if they're at this inn."

Scarcely more than five minutes later he returned to the carriage with a curt "Not here." They drove on down the road to the even larger bulk of the Green Man. Once again, Frank went inside to make inquiries. Charlotte stared out the window at fog rising off the cobblestones and the dark, rambling outline of the inn. It must be getting on toward three. The knot in her stomach had tightened as they drove further from London. Her hands, she realized, were fisted in the folds of the rug. She shifted her position on the seat, trying to ease the cramp in her back.

Frank strode from the inn, a ghostly figure in the fog. He opened the door of the carriage and leaned inside. "They're here."

Chapter 14

Frank took her hand to help her from the carriage. "They arrived about an hour ago. They're calling themselves Mr. and Mrs. Linford."

"So they're sharing a room." She gathered up her skirt and climbed down the steps.

"Yes. But they haven't retired yet. They're still having supper."

"Who did you say we were?" Charlotte asked as they crossed the yard.

"Diana's elder brother and sister-in-law. With an urgent family message."

"The innkeeper didn't question your story?"

"He wouldn't have presumed." Frank glanced down at her. "I learned more than one lesson from Ribard, you know." He caught her arm and detained her for a moment before they went into the inn. "Our first objective is to get her away from Linton. Then . . . we're going to have to find out if there's any chance she's with child."

Charlotte drew a breath. "And if she is?"

"We'll cope with the consequences." He reached for the door handle.

The innkeeper, a portly, gray-haired man, neatly arrayed even at this late hour, was awaiting them in the entrance hall. "The parlor is this way, sir." He indicated a corridor opening off the hall. "The first door on the left. You're sure you don't want me to announce you?"

"Thank you," Frank said, "but my sister will be surprised enough. I prefer to keep it within the family."

The innkeeper glanced down the corridor, then ran a shrewd eye over Frank. Charlotte was sure he didn't believe their story. On the other hand, he would think it best to distance himself from any unpleasantness. "As you wish, sir," he said, face and voice as wooden as the handsome paneling lining the hall.

Frank walked down the corridor and threw open the first door on the left. Charlotte, a step behind him, heard a quick intake of breath, felt the welcome heat of a fire, saw the candlelight waver. She followed him into the room and pushed the door shut against inquiring eyes and ears.

"Francis." Diana made the name a gasp of shock and fear and guilt. She was sitting opposite the door at a square, linen-covered table spread with the remains of a meal. A man in his shirt-sleeves stood at her elbow, a tall, slender man of twenty-five or so, his black hair in an appropriately Corsairlike state of disorder. His hand rested on the back of her chair, but from the flush in Diana's cheeks and the way her gown was slipping from her shoulder, Charlotte was sure that a moment before he had been kissing her neck.

Frank set his hat down on a table by the door and began to strip off his gloves. "Forgive the abrupt intrusion. Under the circumstances I thought the less the innkeeper saw, the better."

Diana put up her chin. "It's no use, Francis. I'm not going back."

Frank tossed his gloves onto the table and walked over to Linton, hand extended. "Hullo, I'm Storbridge. I understand you want to marry my ward."

Christopher Linton swallowed, blinked, and seemed to realize he had no choice but to shake the proffered hand. "Ah . . . yes. I do. Very much."

Diana reached for Linton's free hand. A pearl ring Charlotte had never seen before glinted on the third finger of her left hand. "He's *going* to marry me." She looked at Frank with an imperious lift of her brows.

"Is he." Frank turned to Charlotte. "Allow me to present my wife, Linton."

"Mrs. Storbridge." Linton was obliged to disentangle himself from Diana, step around the table, and make a bow in Charlotte's direction. The light fell full on his face. One could understand what had driven Diana to this rash act. His skin was interestingly pale, his features finely molded, his eyes a deep, compelling blue. Frank had put him on the defensive, but he smiled at Charlotte, a winning, self-deprecating smile. She felt herself almost smiling in return.

"Good, that gets the formalities out of the way." Frank shrugged out of his greatcoat and dropped it over one of the shield-back chairs grouped about the table. "What I can't understand is—" He picked up a half-empty bottle. "You don't mind, do you, Linton? We've been traveling the devil of a long time." He poured the wine into a pair of empty water goblets without waiting for an answer. "What I can't understand is why you didn't apply to me for Diana's hand in the normal fashion."

Diana looked up at her lover. "Christopher—"

"It's all right, my darling." Linton turned to Frank, his handsome features hardening into firm resolve. "See here, Storbridge—I know I'm not what most men would consider a brilliant catch."

"Nor was I when I married Diana's sister." Frank carried one of the goblets over to Charlotte. He smiled as he put it into her hand, a brief, conspiratorial glint of lightning in his eyes.

"My case is rather worse." Linton glanced down at his hands, then looked back at Frank. "My father was the younger son of a baronet—"

"Yes, I fancy your uncle is Sir Horace Linton of Kedelhurst in Buckinghamshire." Frank strolled back to the table.

"He is. My parents died when I was young. My uncle and aunt raised me. I wasn't an easy charge." Linton smiled again, a rueful smile that must have won him forgiveness for a multitude of sins. "Looking back, I expect I was seeking attention, but I make no excuses for myself."

Dear God, the man was far more plausible than Ned had ever been. Diana's gaze was fixed on him, luminous with compassion. Charlotte's insides twisted with equal parts pity and rage.

Linton moved to the fireplace and leaned his arm on the mantel in a pose he must have known showed off his graceful body to maximum advantage. "To cut short a long and dull story, at twenty I was sent down from Cambridge. For dueling."

If he had expected to shock Diana's guardian, he was disappointed. Frank took a sip of wine. "Defending a lady's honor?"

"You could put it that way." Linton looked hard into Frank's eyes. "I shot better than I realized. My opponent died."

"And Christopher nearly died himself." Diana leaned toward Frank, blue-green eyes dark and intense. "He intended to shoot to the side, but his opponent fired before the signal, spoiling his aim. He's told me the whole."

"I daresay he has." Frank regarded Linton for a moment over the heavy rim of the goblet. "So your uncle packed you off to—what did Brandon say? South America?"

"Brazil."

Frank took another sip of wine. "Is that where you first made the acquaintance of Daniel de Ribard, or was that only after you returned to England?"

It was a moment before Linton understood. Charlotte saw the reaction in his eyes: a flare of surprise, followed by a wary narrowing of his lids. "I'm afraid you've lost me, Storbridge." He settled his shoulders against the mantel in a deliberate pose of unconcern.

"Oh, come." Frank splashed some more wine into his goblet—mostly, Charlotte thought, because the gesture maintained his control of the scene. "Daniel de Ribard recently acquired Hawkins's Bank. You don't deny that you are deeply in debt to Hawkins's, do you? I daresay they paid for that very handsome coat—Delcroix, isn't it?—and the pin in your cravat and the charming ring Diana is wearing. Not to mention this excellent claret." He lifted his goblet in an ironic toast.

Linton remained still, but his pale skin went a shade paler. He was silent for a moment, no doubt calculating risks and rewards. Then he gave another smile, with just the right degree of bleakness. "As I said, I'm hardly an eligible parti. I make no pretenses to you. Or to Diana."

Diana smiled at her lover, full lips trembling. Frank continued to watch Linton. "Then you've admitted to Diana that Ribard offered to cancel your debt in exchange for seducing her?"

"Francis!" Diana sprang to her feet.

"I'm sorry, Di. But it's best you hear the truth now."

Linton stepped away from the fireplace. "That's a filthy accusation, Storbridge."

"The truth is frequently filthy." Frank set his glass

down on the table with a force that rattled the dishes. "Going to challenge me to a duel too?"

Linton moved forward. "By God—"

"Christopher, no." Diana put out her arm as though to physically keep the two men apart. She turned to Charlotte. "Why in God's name would your father care anything about me?"

Charlotte's fingers tightened around the stem of her goblet. She had sunk down on a straight-back settee against the wall, distancing herself from the scene. She should have known sooner or later she would have to play her part. She looked into Diana's eyes—troubled, questioning, but not yet disillusioned. She saw herself asking similar questions of Sophie five years ago, unable or unwilling to see a truth that would smash her world to bits. "Because Frank and I went against his wishes and foiled his plans. My fath—Daniel de Ribard is a dangerous man, Diana."

Linton moved to Diana and put his arm around her shoulders. "I love Diana. She has done me the honor of saying she loves me. I mean to marry her."

"Do you?" Frank ran a cool, unconcerned gaze over the pair of them. "An interesting feat. I have it on very good authority that you left a wife in South America."

Charlotte heard a gasp and realized she had made the sound herself. She glanced at Frank, but he was looking at Linton. Linton looked as though he'd just been stabbed in the back at the end of a fight he thought he was winning.

"Christopher?" Diana's voice was hoarse, her eyes pleading.

Linton swallowed. A muscle twitched beside his mouth. "Your guardian must see the strength of our attachment, my love. Why else would he resort to such desperate measures?"

"You deny it?" Frank shrugged. "Very well. I do not wish to stand in the way of Diana's happiness. If there is no impediment, we should do this properly. Let us return to London and send the announcement of your betrothal to the papers. I shall write to your uncle directly."

He had thrown down the gauntlet, as clearly as if they could hear it slap against the oak floorboards. Joy broke across Diana's face, then faded as Linton stared at Frank, eyes dark with rage.

"Checkmate, I think," Frank said.

"Damn you." Linton lunged at Frank.

"Christopher." Diana pulled him around to face her. For a long moment she stared up into his face, searching for clues, for explanations, for a depth that probably wasn't there. "Didn't you want to marry me at all?" she said.

Linton drew a breath, then released it. He looked down into her upturned face. His eyes softened with a tenderness that might, just possibly, have been genuine. He lifted one hand and brushed his fingers against her cheek. "My dearest Diana—a man would have to be a blind fool not to want to marry you. But Storbridge is right. I am not free."

Diana shuddered but did not look away from his face. "And he's right about Daniel de Ribard?"

Linton looked into her eyes. "Yes, God help me."

"I see." Diana's voice trembled. For a moment she continued to look at him, regally self-contained. Then a sob broke from her throat and she turned away, hands pressed to her face.

Charlotte sprang to her feet and gathered Diana into her arms. Frank regarded Linton across the table. "Don't think you can ruin Diana by bandying this story about. Sir Thomas Brandon will swear that he conveyed her safely home to Vaughan House this evening."

"Believe it or not," Linton said, "I have no desire to ruin Diana."

"Even though those were Ribard's orders."

Linton picked up his coat from a chair back and shook it out, staring at the fine, glossy fabric. "Desperation." He slipped the coat on, settling it carefully over his shoulders. "You're a man of the world, Storbridge. Surely by now you've learned that every man has his price."

Frank's expression did not waver. "Yes."

There was a brief silence filled with the harsh sound of Diana's weeping. Linton's gaze rested on her for a moment. Charlotte thought he was going to speak. She could almost feel him struggling to frame the words, though she could not have said what the words would be—an apology, a plea for understanding, an attempt to excuse his criminal folly. In the end he merely inclined his head. Then he turned on his heel and strode from the room.

Diana went still at the sound of the door closing. A single shudder racked her body, followed by a fresh storm of tears.

Frank crossed to their side and laid a hand on Diana's shoulder. "I'm sorry. I wish I could find the words to express how sorry."

Diana's sobs continued unabated. "I'll arrange for a fresh team of horses," Frank said. He squeezed Diana's shoulder and went to the door.

Charlotte and Diana were left alone. Charlotte rocked the younger girl in her arms until Diana's sobs gave way to trembling. At length Diana pulled away, her clear skin blotched and puffy, her bright eyes dull and clouded. "I've been a fool."

"No more than the average twenty-year-old."

"Oh, God." Diana pressed her hands to her face, then let them fall, fighting back fresh tears. "How could I have believed his lies? But how could he—" Her gaze went to the door. She lifted her hand to her neck. Her fingers stilled against her bare skin. She glanced about the room, then knelt beside the chair she had been sitting in and picked up what Charlotte had thought to be a fallen napkin. It proved instead to be a sheer muslin tippet. Diana fingered it for a moment, then wrapped it about her neck and tucked it beneath her kerseymere gown, pulling the folds close about her throat. She swallowed and looked at Charlotte. "You must think me wicked."

"Darling." Charlotte went to the younger girl's side. "No, no, of course not. How could I?" She took Diana's arm and drew her to the settee.

"But I am." Diana sat beside Charlotte without protest, head bent forward, titian curls spilling about her face. "I'm criminally wicked. I gave my trust—my heart—to a liar. I turned my back on my family without a thought of what my actions might mean to them—"

"Doing it much too brown, Diana." Charlotte made her voice deliberately dry. "I saw your letter to Frank. You may have been imprudent, but it sounded as if your family were very much in your thoughts."

Diana lifted her head and looked at Charlotte. "I think a part of me knew how odd it was—Christopher insisting on the elopement, I mean. I kept saying I was sure Francis would listen to his suit if he only explained, but he insisted Francis would throw him from the house and separate us forever." She shook her head. "How could I have believed him? It makes no sense."

"Sense has very little to do with such matters."

"But I should have known." Diana beat her fists in her lap. "I should have been able to distinguish infatuation from . . ."

"Passion?" Charlotte said. "Lust?"

Diana glanced away, cheeks flaming.

Charlotte hesitated. But they had best learn the truth at once. And it was easier to speak of such matters when the wound was still fresh, rather than when it had begun to scar over. "Diana." Charlotte picked up her gloves, which she'd removed when Frank brought her the wine, and twisted them between her fingers. How would she have wanted such a question asked of her? But no one had asked it. That fact had been both a blessing and a curse. She had a sudden image of Sophie's awkwardness the night before she married Frank. She wasn't sure whether to laugh or to cry.

She spread her hands in her lap, smoothing the chestnut lustring between her fingers. "I've no wish to pry into what you wish to keep private. Nor has Frank. But if there's any chance you could be expecting a child—"

"No." Diana looked straight into Charlotte's eyes, face flushed but gaze level. "No. I—we didn't." She looked away, then looked back at Charlotte, eyes bright with a gallant, reckless defiance. "Though if you hadn't come when you did, I expect we would have. I wanted to."

Charlotte forced a smile to her lips. "Naturally. Why else would one elope?"

"But how *could* I have wanted to? He had no finer feelings—"

"If my cousin Sophie were here, she'd say finer feelings enter into it as little as sense."

Diana stared down at her hands. Her gaze fastened on her pearl ring, as though she had just become aware that she still wore it. She tugged the ring from her finger and threw it on the floor. "You were lucky, Charlotte."

Charlotte choked back a desperate laugh. "Lucky?"

"When you were my age you fell in love with Francis."

Charlotte stared at her young sister-in-law. "Who told you that?"

Diana's brows drew together. "But I assumed . . . You met when you were young. . . ."

Charlotte looked down at the warm yellow of her own betrothal ring. "Frank was my father's secretary. I was betrothed to someone else. Frank was . . . Frank was my friend."

Diana studied her. "You never thought of him as more?"

Charlotte's fingers closed over the citrine in her ring. She couldn't honestly say she never had. Not when she remembered the day Frank had kissed her in the garden and the way she had responded. That moment had thrown all her ideas about friendship into turmoil. She looked into Diana's clear blue-green eyes. "I was desperately in love with my betrothed, Diana."

"The man who died." Diana must be piecing together bits of the story she had heard.

"The man who was killed." Five and a half years and she could still hear the sound of the club smashing into Ned's head, still see the dark, sticky blood pooling onto the ink blotter as he collapsed on his desk. "The man who plotted murder. The man who was very nearly as bad as my—as Daniel de Ribard himself. I loved him. I was madly, foolishly, criminally in love with him."

The door opened. With timing that was exquisite or appalling, depending on one's perspective, Frank himself stepped back into the room. "The carriage is ready whenever we are. Do you want some tea before we leave?"

Diana shook her head. She got to her feet and walked toward her brother-in-law. "Thank you, Francis."

He looked down at her pale, tear-stained face. "For bringing you such unhappiness?"

"If you hadn't intervened, I would have known worse." She put her arm around his neck and embraced him briefly, then stepped back. "How did you know? About Christopher's debts and . . . his wife?"

"I didn't. Not completely."

There was a brief silence. Charlotte, watching from the side, saw Diana's eyes widen. "You were *bluffing*?"

"I prefer to think of it as an educated guess." Frank's voice was cool and conversational. "Ribard had to have some hold on Linton; Ribard recently bought Hawkins's Bank; Linton looks like he spends more than he takes in."

"And his wife?"

Frank hesitated for a moment. "Horace Linton is a member of Brooks's. I remember him complaining last year that one of his nephews had made an impossible match."

"Did you know he was speaking of Christopher?"

"Not for a certainty. But Linton spoke the truth, Diana. Any sane man would want you to wife. And that wouldn't achieve Ribard's objective."

"To have me ruined."

"To have Francis Storbridge's ward ruined. Yes. So he had to employ a man who couldn't marry you, however much he might decide he wanted to."

Diana colored again, but this time, Charlotte thought, not with shame. Then she frowned. "Dear God, Francis, if you'd been wrong—"

"I make it a practice not to be."

A faint but unmistakable smile lit Diana's face. "I've been telling Charlotte how lucky she is to have you. Just as Julia was lucky."

The light faded from Frank's eyes. "If nothing else, Diana, this night should have taught you the dangers of romantic fancies."

Diana looked steadily at him. "I understand more than you realize, Francis. And I mean it. My sister was lucky to have you."

Chapter 15

Charlotte tucked the carriage rug about Diana, eased herself off the seat, and picked her way across the carriage to sit by Frank, her arm braced against the silk-lined wall. "She's asleep."

"Thank God for that at least." In the moonlight Frank could only make out the outline of Diana's body, sprawled over more than half the seat now that Charlotte had moved away.

The seat beside him creaked as Charlotte settled herself. She was silent for a moment. "There won't be a child," she said, her voice soft in the darkness.

Frank released his breath. He felt as though he'd been holding it for an eternity. "Thank you for talking to her."

"It was a woman's office, I suppose. I don't know that I handled it very well."

"It's not an easy subject to handle."

"No." Her voice was low and controlled, but he could only guess at the feelings that lay behind the single word.

After that she fell silent. The carriage rattled on, jolting over the occasional deep rut, swaying slightly when the wind quickened. He could not see her face, but he was keenly aware of her beside him. It was as though his nerves were stripped raw in her presence, so that the faintest stirring of her breath or the teasing fragrance of her skin was enough to turn his blood to fire.

She gave what sounded like a muffled yawn. He glanced to the side and saw her head droop. Then, quite suddenly, she slumped backward and slid to the side to collapse against his shoulder.

She was asleep. The even rise and fall of her breathing betrayed that, as did the boneless weight of her body. Besides, awake she would never put her head on his shoulder. He eased his arm out from under her and wrapped it around her shoulders so she was cradled against his chest. Her head fell naturally into the hollow of his collar bone. The hood of her cloak had fallen back. Her thick, soft hair brushed against his cheek. Her full breasts were pillowed on his chest. He could feel the breath stirring through her and the steady beat of her heart.

In its own way, sleeping with another person was as great an act of intimacy as lovemaking. More perhaps. He rarely allowed himself to fall asleep in the beds of any of his mistresses.

There was no tension in Charlotte's body. Sleep had stripped away all her defenses. He held himself very still, afraid of destroying the first moment in over five years when she had shown him perfect trust.

Charlotte was his wife and asleep in his arms. It was more than he had ever thought to have three months ago. It was more, perhaps, than he would have let himself admit he wanted. It was certainly more than he deserved. He felt like a boy again, beset by doubt, suffused with hope. In a world where Charlotte might be able to trust him, perhaps anything was possible.

The miles to London passed too quickly. She stirred occasionally, but did not waken. His arm grew numb, but he didn't care. He looked across the carriage at Diana and thought of what she had been through tonight. He rested his face against Charlotte's hair and thought of what she had been through five years ago. If he and Charlotte had not been able to keep Diana's heart from being broken, they had, he hoped, saved her from permanent scars. It was more than he had been able to do for Charlotte.

The carriage turned into South Audley Street and began to slow. He turned his head and let his lips brush against Charlotte's forehead. Then he gave her shoulders a slight squeeze. "Charlie."

She pressed her face into his shoulder and made a protesting murmur.

"Charlie, we're home."

"Mmm?"

It was a very satisfactory response from a woman in one's arms, but unfortunately not the place for it. "South Audley Street. We live here, remember?"

A tremor of realization ran through her. She sat up and stared at him. In the gaslight slanting through the windows, her eyes were wide and dark and clouded with confusion.

"You fell asleep," he said.

"So it seems." She looked at him for a moment, as though seeking answers to a puzzle she could not quite define. Then she pulled the folds of her cloak close around her, like a shield, and leaned across the carriage to wake Diana.

Charlotte closed the door to Diana's room and hesitated in the corridor. Diana had insisted she would be able to sleep and that Charlotte should do likewise. But Charlotte had the light-headed exhilaration that comes when one is beyond fatigue. Images were jumbled in her mind, like jottings for a formula to which she could not yet see the solution: Frank returning Knightly to her room at St.

John's Court; the fear in his eyes when she awakened after the explosion; the way his face lit up when he knelt to speak to Juliet; his straightforward manner of addressing Bertram; the tenderness he had shown Diana this evening.

However little she understood Francis Storbridge, she could not deny his love for his daughter and his wards. They were all at risk now, thanks to Daniel. Thanks to her. One could argue that she owed him an apology.

She rubbed her arms. Frank hadn't retired to bed when they returned home. He'd gone into his study, perhaps to give her time alone with Diana. He was probably still there.

Less than an hour ago she'd been asleep beside him. No, she'd been asleep with her head on his shoulder. With his arm around her. Her body pressed against his. She had been asleep. But she had to be honest. Two weeks ago she would not have let her head rest on Frank's shoulder, even in sleep.

She should be frightened. She should want to go into her room and bolt the door. She knew the risks. She had felt them that first night in his study, when his gaze stirred feelings she thought she had learned to control. But tonight she had felt something different in his arms. She had felt safe.

She moved to the head of the staircase and paused for a moment, watching the light from the wall sconces spill over the curving stairs, changing the chaste white to molten gold. Then she picked up her skirt and walked down the stairs and along the corridor to Frank's study. The door was ajar. She knocked once and pushed it open.

He was sitting in one of the armchairs in front of the desk. He had taken off his coat and flung it over the back of the chair. His head was resting in his hand, but as she stepped into the room he looked up, his eyes filled with surprise.

She paused just beyond the door and drew a breath. "I'm sorry."

He pushed himself to his feet and rubbed his hand across his forehead. "Sorry?"

She swallowed. "Sorry that I brought you to this. That the children have been hurt. That your factory is threatened."

His mouth twisted. "I think you've got it the wrong way round, my darling. I was the one who insisted on our marriage. Coerced you into it. I knew what I was getting into."

She looked into his eyes. "Why?"

His gaze flickered. "Why what?"

She moved to the other armchair and sat, hands folded in her lap. "Why did you blackmail me into marrying you?"

There was a moment's silence. Frank stood absolutely still. Then he sank back into his chair. The springs creaked softly. "Because I wanted you. And I've learned to take what I want."

Want. Such a weighted word between men and women. It lingered in the air, reverberating with dark, unvoiced associations. A chill ran along her flesh. She gripped her arms. "No."

He lifted a brow. "No?"

She released her arms and stared down at the impression her fingers had made on the black net sleeves of her gown. "You wouldn't have done that."

"*I* wouldn't—"

"The man I've seen in the past two weeks wouldn't have done that."

He gave a laugh that grated like the scrape of iron on iron. "You called me friend for three years and then accused me of being without principles. Now after a fortnight you think I have them?"

"Let's say I've learned to see ambiguities." She sat back and regarded the man who had been her friend, the man she had turned her back on, the man who was now her husband. "Did you think you could protect me from Daniel, was that it?"

He stared at her for a moment. "Oh, Christ." He pushed himself to his feet. "Charlie, don't. Don't turn me into a hero. Not now."

There was a sharpness in his voice that went beyond bitterness. If she had to put a name to it, she would have called it despair. The light from the lamp on the table beside him lit him from below. His face was gray with exhaustion and strain. The cynicism, the self-confidence, the mockery were wiped away. It was as though a sheet of glass had shattered, revealing the boy who had been her closest friend all those years ago when she still believed in humanity.

Before she realized she'd made any sort of decision, she had stood and crossed the stretch of carpet between them and put her hand on his shoulder.

For a moment it was five years ago and they were friends again and life was simple and unclouded. A fleeting, sweet moment, swiftly gone because they weren't the people they had been and life was neither simple nor unclouded. But before she could pull her hand back, Frank had seized it and pressed it to his lips.

A shock went through her. She stood immobile. Unable to move away. Unsure she wanted to. The next instant Frank's arms were around her and his lips were against her hair.

His arms cradled her. His mouth was soft, gentle, feather-light. She closed her eyes and choked back a sob. She wanted to lean into him. She wanted to be held closer. Surely it would be all right. Surely she could surrender but still hang on to some core of herself. Surely she could give comfort and receive it without being swept free of the moorings of reason.

He lifted his head. His eyes were half-apologetic, half-entreating. She hesitated, hovering on the brink between need and fear, desire and the knowledge of what desire could bring.

Frank started to draw back. She put her hand behind his neck and pulled his head down to her own.

Charlotte was in his arms. Charlotte was kissing him, softly, sweetly, God, how sweetly. Space and time rushed away. He was twenty-five again and Charlotte was the eager, joyous, sun-kissed girl who had twisted knots in his heart.

All his senses were heightened. The softness of her lips, the feel of the breath shuddering through her, the smell of vanilla and almond oil. He wanted to deepen the kiss, to explore her mouth, to lose himself in her. But he couldn't. Through the fog of wonder and need and sheer bloody hunger, he knew he couldn't push beyond the limits she had set.

Instead, he lifted his head and looked into her eyes. They were dark, but steady. Her face was pale, but he could see the glow of the blood pulsing beneath her skin. He was afraid speech would break the spell between them. He lifted one hand and skimmed his fingers against her cheek, down the cool, white line of her throat, to the shiny fabric of her gown. It buttoned down the back. He undid the buttons, one at a time, his fingers shaking with the effort at restraint.

The bodice slipped down over her shoulders to reveal the creamy purity of her skin. He leaned forward and brushed his lips over the curve of her shoulder, the hollow of her neck, the delicate, fragile line of her collarbone.

Her fingers clenched on the fabric of his shirt. He closed his eyes and kissed her temples, her cheek, the corner of her mouth.

Her pulse leapt at the base of her throat. She drew in her breath, and that simple sound pushed his need for her over the edge. He lifted her, as he had after the explosion. But this time she was not a deadweight in his arms. This time she wrapped her arm around his neck and pressed her head into the crook of his shoulder. Hardly a passionate caress, but his head swam as if he'd downed half a bottle of whisky.

It was only a few steps to the sofa that stood before the fireplace. The heat of the fire washed over them, but the leather of the sofa was cool and stiff. She deserved lavender-scented linen and goose-down pillows. But he knew whatever had happened between them would not survive if he tried to carry her upstairs. He laid her on the sofa and knelt beside her, kissing her again, burying his face in her hair, wanting more, afraid if he reached for it he would lose everything.

Her arms came around him. Her fingers slid into his hair. He tugged her gown lower and reached beneath her chemise. Her skin was warm and fragrant. Her nipples hardened beneath his touch. His own body responded.

He pushed up the hem of her gown. He felt the heat of desire through the smooth silk of her stockings and the crisp linen of her drawers. He slid his hand up her leg and found the slit in her drawers and the curling nest of hair between her legs. He stroked his fingers against her, wooing, courting, seeking clues to her pleasure. She was trembling. Or he was. Or both.

She drew in her breath. But there was a different quality to the sound than before. It cut through the blood thundering in his head, the need churning within him. Though his senses were overwhelmed, he was aware of a change. A curious . . . lack. Her arms were around him, but she had gone still. Her skin was warm, but the current of response he had felt running through her was gone.

He drew back and looked down at her. Her eyes were open, but where before they had been glowing, now they were blank, as though a shade had been drawn over the thoughts within.

"Charlie." He stroked his fingers against her cheek.

"It's all right." There was a faint tremor in her voice, but she controlled it. "You don't have to stop. I don't mind."

The words were like a douse of cold water. He sat back on his heels. "Don't *mind*?"

"No." She put up her hand, then dropped it without touching him. "I thought—we were both in need of comfort—"

"Comfort, Charlie. Comfort given and taken." He placed his lips over hers, the gentlest pressure, teasing, seeking what had been between them before.

"I can't, Frank." She turned her head away, pushed herself to a sitting position. She was breathing hard. Not from passion, he realized. From fear. Of what—surrender, desire, physical union?

He held himself very still. "I'd never hurt you, Charlie."

"I know. I—" A sob rose up in her throat. She pressed her fist against her mouth. Her gaze was fixed on the carpet. "I'm sorry, Frank. I can't—"

"Give yourself."

She looked at him, as though forcing herself to do so. "I told you I wasn't unwilling."

"You were willing to let me take you. It's a very different thing." He kept his voice low.

"I didn't mean—" She shook her head, tugged her

bodice over her shoulders, fumbled with the buttons at the back of her gown. He could see the marks of his kisses on her neck and shoulders. Damn Ned Rutledge. What had the bastard done to her to make her so afraid of a man's touch?

"Charlotte—" He swallowed, forcing down frustration, regret, need—God, yes, the need was still there. "Here, let me do that."

He moved behind the sofa, putting that protective wall of wood and leather between them, leaned over the back, and did up the buttons. He didn't touch her more than absolutely necessary, but he could feel the stiffness in her body where it had been pliant only moments before. He fastened the last button and rested his hands on the carved wood of the sofa back. "I'm not . . . I'm not unappreciative, Charlie. But while I may be lamentably lacking in morals, I could never take pleasure in a sacrifice."

She turned and looked at him over the sofa back. Her face was a pale oval surrounded by dark hair disarranged by his fingers. Her eyes had never looked deeper or more tormented. "It wasn't—I thought—" She drew a breath. "Frank—"

"Yes?" He tamped down the impulse to reach for her.

She got to her feet, putting the width of the sofa between them. "It doesn't matter."

She was still only an arm's length away. He could reach across the sofa back, grasp her by the shoulders, insist she tell him what Ned Rutledge had done to her. But that would be as much a violation as if he had taken her body. He lifted his hand, then let it fall to his side. "There's more than one office a husband can fulfill. If you ever need to talk, you'll find I make a tolerable listener."

He half expected her to laugh at the idea that she might ever confide in him. Instead, she nodded and gave one of the quick, fleeting smiles that went right to his heart. Then, as though she was afraid to say anything more, she slipped from the room.

Frank stared down into the fire for a long moment. Then he returned to his chair, dropped his head in his hands, and told himself he was a fool.

Chapter 16

Frank paused in the doorway of the coffee room at White's. A gray afternoon light slanted through the long windows, harsher than the glow of the wax tapers at the dining tables. A subdued murmur of conversation and the clink of silver and glasses rose to the white and gold barrel ceiling overhead. His gaze swept past the government ministers, the fashionable young bucks, the red-faced country squires. The man he wanted sat alone at a table against the windows, his strong profile silhouetted against the light, his long fingers curved around the stem of a wineglass.

Frank crossed the room, conscious of a few surprised glances from the other diners, and walked straight to his father-in-law's table.

He thought Ribard noticed him when he was halfway across the room, but he had reached the table before Ribard deigned to look up. "Storbridge. Who let you into a Tory stronghold?"

"Harry Palmerston. He's a good friend, though his political convictions are a bit misguided." Frank pulled out a chair without asking and seated himself. "I was surprised to learn you're still a member."

"You underestimate the conservative instincts of the

membership committee." Ribard blotted his lips with a spotless napkin. "Apparently there was some talk about expelling me five years ago, but cooler heads pointed out that nothing had been proved against me. A glass of claret, Storbridge? You'll find it quite tolerable." He raised his hand and signaled to a waiter, who brought a second glass and filled it from the bottle on the table.

Frank took a sip of the claret. It was even smoother than the vintage Linton had been drinking the night before. "You might be interested to know Diana returned home from the Brandons' last night. She enjoyed her visit, though I'm afraid it was sadly uneventful for a girl of her high spirits."

Ribard picked up his knife and fork and cut into the remains of the beefsteak on his plate. "Yes, I heard she was back in South Audley Street. I understand Christopher Linton left for the Continent this morning."

Frank set down his wineglass with more force than was necessary. "I knew you to be without scruples, Ribard, but I never thought you a coward. Only cowards resort to using the weak."

Ribard sliced a bit of fat from the beefsteak. "I use whomever can serve my purpose, Storbridge. Surely you know that."

"Then before you try to use any other members of my family, I advise you to pay a morning visit to Hyde Park."

Ribard conveyed a piece of beefsteak to his mouth and chewed it thoughtfully. "I am loath to pay a morning visit anywhere. What would I see in Hyde Park?"

"Charlotte walking with my daughter and my youngest ward."

Ribard lifted his brows. "Don't tell me you think my heart—assuming you believe I possess such an organ—would be softened by a sight of their childish charms."

"Hardly. But I think Charlotte's affection for them might give you pause."

Ribard took a sip of wine. "Charlotte has accused me of the most heinous crimes imaginable. Why should anything she might think give me pause?"

"Because she still matters to you."

Ribard's hand did not falter. There was no noticeable change in his breathing. But Frank saw his words register in his former employer's eyes. "An interesting theory. But my actions would hardly seem to bear it out."

"Then I daresay it will mean nothing to you that Charlotte nearly died a week ago when there was an explosion at my blast furnace."

Ribard's knuckles whitened around the stem of his wineglass. For a moment he neither spoke nor met Frank's gaze. "I didn't realize your blast furnace had exploded. My commiserations."

"You don't want to know if she's all right?"

Ribard took a sip of wine. His fingers were not quite steady. "If she wasn't all right you wouldn't have suggested I observe her in the park with the children."

"Unless I wanted to take you off guard."

"My dear fellow." Ribard returned his glass to the table without sloshing the wine. "Do you imagine I haven't had copious reports of your activities—and my daughter's—since you both returned to London?"

"I make no doubt that you have had reports of our activities. That is scarcely the act of a man who is not interested in his daughter's fate."

Ribard sat back in his chair. His eyes lit with appreciative humor, the way Charlotte's sometimes did. "My compliments, Storbridge. You've played a weak hand to perfection." He picked up his glass and twirled the stem between his fingers. "Whatever my sentiments, you are my son-in-law. A far more promising son-in-law than Silverton or those titled fools my elder daughters married. I see no reason we should not come to an accommodation."

"Some might say the fact that you've made every effort to ruin me presents a slight impediment."

Ribard shrugged his shoulders without disturbing the elegant lines of his coat. "I've made my point. It would be vulgar to beat it into the ground. You have something I want, Storbridge. You still sit on the railway committee."

"And now I have Charlotte."

Ribard's eyes narrowed, his tanned skin crinkling up at the corners. He threw back his head and gave a shout of laughter that rose above the subdued murmur of voices in the room. But this was White's. The other well-modulated voices did not falter, and not a head turned in their direction. "By God, Storbridge. So that's why you married her."

"Is it?"

"Because it gives you a hold on me. Or you think it does. I should have seen it sooner."

"An interesting theory."

"You're a realist, Storbridge." Ribard picked up the bottle and refilled their glasses so the rich red of the claret reached the exact same etched mark on the crystal. "Not like my son, whose Jacobin uncle burdened him with an inconvenient weight of ideals. You I could make something of."

Frank lifted the glass and took a sip. The fine claret tasted unexpectedly bitter. "If you're offering me my old job back, I no longer have need of such employment."

"No, not your old job. I have no wish to waste your talents." Ribard leaned forward. "Truce, Storbridge. I can cancel young Vaughan's debt. And your loan could be forgiven into the bargain."

"And in exchange?"

"As you say, you still sit on the railway committee."

"And Chelmsford?"

Ribard's gaze was unwavering. "Invite me to dinner. I'll discuss it with Charlotte."

"Whose opinion means nothing to you."

Ribard lifted his glass, inhaled the aroma of the claret, and took a long sip. "Interpret my actions as you will."

Frank pushed aside his glass. "It's a tempting offer, Ribard. There's just one problem."

Ribard lifted a brow.

Frank pushed back his chair, scraping it against the thick pile of the carpet. "My wife would never forgive me."

Céline dropped her shell-shaped reticule and swansdown muff on the sofa beside her. "You've got black circles under your eyes, Charlie. I take it the honeymoon was a success."

Charlotte bit back an hysterical laugh. In truth, her head was light and her eyes strained from lack of sleep. And if Frank had not drawn back, last night might have seen the consummation of her marriage. She stroked Knightly, who was curled in her lap. "You'd know more about such matters than I, Céline."

"Dear me." Céline unfastened the frogged clasps on her pelisse. "No sisterly confidences? No questions you're longing to have answered? I thought this was one time you might actually need me."

Charlotte picked up the teapot and poured tea into two translucent, pink-and-white porcelain cups. "Don't worry. I daresay I shall be frantically sending to you for advice the first time I'm obliged to give a dinner party."

Céline raised her brows. "Dinner parties hold more mystery than the marriage bed?"

"Sophie explained the marriage bed in exhausting detail before the wedding."

"Yes, she would. She has even less reticence than I do."
Céline shrugged out of her pelisse and let it slither about
her in a swirl of swansdown and blue velvet. "I thought
it had all been explained to me before my own wedding night, yet I know afterward I had dozens of—But
evidently Francis Storbridge knows his way around a
bedchamber."

"Céline!" The milk jug tilted in Charlotte's fingers,
splashing milk onto the glossy surface of the satinwood
table. Knightly gave a protesting mew.

"Oh, don't be such a little puritan, Charlie." Céline began to undo the pearl buttons on her gloves. "You don't
know how lucky you are. Half the women in London
would like to be in Francis Storbridge's bed."

Charlotte pressed her handkerchief over the spilled
milk. "Including you?"

Céline colored beneath her rouge, then laughed and
shook her head. "No. Not now that he's your husband, at
any rate." She peeled her gloves off and laid them on top
of her reticule. "To own the truth, Silverton's not at all
deficient himself in that regard. And in the beginning he
could be quite ardent. But I don't think he's ever looked
at me in quite the way Francis looks at you."

Charlotte paused, her teacup halfway to her lips. "How
does Frank look at me?"

Céline added two lumps of sugar to her tea and stirred
it, eyes on the steaming liquid. "Like you're a prize he
can't believe he's won and can't bear to let go."

Charlotte took a quick swallow of tea. It was hotter
than she expected. Her mouth was scalded. "Don't be
silly. That sounds like something out of a bad novel."

Céline lifted her own cup and took a careful sip. "I

may be an idle, frivolous woman, Charlie, but I'm rather good at reading the look in a man's eyes."

Charlotte ran her fingers through Knightly's fur. The kitten stretched, burrowing his face in the jonquil folds of her skirt. "Frank's a difficult man to read at the best of times." She picked up a plate of biscuits from the table and held it out. "How are the children?"

Céline gave one of those odious smiles that only an elder sister could give. "Oh, Charlie, you'll have to learn to change the subject more adroitly if you're to have a prayer in London society." She took a biscuit and nibbled a small bite. "The boys become more noisy and impossible every day. Lydia burst into tears last night and complained that her new merino is impossibly dowdy, so I have hopes that at last she's beginning to take a passing interest in her appearance."

"I'll bring Serena round to see her. They got on well at the wedding. And the boys were very patient with Juliet."

"You've taken to motherhood."

"Yes." Charlotte broke off a piece of biscuit and fed it to Millamant, who was lying under the table. "What's more surprising is that the children seem to have taken to me."

"Nonsense. Children always take to you. But I can't say I envy you the elder Vaughans. I understand young Bertram lost dreadfully at Marable's while you were away."

"Oh, poison." Charlotte straightened up to look at her sister. "Is the story all over London already?"

"The story was all over London the moment it happened. Everyone knows the play at Marable's is shockingly deep. Silverton used to go there. Thank goodness he's had the sense to stay away since his trouble last autumn."

Charlotte refilled the teacups. "How is Silverton?" she asked, keeping her voice neutral.

"He's been in a fearfully black mood lately. I can't think why, for we've plenty of money for a change." Céline reached for another biscuit, then dropped it back on the plate. "Don't have three children, Charlie. One's waistline is never quite the same." She frowned into her teacup. "I do hate this time of year. Silver insists we come to town in time for the opening of Parliament, but London is far too thin of company to be interesting." She drummed her fingers in her lap. "Do Sophie and Paul still mean to pay you a visit?"

"Yes, in a fortnight or so. I had a letter from Sophie this morning. Robert and Emma will come as well. Their friends the Durwards are coming home from Paris for a visit. Robert and Emma will stay with them, and Sophie and Paul with us. You can help me plan a dinner party."

"With Francis and Silverton glowering at each other, and Paul accusing the pair of them of being without any moral fiber." Céline picked up her teacup. "It would certainly liven things up."

"Just what we need to start the parliamentary session off on the right note," said a voice from the doorway.

"Frank." Charlotte looked up as he strolled into the room. This was the first time she had seen him since last night in the study. Memory spun through her. She wanted to close her arms over her chest and barricade her body. She wanted to stare him down and prove she could do it. She wanted, God help her, to see if his eyes held any hint of the fire she had seen in them last night.

Frank's expression was as impeccably controlled as the folds of his cravat and the smooth charcoal-gray lines of his coat. Her stomach gave a lurch that might have been disappointment. "Céline's called to welcome me to town," she said.

"A delightful surprise, Lady Silverton." Frank gave one of his easy, practiced smiles.

"Céline." Céline held out her hand to him. "We're brother and sister now."

Frank bent over her hand. Charlotte watched his lips brush Céline's white skin, his dark head close to Céline's Marie Stuart bonnet and golden curls. Her insides clenched. For a moment she wished her sister anywhere but in this room, smiling that dazzling smile at her husband.

She shook her head. Frank was her husband only in the most superficial way. It should not matter to her whom he smiled at, whose hand he kissed, whose bed he shared.

Céline settled back on the sofa. "My husband is fearfully annoyed with you—something to do with slavery. I don't mean to sound a horrid idiot, but I thought slavery had been abolished while I was still in the schoolroom."

Frank pulled a straight-back chair away from the table and seated himself. "The slave trade was abolished. That didn't emancipate the slaves already held in our colonies."

"Such as those on Daniel's plantation in Jamaica," Charlotte said.

Céline wrinkled her nose. "Oh, don't mention him. It's bad enough hearing his name in every other drawing room in London." She looked back at Frank. "Silverton says it's shockingly bad timing for you to raise the issue now and you're doing it only to embarrass Canning and the government. I understand you and Silver are going to be hurling insults at each other across the House."

Frank bent down to pet Millamant, who had moved to lie on his feet. "Insults aren't allowed in the House—not in the chamber, at any rate."

"You mean you'll only politely disagree? That's not nearly as interesting." Céline slipped her pelisse back on her shoulders. "I must go. Canning and the Granvilles are dining with us. Oh, dear." She looked up from pulling on her gloves. "That wasn't a political secret, was it? I shall have to learn to guard my tongue now that our families cross political lines."

"Don't worry, Lady Sil—Céline. I know better than to turn a lady's confidences against her." Frank rose and held out his hand.

Céline took his hand, got to her feet, and picked up her reticule and muff. "Good-bye, Charlie." She hugged Charlotte, who was also standing. "You must call soon. We'll take the children on an outing. It will be quite novel. Francis—I'm glad to see you're taking such good care of my sister."

Frank escorted Céline down the steps to where her coachman was patiently waiting. Charlotte watched Frank hand her sister into the carriage with a memory of him doing the same for her the night she agreed to be his wife.

"Thank you," she said when she and Frank had returned to the sitting room. She could hear the edge of irony in her voice.

Frank closed the door behind them. "For being polite to your sister?"

"For being polite to Silverton's wife." She glanced at the closed door. They were alone together for the first time since last night, when her defenses had been stripped away along with her clothing. Her morning dress had a high stiff ruff and long tight sleeves, but her inner defenses were still pitifully battered. And she needed them more than ever. She could still not quite believe she had come so close to surrendering herself to him. Or that he had been the one who had stopped.

"I know," Frank said, leaning against the door. "Almost the only thing as embarrassing as facing someone you've gone to bed with the night before is facing someone you've *not* gone to bed with. Shall I remove to the library?"

His words were as bracing as a blast of cold air, which perhaps was what he'd intended. She looked straight into his eyes. "Oh, don't be silly," she said. "We'll have to muddle through the awkwardness sooner or later." She picked up Knightly, who had taken over her chair, and settled him back in her lap. The silence in the room was suffocating and far too redolent with memory, so she said the first words that came into her head. "Céline thinks you're very attractive."

"I'm flattered."

She looked up at him, regretted the look, regretted her quickly spoken words. He returned to his chair, an arm's length away. "Your sister's a beautiful woman, Charlotte. But she's not quite in my style. And my depravity stops short of bedding my wife's sister."

"Why?" she asked before she could stop herself. "I gave you leave to bed whomever you choose."

"Yes, very considerate of you." He picked up the teapot and poured himself a cup. "But technically it is considered incest, you know."

Charlotte dumped the remains of her tea into the dregs pot. "Somehow I don't think that would stop you. If you wanted her."

"Perhaps not. *If* I wanted her."

Her breath caught. She stared at the wall opposite, watching the firelight wash over the gray-green plaster and dance up the fluted white moldings. Last night he had said he wanted her. Last night she had offered herself to him. And he had refused, because what he wanted was more than she could give.

She spread her hands in her lap. Her palms were damp. "So you're to make your emancipation speech soon?"

He must have seen through her change of subject, but he gave no sign of it. "I saw Brougham this morning. We agreed the time is right."

"You think there's a chance of passing legislation?"

He added lemon to his tea. "Probably not. But we'll make some noise with the opening salvo."

"And then what?"

His mouth curled. "The government—not to mention our own side—will be so alarmed by our radical suggestions that we'll be able to pass some sort of watered-down compromise."

"And the slaves in Jamaica and elsewhere?"

"Will be better off than if we'd made no attempt at all. You take what you can get, Charlotte. I learned that a long time ago." He stirred his tea methodically. She had an acute memory of his fingers moving over her skin. "The government have designated Silverton to fire the answering shots," he added.

She didn't miss the edge in his voice. Its sharpness took her back to the exchange between Frank and Silverton at the wedding breakfast. "Why do you dislike him so much?"

Frank returned the spoon to the saucer with a clatter. "Aren't his politics explanation enough?"

"You don't have the same animosity for Canning or Palmerston or Granville or anyone else in their set."

He took a slow, deliberate sip of tea. "Let's say a number of factors have combined to place Silverton and me in opposition. I won't let it touch you or your relations with your family."

"Then you don't mind if I invite Céline and Silverton to dine with us?"

He hesitated just a fraction of a second. "No. Of course not." He leaned back and crossed his legs. The skintight, pale gray fabric of his pantaloons showed the lean, well-defined muscles of his thighs. "You look exhausted," he said.

"Thank you," she said, her voice tart. For some reason it particularly rankled that Frank should comment on her exhaustion when he had obviously noted that Céline was in her best looks.

The unsettling glint flashed in his eyes. "For the record and at the risk of overstepping the line, I didn't say it was unattractive."

She reached for the teapot and held her hand steady as she refilled her cup. "None of us got much sleep last night. You must be more used to it than I am."

He gave a sudden, appreciative laugh. "Yes, I daresay I am."

She set the teapot down with a thud. Betraying, maddening heat flooded her face. "Oh, bloody hell. I didn't mean—"

"No, I daresay you didn't." There was something unexpectedly kind about his smile. "But it would have been a very clever sally if you had." The smile left his face. "Has Diana come out of her room yet?"

"Briefly." Charlotte took a sip of the hot, astringent tea. "She came into the breakfast parlor and dissolved into tears over the muffin dish. Poor girl. Apparently last night's self-knowledge was short-lived."

Frank's fingers tightened around his cup as though it were Christopher Linton's throat. "Damn the bastard."

"It's a difficult process, growing up. Coming to terms with—" She hesitated, realizing what she had been about to say, not sure she wanted to put it into words.

"Love?" he asked.

She pulled her India shawl closer about her shoulders. "I was going to say passion."

"Ah. Yes, there is that." The word seemed to hang between them for a moment. "Poor Serena's only at the beginning of the whole tangle," Frank continued, as though the air between them had not become suddenly charged. "She seems to be handling the onset of womanhood with amazing equanimity. Or have I missed something?"

"No." Charlotte toyed with the fringe at the end of her shawl, then forced her fingers to be still. "She's remarkably matter-of-fact."

"Serena's always matter-of-fact. She's also insatiably curious. We shall have to find some very informative books for her."

"Frank!" Her hand jerked, tangling her fingers in the fringe.

He lifted his brows. "Wouldn't you rather have her reading about the mysteries between men and women than going out and experimenting for herself?"

Charlotte stared down at her hands. "I'd like to think she could remain a child for a little longer."

"So would I. But physical longings can't be banished simply by being ignored, Charlie."

She looked up at him. His eyes were kind and warm, but she was quite sure he wasn't talking about Serena anymore. She drew a breath, sought the right words, fought against the impulse to retreat.

To her surprise it was Frank who turned away and glanced at the door. "Come in," he called.

It was only when Alan stepped into the room that she realized someone had tapped at the door. The footman held a bouquet of yellow roses. "These were just delivered for you, ma'am." He carried the flowers over to Charlotte, bowed, and withdrew.

She looked at the flowers, pale and perfect and at this season outrageously expensive. A welcome-to-London gift from Céline? There was a card stuck amid the blossoms. She reached for it and gave a start at the familiar, slanted black writing.

> *Charlie,*
> *Please believe that I was desolated to learn of your unfortunate accident.*
> *D.*

She stared at the card for a long moment, beset by an image of Daniel pinning a bunch of yellow roses to her gown the night of her coming-out ball. Then she looked at Frank and willed her voice to be even. "They're from Daniel. He knows about the explosion."

Frank's face showed no surprise. "I saw him this afternoon."

Her fingers tightened about the card. "He sought you out?"

"I sought him out. In the coffee room at White's."

"Why?"

"An attempt to use what pathetically little leverage I have to ward off further attacks."

She set the flowers down beside the tea things, where they wouldn't brush against her. "What leverage?"

Frank's gaze was steady on her face. "You."

She folded her arms over her chest. "You're a fool, Frank, if you think anyone is anything more to Daniel than a pawn."

"He sent you the flowers."

She glanced again at the roses, velvety and beautiful, but lacking in scent, as hothouse flowers often are. They didn't mean anything to her. They *shouldn't* mean anything to her. "The flowers are a challenge. A reminder of what he can do to us."

"Or an apology because he never intended you to be hurt." Frank got to his feet. "I have to write up some notes for the emancipation speech. I'll see you at dinner." He gave a grin full of schoolboy mischief. "And after dinner we can finish that chess game."

Chapter 17

Frank drew a breath and let his gaze sweep the House of Commons. The paneled chamber was still, a taut, expectant stillness. Even the sound of walnuts being cracked on the back benches had stopped. He had them, for the moment at least, held by the force of ideas that many of them considered anathema.

He fixed his gaze across the chamber on the government ministers. "In this day and age it should be impossible for any rational person to justify the right of one class of men to keep another in a state of slavery." He did not shout, but his voice carried clearly, a trick he had learned from the actress who had been his first mistress. "It has been nearly twenty years since we outlawed the taking of slaves. Yet every day in our colonies, children are born into a state of enslavement. I submit to you that this is intolerable. That it flies against the finest principles and best instincts of this country."

He paused again, willing his audience to listen. "I submit to you that we are better than this. I call upon this House to emancipate all slaves now held in the British colonies."

He stood still for a moment, instinct telling him to let the words sink in. Then he resumed his seat.

The silence continued for a few seconds longer. Then the chamber erupted into speech. "Good show, Storbridge," Brougham murmured. "I always say the effect of a speech can be measured by the chaos it causes."

On the opposite side of the chamber, Silverton rose and asked to be recognized by the Speaker.

Brougham cocked an eyebrow at Frank. "Here we go."

Frank leaned back, arms folded across his chest, and looked straight at Charlotte's brother-in-law. Silverton's face was composed, but the fire he usually brought to debates was lacking from his eyes. He cleared his throat. "The government have not the slightest objection to some of the proposals that the honorable member for Howitt has stated with such passion—if perhaps with less rational forethought than is wise."

An equal number of guffaws and cries of protest greeted this last. Silverton raised his voice. "We certainly believe it wise to improve the condition of the slave population and to prepare them for eventual participation in civil rights and privileges."

"Prepare?" Frank was on his feet again. "What sort of preparations does one need to be treated as a human being?"

Their gazes clashed. Past hostilities and other, deeper insults echoed across the chamber between them. "I think," Silverton continued, his voice taut with barely controlled tension, "that the honorable member cannot but be aware that it is not practicable at this time—"

"Ah, *practicable.*" Frank drew the word out. It grated even more harshly than he intended. "That's it, isn't it? The government fear antagonizing the West Indian interest."

Silverton's gaze swept the benches around Frank. "The honorable member would do well to remember that there are slave owners on his own side of the House."

"The honorable member is well aware of that fact. A sin is no less a sin because it is committed by one's friends."

This produced a stir of discontent closer to home. Brougham shot Frank a surprised glance. But Frank was past caring. He felt an exhilarating rush of freedom, like a gallop across an open field on a stormy evening with a breeze blowing hard at one's back.

Silverton's blue eyes narrowed. "The honorable member for Howitt has not been above truckling himself when it suits his purpose—"

"Truckling?" Frank looked straight into Silverton's eyes. "The noble lord and his friends have already *truckled* on the question of Catholic emancipation, purely for the purpose of obtaining office—"

"By God, sir!" Silverton's voice rose to a roar. "That's a false accusation!"

The words were like a pistol shot ringing out in the midst of a tavern brawl. Silence fell over the chamber. Silverton continued to glare at Frank, eyes defiant.

The Speaker turned to Silverton, his long curling wig stirring with the motion. "I must ask the noble lord to retract that expression."

Silverton stood still, gaze level. "I am sorry to have used any word that violates the decorum of the House. But no consideration on earth would induce me to retract the sentiment."

There was a fresh stir of talk. Humphrey Grandison rose from the government side of the House, his face wrinkled with distaste. "Mr. Speaker, the rules of the House have been contravened. I move that both the honorable member for Howitt and the noble lord be committed to the custody of the sergeant at arms."

Frank opened his mouth to speak, but Brougham gripped his wrist.

The Speaker pursed his lips. "The propriety of the honorable member's language depends on whether he spoke of the noble lord in his public capacity or personally."

Canning glanced at Silverton and got to his feet. "Perhaps if the honorable member for Howitt retracted his words, it would assist the noble lord to issue a similar retraction."

Brougham nudged Frank with his foot. Frank swallowed, forcing down his pride. "I should be the last man to wish to see any man censured for his expression. I spoke of political actions." He looked Silverton directly in the eye. "Any personal disagreements between the noble lord and myself are not the province of this chamber."

Silverton met Frank's gaze and gave a stiff nod. "I took the honorable member's words to be a personal aspersion. If he disavows that, I will disavow my subsequent statement."

Palmerston whispered something to Canning, then rose as well. "The House should be satisfied." His face was serious, but there was a gleam in his eyes. "The honorable member was misinterpreted. And the noble lord did no truckling."

Henry Brougham flung himself back in his chair and took a swig of geneva. "By God, Francis, I think this is the first time I've seen you lose your temper. Usually you've got all that fire under firm control."

Frank reached for his own tankard. "It wasn't my finest hour. I'm sorry, Henry. I didn't do the cause much good."

Brougham shrugged. "We wanted to get their attention, and we've done that. We'll try again in a few months, with a slightly less ambitious proposal. Something along the lines of freeing slaves born after a certain date."

Frank clunked his tankard down on the table. "Christ."

"It's a good strategy. Stake out an extreme position, then make it look as if we're compromising."

"We are compromising."

"We're seeking an objective we can win." Brougham pushed aside his tankard and leaned forward, arms on the table. "What I've always admired about you, Francis, is the way your passion is tempered by pragmatism. You know as well as I that you have to play the game if you're to have a chance of winning it."

Frank stared at the liquor that had splashed out of the tankard onto the scarred table. The tavern door swung open, disturbing the buzz of conversation around them. A blast of chill wind cut through air choked with tobacco smoke and the stench of damp wool. The rain was so fierce that many of the House members had repaired to this tavern, snug by Westminster, instead of driving to their clubs in St. James.

"When I was Daniel de Ribard's secretary I handled correspondence with his plantation in Jamaica," Frank said, gaze fixed on the initials some long-forgotten politician had scratched into the tabletop. "Runaway slaves were identified by marks from branding and flogging. If your children could be flogged and branded, if your family could be ripped apart at a slave sale, would you be content to wait while we played the game?"

"If I were a slave I wouldn't have any choice." Brougham spread his hands on the table. His narrow face was stripped of artifice. "Good God, Francis, don't you think it bothers me too? We share the same goal, but we won't achieve it by banging our heads against a stone wall." He pushed back his chair. "We all suffer from bouts of self-reproach at times. I daresay it's good for the soul, as long as you don't indulge to excess." He stood and took his greatcoat from a peg on the wall behind them. "I promised Dolly I'd look in at Granby House. Care to come with me?"

Frank splashed some more geneva into his tankard. "I'll stay here a bit longer."

"Well, don't drink too much. No sense in having a bad head as well as an attack of conscience." Brougham picked up his hat. "Go home to your pretty new wife, Francis. The blue devils will pass. Then you can get back to the business of changing the world."

Frank took a long sip of geneva. The fire of the liquor did nothing to extinquish the embers of anger in his gut. The room was thick with shouts and laughter, the slosh of drink, the heavy tread of booted feet, the clatter of tankards and plates. Fortunately his table was in a secluded corner. He was in a mood for solitude.

He stared into his tankard, contemplating his loss of control tonight and all that had led up to it. It was as though Daniel de Ribard's return to England had thrown a looking glass up in front of his face. Men who sold their soul to the devil were supposed to lose their reflection. What was worse, to look into a mirror and see nothing or to look into it and see Daniel de Ribard?

Frank took a deep draught of geneva. Ribard had driven Charlotte back to him. And he had proved her worst suspicions of him right, by turning the information she gave him against her to get what he wanted, just as Ribard would have done.

And then, when he thought perhaps there was a spark of hope for their marriage, he had got it all wrong. He had thought, with blind, arrogant stupidity, that if he could seduce her into his bed, physical love could breach the gulf of mistrust between them. Instead, their unfinished lovemaking had revealed the extent of the chasm.

Even more than Charlotte's passion, he wanted her trust. And Charlotte couldn't even trust him enough to let herself accept pleasure from him.

Frank shifted the tankard in his hands and watched a trace of liquor trickle down the pewter. He didn't realize anyone had approached the table until a voice broke in on his reflections. "I don't know which of us owes the other an apology. But I do know I'm not proud of my actions tonight."

Frank looked up. Silverton stood before him, his fair hair gilded by the firelight, his face in shadow. Frank passed his hand over his eyes. "I can't say I am either."

Silverton dropped into Brougham's vacated chair. "The damnable thing is, you were right. I've no love for slavery, though I think you're a starry-eyed idealist to believe it can be ended in one fell swoop. I was angry that you chose to force the issue, but from your perspective it's probably a clever time."

Frank stared at Silverton. The light fell slantwise across his face now, but Frank still could not read the motives behind that elegant, affable smile. "What brought this change about?"

"You'll always be my political opponent, Storbridge. But now you're my brother-in-law as well. We may never be friends, but for our wives' sake I hope we can contrive to be less-bitter enemies."

"There's no reason our disagreement should affect our wives."

"My dear fellow, it already has. You saw Charlotte's expression when we met at the wedding." Silverton leaned back in his chair and crossed his legs. "Where did it start, Storbridge? I know we often oppose each other in debate. But when did it become so virulent? Can you remember? For I swear I can't."

Frank reached for his tankard. "Can't you?"

Silverton laughed and shook his head. "I can't even remember which of us started it."

Frank's fingers clenched around the handle of the tankard, so hard the pewter cut into his skin. "You know damn well when it started."

"No, I don't, I assure you." Silverton's voice was light, even surprised. "Your memory must be better than mine."

That was too much. Rage boiled up, hot and molten. Frank looked straight into Silverton's cool, questioning blue eyes. "You'll forgive me. I find it hard to feel charitable toward the man who seduced my wife."

Silverton's eyes widened. *"What?"* He drew a breath. "What sort of degenerate do you think I am? It's true I'm fond of Charlie. But if you think I ever laid a hand on her—"

"I'm not talking about Charlotte."

The flickering light from the wrought-iron chandelier overhead caught the flare of shock in Silverton's eyes. "Good God, *Lady Julia*?"

Frank cast a quick, belated glance around the room. But five years in Westminster had taught him that a noisy tavern afforded more privacy than a secluded chamber. No one was looking their way, and it was impossible for voices to carry more than a few feet in the babble of sound. He leaned across the table. "It's no good lying, Silverton. Julia told me the whole before she died."

"Told you the whole what? Storbridge, I swear—"

"There's no sense in denying it." Now that the words were out, Frank felt almost tired. He slumped back in his chair, the tankard between his fingers. "I wouldn't soil my hands by challenging you."

"You were married less than a year, and she was with child—"

Silverton broke off. Frank continued to look at him.

"Oh, Christ," Silverton said in a soft voice. "The little girl isn't yours, is she?"

Frank twisted the tankard in his hands, watching the candlelight strike the dull pewter. "You'd know the answer better than I."

Silverton drew a breath. "Look here, Storbridge." He leaned forward, gripping the table. "I've never claimed to be a model husband like your friend the Duke of Howitt. I've never even claimed to be a faithful husband. But I stop short of tampering with virgins."

"Don't lie. It demeans us both." Frank's voice was low, but he could taste the bitterness on his tongue. "The truth is the least you owe Julia. Not to mention Juliet."

Silverton raked his fingers through his hair, disturbing the carefully arranged golden waves. "What the devil did she say to you?"

Frank saw Julia's pale face lying against linen embroidered with the Vaughan crest, titian hair damp with sweat, skin like parchment, eyes glazed with pain. "Enough. I didn't press her for details. She was dying."

"She was dying and you asked her to name her child's father."

"Yes."

"And she didn't want to tell you the truth."

Frank reached across the table and gripped Silverton's arm. "Damn you, you bastard, can't you at least own up to one of your crimes?"

Silverton stared down at Frank's fingers on his sleeve, but made no effort to pull away. "Hell. Bloody, bloody hell. There's nothing I can say to convince you, is there?"

Frank released him and sat back. "No."

Silverton smoothed the creases from his sleeve one at a time. "I don't expect you to believe me. I doubt I would were our situations reversed." He tugged his signet ring from his fingers and held it up. "But I swear to you, on the honor of my family, that I never touched Lady Julia, before or after your marriage."

Someone threw a log on the fire, sending up a shower of sparks. Words of contempt rose in Frank's throat, but he didn't speak them. He stared at Silverton, trying to see him without the gloss of resentment that had accumulated through the years. "You can't deny you flirted with her. I saw you dancing together a score of times."

"I don't deny it. She was a lovely girl. But I like my mistresses older and more experienced—as you have cause to know."

"Why would she lie to me?"

Silverton's eyes softened with what might almost have been sympathy. "My dear fellow, it's obvious. She was protecting her lover."

A waiter passed by carrying a tray of beef and a pitcher of ale. Frank stared down at his hands, peering back into a past that was as murky as the smoky, steaming air of the tavern. For all the months of her pregnancy, Julia had refused to name her lover. Frank had felt compelled to ask when she lay on her deathbed, but he had been surprised himself when she gave him the name so readily.

Too readily. He looked up at Silverton. "You're right. There's no reason for me to believe you. But I think perhaps I do."

Silverton released his breath very slowly. "You may be misguided, but you're a decent man, Storbridge. Lady Julia was fortunate."

"I didn't do badly out of the arrangement."

"You didn't have to love her daughter."

Frank picked up the flagon of geneva. "One of the few things I've always liked about you, Silverton, is your lack of sentimentality. Have a drink." He filled Brougham's empty tankard.

Silverton reached for the tankard. "Don't tell me we're drinking to friendship."

"Let's say to being brothers-in-law." Frank lifted his own tankard and clinked it against Silverton's.

Silverton took a drink. "No wonder you lost your temper with me tonight. I'm surprised it didn't happen sooner."

"It wasn't just Julia. I had this urge to speak my mind. I was tired of—"

"Truckling?" Silverton smiled.

"Precisely." Frank found himself returning the smile.

"Yes. Truckling." The smile faded from Silverton's eyes. A bleak look passed over his face, draining it of color and animation, making him look unexpectedly older. "I was in a black mood myself tonight. I've been in a black mood for weeks."

"I could make a remark about the stands your party forces you to take. But in view of our rapprochement I'll let the opportunity pass."

"It's not my party. Not this time." Silverton slid his signet ring back onto his finger and looked at it for a moment, as though weighing a decision. Then he looked up at Frank. "See here, Storbridge." His voice turned low and urgent. "The surveyor's report for the proposed Lancaster and Liverpool Railway. It's not . . . it's not wholly accurate."

Frank bit back a comment and lifted his brows. "How do you know?"

Silverton's mouth tightened. "Because Henry Sunderland paid me five thousand pounds to see that it wasn't." He regarded Frank in silence for a long interval. "There. Now you've the power to ruin me. I'm not sure why the devil I told you. Something on the order of letting blood to cure an infection."

"It's all right. I already knew."

"You—" Silverton shook his head as though to clear it. "How?"

Frank poured Silverton some more geneva. "Ribard offered to sell me a note you wrote to Sunderland in exchange for my support of his railway."

"How the devil—" Silverton's face went paler still. "Ribard has the note?"

"Not anymore. He gave it to me."

"In exchange for your support of the railway?"

"He thought so. I told him he'd have my support of the railway when I used the letter. I burned it instead."

"Christ." The candlelight flickered over Silverton's drained features. "I owe you a debt I can't possibly repay." He stared at Frank for a moment. "And you did all this thinking that I—in God's name, why?"

"I had my reasons."

Silverton scanned his face. "I didn't realize how much you loved her," he said after a moment.

"Who?"

"Charlotte. You must have done it for her."

Frank stilled his fingers before Silverton could notice they were trembling. "In a way—though not precisely the way you're thinking. I don't like to give Ribard any advantage." He took a sip of geneva. "Do you have any idea how Ribard came by the letter?"

Silverton shook his head. "He and Sunderland have been thick as thieves lately, but I can't see Sunderland giving him the note. He wouldn't want it made public either. In fact, the damn fool should have burned it. Ribard must have stolen it from his house."

"Sunderland approached you with the arrangement? Or did you suggest it?"

"I'm not quite so steeped in corruption."

"Then the offer came from Sunderland?"

Silverton hesitated. "In a manner of speaking."

"He used a go-between? Come, man, after tonight's revelations there's no sense in secrets."

Silverton took a long drink. "If you must know, Sunderland made the approach through his sister."

"Ianthe?" Frank frowned. "Why would she want to involve herself in something like that?"

"She is Sunderland's sister."

"She makes it a point to steer clear of him and anything that smacks of trade. I can't see her risking involvement in a scandal to do him a favor. Or you."

"Thank you."

"Or me or any other man who happened to be her lover." Frank tilted his head back and stared at the ceiling, shifting pieces of information in his head. Ianthe's return to England. Her affair with Silverton, swiftly begun and ended. The blatant way—he had to admit it had been flattering—she had initiated her affair with himself. The incisive questions she would ask before retreating into a pose of languid gossip. "Christ, I should have thought of it sooner."

"What?"

Frank tapped his fingers on the tabletop. "Ianthe lived in Brazil until last winter. Ribard's stay in South America overlapped with hers. He has a coffee plantation in Brazil."

"Yes, I know. But he and Ianthe never met."

"So they say. Which in itself is odd. Brazilian society isn't that large. And I wouldn't say either of them is known for their truthfulness, would you?"

"No, but—"

"Ianthe's brother is the first person Ribard was seen with after his return to England. He and Ribard became business partners in the railway with which Ribard means to reestablish himself. And through Ianthe you were drawn into a scheme that gave Ribard a hold over you."

Silverton was silent for a moment. "If you're right— Ianthe took me as a lover because Ribard wanted to use me."

"If I'm right she probably took me as a lover for the same reason. Only I ended the affair before she and Ribard could entrap me."

Silverton's eyes narrowed. "How much more do you know about Ribard?"

Frank tossed some coins on the table. "Come home with me. Charlotte should hear this as well."

Silverton got to his feet. "Do you think Ianthe is Ribard's mistress?"

"If we're right that they're working together, I don't doubt it."

Silverton stared down at the table. "That means we both shared a mistress with our father-in-law."

Frank reached for his greatcoat. "If that's the greatest sin you can call down on either of our heads, you're blinder than I thought. Let's go, Silverton. There's work to be done."

Charlotte set down her pen and stared at the columns of figures before her. Income, expenditures, potential economies. She stretched her cramped fingers. Millamant stirred at her feet. She reached down to pet the dog, careful not to disturb Knightly, who was asleep in her lap. It was little more than a week since she and Frank had brought Diana back from her ill-fated elopement. Diana had ceased to hide tearfully in her room, though her face was still pale and she had lost her vivacity. Serena's spirits were undimmed, and she asked entirely too many questions. Bertram was itching for action. Frank had managed to keep Diana's elopement secret from him, or he'd want to race off to the Continent and challenge Linton to a duel.

As for Juliet—Charlotte smiled for a moment, remembering the way Juliet had reached up to touch her face when she tucked the little girl into bed this evening. She was beginning, against all expectations, to feel like a mother. Juliet seemed to be beginning to feel like a daughter. The young Vaughans at least viewed her as a friend.

And Frank—Charlotte looked down at the neatly ruled columns of figures before her. She was at a loss to define what Frank was to her. Husband. Friend. Ally. Enemy. Some of all those things, and all of none of them. The only thing he unequivocally was not was her lover.

She folded her arms over her chest. She had been a fool. She had thought she could comfort Frank and take comfort from him without giving way to her own baser longings. She should have known desire could not be made to run on an even keel. She had felt the insidious danger that flared between them, but she had let herself go on. And then, as his hands and lips swept her from the moorings of reason, the image of Ned's face had flashed before her eyes. Perhaps her mind had lashed out in panic, defending itself in the only way possible as it felt itself drowned by the demands of her body. She had retreated to a safe place deep inside herself, numb to all feeling.

She wondered sometimes what would have happened if Frank hadn't ended the lovemaking. Whether she would have been able to quench her response to him or if he would have pulled her with him over the edge. There were moments when she wished she could find out and others when she was desperately glad she had not been put to the test. She woke nightly from sweat-drenched dreams she would not allow herself to remember, facing an abyss she could not allow herself to contemplate.

The door opened behind her. Millamant barked and jumped up. Knightly raised his head. "Frank." Charlotte got to her feet, braced for the shock of his presence. "How was the debate? Did—" She broke off at the sight of Silverton standing beside her husband.

"Hullo, Charlie." Silverton looked pale and haggard, but his face lightened as he smiled at her. "Your husband was kind enough to invite me home."

"I'm delighted." She walked forward, took Silverton's hands, and kissed him on the cheek. "Surprised, but delighted."

His fingers clenched around her own. "I owe you a debt, Charlie. A debt I can't possibly repay. I was never proud of my actions. But I had no idea you would ever be embroiled in my sins."

Charlotte scanned his face. There was a time when she had wanted nothing more than to take him to task for his crimes. But it looked as if he had been doing plenty of that himself. "It was Daniel who did the embroiling." She squeezed his hands. "There's no sense in dwelling on past mistakes, Silver. But I'm glad you and Frank were able to talk."

She released Silverton and looked at Frank directly for the first time, though she had been aware of him from the moment he walked into the room. She was aware of him whenever he walked into a room now, aware of his gaze upon her, of subtle changes in his breathing. For all their marriage remained unconsummated, the one night they had almost spent together had branded them both with knowledge of the other.

Tonight he appeared as drained as Silverton, but he, too, smiled. He made no move to touch her. He hadn't touched her, save when absolutely necessary, since the night he had touched her in the most intimate ways. "A lot of things have changed, Charlie," he said. "Sit down and we'll tell you about it."

He added another log to the fire and they clustered around it and told her. Not everything that had passed between them this night—Charlotte was sure of that. They never quite explained what had brought about the rapprochement between them. But they told her their conjectures about Daniel and Ianthe de Cazes and Henry Sunderland. Silverton colored and looked at the floor when speaking of Ianthe. Frank looked Charlotte straight in the eye. Unbidden images clouded her mind—images of Frank kneeling beside a sofa, caressing Ianthe de Cazes as he had caressed her.

"I don't know how I could have been such a fool," Silverton muttered, gaze on the moss roses on the carpet.

"Daniel has a way of making people act like fools." Charlotte looked at Frank, pushing the images of him and Ianthe to the back of her mind. "He appears to be making a habit of blackmail."

"It's nothing new," Frank said. "I'm quite sure he did the same when I was his secretary, though for what it's worth I never actually saw anything in writing."

She swallowed. "I didn't say you had."

He watched her for a moment, then glanced away. "People who were opposed to him had a strange way of changing their positions. I wouldn't be surprised if he has a hold on half the Cabinet. Or has tried to develop one— oh, good God."

"What?" Charlotte looked at him and the same instant put the same pieces together in her own mind. She drew an uneven breath. "You can't think—"

"I think it's possible." Frank's mouth had gone grim. "Likely even."

"What's likely?" Silverton looked from Frank to her in bewilderment.

"The Foreign Secretary's suicide," Charlotte said.

"But—" Silverton sat back in his chair. His eyes widened as he took in what they were implying about the late Foreign Secretary. "Christ. Ribard was in South America when Castlereagh killed himself."

"Mere geographical distance doesn't stop Ribard from pulling strings." Frank stared at his hands, his gaze intent. "We've all heard the rumors that Castlereagh killed himself because someone was trying to blackmail him over a supposed love affair with another man. A complete fabrication to the best of everyone's knowledge, but Castlereagh's mind was already unstable. The blackmail broke him. No one has ever been quite sure of the blackmailer's purpose."

Silverton frowned. "In the old days Ribard thought of Castlereagh as an ally."

Frank nodded. "But despite being an impossible reactionary, Castlereagh stuck by his principles. Ribard was never able to bend him to his will."

"Castlereagh was about to go off to the Congress of Verona when he killed himself," Charlotte said, recalling the events of the previous summer. "Daniel must have been plotting his return to England then. If he wanted to influence Castlereagh to make certain moves at the Congress—"

"He might have hired someone to forge incriminating letters," Frank concluded. "Very much in character. Only Ribard didn't realize how fragile Castlereagh's mental health had become. Instead of knuckling under, Castlereagh killed himself, and Ribard got Canning as Foreign Secretary, who I imagine is much less to his taste. On the other hand, it moved you into a position where you could be useful to him, Silverton."

"So he set his mistress to develop a hold on me." Silverton looked as though he were going to be sick. "If this is true—He's got to be stopped."

"That goes without saying." Charlotte looked at Frank and felt the burst of elation that comes from a shared goal. "We can't simply wait for him to strike again. We have to go after him."

"I'll help." Silverton looked up. "I'll do anything in my power to make up for my share in this debacle."

"Good." Charlotte tore her gaze away from Frank. The brightness in his eyes singed her. A plan, that was what she needed, something to focus on, to ward off the threat not only from Daniel but from her own weakness. "The advantage of having been raised by Daniel is that I know just how to get to him." She sat back and looked from one man to the other. "Through his greed."

Chapter 18

Sophie watched Charlotte move down the length of the dining-room table, pausing to straighten an ivory-handled knife, to twitch a linen napkin into place, to align a wineglass more precisely. "You look thoroughly at home as the lady of the house. I doubt I'd have settled in so quickly."

Charlotte looked up, fingering the fluted stem of a glass as though not quite willing to acknowledge ownership of it. "I don't feel particularly settled. I never knew giving a simple dinner could be so complicated."

"You do it all the time at Chelmsford."

Charlotte set the glass above the appropriate knife. "That's just family."

"This is just family."

Charlotte's fingers stilled on the crystal for a moment, as though she were digesting the reality of this remark. "Yes, well, the family's got larger and more complicated in recent months." She adjusted the vase of dried flowers in the center of the table. "I've put Céline next to Frank, and Silverton next to me. It seemed diplomatic, though I'm afraid Paul will be terribly disappointed in me when he learns I've seated people according to precedence."

Sophie smiled. "Even Paul has to admit there are times one must observe the forms. What about the children?"

"I've put them together at one end—Serena and Kirsty and Lydia and Emily Durward. It's a pity there aren't any young men for them, what with Val at Harrow and Dugal and David at university in Edinburgh." Charlotte glanced at Sophie. "I'm sorry Amy decided to stay in Edinburgh with them. I miss her."

"So do I." Not for the first time since they'd left home, Sophie thought of her self-possessed nineteen-year-old ward and felt a small pang. "To own the truth, I think there's a young man at university Amy's more than passingly interested in. They do grow up so very quickly."

"I'm beginning to realize that with Serena. For all Céline longs to have Lydia behave like a grown-up young lady, I daresay she'll go into nervous spasms when she actually does." Charlotte glanced at the table, then looked back at Sophie, her face intent. "Diana's going to keep the younger people occupied after dinner so the rest of us can talk." She smoothed the ends of cream satin sash that tied at the front of her gown. "Sophie—what Frank and Silver and I are going to ask all of you to do tonight—I don't want any of you to agree to the plan out of a sense of obligation."

Sophie righted an unlit wax taper that was tilting in one of the silver candelabra. When she and Paul had arrived at Vaughan House last night, Charlotte told them she and Frank and Silverton had a plan to check Daniel. But the details of the plan were to wait until after tonight's dinner, when Robert and Emma and their friends Adam and Caroline Durward would be present as well. "I don't know what you mean by obligation." Sophie pushed the taper more firmly into its filigree base. "Paul and I aren't given to foolish decisions. Nor are Robert and Emma or Adam and Caroline."

"I thought perhaps Adam would think he should help us because he owed some sort of debt to Robert."

"You mean because Robert saved his life? But Adam's saved Robert's life as well. I think they would both say all obligations are cleared, save those of friendship." Adam Durward, now an attaché at the British Embassy in Paris, had been a British spy during the war in the Peninsula, when Robert had been a spy for the French. Though on opposite sides, the two had formed an unlikely friendship that had outlived the war. "Adam will want to help for your sake, Charlie; he's very fond of you. But you can trust him to judge risks for himself. What surprises me more is that you can count on Silverton as an ally."

"A lot of things have changed quickly. I haven't even had a chance to talk to Céline about it yet." Charlotte smoothed a crease from the tablecloth. "You do think it's safe to include Céline in the plans, don't you?"

"Considering I know nothing about the nature of the plans? No, I won't tease you, I'll know soon enough. Whatever the plan, I do think it's safe to include Céline. She's far more sensible than she lets on."

"She is, isn't she?" Charlotte stared down at the table for a moment. "Do you think she minds about Silverton?"

"About his wandering eye? Céline's done her own share of wandering."

"Yes, I know, I'm not blind." Charlotte studied the Wedgwood plate before her, as though answers might be found in the intricate blue and white landscape pattern. "I always took it for granted that they were both happy with the arrangement, but lately I've begun to wonder."

Sophie watched her cousin, trying to search for clues in Charlotte's countenance without revealing that she was doing so. "Since you've been married yourself?"

"No." Charlotte looked up quickly. "That is, yes, but that isn't why I've begun to wonder." She twisted her pearl bracelet around her wrist. "I was Serena's age when they got married. Were they happy then?"

Sophie gave the question honest consideration, though at the moment she was more concerned with the state of Charlotte's marriage than Céline's. "Céline certainly would have said she loved him."

"But you don't think she really did?"

Sophie smiled. "Who's to say what's love and what isn't? But I doubt either of them would have dreamed of the match if the other hadn't met all the qualifications of rank and fortune."

Charlotte disengaged a fold of her gauze overdress that had caught on a chair back. "Even if Céline wasn't desperately in love with him when they became betrothed, one's feelings can change after marriage."

Sophie studied her cousin, pale and classically elegant in pearls and cream-colored gauze, yet somehow as vulnerable as the delicate glassware on the table before them. "Oh, yes. They most certainly can."

Charlotte's gaze hardened. So much for attempting subtlety. "I just don't like to think of Céline being unhappy. There." She stepped back from the table. "Will it do?"

Sophie knew when to let a matter rest. She ran her eye over the gleaming dishes, the polished silver, the sparkling crystal. "Admirably. The flowers add just the right touch of informality. And the dried lavender smells heavenly. Charlie—come here a minute."

Charlotte smoothed her gown. "What's wrong?"

"Your hair. It's a pretty style, but much too severe. When did you start pulling it back so ruthlessly?" Sophie loosened the pins so the curls fell softly about Charlotte's face.

"Oh, Sophie, now it will all fall down."

"No, it looks charmingly disheveled." Sophie twisted

Charlotte around so she could see herself in the gilt-framed mirror over the mantel. The heavy, tousled dark waves fell against her creamy skin, emphasizing the deep mystery of her eyes, the dark wings of her brows, the ripe fullness of her lips. There was something distinctly French about Charlotte's face. There was also, Sophie realized, an innate sensuality, which all Charlotte's best efforts had not been able to suppress.

"It will never stay."

Sophie squeezed her shoulders. "Take a risk, Charlie. Sometimes it's worth it."

A fire crackled in the library fireplace. Candlelight flickered against the gilded spines of books and gilded frames holding Vaughan ancestral paintings. The heavy crimson brocade curtains were drawn across the windows, isolating the long room from the outside world.

Charlotte sat in a lyre-back chair, hands folded in her lap, gripped more tightly than she would have cared to let anyone know. Frank stood by the fireplace, stirring the coals. Their guests—their potential fellow conspirators—were grouped about them. Adam and Caroline Durward and Robert and Emma on one of the crimson velvet sofas; Sophie, Paul, and Céline on the other; Silverton alone in a chair. Only an hour before they had been laughing around her dining table with the younger members of the party. Now they were all quiet. Waiting.

Frank set down the poker and leaned his arm against the mantel. He had, Charlotte had come to realize, a superb sense of setting. "This is a long story." His gaze swept the company. He made the words conversational, as though he were addressing each individually. "But you'll have to understand the whole if you're to understand what we're asking of you. Then you can judge for yourselves."

He paused, just long enough to let the words sink in. "It begins over five years ago, before Daniel de Ribard left England. I think we're all familiar with those events."

Adam and Caroline, the least acquainted with the details of the past, nodded. Paul's mouth went taut and his arm tightened around Sophie.

"Ribard went to Jamaica," Frank continued. "From there he traveled a good deal, visiting his various foreign investments. Two years ago he visited Brazil. And I believe that in Brazil he made the acquaintance of Ianthe de Cazes."

There was a stir of surprise. Céline swung her head around to look at Silverton. Paul raised his brows.

"Ianthe is the widow of a Brazilian *conde*," Frank went on. "Her father was the younger son of a country squire. Her brother, Henry Sunderland, made a fortune in drapery. He has ambitions to move in the first circles. He also has a passion for railways. Silver?"

Silverton nodded and took up the story. Like Frank, he knew how to hold his audience, but his face was pale. Lines Charlotte had never before noticed stood out against his fair skin. He looked down at his hands more than once when speaking of Ianthe, but when it came to his bribe over the railway survey he looked the others straight in the eye, like an injured man deliberately putting weight on a wounded limb.

When he had finished with his account of Ianthe and the bribe, there was a brief silence. Céline snapped the ivory sticks of her fan together. "Good heavens, Silverton, why didn't you tell me? I could have pawned my diamonds."

Silverton looked into her eyes. Good God, Charlotte

realized, he hadn't told her until tonight. He'd preferred to have her learn the story in this public setting. Charlotte would box Frank's ears if he kept such a secret from her.

"It wasn't your problem," Silverton said to Céline.

"That's a bird-witted and typically male response, Silver." The slashed gold satin on Céline's sleeves shimmered in the candlelight as she threw up her hands. "Taking a bribe is likely to lead to all sorts of problems for the whole family."

Robert regarded Silverton with appraising eyes. "I won't presume to judge your actions over the bribe, but talking of it as you just did, in front of a pack of journalists, took considerable courage."

Silverton looked at him without flinching. "I'm not asking for special treatment."

"No, you're too intelligent to expect it from us. On the other hand, I suspect exposing the story would play right into Ribard's hands."

"Yes." Charlotte leaned forward. "Daniel got possession of a note Silverton had written to Sunderland. He offered it to me if I'd sell him Chelmsford."

Paul's gaze flickered toward Silverton, then back to Charlotte. "And if you didn't?"

She drew a breath and cast a quick glance at Frank. He looked steadily back at her. They'd agreed that the whole story had to come out. "He said he'd give the note to Frank."

Charlotte watched as, inevitably, the pieces fell together in her brother's mind. He looked at Frank. "And what did you say to that, Storbridge?"

Frank returned Paul's regard, his gaze cool, level, unapologetic. "I said I'd get the letter from Ribard if she'd marry me."

The brief, stunned silence was broken as Paul pushed himself to his feet. "By God, Storbridge—"

Silverton, who hadn't been told this last and unlike Paul hadn't guessed, stared at Charlotte. "Charlie—"

"Paul." Charlotte stood. "Frank's reasons for wanting to marry me are his own affair, as are mine for accepting him."

Paul swung his head around to look at her. "Why the hell—"

Charlotte looked into her brother's eyes. "Don't you think this is just what Daniel wants? To have us fighting among ourselves?"

That silenced Paul. He drew a long, harsh breath and resumed his seat, though his gaze was anything but tranquil. "We can discuss this later, Storbridge."

"Quite," said Frank.

Sophie said nothing, but Charlotte could feel her cousin's gaze upon her. Frank continued with the story in the same measured voice. His bargain with Daniel, the burning of the note, the sabotage at the factory—here Charlotte felt both Paul and Sophie watching her—the incidents with Bertram and Diana. Finally, their suspicion that Daniel had played a role in the Foreign Secretary's suicide the previous summer.

"Dear God." Emma put her hand to her mouth, as though she felt ill.

Sophie smoothed the sea-green velvet of her gown between her fingers. "I wouldn't have thought anything Uncle Daniel could do could surprise me. But I'd forgotten how devious he can be." She looked at Frank. "What is it you're planning?"

Frank's mouth lifted in a faint smile. "I appreciate your directness." His gaze swept the others. "We have no right to ask for your help—"

"There's no need to protest on my account, Storbridge." Adam Durward spoke up for the first time. His dark eyes were even more intent than usual. "I can't speak for the others, but after what you've told us, I'll do whatever it is for Charlotte, if not for you."

Sophie smiled. "I suspect that just about sums up everyone's feelings. But perhaps you'd better tell us about this plan, so we know what we're getting into."

"Charlie?" Frank said. "It's your plan."

Charlotte drew a breath. "Everyone has a weak point. The trick is knowing where to find it. Daniel told me that, and he was right, as he so often is. His weak point is greed."

The silence in the room shifted. Paul's eyes narrowed. Sophie cupped her chin in her hand. Céline gripped her fan tightly.

"We need evidence of Daniel's corruption," Charlotte continued. "But it won't be easy to find. So we have to go out and create it."

"How?" Robert asked.

Charlotte leaned forward. Her hair, loosened by Sophie, fell haphazardly about her face. "Daniel thinks railways are the key to rebuilding his power. He's already got many powerful men from both parties to invest in the proposed Lancaster and Liverpool Railway." She pushed her wayward hair back from her face. "As railways develop, the demand for iron will soar. Daniel must know that. He already controls some iron reserves in Brazil, but they're comparatively small. If he heard there was a Peruvian count in London with iron reserves on his estates, who wanted to meet him, I think he'd take the bait."

Céline frowned. "Who is this count?"

Charlotte looked across the room. "Adam, if he's willing."

"Ah." Adam gave one of his unexpectedly sweet smiles. "I was beginning to suspect as much. I did pose as a Peruvian once on a mission in Spain."

"Yes, Robert told us. We thought of asking Robert to do it, but Daniel's met him. He's never seen you."

"And my coloring is . . . not British." Adam smiled again, a little less sweetly. His mother had been a Hindu from India. He had her tawny skin and dark hair and, Charlotte knew, bore inner scars from years of being an outsider.

Caroline Durward—blond, fine-boned, every inch the squire's daughter—scanned Charlotte with anxious eyes. "And after Adam pretends to be this Peruvian? What then?"

Charlotte drew a breath, glanced at her friends and relations, and outlined her plan step by step.

There was a moment's silence when she finished. "Q.E.D.," Robert said. "That's as brilliant as one of your most complicated proofs."

Charlotte felt herself flush with pride, then told herself she was being silly. "I wish I could be as sure it would lead to the intended outcome. People aren't nearly as predictable as numbers."

Sophie twisted her cameo bracelet around her wrist. "Uncle Daniel will be sure to check into the background of the Peruvian count."

"That shouldn't be a problem." Robert exchanged glances with Adam. "We know a thing or two about how to plant a good cover story." He leaned back into the sofa, smiling. "We'll have to engage a suite of rooms at an hotel and find a strategic number of people to vouch for you."

Adam nodded. "I still know some people in London who can help with documents."

Caroline turned to her husband, gilt ringlets stirring about her face. "Adam Durward, you're enjoying this."

Adam grinned at her. "It does make for a change from diplomatic minutia."

Emma, probably the most practical person in the room, gave a mock sigh. "All this plotting makes me feel quite ten years younger. I must own to a selfish wish that your plan gave me a greater role to play."

"I suspect in the end there'll be more than enough for all of us to do." Frank glanced about the room and gave a full, genuine smile for the first time since they'd entered the library. "If we're in agreement, let me pour some brandy. I think it's time for a toast."

Chapter 19

Céline rapped on the door of her husband's bedchamber, then turned the handle without waiting for an answer. "Silverton? We have to talk."

He was standing in front of the fireplace, one foot on the fender, staring down at the coals. He was wearing a patterned blue silk dressing gown she didn't think she'd seen before. He looked up as she walked into the room, surprise written on his face.

"We have to talk," she said again. "Surely you realize that."

He adjusted the tie on his dressing gown. "You were perfectly quiet on the drive home."

"I had to think. You must admit it was all something of a shock." She dropped into an armchair with a deliberate *swish* of her damask peignoir. "Why the devil didn't you tell me?"

"I told you." He slicked his hair back from his forehead. "That is, I told you why I didn't tell you. I didn't want to worry you."

"Yes, and I can understand that—barely—though it still strikes me as idiotic. But afterward—knowing I'd hear it all tonight. Why did you say nothing to me beforehand?" Her voice trembled a little on this last. She stilled it with an effort. It wouldn't do for him to know quite how badly he'd hurt her.

Silverton crossed the carpet, fists jammed into the pockets of his dressing gown. "I told myself it would be easier for you to hear the whole at one time— Storbridge's and Charlotte's sides of the story as well as mine. But the truth is, I was a coward." He stopped and looked down at the pattern on the Wilton Carpet. "I'm not very proud of my actions, Céline."

She had an unexpected impulse to go to him and stroke his hair, as she would with her sons. But she hadn't the least idea what her husband would make of such an action. "If it's any comfort, you aren't alone." She smoothed her peignoir, staring at the figured violet damask between her fingers. She had removed most of her jewels, but she was still wearing a favorite sapphire ring. "I suppose I spend a great deal of money."

"We're both accustomed to living lavishly. You had a large dowry."

"Thanks to my father."

"True. We've both done well off Ribard."

Céline swallowed. "I know we've never lived in each other's pockets. But I would like to think you would come to me when we faced a problem."

He turned toward her. "We haven't faced many problems, have we? We've both been privileged from the cradle." He was silent for a moment. "When I first stood for the House I thought it was something of a lark. An extension of cricket at Eton or racing horses on Rotten Row. Something to keep me busy until I inherited Father's title someday and started running the estates and sitting in the Lords. When I met Canning I was amazed at how seriously he took everything." He smiled, though the smile did not reach his eyes. "It was a novel experience, taking something seriously."

"Heavens, yes." She tried to make her voice playful, but it came out sounding thin and hollow. "Silver—"

"When I took that damn bribe I knew it was wrong, but I didn't realize the line I was crossing over. . . . I suppose the truth is, one approaches it by inches, so that it's only when you look back that you realize how far you've gone. I haven't been very happy with myself these last months. I didn't want to inflict that on you."

She glanced away, toward the bed. Her view of the blue velvet hangings and mahogany posts wavered. They'd made love in that bed once or twice, in the early days of their marriage. Now Silverton mostly visited her bedchamber, after first discreetly asking her permission. And in recent months he had ceased to visit much at all. "Charlotte knew. Before I did. My younger sister knew."

"Storbridge wanted to tell her."

She looked him full in the face. "They've been married less than two months. I'm not sure I even understand their marriage. And yet *he* confides in *her*."

"I don't think he had much choice. Charlie's at the heart of the conflict."

"She would be. Whatever *Papa* is doing. She's the only one of us he ever spared a second thought for. It shouldn't bother me. I never thought it bothered me." Céline twisted her ring around her finger. "But I rather suspect Francis would have told Charlie even if Daniel had had nothing to do with the problem. I'm sure Paul would have told Sophie. Silverton." Céline looked at him, the words coming unbidden. "Why did you offer for me?"

His eyes went wide. "My dear—"

"It's a fair question. I think after tonight I at least deserve honesty."

He took a step toward her, then checked himself, his gaze moving over her skin. "You were the loveliest girl I'd ever seen."

"And your parents were insisting it was time you got married."

"I didn't say that."

"No, I did."

He watched her, a strange light in his eyes. "Does it matter so much?"

He was close enough that she could smell the sandalwood of his shaving soap. For a mad moment she wanted to burrow into that scent. "No," she said, "of course not. Not now." She got to her feet, the cool folds of her peignoir rustling about her. "Forgive me, Silver, the shock's overset me. I really only wanted you to promise that from now on you won't keep anything from me." She felt herself color, but she did not glance away. "Anything relating to this business with Daniel, that is."

"Of course." He drew a breath. "Céline—"

"Yes?" Her voice was quick and breathy.

"Nothing. Except . . . I'm sorry."

She forced a smile to her lips. "I'm sure there's plenty of cause for apology on both sides."

He looked at her for a moment, then crossed to her side, took her hand, and pressed it to his lips. A shock ran along her skin. For a moment she thought he meant to take her in his arms. Instead, he released her. She hesitated a moment longer. But tonight of all nights he would scarcely want her to stay. She moved to the door. "Good night, Silver."

Silverton inclined his head with careful formality. "Good night, Céline."

Frank hesitated, his gaze moving over the mahogany door panels. Charlotte's room, separated from his own by a simple connecting door. They should discuss tonight's events. But the discussion could wait. They could talk in the morning, amid the trivialities of coffeecups and muffin dishes. Or in his study, surrounded by the smell of ink and a litter of parliamentary papers. Or in the sitting room, with its long sparkling windows and airy expanse of carpet.

But he didn't want to wait. He had an excuse, for the first time in his marriage, to knock on the door of his wife's bedchamber. And he had never been good at resisting temptation.

The fingers of his right hand curled into a fist. He raised his hand to knock. He hesitated a moment longer, then rapped on the door. "Charlotte? We should talk."

He half expected her to say no. Silence dragged on, pressing in upon him. Perhaps she intended to make no answer at all. It was even possible she was asleep and hadn't heard him. In any case, he had very little choice but to—

"Yes, all right." Her voice was level, even, carefully controlled.

He drew a breath, turned the handle, and walked into his wife's bedchamber.

She was sitting at her dressing table, her unpinned hair gilded with honey by the light of the tapers that burned on either side of the looking glass. She turned her head as he stepped into the room. Her gaze was armored with determination. He wondered if she had let him into the room just to prove she could face him with equanimity in such a setting.

"It went well tonight." Her tone was conversational.

"Yes." He was surprised to find his own voice nearly as level and only a shade breathless. "All things considered, it could scarcely have gone better. You're fortunate in your friends and relations."

"They're your relations now as well." Her silver-backed brush flashed in the candlelight as she set it down on the dressing table. "Do you think it will work?"

"I think there's a good chance it will." He moved into the room, avoiding the white-clad mass of the bed, and seated himself in a wing-back chair. He was far enough from the dressing table that there was no way he could touch her, but close enough that he could smell the vanilla and almond scent of her skin. He wondered what would happen if he crossed to her side and pulled her into his arms. Yet even as the thought crossed his mind, he knew it was no kind of answer. He had tried that path and found it set with mines.

Charlotte turned in her chair to look at him. She was wrapped in a voluminous peach-colored garment that covered far more of her than the gown she had worn at dinner. But it was a dressing gown, and he could not deny that the knowledge lent an erotic edge to the sight. "I wish we could have kept our bargain from Paul," she said.

"You needn't worry. Your brother doesn't strike me as the sort to fight a duel."

"No, but I hate to have him think me such a poor-spirited creature as to give way to blackmail."

A vinegar-sharp taste welled up on his tongue. It might have been self-reproach. "You're anything but poor-spirited, Charlotte."

She drew a breath. He could see the stirring of her breasts beneath the loose fabric of the dressing gown. "I think Paul likes you more than he'll admit. Or he'd never trust you with the plan against Daniel."

Frank crossed one leg over the other. "Do you?"

"Do I what?"

He rested his elbows on the chair arms and tented his

fingers together. "Trust me. To follow through on what we've set out to do. I might decide it's more expedient simply to join forces with Ribard."

She regarded him for a moment, then shook her head. "No."

He returned her regard, searching her eyes for something he would scarcely let himself put into words, though he hungered for it with the intensity of physical desire. "Why?"

A smile played about her lips. "Because if you wanted to join forces with Daniel, why not simply do so? Why go through the charade of pretending you wanted to bring him down?"

Such a simple answer, so much more straightforward than if she'd said she knew he wouldn't betray them because she believed in him. And yet he'd hoped—Strange how disappointment could bite one in the throat, a sharp, bitter pang. He smiled back, wondering if the bitterness showed in the curve of his mouth. "To put you all off your guard?"

Her smile deepened. "Doing it much too brown, Frank. We don't pose enough of a threat for you to go to such lengths to put us off our guard."

"Don't underestimate yourself, Charlotte. The mind that conceived a plan to outwit Daniel de Ribard is formidable indeed."

Her smile faded. She turned back to the mirror. Her face was reflected threefold in the looking-glass panels, pale and heart-shaped, her eyes dark and troubled beneath her thick brows. "Do you know what I see when I look into my glass, Frank?" There was a harshness to her voice, like the rasp of steel against stone. She pushed both hands into her hair, so that her fingers stood out starkly, white against the dark strands. "I see his eyes, his brows, his mouth. There are moments when I want to smash my fist into the glass and break the image to pieces."

Frank was on his feet, but he checked himself before he crossed the carpet to her. "Do you know what I see?" He kept his voice mild with an effort. "Kindness. Loyalty. Sweetness."

She shook her head. "We're none of us so simple, Frank. We all have our dark sides." Her fingers pressed into her scalp, so tightly her knuckles turned white. "Surely you know that."

"Who better?" He watched her, knowing no false reassurance would do. "But it's our actions that matter, not whatever thoughts lurk in the recesses of our minds. You have nothing to reproach yourself with."

Her gaze met his own in the mirror. Her deep-set eyes were as unfathomable as the darkest water. "You can't know that, Frank. No one can ever really know another person. I once thought I knew Daniel. And Ned."

She dropped her hands to the walnut surface of the dressing table. "Do you remember when we used to talk about our parents? I'd think how lucky I was because I wasn't at war with Daniel's expectations for me, the way you were with your father's. What a fool I was."

Frank heard the breath rush from his lungs. It was the first time she'd referred to that other world in which they'd been friends. A small rent had been made in the curtain that had hung between them since his ill-timed proposal in Edinburgh.

He dropped back into the chair. "It's true, I've never had to worry I'd inherit my father's character. I knew all too well that I had not."

She turned from the mirror to look at him. "No? From

what I know of your father, in some ways you're very like him. Isn't the principle behind your factory much the same as your father's school?"

"On the contrary." For a moment his father came vividly to mind—the thin face, the mild voice, the thread-bare brown coat he always wore. Frank glanced down at the rich paisley silk of his dressing gown. "What does my factory require beyond an outlay of capital and quarterly visits? The school was my father's life. That and his parish."

"And he wanted you to follow in his footsteps." She pushed her hair back from her face and rested her elbow on the chair back. The loose sleeve of her dressing gown fell back, revealing the curve of her arm. "As I recall, you quarreled every time you went home for a visit."

For a moment they were back at Rossmere, walking along the leafy streambank, exchanging earnest, intent confidences. Frank closed his eyes for a moment. They'd had this discussion before, but it was more important than ever that he make her understand. "He said that if I really wanted to help people I should go into the church. I said I could be of more help to the downtrodden in West-minster than I'd ever be in Spitalfields. He said you only got that sort of power by destroying your soul. Perhaps he was right." He paused and stared down at his hands. There was a trace of ink on one of his fingers. He rubbed it out. "But even as a clergyman I'd never have measured up to his standards."

"Are you saying it's more difficult to have a saint for a father than a sinner?"

He looked up. "I wouldn't presume to make that claim. But I was never as central to my father's life as you were to Ribard's."

"Don't you see, that's just it." The words burst from

Charlotte. She swallowed. A pulse beat wildly in her throat. "That's the part of me I'd like to smash. The part I'd like to reach inside and tear out."

"The part that Ribard loves?"

"No." She turned back to the mirror and stared at her reflection. "The part that still loves him."

Chapter 20

"There's the Marquis de Ribard." Serena leaned over the rail of the box, crushing her new Pomona green sarcenet. "On the other side of the theater. He just came in with the Sunderlands—oh, goodness, Ianthe de Cazes is with them."

"The dark-haired woman?" Kirsty joined Serena at the rail. "She's very striking."

"She's too obvious." Serena glanced back over her shoulder to where Charlotte stood talking with Sophie and Emma. "She's not half as pretty as Charlotte."

"Don't tell lies, Serena," Charlotte said. "It's a shockingly bad habit." She followed Serena's gaze across the theater. Henry Sunderland, his florid face pushed up by overstarched shirt points, and his wife, swathed in Brussels lace and diamonds, had stepped to the front of the box. Daniel and Ianthe were just behind them, Daniel immaculate in a black coat and cream-colored breeches, Ianthe brilliant in unadorned white satin and rubies.

"So that's Ianthe de Cazes," Sophie said. "She certainly has an air about her."

"Yes." Charlotte's voice sounded unnaturally bright to her own ears, like overpolished silver plate that was beginning to wear thin. She'd seen Ianthe once or twice at

entertainments in London, but she'd forgotten how white
her skin was, how dark her hair, how deep green her eyes.
She looked at once a temptress and a queen. Charlotte
fingered the amber *gros de Naples* of her own gown. With
a woman like that in his bed, how could Frank have
thought of marrying anyone, let alone her?

Sophie pressed Charlotte's arm. "Clever of them to arrive at the first interval when they can create the maximum stir. I used to employ that trick myself, but I always
hated missing the first act."

Frank was at the back of the box with Caroline. He
turned and ran his gaze over the Sunderland party, then
turned away. With the intensity of a sudden thirst, Charlotte wanted him to look at her. She wanted some spark in
his eyes, some clue that Ianthe was no more to him than a
former mistress.

But that was silly. If their ploy with Daniel was to
work, Frank could not act as though he cared about her
opinion. Besides, she didn't want him to care about
her opinion. She'd given him her permission to have mistresses. She'd encouraged it. It would be far better for
him to have a mistress, for then that dark, dangerous intensity would not be bent on her. They might be allies
now. They might even be something approaching friends.
But fundamentally nothing had changed. She could hardly blame him for seeking from another woman what she
wasn't able to give him herself.

Daniel was watching her. She could feel the pressure
of his gaze across the crowded expanse of the theater,
cutting through layers of pretense and defense, like a diamond slicing through glass.

"Who's that third man?" Serena asked. "I've never
seen him before."

Another man had come into the box behind Daniel and

Ianthe. Charlotte had expected to see him. She knew perfectly well who he was. Yet for a moment she thought her eyes were playing tricks on her. Surely this stout, barrel-chested man with gray-streaked hair, neatly clipped side whiskers, and a flowing mustache could not be Adam Durward. Even his face looked fuller. As she watched, he walked forward with a purposeful, ponderous gait, very unlike Adam's quicksilver agility.

Serena showed no sign that she recognized him. Nor did Kirsty, who knew Adam far better. Charlotte glanced at the adjoining box, where Adam and Caroline's daughter, Emily, was talking to Bertram and Diana. Like the other young girls, Emily was looking at the Sunderlands' box. Her gaze flickered briefly in Adam's direction. Then she returned to studying Ianthe's gown. Charlotte breathed an inward sigh of relief. If Adam could fool his own daughter, he could fool anyone else in the theater who might happen to know him.

Behind her, Frank murmured something to Caroline and pushed aside the blue velvet curtain to leave the box.

Serena whirled around. "Where are you going?"

Frank lifted his brows. "To conduct deep dark business, brat. Much too deep and dark for eleven-year-olds."

"But the interval's nearly over. You'll miss the next act."

"Then you'll have to take notes for me. Let me know if Charles Surface is as attractive as they say. If you'll excuse me." He nodded to the others and slipped from the box.

"Well, I call that shabby." Serena stared after him. "This was supposed to be a family party."

In the adjoining box, Bertram looked up from talking to Diana and Emily. A shadow crossed his face. A thick silence settled over both boxes. The younger people were worried about Frank disappearing so soon after the arrival of his former mistress. The elder members of the party—who knew perfectly well what Frank was about—were pretending to be worried. Charlotte knew she belonged in the latter category, yet she had an unaccountable knot in the pit of her stomach.

She smiled and held out her hands to Serena and Kirsty. "I think we just have time to fetch some ices before the interval ends. Shall we?"

Frank made his way along the curving corridor that ran behind the boxes in the Bedford Theater. Thus far the plan was proceeding with the precision of a Swiss time-piece. Which did not explain the flicker of unease he'd seen in Charlotte's eyes before he left the box. Discomfort at facing her father? Consummate acting? Worry about the success of their plan? Or had she possibly been unsettled by the sight of her husband's former mistress? There was an unworthy part of him that hoped this last was the answer. For that would mean that she cared about her husband's opinion.

He was stopped by Lord John Russell, who wanted to discuss the prospects for a new emancipation proposal, by Dolly Granby, who insisted he must bring his charming new wife to her rout on Friday next, and by Mr. Creevey, who was eager for gossip about Daniel de Ribard. At last he reached the outer door to the Sunderland box. It was ajar. He stepped into the anteroom, warm with the heat of candles and close-pressed bodies. Sunderland was sitting on a gold sofa, surrounded by four or five cronies, his hearty laugh echoing through the room. A knot of men were clustered around the open doorway to the box itself.

Frank nodded to Sunderland with familiarity, strolled

toward the doorway, touched a man on the shoulder, murmured a greeting to another, and slipped through the crowd into the box. Ianthe was sitting where he had known she would be, with a favored few men clustered about her in addition to the crowd in the doorway. Her chair was turned so her profile was revealed to the theater at large. Ribard was on the other side of the box, talking quietly with Mrs. Sunderland and Adam. But for the moment Ribard could wait. It gave the enemy an advantage if one rushed an attack.

Ianthe looked up as he stepped into the box. Her eyes lit with mischief and reproach. She turned deliberately away and took a sip of champagne, then looked back at him. "Francis. I was beginning to think you'd quite given up your old friends. It's kind of Mrs. Storbridge to spare you."

Frank bent over her hand. The scent of lilies washed over him, rousing memories but not desire. "You'd best sheathe your claws, my sweet. Malice doesn't flatter your complexion."

Ianthe snatched her hand away. "Tiresome man. But you're not going to provoke me. I have far too much consolation." She looked from the flaxen-haired gentleman on her left to the red-headed gentleman on her right with a dazzling smile.

The curtain was going up. The buzz of conversation in the theater diminished, but did not cease. Mrs. Sunderland returned to her seat. Frank met Ribard's gaze for the briefest of moments, then made his way out of the box and through the anteroom to the corridor. There were still a few knots of people talking, but the crowd had thinned. He leaned against the wall, contemplating a framed theatrical print. The assassination scene from *Julius Caesar*. Appropriate.

A few minutes later Ribard strolled out of the box and

came to stand beside him. "I trust you have something important to say to me, Storbridge. I'm rather partial to *School for Scandal*, and I understand Mrs. Ralston is particularly fetching as Lady Teazle."

Frank turned to look at Charlotte's father. "Then by all means return to the play. I was under the impression that you valued my assistance, but if you prefer to watch Sheridan that's quite your own affair."

Ribard leaned against the wall beside him. "As I recall you refused to give me your assistance, in rather high-flown language. Do you expect me to believe something has changed?"

"I never know what to expect of you, Ribard. You made me an offer the last time we met. Is that offer still open to negotiation?"

Ribard's dark, slanting brows drew together. In his eyes, Frank caught the same look Charlotte had when she was trying to puzzle out his motives. "Why?"

Frank rested his head against the silk-covered wall behind him. "What do my reasons matter?"

"A great deal if you want me to believe you're sincere."

Frank met the other man's gaze. "I'm probably sincere about as often as you are, Ribard." He glanced at the gilded gas lamp across the corridor casting a yellow glow on the peacock-striped silk. "*High-flown* pretty accurately describes it. If you must know, I thought I could curry favor with Charlotte by rejecting your offer." He grimaced with a bitterness that was only partly feigned. "I should have known nothing I can do will change Charlotte's opinion of me."

He turned to find Ribard watching him. "Yes." There was something new in the older man's eyes—not warmth, not sympathy, but certainly understanding. "Charlie's remarkably clear-sighted. There's no bamboozling her. And once she's made up her mind she sticks by her guns."

"However did you manage to produce such a child?"

Ribard's mouth curved in a half smile. "Paul once said something similar to me. 'Good to the core' was how he described her—implying, of course, that I'm the opposite. In truth, I haven't the least idea how Charlotte became the woman she is. She is either my greatest success or my most egregious failure. I can never be sure which."

"I won't bore you with a discourse on the state of our marriage. Suffice it to say, while I may have secured her hand—thanks to the rather crude methods of persuasion you yourself tried on her—I don't have a hope in hell of securing her affections." This last rang true with bell-like clarity.

Ribard considered for a moment. "Does that account for your exchange with Ianthe? I don't think she's best pleased that you didn't stay longer, by the way."

"I had to have some excuse for coming into the box." Frank shifted his shoulders against the wall. "You and Ianthe make a handsome couple."

Ribard lifted his brows. "I wasn't aware that giving a woman one's arm automatically leg-shackled one."

"It wasn't the fact that you'd given her your arm. It was the rather proprietary way she was holding it. When I introduced the two of you at Lady Granby's, I didn't realize I was playing matchmaker—to avoid a more vulgar term." Frank glanced down at his hands. "I must say I'm not sure I care for the thought of sharing a mistress with my father-in-law."

"Spare me the moral outrage, Storbridge. It's a stretch." Ribard twisted his signet ring on his finger. "You said you were willing to reconsider my proposal. I'm willing to listen to what you have in mind." He glanced up and down the corridor, then jerked his head to the right. They walked down the corridor in silence until they reached a shallow embrasure. Ribard folded his arms across his chest and waited for Frank to speak.

"I give my support to the Lancaster and Liverpool Railway," Frank said. "You instruct Hawkins's to extend my loan when it falls due and to advance me whatever other monies I require. The accidents at my factory stop, as do the attacks on my family."

"That's the proposal I made over a fortnight ago. I don't leave my offers open indefinitely. If you want me to reconsider, you'll have to offer a greater inducement."

"And as it happens I can." Frank paused, enjoying the moment. "That was the *Conde* d'Amarante in the box with you, wasn't it?"

Ribard's eyes narrowed. "I didn't know you knew the *conde*."

"We haven't met, but there's been talk about him at Brooks's. Rumor has it he's come to England on an unofficial mission seeking recognition of Peru's independence from Spain."

"I'm afraid I can't comment on that. The *conde* has cousins who are friends of friends of mine in Brazil. He sought me out to give me greetings from them. He's living quietly while he's in London, but we persuaded him to come to the theater with us tonight."

Frank glanced beyond Ribard at the wall opposite. "I've also heard rumors that the *conde* has some of the largest iron reserves in Peru. I assume I don't need to tell you how valuable iron will become in the next years if you're right about railways."

"I'm seldom wrong about economic prospects." Ribard took out an enamel snuffbox, took a pinch of snuff, and sneezed, managing to do even this with elegance. "I've decided to sell the plantation in Jamaica, by the way. I have the tiresome feeling that you and your friends are going to get your way over emancipation in the next few years."

"Brougham will be pleased to hear it. But to return to the iron. It strikes me that a man who could help the *conde* further his cause with the British government might be able to secure the iron at an advantageous price. If you were to do so, you could sell the iron at a discount to my now sorely beleagered factory. I, in turn, could offer you rails for the Lancaster and Liverpool Railway for far less than any other iron founder. And I don't have to tell you the profit you could make on the rest of the iron."

"An interesting idea. What a pity it is neither you nor I is in a position to influence Britain's foreign policy."

"No, but Silverton is."

Ribard paused in the midst of returning the snuffbox to his pocket. "I was under the impression that you and Silverton weren't on speaking terms."

"I wouldn't go that far. Charlotte actually had him and Céline to dine recently. We even managed to be civil to each other. But I was thinking of Silverton's note. The note Charlotte was so desperate to recover that she risked her eternal soul by becoming my wife. The note you still probably haven't forgiven me for taking and then reneging on our bargain."

Ribard tapped the snuffbox against his hand. "I get the general picture."

"I had to get the letter to get Charlotte. Obviously I couldn't use it publicly. But it was far too valuable to destroy."

Ribard's eyes narrowed. "Where's the letter now?"

"Here." Frank drew a paper out from within his coat. He kept hold of the note while Ribard scanned it. It had been simple enough for Silverton to recreate the words, but he had had to write it on a more recent bill from his bootmaker. It had been some weeks since Ribard had seen the note, but his memory was uncannily sharp. Frank watched in as good a pose of detachment as he could muster until Ribard looked up from the letter.

Ribard surveyed him for a long, inscrutable moment before he spoke. Then he gave a quick, gleaming smile. "For once I underestimated you, Storbridge. It seems we can be of use to each other after all."

"Come on, love, you're dropping on your feet." Diana put her arm around Serena and steered her toward the stairs. "I think Francis gave you too many sips of champagne at supper."

"He didn't. I'm not." Serena turned at the foot of the stairs and swept a curtsy in the manner of Mrs. Ralston as Lady Teazle. "Good night, everyone. It was an *enchanting* evening."

She whirled around with a *swish* of her crumpled skirts and followed Diana up the stairs, trailing her slightly grimy white-gloved fingers along the polished mahogany stair rail.

"Oh, to be eleven. I hope Fenella's as free-spirited at the same age." Sophie relinquished her black velvet cloak to the footman. "I think we'll go up as well, Charlie. It was a lovely evening."

Sophie and Paul started up the stairs. The footman disappeared into the back of the hall, laden with cloaks and greatcoats. Charlotte moved to the marble-topped table by the stairs to take a candle. She deliberately took her time lighting the candle from the single taper on the table. If Bertram would go up, she could question Frank about his talk with Daniel. Otherwise she would have to go to Frank's room for a report. And she was not sure that would be wise.

But Bertram lingered, warming his hands at the fireplace for what seemed an unconscionably long time. Millamant and Knightly lay on the marble tiles, watching the humans. Frank moved to Charlotte's side, stifling a yawn. "All in all a very successful evening. Shall we, my dear?"

He held out his hand. Charlotte hesitated a moment, then put her own into it. He had removed his gloves. His fingers closed around her own, warm and steady. He smiled at her. A friendly, undemanding smile, but it sent a chill along her nerves.

"Just a minute." Bertram's voice rang out, echoing off the scagliola columns. "No, Charlotte, stay, you should hear this too. It concerns your father." He strode across the room. "I saw you with Ribard at the theater, Storbridge. What the hell are you playing at?"

Chapter 21

Frank surveyed his brother-in-law. "Skulking about the corridors of the Bedford, Bertram? Isn't that a bit beneath a Vaughan?"

"Damn it, Storbridge." Bertram faced him, hands clenched at his sides. "I don't know the whole story about Ribard. No one's seen fit to tell me. But I know you claim he's behind my debts and the damage at your factory and whyever Diana's been crying her eyes out. I know Charlotte doesn't trust him. I thought you didn't either."

"I don't."

"Then why the bloody hell were you talking to him? Behind all of our backs."

Frank felt Charlotte cast a questioning glance at him. He was still holding her hand, and she had made no move to disengage her fingers. He hesitated. Responsibility would be good for Bertram. But trusting someone so young and so hotheaded with something as delicate as their plan seemed foolhardy in the extreme. Especially tonight. Bertram's fair skin was flushed and his eyes unnaturally bright. He had drunk more than his share of champagne during their supper party at the Clarendon after the play.

"I should have known." Bertram's voice filled the silence, shaking with the bitterness of disappointment. "I should have known you were plotting something."

"Much as it desolates me to admit it, you have a point." Frank squeezed Charlotte's fingers and released her hand. "It's true, I am plotting something. But not what you think. Perhaps—"

"Oh, no." Bertram waved his arm in a wide arc. "No more of your sophistry, Storbridge. Christ, you could talk your way around anyone. For a while you almost had me trusting you." He took an angry turn about the hall and then froze, staring up at the portrait of Julia over the fireplace. The light from the chandelier slanted across the picture, making the pearly tones Thomas Lawrence had used on her face glow with luminescent purity. "I should have known. I should have remembered. What did you say to her?" He looked back over his shoulder, pinning Frank with his gaze. "How did you trick my sister into your bed?"

Frank deflected the stare like a rapier thrust. "What happened between Julia and me has nothing to do with my meeting with Ribard."

"It has everything to do with it." Bertram strode forward until he was an arm's length from Frank. "You say one thing and mean another. Your motives are as slippery as a damn eel. You made us think Ribard is the enemy, and now you're plotting with him behind our backs. You made Julia think you loved her, and all the time you only wanted Father to get you into Parliament."

Frank folded his arms across his chest. Beside him, Charlotte had gone very still. He could not tell what she was thinking. "A rather strained comparison, Bertram. But for the record, I never lied to you about Ribard. And I never lied to Julia about my feelings for her."

"Damn you, you coldhearted bastard." Bertram aimed

a blow at Frank's chin. Frank ducked and crashed into the marble table. Heat seared his arm. The smell of burned wool filled the air. The taper rolled off the table and fell, hissing, to the floor. Millamant began to bark.

Frank reached for the taper. Bertram's fist smashed into his jaw. As he slipped to the floor, Frank grabbed Bertram's arm and twisted. Bertram thudded to the floor in front of him, his arm pinned behind his back.

"For heaven's sake, stop or you'll break the porcelain. Not to mention your heads." Charlotte stood over them, clutching both the taper and a wriggling kitten.

Frank adjusted his hold on Bertram's arm. "You have a powerful right, Bertram. But I grew up in Spitalfields. The local lads taught me a few tricks quite unknown to you Harrovians."

Bertram tugged against Frank's hold. "I'm not sorry, Storbridge. I should have done that years ago."

Millamant jumped on Frank and licked his face. Bertram chose the same moment to lunge forward. Millamant threw Frank off balance. He lost his purchase on Bertram's arm. Bertram broke free, turned on his knees, and grabbed Frank by the lapels of his coat.

Millamant growled. Bertram didn't seem to notice. "What you did to my sister—"

"Bertram, no, don't be an idiot." Diana's voice came from above. Her slippered feet sounded against the marble stairs.

"Stay out of this, Di." Bertram, still gripping Frank's coat, looked up at his sister. "Go back to bed."

"I'm not sleepy." From the bottom step Diana glared at them over the stair rail. "I came down to get a book. I can see now that it's a very good thing I did."

"A timely intervention, Diana." Frank detached himself from Bertram's grip and got to his feet. "Easy, Millamant. Bertram and I were just playing."

"*Damn* you, Storbridge—" Bertram scrambled to his feet.

"Stop it, Ber." Diana ran to her brother.

"You don't understand, Di. I owe it to Julia."

"No, *you* don't understand." Diana gripped her brother's arm.

"It's all right, Diana." Frank scooped up Millamant. "Bertram has one salient point. We should all go to bed."

"You and I are going to have this out, Storbridge."

"Bertram, you prize idiot." Diana pulled her brother around to face her. "Hasn't it ever occurred to you?"

"Hasn't what ever occurred to me?"

Diana looked up at him. The light of the chandelier burnished the titian hair of brother and sister. "That Francis isn't Juliet's father."

Silence fell over the circular hall like a tangible force. The fire crackled in the fireplace. The long shadows of the scagliola columns shifted with the wavering blaze. "Not entirely accurate," Frank said. "Juliet *is* my daughter, regardless of who performed the biological deed. Perhaps we'd better remove to the library."

Bertram opened his mouth as though to protest, then closed it and stalked to the library door. Diana looked over her shoulder at Frank. There was a spark in her eye Frank hadn't seen since the elopement and a maturity he had never before glimpsed. "I'm sorry," she said. "But it was time he learned the truth."

"Yes," Frank said. "I believe you're right." He looked at Charlotte. She was regarding him as though trying to arrange fresh pieces of a puzzle in her mind. There were dozens of things he would have liked to say to her, all hovering half-formed at the back of his mind. He said none of them. Instead, he held out his arm for the women to precede him to the library.

A lamp had been left burning on the library table in

case any of the family came down for a book, but the coals in the fireplace had grown cold. Frank closed the heavy door to the hall. Bertram faced him, arms folded, chin jutting. Diana stood with one hand on the sofa back, her color high, her breathing quickened. Charlotte had sunk into a chair, still cradling the kitten. Frank felt her gaze upon him, wide and dark and questioning.

"I owe you all an apology," Frank said. "I thought it was best to let the truth remain in the past. Perhaps I was wrong. I certainly didn't realize Diana knew it already." He gave her a faint smile.

Diana returned the smile, though her eyes remained serious. "Julia told me. Not at first, but I guessed some of it and she admitted the rest. I think she was glad to be able to talk."

Bertram's gaze fastened on his sister. "*What* did she tell you?" He looked at Frank. "You stay out of this, Storbridge. I want to hear it from Diana."

Frank clasped his hands behind his back and leaned against the closed door.

Diana's fingers tightened on the crimson velvet of the sofa. "I didn't learn the truth until after they were married. Julia told me that she had found herself with child and couldn't marry the father. There was no one to whom she could turn. You know how Papa lost his temper at the least scrape, let alone anything serious. So in the end she confided in Francis."

Bertram's brows drew together. "Why the hell would she confide in Father's secretary?"

"Who else was there?" Diana leaned forward across the sofa back. "You were at Cambridge. I was only seventeen. Marianne was in the country about to have a baby of her own. I can't imagine her going to Aunt Henrietta with such a story, any more than to Papa. Besides, I think she knew Francis had always cared for her." Diana smiled at Frank again.

Frank stilled an instinctive protest. Julia had embroidered the story considerably, no doubt to smooth over the unsavory edges. But denial would only tarnish her memory.

Diana turned to Charlotte. "I'm sorry. It can't be pleasant to hear about your husband's first wife."

Charlotte dug her fingers into Knightly's silver-gray fur. "On the contrary. The story is very illuminating. I'm honored you flatter me with your confidence."

Diana smiled with evident relief. "You should know, and I can't imagine Francis ever bringing himself to speak of it. You can be very proud of how chivalrously he treated my sister."

Bertram shot another, more appraising glance at Frank, then returned his gaze to Diana. "What happened after Julia confided in Storbridge?"

"Francis offered to marry her." Diana looked at Frank. Her eyes shone like the aquamarines she wore about her neck. "It was splendid of you. I've always wanted to be able to say so." She drew a breath. "I hope one day to find a man who loves me as much."

Bertram walked to the fireplace, out of the circle of light cast by the lamp. "Who was the father?"

Diana shook her head. "Julia wouldn't tell me. I think—I think he was married already."

Bertram looked Frank full in the face. "Did Julia tell you?"

Four simple words. Bertram might not realize it, but with that question he had crossed the line from disbelief to acceptance. Frank unclenched his hands, which he had been gripping together behind his back. "No."

Bertram's eyes widened, perhaps with the realization

that he had accepted the truth of the story. He released his breath with the sigh of a winded man who finds he has been shadowboxing a phantom. "The bastard." He brought his fist down on the black marble of the mantel. "The goddamned, lily-livered, spineless bastard. If I knew his name I'd kill him."

"I understand the feeling," Frank said. "But it would do Julia little good."

"Did Father ever learn? About the baby?"

"I told him before our marriage. Julia asked me to." That was true, as far as it went, but it left out certain pertinent details of the conversation. "I doubt he'd have given his permission otherwise," Frank added. "Like you, he would have preferred a more brilliant match for Julia."

Bertram dragged his hands over his face. "I've done you a great wrong, Storbridge."

Frank suppressed an ironic smile. With typical Vaughan extravagance, the boy had rushed from one emotional extreme to another. "Your feelings were very understandable in the circumstances." He regarded Bertram for a moment. "Be careful you don't misjudge me again. I may not be the blackguard you thought me, but I'm no saint either."

"You came to my sister's rescue. I should have done so myself."

"This is one office you could scarcely have performed. Marriage to Julia was no sacrifice, believe me."

"Papa couldn't have allowed his son-in-law to remain a mere secretary." Diana perched on the sofa arm with the relief of one who has won her point. "Julia herself asked the duke, as Marianne's husband, to sponsor Frank for the seat at Howitt. It was the least the family owed him."

Bertram dropped down on the sofa opposite Diana. He sank his head into his hands, his blue superfine shoulders hunched into wrinkles. Charlotte said nothing. Her fingers stroked rhythmically through the kitten's fur, but other than that she had scarcely moved a muscle since they came into the library. And yet, all the time he spoke to Bertram and Diana, Frank had been aware of her, like a shaft of moonlight shimmering through tree branches, just beyond view.

Bertram dropped his hands and jerked his head up. "What about Ribard?"

Charlotte looked at Frank and spoke for the first time. "I think they both deserve to hear the story."

Frank nodded. "Yes, I believe you're right. We've just seen what folly comes from the keeping of secrets."

With as much economy and as little melodrama as possible, he told them the story of Daniel de Ribard. When it came to Bertram's debts and Diana's elopement, he left it up to each to tell the other what he or she would. Both were disarmingly frank, with that straightforward, reckless honesty that was also a family trait. Diana took the news of Bertram's gaming in stride, but Bertram's face darkened at her account of her elopement with Linton. He swung his head around to look at Frank. "You should have called the fellow out."

"Possibly, if vengeance was my goal." Frank was standing with his arm resting on the mantel. "I was more concerned with keeping the events quiet. Duels have a tiresome way of getting talked about."

"But—"

"Oh, don't be an idiot, Bertram." Diana's fingers were curled tightly against the shiny blue stuff of her gown, but her voice was cool with sisterly mockery. "I know you'd like to thrash Christopher in place of Julia's seducer, but you haven't the same cause, I assure you."

Bertram flushed. "I know that, Di. That is—of course I believe you. It's not what he did, it's what he tried to do." He subsided into the sofa cushions, though it was by no means clear that he had given up the thought of duels. Frank contented himself with the thought that Linton was out of the country and therefore beyond Bertram's reach.

Frank went on to describe what he and Charlotte and the others were planning to counter Ribard's moves. When he finished, Bertram was on his feet. "I want to help."

Frank regarded his brother-in-law for a long moment. "All right."

Bertram gave an involuntary start. "All right?"

Frank nodded. "It will be far more productive than fighting duels. Congratulations, Bertram. You've just become my new secretary."

"You've never had a secretary."

"No, and it's high time I did. I need someone to record the details of the meeting when Ribard and I wait on Silverton on Friday next to persuade him to cooperate with our plans."

A slow smile spread across Bertram's face. "Thank you, Francis."

Frank returned the smile. "I believe that's the first time you've called me Francis. It appears we've made progress this evening after all."

Bertram gave a sheepish smile, then turned serious. "I won't disappoint you."

"No," said Frank, looking straight into Bertram's blue-green eyes, "I don't believe you will."

Diana drummed her fingers on the sofa arm. "It's all very well for you. I wish—"

"I know," Charlotte said. "The problem with this scheme is that it leaves disgustingly little for the women to do."

"Which makes it all the more remarkable," said Frank, "that I actually believe it has a chance of success."

A relieved laugh cut through the tension that had hung

over the library since they entered it. Diana got to her feet and said she must go up or she would never wake for her morning ride with Serena. Bertram, too, said his good nights. Charlotte lingered in the library. Frank was not sure whether he was glad or sorry.

He accompanied Diana and Bertram to the door. When the young Vaughans had left the room, he turned to find Charlotte watching him as though he were a picture she had just shifted to see from a different angle.

"That can't have been easy for you, but I think it was worth it," she said.

"Yes." Frank moved to the table. "As usual, Diana puts a romantic gloss on everything."

He could feel the steady pressure of Charlotte's gaze upon him. The light of the lamp on the library table fell half across her face, leaving the rest in shadow. "But even when that gloss is stripped away, the facts of the case— for once—seem to be in your favor," she said.

Frank turned up the wick on the lamp, stalling for time as he searched for the right words. "Facts have a way of shifting with the interpretation."

The light from the lamp spilled across the red and gold carpet. The irony had faded from Charlotte's eyes, replaced by a glow that twisted his guts. "Diana's right," she said. "Julia Vaughan was fortunate. And Juliet is fortunate to have you for a father."

Frank spread his hands palm down on the cool, finely textured leather of the tabletop. It had been one thing to let Diana's story stand when Diana and Bertram were in the room. Preserving Julia's memory as Julia would have wanted it and concern for the youthful vulnerability of Diana and Bertram had all played neatly into his hand. Charlotte was another matter. Charlotte was not Julia's sister, and God knew her eyes were already open to human frailty. Especially his.

And there was the rub. "Julia wasn't in love with me," he said, his gaze on his hands. "I wasn't in love with her. We scarcely knew each other."

"Yet she trusted you enough to turn to you. And you love her daughter as if she were your own."

Frank looked up. Shadows nestled in the amber folds of Charlotte's gown, but her face glowed like the moonstone earrings that swayed against her skin. Five years ago he would have given all his worldly ambitions to have her smile at him like that. Then as now she had looked at his behavior through a warped glass. Five years ago she had condemned him. Tonight she was smiling at him. But her image of him was as distorted now as it had been then. The irony of the moment bit him sharp in the throat.

And yet even gilded brass could dazzle the eye and warm the soul. He could not bring himself to destroy the glow in her eyes, however false the reasons for it. "Juliet's an easy child to love," he said.

"Yes." Charlotte's betrothal ring flashed in the light as she toyed with the kitten's fur. "Do you—forgive me, you needn't answer if you don't wish to—but do you really not know who the father is?"

He moved to the sofa opposite her. "Until a few weeks ago, I thought it was Silverton."

"Good God." Charlotte stared at him. "So that was why—oh, Frank, no wonder you were so disgusted when I asked you to rescue him."

Frank bent down to pet Millamant, who was lying by his feet. "I confess that at the time I thought Silverton not particularly worthy of assistance."

"And now?"

He picked up Millamant and settled her in his lap. "The bribe was a mistake, but he's beaten himself up enough about it. I doubt he's more corrupt than the average man in Westminster. Despite his misguided party affiliation, we could almost be friends."

Charlotte laced her fingers together over the kitten's back. "What made you think it was Silverton?"

Frank pulled on Millamant's long ears. "Julia told me. She'd always refused to talk about the baby's father, but when she was dying I had some mad impulse to know. I told myself it was for Juliet's sake, but in truth it was for my own. She whispered Silverton's name. I took her at her word. I should have known that even then she was trying to protect her lover. She was as singled-minded in her passions as Diana, and she had less sense to balance her sensibilities."

Charlotte smiled. "Don't tell me you've become an admirer of Miss Austen. When I think of how I teased you to try *Pride and Prejudice* and how stubbornly you resisted."

He smiled back. "My tastes have broadened."

They looked at each other in a moment of rare amity, sweet as canary wine. Charlotte lowered her gaze, as though discomfited by the intimacy. "You must have loathed Silverton as much as Bertram once loathed you. And yet you still agreed—" She shook her head, honey-brown curls falling about her face. "I'll never understand you, Frank."

He continued to smile, though he could feel self-mockery creep into his expression. "I rarely understand myself."

Her dark brows drew together. With typical honesty she pushed through the problem instead of shying away from it. "You married Julia and saved her from disgrace. You forced me to marry you by agreeing to save the man you thought had seduced Juliet's mother. I still don't understand why you did it."

She was leaning forward. Her lips were parted slightly.

He could taste the remembered sweetness of their kiss. Sometimes it seemed that the closer they grew, the more she remained out of reach. He set Millamant down and got to his feet. To be alone with Charlotte in this lamplit intimacy was suddenly a torture like ice on bare skin. "Diana would no doubt say I did it because I fell in love with you the first time I saw you and have never recovered. Not sharing Diana's romantic view of the world, I am unable to give an answer."

Charlotte's eyes went very wide, still as a Highland loch on a windless day.

He looked at her a moment longer, then turned on his heel and left the room.

Chapter 22

Silverton rapped on the door of Céline's boudoir, hesitated a moment in the hushed, candlelit silence of the corridor, then turned the handle and opened the door.

His wife was stretched out on her chaise longue, one arm resting on the back, supporting her head, the other holding a book. She didn't seem to have heard his knock or the opening of the door. He lingered in the doorway, watching the curve of her head bent over the book, the flutter of her finger turning the page, the soft rise and fall of her breasts. Her hair was pinned back from her face and tumbled girlishly down her back. The lacy skirt of her peignoir was rucked up, revealing a coltish length of bare leg. The light from the brace of candles on the table beside the chaise longue glinted off her hair and cast a soft glow over her skin.

Fifteen years melted away. He was looking at the girl he had first glimpsed at Lady Harrowby's breakfast, giggling with her cousin Sophie. A pang of loss tightened his throat, sharp and bittersweet. The loss of something he had never known he had or realized he wanted.

"Silverton." Céline looked up with a start. "I didn't realize you were there."

"You said—" He swallowed, surprised to find his

mouth had gone dry. "You said you wanted me to keep you informed."

"Yes." She closed the book and swung her legs to the floor, regrettably smoothing her skirt over them. "The meeting went well?"

Silverton smiled in spite of himself. "Ribard and Storbridge sought me out at White's after the House rose this evening. Young Bertram was with them. Storbridge has made him his secretary."

"Bertram Vaughan?"

Silverton moved to a chair near the chaise longue. "A new Bertram Vaughan. Sober and serious and determined to live up to his responsibilities. Storbridge has taken him into his confidence. He sent me a note about it earlier in the day."

Céline raised her pale brows. "I'd have sworn Bertram resented Francis too much to make a decent fellow conspirator."

"Storbridge seems to have won him over."

"I suspect Francis Storbridge is rather good at winning people over." Céline's mouth curved in an appreciative smile.

Silverton didn't care for the smile or the warmth in his wife's voice. "He knows how to employ charm."

"So do you, my sweet."

He wasn't sure whether this was a compliment or a rebuke. He wasn't sure he wanted to know. He clasped his hands together. "At all events, I don't think we need worry about Bertram."

Céline smoothed the shimmering violet fabric of her skirt. "*Pa*—Daniel behaved according to expectation?"

Silverton rested his head against the chair back. It was hard and stiff, despite the figured damask upholstery. "Insofar as one can ever know what Ribard is thinking. He let Storbridge do most of the talking. Storbridge produced my note to Sunderland. I went suitably pale—it wasn't hard, I can't stand the sight of the damn thing. Storbridge outlined the influence they wanted me to exert on behalf of their Peruvian friend. I made affronted noises, then relented. It was rather a lark. It reminded me of those theatricals we got up at Morland a few Christmases ago."

"She Stoops to Conquer." Céline's eyes lit with the memory. "I'd forgotten. You made an admirable Charles Marlow."

"And you were a very fetching Kate Hardcastle. Though everyone said it was a great waste for a husband and wife to play opposite each other."

Céline gave a quick, involuntary smile, then looked down at her hands. "How did the meeting with Daniel end?"

"I'm supposedly going to talk to Canning. We're to finalize the negotiations Tuesday next with Durward—I mean, the *conde*. At a dinner at Charlotte and Storbridge's. Ribard's idea."

Céline sat up very straight. "Good God, Sophie and Paul will be there."

"That would hardly stop Ribard. He suggested Storbridge invite Emma and Robert as well. Make it look like a family party."

"But surely—surely it's a bit much even for Daniel to conduct illicit business under the nose of a pair of journalists."

"Ribard would say that's just where no one would expect him to conduct illicit business. But the truth is, I think he wants to see all of them together—Storbridge and Charlotte and all Charlotte's radical relatives. So he can test who's really on which side."

Céline gripped her hands together. "It won't be easy for Charlie."

"No, but she managed at the wedding breakfast, and then she didn't have any warning." Silverton studied his wife for a moment. They had never really discussed her feelings for her father. "For the look of the thing, you should be there as well. Do you mind?"

"No, of course not. That is—" She rubbed her arms, her white fingers pressing into the silk and lace. "I can't deny I'm uncomfortable in his presence. My skin crawls. I suppose I still can't quite accept what he did. But I don't want to run away." She loosened her hold and smoothed the crushed fabric. "Will it be over after that?"

"Storbridge thinks so."

Céline looked down at her hands. "I'm proud of you, Silver."

A bitter taste welled up on his tongue. "I've done little enough."

She looked up at him. "You've owned up to your mistakes. That's more than most people do."

"In the circumstances it was the *least* I could do."

Silence fell over the boudoir. He found himself searching for something more to say, wanting to prolong the discussion, unable to find a reason to do so. He gripped the arms of his chair and leaned forward. He knew he should leave, but somehow he could not quite manage to push himself to his feet. "I just wanted to be sure you knew."

She pressed her finger over a wrinkle that remained in her sleeve. "Thank you."

Silence again. There was really no excuse to linger. He would only embarrass her. He pushed himself to his feet.

Céline looked up. "It's a long time since we've talked so freely."

"Too long." He went still, looking down at her. The light of the candles and the flickering of the fire encircled them in unexpected intimacy.

Céline toyed with the lace frill on her sleeve. "When did we stop? Talking to each other, I mean." Her fingers tightened on the lace. "Or did we ever talk?"

He squelched the facile answer that sprang to his lips. "I don't know." He dropped back into his chair.

"It's a betrayal of its own, isn't it? Not talking. As real as—as the other."

"Yes, I suppose you're right." He sat forward on the edge of the chair.

Her nail snagged on the lace. She tugged it free. "When we first married . . . did you always assume you wouldn't . . . that is . . . oh, the devil, why is it so hard to say? Did you always assume you'd keep a mistress?"

He sucked in his breath. "I don't believe I thought about it much one way or the other." His voice was stripped raw with honesty. He scarcely recognized it.

She looked up at him, her eyes blue and candid and incredibly beautiful. "Nor did I. That is, I didn't assume I'd take lovers. It just came to seem inevitable. Not so much because I wanted to as because—"

"Everyone else did?"

They regarded each other in silence. In that moment there was perhaps less pretense than at any point in their marriage. "Yes," she said.

Silence stretched between them again, but a different silence—thoughtful, tentative, shimmering with hope, like the candlelight striking the damask upholstery.

"Silver—" Céline put out her hand. "If we've learned nothing else from all this, surely we've learned that it's possible to change."

He chose his words with care. He already felt as vulnerable as if his skin was exposed to the elements. "Are you saying you want to change?"

He could see in her face that she, too, was picking her way through uncharted territory, wary of the traps it might hold. "I think I'm saying that when I'm married to one of the more interesting and attractive men in London, it seems foolish to seek consolation elsewhere."

Beneath the light, brittle voice lay something unsought, undreamed of, and unbearably sweet. Silverton dropped to his knees at her feet. "My darling. I don't know whether I've been mad or blind or simply too afraid to admit what I wanted. I've been such a fool."

Her arm came around his shoulders. She bent over him. Her hair brushed his skin, and the scent of jasmine and tuberose washed over him. "Then at least we can be fools together," she said, and pressed her lips against his forehead.

"He'll come early. A quarter hour." Charlotte stopped pacing the Aubusson drawing-room carpet to adjust the clasp on her pearl bracelet beneath the rose-shaded light of a lamp. "So he can catch us on our own before the other guests arrive."

"Twenty minutes, not fifteen," said Frank.

"Why twenty?" The silver clasp slipped from her hold, jabbing her in the finger.

"Because he knows you'll be expecting fifteen. Here, let me do that."

He crossed to her side. She made no protest and held herself still while he snapped the clasp into place. She could feel his fingers skimming her skin through the kid of her gloves. She was trembling, but the trembling was so deep inside she didn't think he could be aware of it. "You're very good at that," she said, speaking through her rapid breathing.

"I've had my share of practice." He released her wrist, but stood looking down at her. "You look beautiful."

She felt an absurd flush of gratification. She was wearing a new dress Sophie had helped her choose, French lace over a slip of primrose satin. The neck was lower than she was used to, but the fashionable style gave her much-needed confidence. "Do you always know just what to say to a lady?" she asked, the playful words coming to her mouth unbidden.

"On the contrary. With you in particular, I frequently get it abysmally wrong." He looked at her for a moment. "Are you sure you're ready for this, Charlie?"

She took a step away, on the pretext of adjusting the vase of dried flowers on the Pembroke table. "If I were going to dissolve into hysterics at the sight of Daniel, I'd have done it by now."

His gaze moved over her face, probing yet uncharacteristically soft. "It's wise to hide weakness from an opponent, but it's generally thought prudent to admit it to an ally."

She crumbled a bit of flower between her fingers. The pungent scent of dried lavender filled the room, as potent as memories. "I can face Daniel, Frank. I'll never be able to live with myself if I don't."

"Yes, I rather thought so," he said, coming to stand beside her. "It's my one justification for putting you through this."

She looked up at him, raising her chin. "I'm putting myself through it."

The corner of his mouth lifted in a smile. "Of course." He brushed his fingers against her cheek, the way he sometimes did. Her body tightened with conflicting impulses. Yet there was something unexpectedly comforting about the familiar gesture. And that, perhaps, was more unsettling than anything. Three months ago she would never have believed that she and Frank could possibly develop a physical vocabulary of their own.

The door swung open, stirring the candlelight and

lavender-scented air. There was a rustle of silk as Sophie and Diana stepped into the room, Paul and Bertram just behind them.

Sophie swept forward with the confidence of an actress on a first night. She was dressed with defiant brilliance in geranium-red figured levantine. "Well?" she said, her voice bright. "Are all the props in place?"

Frank turned from Charlotte, his composure seemingly in place. "Tonight's performance doesn't rely on props. We succeed or fail based on sheer acting ability."

Bertram moved to the fireplace. His eyes glittered, not from drink for once but from excitement. "We won't fail. We've got Ribard completely taken in."

Frank turned to his brother-in-law. "No one's better at double-dealing than Ribard, Bertram. Never underestimate him."

Diana dropped down on the sofa. "I can't believe we have to sit down to dinner with him and be civilized. I'd like to scratch his eyes out."

"I understand the impulse." Sophie stopped in front of a pier glass to adust a ringlet that had escaped her silver bandeau. "But it would do little good. I sometimes think Uncle Daniel is indestructible."

"On the contrary." Paul had wandered across the room and was staring at a painting of the first Earl Vaughan as though he didn't really see it. "Ribard is as human as the rest of us. He could have died five years ago. He would have if I hadn't intervened. Then, of course, we'd be missing out on all this excitement."

Charlotte studied her brother's face, which could be so like Daniel's at times and yet was so very different. She walked across the room and laid a hand on his arm. "If you hadn't saved Daniel, you would have destroyed something within yourself. That would have been worse."

Paul squeezed her fingers. "Would it? You'll forgive me if there are times when I wonder."

Charlotte returned the pressure of his hand and glanced at the ormolu clock that stood on the mantel between a pair of gleaming black basaltware candelabra. The delicate filigree hands pointed to ten minutes past seven. Twenty minutes before Daniel was due to arrive. Through her gloves, she could feel a film of sweat break out on her palms.

Two minutes later, give or take a second or two, the drawing-room door opened. "The Marquis de Ribard," Alan announced. Charlotte wondered if there was sympathy in the footman's gaze or if she was imagining it.

Daniel strolled into the room at a leisurely, unhurried pace, quite as if he were entering one of his own homes. He was always at his magnetic best in evening dress, sleek and dark and unruffled.

"Ribard." Frank walked forward, his hand extended. "Glad you could join us."

"On the contrary." Daniel clasped Frank's hand. "It's I who owe you thanks for the invitation." He looked at Charlotte for the first time. "Charlie." His voice was friendly, his eyes smiling, his manner all affable, faintly rueful courtesy. "You're looking very lovely. Marriage seems to agree with you."

Once a compliment from her father had flushed her with pride and given her the confidence to stand beside her regal mother and ravishing sisters. Now she walked deliberately toward him and stopped a half dozen feet away, close enough to see the lines about his eyes and forehead that had not been there when she was a child. "Let me make this clear, Daniel. I don't want you here. I don't want to be here. I don't want you to sit down to dinner with my family. The only reason you're in this house is because my *husband*"—she flashed a glance at Frank—"insisted on it."

Frank deflected her glare. "You'll have to forgive us, Ribard. You've come in on a domestic dispute."

"You've come in on a war," Charlotte said.

"I see." Daniel's gaze shifted from her to Frank, as though he were observing a tennis match. "I won't pretend I'm surprised, *ma chère*."

His voice warmed on the French inflection, slashing unexpectedly at her defenses. She held herself still, refusing to give ground.

It was Daniel who turned away to greet the others. "Sophie, my dear. I'm glad you still find time to visit London."

"Uncle Daniel." Sophie gave him a smile that was as dazzling and impenetrable as polished armor. "I trust you don't expect me to shake hands."

Daniel returned the smile with disgusting ease. "Hypocrisy would only diminish us both, *chérie*." He inclined his head at the others. "Lady Diana, a pleasure. Vaughan, I'm grateful for your hospitality." He looked last at Paul. "Lescaut. I'd have given it as even money whether or not you'd join us."

Paul was standing close at Sophie's side, his arm around her waist. "You can't think me much of a brother if you imagine I'd leave Charlotte to face you alone."

"Of course. Forgive me." Daniel regarded Paul for a long moment. "I know you want nothing from me. But you must allow me to thank you for taking such good care of Charlie."

Paul returned Daniel's regard. From the side, Charlotte saw the two profiles, the identical slanting brows, the firmly set chins, the straight, arrogant noses. "Charlie can take care of herself," Paul said. "But anything I have done for her has been for her sake alone."

"Of course," Daniel said. His gaze shifted to Sophie. "At the wedding breakfast I didn't get a chance to congratulate you on the birth of your son. What have you called him?"

"Gerry." Sophie's gaze was blue and bright and unwavering. "After Paul's Uncle Gerard, who raised him."

"Of course." There was the faintest softness in Daniel's eyes, almost a touch of well-concealed wistfulness. "I won't presume to ask to see him. But I trust you'll let me say I took a certain delight in hearing of his birth. The only son of an only son."

Charlotte sucked in her breath. For over thirty years Daniel had refused to acknowledge Paul's paternity. Now he admitted it with simple, disarming candor. How diabolical. Yet for an instant she saw that he had slipped under Paul's guard. As he had slipped under her own.

"There's hardly a parallel." Paul's voice was as caustic as lye. "Gerry has the good fortune to know who his father is, rather than being obliged to guess."

Daniel inclined his head. "A crude blow. But effective. You haven't lost your sting."

"In one respect," Sophie said, "Paul is very like you."

The door opened again on the silence that followed this remark. Alan announced Lord and Lady Silverton and Mr. and Mrs. Robert Lescaut, who had apparently arrived at Vaughan House simultaneously. Charlotte went forward to greet them. Silverton appeared nervous and edgy, a good display of acting talent—though in truth, he had plenty of reason to appear nervous and edgy. Céline, whom Charlotte had expected to reflect some of her own strain, was unexpectedly serene. She was also clinging to Silverton's arm in an uncharacteristic manner. Robert surveyed Daniel with frankly appraising eyes. Emma pressed Charlotte's hand with a sympathy that was at once genuine and a good show for Daniel.

The company disposed themselves about the room. The tension was as thick as Devonshire cream. Charlotte could feel it pressing against the watered-silk walls. It was difficult to remember that she was not supposed to smooth things over, that this was precisely the effect they had been striving for.

The door opened again. "The *Conde* d'Amarante," Alan announced.

Adam entered the room with measured, courtly dignity. "Mr. Storbridge, so kind of you to invite me to your excellent house. I am enchanted by the building. A trifle cold, yes, but so grand, so formal, so very English. And this must be the charming Mrs. Storbridge?"

Frank inclined his head. "Charlotte, the *Conde* d'Amarante."

Adam bowed over Charlotte's hand with practiced gallantry, yet there was something about the gesture that was as reassuring as if he had winked at her. "An English rose." He glanced at Frank. "It is permitted to say so? The English rules of gallantry, they are a mystery to me."

Charlotte cast a glance at Frank. "Pay no attention to what my husband may say. I find it charming. Come and meet the rest of the guests."

She drew Adam forward. The game was under way.

Chapter 23

Adam accepted a glass of whisky from Frank and settled back on the library sofa with the dignified elegance of the *Conde* d'Amarante. "A splendid drink. Another delightful invention of your country. Though I understand it comes not from England but from your colony to the north."

Bertram choked on his own whisky. "Scotland's a part of Britain, not a colony."

Adam shrugged. "Labels. You will forgive me if I express sympathy for any country that does not possess national sovereignty."

Ribard leaned back and crossed his legs. "Personally, much as I love my adoptive country, I shall never find anything to equal good French brandy."

Frank moved a chair between Bertram and the silent Silverton. The five of them had removed to the library after dinner to conclude their business, while Charlotte entertained the other guests in the drawing room. "Perhaps we should progress to the subject at hand," Frank said.

"By all means." Adam twisted his glass between his hands. The candlelight played off the etched glass, refracted into myriad, shifting patterns. "It would seem to be a simple enough proposition. I want recognition for my country. My lord Ribard wants to mine the iron on my land."

"That's it in a nutshell," Frank agreed.

"My lord Ribard, as I understand, has no influence over the government," Adam continued.

"No direct influence." A smile played about Ribard's lips. "But you, my lord Silverton. You do."

Silverton squared his shoulders. "I am a junior minister."

"Quite so. And you wish to help your father-in-law?"

Silverton's jaw clenched. He was playing the scene to perfection. "I will provide the assistance he has requested."

Adam lifted his brows and glanced from Ribard to Silverton, then shrugged. "How you arrived at the accommodation is your own affair. In my family we pride ourselves on strong ties of the blood."

Ribard set down his glass. "In our family we pride ourselves on practical arrangements."

Frank leaned forward. "And in the name of practicality I suggest that the arrangements be in writing. So it is quite clear who has agreed to what."

Adam relaxed back into the crimson velvet of the sofa. "Not a pleasant thing for me to put in your hands."

Ribard took a sip of old Lord Vaughan's best brandy. "Those were my thoughts at first, d'Amarante. But Storbridge pointed out that we'd all be equally at risk if the paper ever became public." He flicked a glance at Frank. "I must say, at times Storbridge can be quite convincing."

Adam pulled at his very authentic-looking mustache. "If we put the agreement in writing, then we both retain copies."

Ribard nodded. "Agreed. And we all sign it. Storbridge and Vaughan as well."

"Why?" Bertram looked up from his own drink. "Storbridge isn't agreeing to anything. And I'm just acting as his secretary."

"So none of us can afford to turn the information against the others," Frank said. "How trusting, Ribard."

"I trust you as much as you trust me, Storbridge. I take it I have your agreement?"

"We've already discussed this," Frank said. "I'm in agreement provided you sign as well."

"Silverton?"

Silverton grimaced. "I'm in no position to protest."

Adam hesitated just the right amount of time. Then he tossed off the last of his whisky. "Very well."

Ribard glanced at Frank. "I trust you have pen and ink handy, Storbridge. Let's get this done. Then we can have another drink to seal the bargain."

"Bertram?" Frank said.

Bertram stood and walked to his father's Sheraton writing desk, as though conscious of the gravity of the moment. Frank watched as his brother-in-law wrote out two copies of the terms they had agreed to. Ribard and Adam remained by the fire and talked quietly about trivialities. Silverton was silent.

When Bertram was done, they all moved to the desk. Ribard signed the documents with a flourish, Adam with precision, Silverton with an air of grudging acceptance. Bertram cast a questioning look at Frank, then added his own name. Finally Frank signed at the bottom of both papers.

"There." Frank stepped back from the desk. "Shall we—"

Adam was staring down at the two pieces of paper, a look of distaste on his face. "So." He glanced at Ribard. "You were right. I couldn't believe two such seemingly upright young men were capable of such corruption until I saw it with my own eyes." His gaze went from Frank to Silverton, as though they were some particularly low form of vermin.

Ribard rested one hand on the desk and met Frank's gaze. "You disappoint me, Storbridge. I thought I'd trained you better. I'll admit you and Silverton kept up a pretense of enmity remarkably well. But did you really think I'd be so careless as not to note the date on that all-important bill from the bootmaker?"

Frank looked straight into Ribard's eyes. "I don't suppose it would do any good to say I haven't the least idea what you're talking about?"

Ribard smiled. "None. At least you know when to cut your losses. Commendable."

"See here—" Silverton began.

"It is not a humorous matter." Adam drew himself up very tall. His mustache quivered with indignation. "You have violated the sacred trust placed in you by your country. I may be a stranger here, but I am not so lacking in connections as you think. I shall take this"—he snatched up his copy of the document—"and show your political superiors how willing you are to sell your favors."

Frank turned to Adam with a carefully calculated look of alarm tempered by self-control. "My lord, I don't think you realize—"

"No." Adam flung up a hand. "Do not attempt to make excuses for yourself. I shall see myself out. My compliments to the charming Mrs. Storbridge. For her sake I am glad she is ignorant of these events."

He strode from the room, leaving silence in his wake. Ribard lifted the second copy of the document and tapped it against the writing desk. "I quite see your objective, Storbridge. And yours, Silverton. You thought if you could get me to put my name to something incriminating, you would be able to order my actions to your liking. Your mistake was not being sure which way the *conde* would jump. He's a very moral man, as I made sure to discover before I committed myself."

Bertram was frowning. "But your name's on the document as well. Surely if the *conde* shows it to anyone—"

"He will say that I was simply attempting to obtain proof of my sons-in-law's corruption. It saddens me to expose them, but my duty to the country comes first."

Silverton dropped into a chair. "Oh, Christ. Stop gloating, Ribard. It's disgusting."

"You needn't look so tragic, Silver." Ribard folded the paper and put it inside his coat. "I can assure the *conde* that my sons-in-law are repentant and that I wish to rescue them for my daughters' sake. I believe I can convince him to give me the other copy of the document."

Frank folded his arms across his chest. "For what price?"

Ribard looked at him with weary patience. "It's really quite simple. You and Silverton throw your support behind the Lancaster and Liverpool Railway. That, if you'll remember, has been my objective all along. If the two of you had gone along with my plans from the first, we could have been spared all this tiresome game-playing."

Bertram looked at Frank. "You can't agree."

Frank looked at Silverton. "On the contrary. I don't see that we can do anything else."

Bertram opened his eyes very wide. "But—"

"One of the first lessons of politics, Bertram, is to know when you're beaten."

"I'm delighted to hear it." Ribard moved toward the door. "I won't stay longer. I trust our future dealings will be somewhat less convoluted than these negotiations." He turned, his hand on the doorknob, and smiled at the three of them with punctilious politeness. "Thank Charlie for the excellent dinner."

The door closed behind Daniel de Ribard. Frank, Silverton, and Bertram remained where they were for a long moment, none daring to move. At last Frank raised his head from a contemplation of the medallions on the carpet. Silverton met his gaze, and then Bertram. At the same moment, all three of them burst into triumphant whoops of laughter.

"I still don't understand part of the plan." Diana set down her gold-rimmed teacup and looked from Frank and Silverton to the other conspirators gathered in the drawing room. "How can you use the paper against Ribard when he made all of you sign it?"

Frank, who was standing by the fireplace, gave a slow smile. Damn the man, Charlotte thought—her own nerves frayed to the breaking point—he was enjoying this. "But we have Adam," he said. "Ribard thinks the *conde* will support the story that they were both acting to entrap us. In fact, Adam will support that *we* were acting to entrap Ribard. How could we have meant to make corrupt deals to obtain the *conde*'s iron when we knew all along that the *conde* is Adam Durward? Adam may be a maverick, but there are a number of people in the government who owe him favors. They'll listen."

Sophie sent a smile of congratulations to Frank and Silverton and Bertram. "Caroline will be glad when Adam can move home from Mivart's Hotel."

Céline toyed with the scalloped end of her lace scarf. "I still can't quite believe Daniel was taken in by the *conde*. He's bound to have investigated all of us exhaustively. He must know Robert and Adam worked in Spain and that Adam supposedly was called back to France just before the *conde* arrived in England—"

"It's possible." Robert exchanged glances with Emma. Charlotte was reminded of children, gleefully triumphant at having pulled the wool over the adults' eyes. "But he'll also have investigated the *Conde* d'Amarante exhaustively."

"And?" Céline asked.

Emma smoothed her willow green skirt. "He'll have found an innkeeper in Dover who swears he saw the *conde* disembark from the *Golden Lion*, two postboys along the Dover road who waited on him, and a serving maid who distinctly remembers the *conde* cursing the execrable Burgundy served at the White Hart in Gravesend."

"Not to mention a tailor in Bond Street from whom the *conde* ordered his very fashionable British clothes," Robert said. "And a prostitute in one of the best houses in Covent Garden who entertained the *conde* on more than one occasion."

Emma turned her head to look at her husband. Her wrought gold earrings swung beside her face. "I didn't know about that last. The lengths to which you'll go in the line of duty, darling."

Robert's smile was a private sort of answer, more reassuring than any words. "Old contacts. Delighted to help out. For a fee."

Emma lifted her brows. "A monetary fee?"

"What else do I have to offer?"

Emma reached for his hand. "I'll enlighten you sometime when we're alone."

Silverton turned to Frank. "What do we do next?"

"Lay the whole before Parliament. We knew Ribard was up to no good, but we had no proof, so we set a trap to catch him."

Silverton settled back on the sofa. He was sitting beside Céline—in fact, Charlotte noticed with belated surprise, he had his arm around Céline. His fingers were skimming against the bare skin above the ruched neck of her gown. Charlotte couldn't remember when she had last seen them sit thus. "When do we make our move?" he asked.

Frank picked up the poker and pushed a fallen coal into the fire. "Howitt should be back from Italy by the end of the week. I want to speak to him first. It will help to have a strong presence in the Upper Chamber behind us."

Robert got to his feet and held out his hand to Emma. "We'd best go. Ribard may have someone watching the house. To linger too long would give the impression that we're all in collusion."

Emma took his hand. "Who on earth could be mad enough to think that?"

Charlotte stepped through the nursery doorway. After the evening with Daniel, which she could still not quite believe was over, she had felt a sudden need to see her stepdaughter. Juliet was asleep, flopped on her back, legs splayed out, one arm thrown over her head. The night-light made hills and valleys of shadow out of the bedclothes.

Charlotte smoothed the covers. In the few short weeks since the wedding, Juliet seemed to have grown an inordinate amount. Her body had lengthened, her face was thinner and more defined, her hair longer, curling against the nape of her neck and over her ears. She seemed to learn new words every day. Sometimes the thought that she had not been there for the first two years of Juliet's life brought a sharp ache to Charlotte's chest.

Juliet's blue eyes flickered open. "Mummy." She reached out a hand and touched Charlotte's lace skirt. "Pretty dress."

So much for thinking she could slip quietly into the nursery. Charlotte sat on the edge of the bed. "I'm sorry I woke you, darling."

Juliet pushed herself up against the pillows. "Get up?"

"No, it's still nighttime."

Juliet's chin took on a stubborn set, in a way that reminded Charlotte of Frank. "Not sleepy."

Charlotte patted the pale pink chintz quilt. "I know it's terribly boring, but you need to try."

"Ter'bly boring," Juliet repeated, trying out the new phrase. Her mouth widened in a smile. "Ter'bly boring."

"Careful where you say those words, poppet. They can get you into trouble."

Charlotte started. Frank was standing in the doorway behind them. He strolled into the room, smiling.

Juliet looked at him, eyes sapphire bright with hope. "Get up?"

"No, sweetheart, Mummy's right. It's nighttime." Frank dropped down on the bed opposite Charlotte.

Juliet settled back against the pillows. "I need story."

Charlotte suppressed a smile. *Need* was a favorite word with Juliet. Frank hooked his hands around his knees and launched into what sounded like a simplified version of *As You Like It* mixed with bits of *Robin Hood*. With his attention on his daughter, Charlotte had rare leisure to watch him. In the warm glow of the night-light, his face was relaxed and unguarded as it seldom was. His voice rose and fell with a soft cadence that held Juliet enthralled. Charlotte felt it having the same effect on her.

Juliet's eyes drifted closed. Frank let his voice trail off. He glanced up and met Charlotte's gaze. Charlotte flushed, realizing he would know she'd been watching him. He looked at her a moment, an unspoken question in his eyes. Then he eased himself off the bed, his finger to his lips.

They left the room in silence. "I'm sorry," Charlotte said, as he pulled the door shut on the lamplit warmth of the nursery. "I should have known she might wake if I went in. I gave way to selfishness. I wanted to see her."

Frank smiled. It was deceptive, that smile. It slipped under her guard like the deadly, quicksilver flash of a rapier. The smile faded and he looked at her for a moment. "Do you want to talk?"

"No. Yes. I'm not sure what there is to say." She moved into the corridor. Unlike the arrangement in most houses, Juliet's nursery was on the first floor with the other bed-chambers. Charlotte did not have to go far to reach her own room, but her legs had grown heavy and it seemed a great effort to move. She was cold. Her body ached as though from some great exertion. Was this how a prize-fighter felt after a long bout?

Too swift for thought, Frank's hands were on her shoulders. "Charlie, you're exhausted. Tonight was harder even than you realize."

Through the fatigue she felt the shock of the contact. The pressure of his fingers struck hammer blows on her heart. But she was too tired to pull away. No, that was untrue. She didn't want to pull away.

He steered her to a green satin bench on the opposite side of the corridor. She sank down on the smooth, cool fabric, not sure she could stand much longer, let alone walk. "I won't dispute the difficulties of the evening, but I'm not sure why it should bother me so much. I've faced Daniel before."

He sat beside her. "Guilt?"

She checked an instinctive denial and turned the possibility over in her mind. "Sometimes he can make me forget. I lose track of where I am—not geographically, but in relation to other people. Or if I know, I don't feel the things I should."

Frank smiled again. "People seldom do."

She stared down at her hands. She had got a tea stain on one of the fingers of her glove. "When I was ten years old Daniel hired a box at Drury Lane and took us all to see *King Lear*. Toward the end I desperately wanted Edmund and Edgar to shake hands and embrace as brothers. I quite forgot that Edmund had put out poor Gloucester's eyes only a few scenes before. Sometimes I feel the same way about Daniel."

"He's your father."

For once she didn't try to deny it. "Yes."

Frank was still for a moment. Then his arms encircled her shoulders with a light touch that asked for nothing more. "All right?" he murmured.

"Yes." She released her breath and let herself relax back against him. It felt amazingly right to have his arms around her. In the dangerous thicket between them they had found a small, sweet clearing of safety. She closed her eyes for a moment and felt the prickle of tears behind her lashes. She hadn't realized how much she needed to be held. "Will the plan work?" she asked.

"It's a risk." Frank's voice was muffled by her hair. "Ribard won't give in without a fight. A lot of the people who've invested in his railway will want to defend him. But we'll have allies of our own. With luck Silverton will bring Canning round to our side. And Howitt wields considerable power."

Frank's voice always warmed when he spoke of his patron. "You consider Howitt a good friend, don't you?" Charlotte said.

He gave a laugh that vibrated against her. "When we first met, I thought he was a stiff-necked puritan and he thought I was a degenerate reprobate. But in the intervening years I think we've both come to appreciate each other."

"I met him once years ago at a party in London. Lady Marianne was with him—they hadn't been married very long. But they were both very much on their dignity, in spite of being newlyweds."

"A duke and duchess have little escape from dignity. Annabel's the same way."

"Annabel?"

"Howitt's younger sister." Frank shifted his hands to a more comfortable hold. The satin and lace of her gown rustled beneath his touch. "Both families have always hoped she and Bertram will make a match of it, but neither Annabel nor Bertram have shown much interest in the prospect."

Charlotte let her head sink into the curve of his collarbone. "Are Howitt and Marianne happy?" It was a strange question to be asking of Frank, but the words were out before she could think twice about them.

Frank rested his chin on her hair. "I think so, when they let themselves be. Howitt's never kept a mistress. He has an appreciation of Whig principles, but a horror of Whig morality. The poor man doesn't quite know where to look when his friends start swapping stories over a late-night brandy at Brooks's."

Charlotte thought of some of the gossip she'd heard growing up. There was no shortage of profligacy among Tories either, but for many of the great Whig aristocrats it was a matter of family pride, from the scandalous ménage à trois at Devonshire House to the current generation like Caroline Lamb and Emily Cowper. She found herself wondering if Frank had bedded either of those ladies. The thought made her feel hollow inside. "Poor Howitt," she said, making her voice light with an effort. "What on earth do the two of you find to talk about?"

"Oh, the state of the world. Working conditions in factories. The need for better schools. Howitt may have been born to privilege, but he understands the plight of the unfortunate. And being born to power gives him one great advantage."

"What?" she asked.

He lifted a hand to disentangle a loose curl from one of her moonstone-and-seed pearl earrings. "He hasn't had to make compromises to acquire it."

She frowned. "Are you saying only the powerful can afford to be incorruptible?"

"I think Ribard disproves that."

She was silent for a moment, thinking of Daniel, and what they had done, and what might lie ahead.

"It isn't over," Frank said. "But for the moment we have the upper hand."

Despite everything, she felt a smile break across her face. She drew a breath, savoring the moment. The cedar scent of his skin washed over her. His breath ruffled her hair. All at once her blood quickened as though answering some primitive call.

Her skin felt raw, exposed, chilled, and scalded at once. Dear God, how could the line between tenderness and the baser cravings of the body be so frighteningly easy to cross? She felt the welling of panic that always overwhelmed her at the prospect of losing her self-control. And yet she didn't want to leave the haven of his embrace, however treacherous it had become. Ambivalence held her motionless. Perhaps tonight it would be all right. Perhaps they were both drained enough by the night's events that he wouldn't mind that she couldn't respond to him as he wanted.

He drew a long, uneven breath. Then he squeezed her shoulders and released her. She had the strangest feeling that he was proving to them both that he could do so. "Good night, Charlotte."

Chapter 24

"Francis, it is good to see you." Marianne, Duchess of Howitt, pressed a decorous, violet-scented kiss to Frank's cheek. "Dear Bertram." She moved on to embrace her brother. "I trust you haven't got into any scrapes that are too dreadful."

Bertram, Frank was pleased to see, did not color beyond a faint flush in his cheeks. "Welcome home, Mari." He gave his sister a hearty embrace. "We've missed you. Both of you," he added, looking beyond her to her husband.

"It's good to be home." William, Duke of Howitt, clasped Bertram's hand and then Frank's. The light from the Howitt House library windows fell across his face. Frank was surprised to see lines he had not remembered. Howitt's face had an austere look at the best of times, but now his nose seemed sharper, his cheekbones more pronounced, his mouth more set. He did not look like a man who had spent the last seven months on holiday in warmer climates. But then it was to be expected that he would be quick to resume the mantel of the dukedom.

"Much as I enjoyed Italy, it's a relief to be back in England." Marianne settled her Florentine silk shawl more precisely over her arms. "I never feel quite *settled* on foreign soil."

"You're looking very well for the journey," Frank said. He was pleased to see that the words brightened Marianne's face. At twenty-five she was a paler, more refined version of Diana. Her fair hair had only a hint of the Vaughan titian, her eyes were blue-gray rather than aquamarine, her manner quiet and reserved. She had married before Frank came to Vaughan House. He had never been sure if she had been born more sober than her siblings or if marriage to one of England's foremost peers and the swift birth of four children had tempered her spirits.

"I'll leave you," Marianne said, smiling at her husband. "I know William is longing to talk over all the details of the parliamentary session, and it's sure to take hours. Annabel and I are going to call on your wife tomorrow, Francis, since you were so disobliging as not to bring her yourself. Diana wrote me that she's quite transformed the atmosphere at Vaughan House."

Marianne was gone with a swish of her elaborately flounced gown. Howitt smiled at Frank, though the bleak look remained in his eyes. "We were sorry to miss the wedding."

"We were sorry not to have you there." Frank studied Howitt for a moment. William had always taken the responsibilities of his position seriously. He had succeeded to the dukedom at the age of fourteen, and there had been little escape from the role. Even the library, his retreat, was weighted with marble and a heavily carved cornice displaying the Howitt arms. Yet usually with his friends Howitt relaxed his guard somewhat. Today he seemed as armored by his role as if he were in full ducal regalia. "Is anything the matter, William?" Frank asked.

"The matter? No, just the general disorienting experience of returning from a long trip. You try crossing the channel with four children in tow." Howitt laughed, a shade too heartily, and waved his arm toward a grouping of sofas and chairs in a recess created by the columns that ran the length of the room. "Let's sit down. Marianne's right. I want to hear about the parliamentary session." He moved to an ebony-inlaid table and poured three glasses of sherry. The Howitt crest glinted again off the crystal of the decanter. "It was odd to be away when the session started." He carried two of the glasses over to Frank and Bertram. "I was tempted to come back early, but Marianne and Annabel were set on seeing Florence." He dropped into a chair opposite them. "You spoke on emancipation?"

"To singularly little effect. We're to try again in the spring." Frank sipped the sherry—a trifle sweet, but rich and mellow and aged to perfection. It was a taste he had associated with Howitt House ever since he had first accompanied Lord Vaughan on a visit to the duke. "Emancipation may be the most significant matter we discussed, but on a personal level there were matters of equal weight."

Howitt lifted his brows.

Frank set down his glass. "It's a long story, William, and not a pretty one." He proceeded to outline the events of the past two months, omitting only the details of his bargain with Charlotte. He had an impulse to tell his friend even that, but not in front of Bertram.

Howitt listened in sober silence, masking his surprise even better than Frank would have expected.

"I'm going to lay out the whole in a speech in the Commons tomorrow," Frank concluded. "There'll be the devil of a ruckus. Ribard has some prominent members of both parties as investors in his railway."

"Francis." Howitt turned his empty glass between his hands. His mouth was curled with distaste. Frank had seen the same look on his face once when they walked through one of the slummier parts of Covent Garden.

"I know," Frank said, "deception isn't particularly

heroic. But there was no other way we felt we could stop Ribard. And he has to be stopped. Not just for my sake and Charlotte's. I don't care to think of what he might do if he succeeds in reestablishing his base of power. Especially if our suspicions about Castlereagh's suicide are correct."

Howitt coughed and stared down into his empty glass. "That isn't—" He drew a breath. "Francis, I don't want you to do it."

Frank was rarely taken by surprise and almost never by Howitt, whom he had learned to read well. He stared at his friend. "Don't want me to do what?"

Howitt wiped a trace of sherry from the side of his glass. "I don't want you to make the speech."

For a moment Frank wasn't sure he had heard correctly. He sat back in the chair, his fingers closed on the carved arms. "Why not?"

Howitt stared into the cold, empty crystal of the glass. "That's my business."

Bertram sat forward in his chair. "What the bloody hell are you playing at, William? Don't you know how hard—"

Howitt continued to look at the glass. "This isn't your affair, Bertram."

Frank studied the man he had come to think of as one of his closest friends. Howitt's dark hair was combed perfectly into place. His sharp-boned face was intent and determined. How many times had Frank seen that determined intensity put to a noble end? "You're advising me as a friend that to denounce Ribard publicly may be dangerous?"

Howitt looked up. His eyes had gone flinty. "I'm telling you as your patron that you aren't to make the speech."

For a moment all Frank was aware of was the hard

wood of the chair arms, the thick upholstery of the chair, the heavy pile of the carpet. His brain refused to make sense of words that were beyond his comprehension. "You're *telling* me—"

"You could say it's an order."

Bertram gasped. Frank stared at Howitt. Howitt stared back, pale but unflinching. The door from the study swung open. The far end of the room was in shadow. But as footfalls sounded on the carpet, Frank suddenly knew whom he would see. He stared into the shadows and spoke over blinding anger, nausea, and self-disgust. "Hullo, Ribard. I should have known you couldn't be so easily deceived. But how the devil did you arrange this?"

"Surprised, Storbridge?" Ribard stepped into the light.

Frank looked straight into Ribard's eyes. "I shouldn't be. Though I confess I thought we had you taken in."

"You did." Ribard moved to the table where the sherry was set out. "May I, Howitt? Thank you." He poured himself a glass. "I quite believed the *Conde* d'Amarante. You must give Durward my compliments on his acting technique. And I don't believe I've ever seen such a well-laid cover story. But I felt it wise to be prepared for any eventuality. If you and Howitt had spoken only of the weather, I would have remained in the study. As it is—" He shrugged.

Bertram, who had been momentarily struck dumb, found his voice and pushed himself to his feet. "How dare you? How dare you stand there and—William, tell him to get the hell out of your house."

"I think that's the problem, Bertram," Frank said. "William invited him in." He looked at Howitt. "Well, old friend? What was your price? Surely that's the least we deserve to know."

Howitt blanched, but did not look away. Now that the

truth was out, pride or arrogance kept his gaze steady and his expression firm. "You must understand that I cannot afford to have Ribard injured. I recently agreed to his offer for Annabel's hand."

"What?" Bertram stared at Howitt as though he had taken leave of his senses. "You're going to let that monster marry Annabel—"

"You'd be wise to stay out of what you don't understand, Bertram." Howitt's voice was suddenly sharp.

"My God." Frank's last vestiges of sangfroid deserted him in a rush of cold rage. "What hold does Ribard have over you? What dark secret can't you afford to have sully the Howitt name?"

"That's enough, Storbridge." Howitt's voice cut with ducal force. "You will return the paper Ribard signed and say nothing more of the matter. Ribard will do nothing further to injure you or your family. The matter is closed."

"If you think I'm going to stand by and watch Ribard—"

"And if you persist in this matter, I shall be forced to ask you to stand down as the member for Howitt."

"Why you—" Bertram lunged forward.

Frank gripped Bertram's arm and pulled him back into his chair. "That won't help."

Ribard, who had been standing a little apart, moved to a chair between Howitt and Frank, once again dominating the scene. "In case loss of your seat isn't inducement enough, I can offer another incentive. As Charlie is part of this plot, I take it you are now on better terms— despite her performance last Tuesday, which was really quite remarkable. I gather that my daughter is rather important to you. You would not, I assume, wish to have the relations between you take a turn for the worse."

Frank looked at Ribard, relaxed in his chair like a serpent coiled to strike. "Whatever my relationship with Charlotte, it is one thing you can't touch."

"No? You'll have to be the judge of that." Ribard took a sip of sherry. "You're very fond of written agreements, aren't you, Storbridge? One would think from your attempt to trap me that you realized how dangerous they could be. Was your bargain with Charlotte in writing, I wonder? I should be interested to see how you worded it. I wonder what your first wife would make of your new marriage. And I wonder what Charlotte would think if she saw the agreement you entered into at the time you married Julia Vaughan."

Despite the fire blazing beneath the pedimented mantel, the room had grown cold. Frank did not speak, because there was nothing, really, that he could say.

Into the silence Bertram said, "What agreement?"

"Ah." Ribard turned his smile on Bertram. "You'll be interested as well, Vaughan. I don't suppose he's told you either. Storbridge signed an agreement with your father before he married your charming sister. He agreed to give a name to her child and keep silent about its true parentage, provided your father got him a seat in Parliament."

"Julia was in trouble." Bertram's voice was as stiff as his posture. "Francis came to her assistance. I'm very grateful to him."

Ribard smiled affably at Julia's brother. "You could argue that he came to her assistance. But was his goal to help her—or to turn the situation to his own advantage? How can one possibly guess at another's motives, you might say. But if Storbridge's chief aim was to protect your sister, then why did he insist that your father put in writing precisely what he would do to further his political career?"

The certainty in Bertram's eyes wavered. He looked at Frank. "Diana said it was Julia who asked William to find you a seat." He paused, a silent beat that marked the death knell of dawning friendship. "That isn't how it happened?"

Frank looked into the blue-green Vaughan eyes. "No. Julia was in no state to speak to your father about anything. I went to him with the story. I told him my price was a seat in Parliament. I got it in writing."

Bertram's eyes were filled with confusion, like a puppy who can't quite comprehend that it has been kicked. "You lied to us."

Frank kept his gaze steady. "Julia was in trouble. She told me. I offered her a way out. I didn't lie about any of that."

"But you twisted it." The confusion in Bertram's eyes gave way to the anger of the betrayed. "You made it sound like some romantic novel."

"I think it was Diana who did that."

"And you let her."

"Yes. I let her. Would she be happier if I hadn't?"

"It's always lies, never the truth." Bertram pushed himself to his feet. "Diana said you loved Julia. Did you?"

"Bertram—"

"Did you?"

Truth, lies, the time of reckoning. Frank looked at Julia's brother without flinching. "No."

Bertram drew a long, shuddering breath. For a moment Frank thought the boy was going to hit him. God knew he had a right to. Instead, Bertram turned on his heel and strode from the room.

"You bastard." As the heavy library door crashed closed, Frank looked not at Ribard but at Howitt. "You'd put a paper into Ribard's hands that could destroy Julia's memory. And my daughter's future. I might forgive everything else, but not that."

Howitt had gone as pale as the alabaster of the mantel. He had never looked so weak and so much a duke.

"You're not a man to repine over what can't be helped, Storbridge," Ribard said. "I have the paper. You've seen young Vaughan react to it. Do you really want Charlotte to do the same?"

"Brooding again, Storbridge? I saw you slip out of the House. I can't say I blame you. It was a cursed dull debate. But usually you can find a more interesting refuge than the morning room at Brooks's."

Frank drew a breath and steeled himself to face Henry Brougham. "How did you know I was brooding?"

"Because you never read the *mirror of fashion*. Good God," Brougham added as Frank lowered the paper. "My dear chap, what's the matter?"

So much for trying to keep up a facade. "I had an unwelcome surprise," Frank said. The paper crackled between his fingers.

Brougham dropped into a chair separated from Frank's chair by a small table. "Where's your young secretary?"

Frank felt his mouth tighten. "Being rescued from his own folly by Silverton and Paul Lescaut. At least, I hope to God he is."

Brougham's thick, fair brows drew together. "You think he's in trouble? Why aren't you rescuing him yourself?"

"Because I'm the last person in the world he wants to see just now." Frank folded the paper. The dry, brittle feel of the newsprint and the lingering smell of ink reminded him of his talk with Paul Lescaut in the print shop in Edinburgh. He wondered what his brother-in-law would say

to him in his present dilemma. No, he knew perfectly
well what Paul would say. "Henry—" He looked at
Brougham, who was not Paul Lescaut and was no
stranger to compromise and ambition. "What would you
do if you were faced with a choice between losing your
honor or losing your seat in Parliament and all that went
with it?"

"That's melodramatic talk coming from you, Francis. Are we talking about hypotheticals or something in
particular?"

"We're talking."

"I see." Brougham stretched out his legs and contem-
plated the toes of his shoes. "I suppose first you'd have to
define *honor*. We bandy the word about a good deal, but
we rarely come up against its meaning."

"That's the question, isn't it?" Frank set the paper on
the table between them, carefully smoothing the wrinkles
from the pages. "Can it be defined? Does it exist at all?
Or does any politician worth his salt compromise himself
out of it at his first election?"

"Oh, no, not in the least. It takes years." Brougham
glanced up. "Sorry, bad joke."

"Perhaps a singularly apt joke."

"Look here, Francis." Brougham leaned across the table, crushing the paper beneath his elbow. "I don't know
what you're contemplating. But I do know that you can't
hope to do any good in the world unless you first acquire
the power to achieve your ends."

"Yes. Or so I always thought." Frank glanced around
the morning room. The middle-aged man snoring by the
fire would be a cabinet minister if the Whigs were in
power. The young men arguing over the rival merits of
two opera dancers were scions of two of the most powerful Whig families. Lord Vaughan had put Frank up for

membership at Brooks's when he and Julia became betrothed. It had seemed a milestone, almost as much a step into the inner sanctum of Whig politics as his election to Westminster. Frank turned his gaze back to Brougham. "But how do you know at what point you've compromised your ideals clean away?"

Brougham regarded him, his eyes shrewd and candid. "I don't know." He frowned, a quick contraction of his brows. "I'd be the last to claim I'm a saint. But I don't think I could go on if I stopped having some sort of faith in myself, however misguided."

Frank returned Brougham's regard, letting the words resonate in his head. Brougham, of course, did not know how very much more was at stake beyond his seat in Parliament. But the principle remained the same. He pushed himself to his feet. "Thank you, Henry."

"You've made a decision?"

"You've helped me make it. Please excuse me. I need to talk to my wife."

Brougham grinned. "That desperate, eh?"

"You could say so. If I don't talk to her, what faith I have left in myself will be quite destroyed."

"It's from Paul." Sophie nodded to the footman to withdraw as she slit open the note he had brought her.

Charlotte was on her feet without realizing she'd moved. "Have they found Bertram?"

Sophie scanned the single sheet of paper. "They've found him. At a coffeehouse in Covent Garden. Terribly foxed, but otherwise none the worse for wear. They're going to try to sober him up a bit and then bring him home."

"Does Paul tell us not to worry?"

Sophie smiled. *"Silverton said to tell you not to worry,"* she read from the letter, *"but I said that would only ensure that you worried, out of sheer bloody-mind-edness if nothing else. Please believe that I have no more idea what's going on than you do."*

Charlotte smiled at her brother's words, then felt the smile fade. "I wish Frank had told us something, instead of just sending word for Paul to go rescue Bertram. I wish Frank had come home himself. I wish we knew what had gone wrong."

"I won't argue with you there." Sophie returned to the sofa in Charlotte's boudoir, where they had been sitting. "But we're bound to know soon enough." She dropped down on the sofa, picking her way around Millamant, who was asleep on the floor. "At least the immediate crisis has been averted. There was a time when I would have laughed at the thought of Paul and Silverton working together so ably."

"Yes." Charlotte sat beside her cousin. "I suppose we must be grateful for small mercies." She stroked Knightly, who had jumped up beside her and was trying to play with the end of her bronze satin sash. "Sophie, have you noticed that Céline and Silverton seem . . . well . . ."

Sophie met her gaze, eyes laughing. "Yes, I have. Very much. This past week they've scarcely seemed able to keep their hands off each other. I always have the feeling they want to slip off and find a dark corner."

"Sophie!"

"Don't be missish, Charlie." Sophie picked up the teapot from the Pembroke table and refilled their teacups with a steady hand. "Newlyweds don't have a monopoly on delights in bed, you know. Or out of it."

"I didn't mean that." Charlotte reached for her teacup. The heat burned her fingers through the thin porcelain. She set the cup down and added a liberal amount of milk. "It just seems vaguely indecent to be talking about it."

She picked up a little silver spoon and kept her gaze on

her tea as she stirred it, but she could feel Sophie watching her. "What happens between two people in bed should never seem indecent, dearest, provided the pleasure is mutual," Sophie said. "It took me rather a long time to work that out. I'm afraid I wasted a good many years."

"You?" Charlotte was startled into looking up.

Sophie smiled with characteristic self-mockery. "In a lot of ways I was a hopelessly naive bride." She reached up to touch the lapis lazuli pendant, a gift from Paul, that she wore on a blue velvet ribbon around her throat. Her face went serious. "Tom—my first husband—and I were ill-matched from the first. You could say bed was practically the only place we were compatible."

Charlotte felt her face grow warm. "Sophie, you don't have to—"

"Don't blush, love. I'm not trying to shock you, I'm trying to make a point. Even when things were at their worst with Tom—even when he'd come home reeking of another woman's perfume and I knew she was very likely a friend of mine and we'd have the most blazing row— we'd somehow end up in bed. And I enjoyed it. I prided myself on being a sophisticated woman, but I was sure there must be something wrong with me for taking such pleasure from a man I couldn't respect. When I met Paul—when I realized how much he meant to me—it was hard to reconcile how the man I loved could rouse the same feelings as the man I'd come to despise."

Charlotte's fingers curled tightly around her teacup. Even with the added milk, the heat of the cup scalded her flesh. "Why are you telling me this?"

Sophie looked into her eyes and smiled—a simple, disarming smile. "Because I thought it might help. At the very least I knew it wouldn't hurt."

"Sophie—" Words clogged her throat, straining to

break free, but she couldn't find a way to give them voice. Perhaps Sophie had guessed. But perhaps she hadn't. And if not, Charlotte couldn't face putting the truth into words. Perhaps she had buried it too deeply ever to be able to dredge it up.

A rap sounded on the door. Charlotte started, spilling the tea. Knightly mewed and looked at her reproachfully.

Frank stepped into the room.

"Thank goodness." Charlotte sprang to her feet.

Even in the soft candlelight she could see that Frank's face was etched with weariness, but his mouth lifted in one of his customary smiles. "Forgive me for interrupting. I must confess to a burning desire for news of my scapegrace secretary."

"Bertram's fine." Charlotte went to Frank and took his arm. It seemed natural. She didn't even think about the fact that she had touched him until she felt his muscles go taut beneath her hand. Instead of pulling back, she smiled into his tired face. "Paul and Silverton are with him in a coffeehouse in Covent Garden. Is it very bad?"

He smiled again, but this time she noticed the shadows in his eyes. "Fair to middling." He bent down to acknowledge Millamant, who had run over and put her paws up on his leg.

Sophie got to her feet and walked over to them. "You want to tell Charlotte about it, and I have a feeling it's going to take rather a long time. I'll go down and wait for Paul and Silverton. They may need help with Bertram. Fortunately, I was once married to a rakehell. I know something about coping with inebriated young men."

Frank pressed her hand. "You're a remarkable woman, Sophie."

Sophie smiled. "I warn you, we're all going to want the story in the morning."

Sophie left the room with a characteristic whisper of silk and rose scent. Charlotte remained where she was, her hand on Frank's arm.

Frank looked down at her, as though searching for something. The look in his eyes stopped her from speaking. "Charlie. I have a story to tell you. Or perhaps it's a confession. You can be the judge."

Chapter 25

The tone and the set of his face told her just how grave this confession was. Impatience and fear roiled in her stomach. She forced them down and summoned up a smile. "Then we'd better sit down."

She returned to the sofa. Frank hesitated, then seated himself in a chair beside her. Close, but beyond touching distance.

There was an empty cup on the tea tray. Charlotte filled it, grateful to have something to do with her hands, and passed it to Frank. "You look as if you could do with something stronger, but I'm afraid this will have to suffice."

He smiled, a sweet, open smile, and took a long gulp of tea. He set down the cup and looked directly at her. "Ribard guessed. Or at least suspected. He got to Howitt ahead of me."

For a moment Charlotte thought she was going to be sick. She picked up Knightly and hugged him close to her chest. "How could he? Why would Howitt listen to him?"

"Ribard has something on William. William the incorruptible. He's agreed to let Ribard marry his sister."

"But—" Charlotte stared at her husband. "She must be younger than I am."

"By a few years, I would guess. She's one of the more eligible heiresses in London."

"An alliance with one of England's oldest families. He must have been planning this from the first. Respectability. Acceptance. Power. What's Annabel like?"

"Moderately clever. Overly conscious of the meaning of the Howitt name. She'll make a perfect hostess."

"And she can give him an heir. Maybe even a legitimate son this time." She pulled Knightly closer. "Howitt told you not to make the speech?"

"He said that if I denounce Ribard he will be forced to ask me to stand down as the representative of his pocket borough."

His mouth curled around the words *pocket borough*. Charlotte looked into his eyes. "Oh, Frank."

"But there's more, I'm afraid." Frank tossed off the last of his tea as though he wished it were whisky. "Ribard was there as well. He added his own inducement."

Her gaze did not leave his face. "What?"

He returned his teacup to the Pembroke table with deliberate care. "What I told you—what Diana told you— what I allowed you to believe about my first marriage wasn't entirely true. Wasn't true at all."

Knightly made a protesting mew. Charlotte loosed her hands. The kitten jumped down and curled up beside Millamant. "No?" she said after a long moment. "Do you want to tell me what is true?"

"I think I must. I think it's long overdue." He linked his hands together and stared down at them for a moment. "Julia was with child. But she didn't confide in me. I found her being sick into a Sèvres vase in the rose parlor. I guessed. She admitted."

Fragments of the past, never really settled, once more rearranged themselves in her head. "And?"

"I told her I thought I saw a way out. I was sorry for her—who wouldn't be? But I also saw the key to all my ambitions. If she'd been a country parson's daughter—if her father hadn't been able to give me everything I wanted—would I have offered for her? I doubt it. No, I know I wouldn't."

He looked up, straight into her eyes, as though it were a kind of penance. "What then?" she said.

"I went to Vaughan. I told him of his daughter's plight. I told him I was willing to marry her—for a price. I told him I wanted it in writing."

"I see. And Daniel has hold of whatever was written down?"

"Quick as always, Charlie." Frank dug his fingers into his hair. The candlelight glinted off a sheen of sweat on his forehead, but his voice was cool and steady. "Vaughan was angry—angry with Julia for getting herself in trouble, angry with me for my audacity. But he was a good negotiator. He was shrewd enough to see that this was a way out. He told me Howitt had a pocket borough vacant and might be willing to help for the sake of Marianne's sister. I told him I wanted a guarantee. We drew up a contract. Howitt witnessed it and kept a copy. Which he's now shown to Ribard, damn his soul to hell."

Charlotte fingered the russet terry velvet of her skirt. "So that's why Bertram ran off. And why you didn't think you could go after him."

Frank grimaced. "He was angry enough to start a fight with me and spill the whole story in a Covent Garden coffeehouse."

"Sensible of you not to risk it. Poor Bertram. You're obviously very important to him. His view of you can swing from admiration to loathing at the least provocation." She toyed with one of the velvet ribbons that confined her long gauze sleeves. "Daniel wasted some of his bargaining chips by telling Bertram. What else did he threaten—to make the whole story public?"

"He threatened to tell you."

She looked back at him, unblinking. "I see. He must think my opinion is of great value to you."

"Yes." His gaze shifted to the print on the opposite wall, an innocuous grotto with a waterfall. Charlotte was convinced that something in it reminded him of Julia. "I always said I didn't have enough money to buy my way into politics. But, you see, in the end I did buy my way in. I just used a different coin than most."

"Frank—"

He looked at her. "You said I was cut from the same cloth as Ribard. Even then I knew there was more than a grain of truth to it. But it took years for me to realize how much. I used Julia to give me the power and position I wanted. Just as Ribard is using Annabel Howitt."

She folded her hands in her lap. "Let me understand this. You're saying Lady Annabel is with child and Daniel is using that knowledge to force the marriage?"

"No. At least not to my knowledge. Ribard's hold seems to be on Howitt himself."

Charlotte sat back in her chair. "Your arrangement with Julia was a fair exchange. You got a seat in Parliament; she got a father for her child. Daniel is getting Lady Annabel's hand in exchange for his silence about some peccadillo of the Duke of Howitt's. Poor Lady Annabel doesn't gain anything at all, except the dubious honor of being Daniel's wife. From a woman's perspective the two cases are completely dissimilar."

"Are they? Or did Ribard and I just use different leverage?"

"If Julia hadn't been with child—if instead you'd learned something to Lord Vaughan's disadvantage—

would you have used that leverage to force him to agree to the marriage?"

He was silent for a long moment. The candlelight flickered over his drawn face, his tightly clenched, long-fingered hands. "No," he said at last. "I don't think I would. But I did use something to Silverton's disadvantage to force you to marry me."

His gaze met hers and held, dark, challenging. And yet she was suddenly reminded of Céline's boys when, in perverse moments, they wanted to prove to her just how naughty they had been. "Let me ask you something, Frank. If I'd walked out of your study that night and refused the bargain, what would you have done when Daniel offered you the letter?"

He released his breath in a harsh exhalation. "We'll never know, will we?"

"I think we do. I think I do. I think you'd have taken the letter from Daniel and burned it, just as you did with my help."

His gaze was steady and a little bleak. "That's Bertram's specialty, Charlie, rushing from one extreme judgment to another. You're too clever for that."

"You won't say it? All right, I will. I don't think your proposal was a proposal at all. I think it was a challenge. You wanted to see how far I would go. You wanted to see if I'd get down in the dirt and soil my hands in the game you'd been playing for so long. I think you were shocked when I agreed. Poor man. You found yourself married when all you'd been trying to do was tweak me on my sense of morality."

The candlelight wavered in his eyes. "Rubbish. I could have canceled the bargain in a minute. I would have, if I'd had a shred of honor left."

"You could have canceled the bargain. I'm not absolving you of guilt. But if you hadn't a shred of honor left, you'd never have told me about Julia." She leaned forward. "I was wrong five years ago. No, listen, Frank, this is important. Five years ago when you came to Edinburgh . . . I was cast totally adrift. Daniel went from seeming everything good to me to everything rotten. Ned too. And so I began to divide everything up into good and bad. I couldn't *see* anything in between. But the world is so much more gray than that. You've taught me that."

He gave a shout of laughter. "Have I? What a dreary lesson. The problem with living in a gray world, my darling, is that it becomes difficult to tell where light ends and dark begins. Until you become like Ribard, who doesn't know the difference. Or doesn't care."

"No, that's where you're wrong." She gripped his hands, willing him to understand. "You make compromises, it's true. But you couldn't be more different from Daniel. He has no moral center. There's a core of you that's untouched. If you can't see that, I can."

Frank sat absolutely still. A light flared in his eyes—disbelief, surprise, wonder? "And to think I always gave you credit for being insightful." The customary irony was still in his voice, but it was worn threadbare.

"Frank." She tightened her grip on his hands. "What you tell Daniel and Howitt—whether or not you make the speech—it's your decision."

His mouth lifted in a smile that was dry, but not bitter. "If you've guessed so much, surely you know the answer to that."

His gaze, for once, was as open as clear water. "Perhaps I'm the one who doesn't want to see you give up your career," she said.

"I don't want to give it up. Make no mistake." His mouth went hard, and in his eyes she could see the ache of loss. "You can question my motives—perhaps it's merely that I can't bear to let Ribard win. But I'm going to make the speech. Do you think you can accustom yourself to being married to a man whose only asset is a badly encumbered factory?"

"I think I could come to be rather proud of being married to you."

He lifted one hand and brushed it against her cheek. His fingers were warm, and she had a clear memory of them on other parts of her body. There was something new in his eyes, something hot and sweet and dangerous. She sucked in her breath.

He dropped his hand. His fingers clenched, then loosed as though with a deliberate effort. "Charlie—what in God's name did Rutledge do to you? What did that bastard do to you to make you so afraid?"

It was a moment before she understood. She stared at him. "How—"

Only then did he seem to realize what he had said. "Ribard told me. At the wedding breakfast."

"Oh, dear God, of course." She sat back. Even now Daniel could find ways to touch her. "Ned would have told him. That was the whole reason he did it, you know. Seduced me. Not that it took a lot of seduction. He told me he couldn't wait. That he was desperate for—for us to be together. But that wasn't the real reason. His schemes with Daniel were already collapsing. He guessed—rightly—that Daniel might leave him to take the blame. He wanted to have one more hold on Daniel. Blackmail again. That seems so obvious now. But at the time . . ."

Frank watched her. "Charlie, if he hurt you—"

"That's just it, Frank. He didn't hurt me. It was wonderful." The words came out in a furious rush. She put up her hand as though to call them back, but she was powerless to stop the torrent now that the dam had broken. "I thought Ned was wonderful. I couldn't see the truth. Not even when we were as intimate as two people can be. I only felt . . . delight."

The images were so vivid, for all she'd attempted to excise them from memory—the warmth of the September day, the cold marble of the bench in the garden folly, the heat of his hands, the soaring, intoxicating release. "Afterward I couldn't stop thinking about it. It was as though my body had discovered a will of its own. I came alive when I was with him." She pressed her hands over her face, though she could not shut out the images that were locked inside. "Even that last night when I went to confront him, when I knew what he was, I could feel the force of it. If he'd only had the sense to take me in his arms, he could have got me to do, to believe, whatever he wanted." A shudder racked her body. "What's wrong with me?" she said into her hands. "How could I take such pleasure from a murderer's touch?"

Frank pulled her hands from her face and brushed his fingers against her cheeks. She'd never seen such gentleness in his eyes. "Nothing's wrong with you except an open heart and a passionate nature. Thank God Rutledge wasn't able to destroy either one."

She looked into his eyes, seeking understanding. "When you kissed me that day in the garden I got hopelessly confused. Here I was responding to my friend the same way I had to my betrothed. I thought I was turning into a wanton."

He grimaced. "And so by the time you learned the truth about Rutledge, I'd made it impossible for you to confide in me."

"I suppose so. I couldn't think of you as just a friend anymore. I wanted desperately to go back to being the girl I'd been before, but I couldn't."

His fingers moved against her face. "Physical desire

isn't something that can conveniently be turned on and off."

"But how could Ned, of all people, have made me—"

"Rutledge only tapped something that was already inside you, Charlie. One doesn't have to love someone or even like them to feel desire. After all, I shared a very pleasant interval with Ianthe de Cazes." He dropped his hands and gave her a smile that demanded nothing in return. "And a few weeks ago you very nearly went to bed with me."

The room seemed to have gone very still. She could smell his shaving soap and the scent of the candles and the oil in the lamps. "The problem wasn't not liking you. Not then." She swallowed. "The problem wasn't not being . . . attracted to you."

"No. I begin to understand what the problem was. You didn't want to give yourself to anyone." He hesitated, as though perhaps he meant to say no more. At last he added, "Perhaps one day you'll trust me enough that you won't be afraid."

They had made themselves vulnerable to each other in every way but one. She looked into his eyes and spoke before she could let herself think too much. "If I'm afraid it's only of myself. And I do trust you." She swallowed. Her mouth was dry, as though it was parched for something she couldn't name. "Frank. Make love to me."

She could hear the change in his breathing. She could sense just how close he came to seizing her in his arms, which would have made the whole thing so much easier. But he didn't. He drew back. "Charlotte, no. Not like this. Not to prove something."

"Not to prove something." She kept her gaze steady on his own, though she could feel the erratic leap of her pulse and the pounding of the blood in her veins. "Because I want you to."

He was silent for so long she didn't think she could stand it, though she knew there was no way now she would turn back. Then he reached out and seized her hands.

His fingers closed convulsively around her own. His grip slackened to the lightest of touches and he drew her to her feet.

He didn't speak. He didn't kiss her. Holding her hand, he drew her across the room and through the door to her bedchamber.

She was dimly aware that the maids had made up the fire. She could feel its heat. Or perhaps the heat came from inside her. There was a brace of candles burning on the dressing table. He stopped where the warm light pooled on the carpet and fell across both their faces. He rested his hands lightly on her shoulders and looked down into her eyes, his own intent and strangely vulnerable. "Tell me if there's anything that . . . makes you uncomfortable." *Stirs unwelcome memories,* that's what he meant, but he wasn't going to refer to Ned even obliquely. He hesitated a moment. "If you want to stop, say so. And I will, I swear I will." He gave a shaky laugh. "If I don't, hit me."

"Last time you were the one who stopped. I don't remember your asking my permission." She tilted her head back and looked up at him. "Don't you think it's time you kissed me?"

She felt his warm, uneven breath on her skin as he bent his head. His lips brushed over her hair, her forehead, her cheek, and at last closed over her mouth.

It was the lightest of kisses, but she felt it to the tips of her ungloved fingers, to the soles of her satin-slippered feet. The needs she had buried for so long broke free, scalding, blinding, racking her body with an intensity almost too great for her to bear.

"Charlotte?" he murmured into her hair.

"Don't stop—I can't—Oh, Frank."

He found the buttons on the back of her gown and undid them so effortlessly that she didn't realize it until she felt his fingers playing against the nape of her neck and skimming over her shoulders.

He was good at this. She had known that. Even on the night of their bargain she had been both frightened and stirred by the sensual promise in his eyes. But she hadn't realized just how skilled he was. Her gown slid to the floor. Her chemise was drawn over her head. Her hair tumbled about her shoulders. Every touch was a caress, as smooth and fluid as soft, lapping water that carried her on its current. Only his uneven breathing told her how fragile his control was.

He lifted her in his arms and carried her to the bed. His coat and neckcloth were discarded, his waistcoat unbuttoned. She wasn't sure if she had done that or if he had, though she had a vague memory of her fingers fumbling with buttons and tangling in folds of linen.

She fell back against the smooth damask coverlet. He bent and kissed her while his hands slid lower, disposing of drawers and slippers and stockings. His fingers tangled in the hair between her legs and slipped inside her, and then his mouth was where his hand had been.

She sucked in her breath. Ned had never done this to her. She hadn't known people *did* do it. Dear God in heaven. She clenched handfuls of the coverlet. There was a darker edge to the sweetness now. Barriers slammed up inside her, resisting, severing her mind from the needs of her body.

Frank raised his head and looked at her, his gaze questioning.

"I'm sorry." She turned her face into the crushed linen of the pillowcase. "I can't. . . . It was too much."

He lay down next to her and propped himself on one elbow. "Tell me what you want."

To find solace in the darkness of his embrace. To escape into the shell she had built for herself. But she knew that if she drew back now, he would never believe she trusted him. She swallowed. "I think I want you inside me."

He sucked in his breath. His gaze not leaving her face, he stood and stripped off the rest of his clothes. Then he lay down, not on her, but beside her. He touched her, with light, sure fingers, and lifted her over him and sheathed himself inside her.

She was trembling, but whether from passion or the effort to control it she couldn't have said. His hands were around her waist, but it was up to her whether to move or not. She did, with that powerful, terrible instinct she had tried so hard to deny. She forced herself not to retreat, not to pull back from the sensation. The slide of skin against skin, the feel of his body pulsing deep inside her own, the harsh mingled sound of their breathing. Tension built within her, a pulsing chord tuned higher than she could bear.

"Charlie." He pulled her head down to his for a kiss. "Let go."

His mouth was sweet. She wanted to give this to him, she did, but she couldn't. Darkness hovered too close. The only way to escape it was to retreat behind the barriers she had built to protect herself.

He reached between them and touched the spot he had found earlier with his lips. She sobbed once and the barriers gave way, and she was flooded not with darkness but with blinding light.

She lay with her head on Frank's chest and his arms wrapped around her. Their bodies were still joined, but that intimacy seemed scarcely less than the intimacy of their minds. She could not put a name to what she felt, save that something within her had been cut loose and set soaring.

She lifted her head and looked down at him. "Thank you."

He loosed one of his hands and pushed her sweat-dampened hair back from her face. "I would say the pleasure was mutual."

What could she say? *I gave myself to heal you, but I was the one who was healed.* Perhaps it didn't need to be said. Perhaps he understood. Perhaps she was not the only one who had been healed. Even in the shade of the canopy, she could see that the shadows were gone from around his eyes.

He smiled suddenly.

"What?" she asked.

His fingers brushed over her shoulder. "I've had a varied career in the bedchamber. And yet this is the first time I've bedded a woman I called wife."

She felt her eyes widen.

His face went serious. "Julia was already with child when we married. She wasn't well. And we scarcely knew each other. It would hardly have been appropriate—"

She smiled down at him. "I think you're wonderful, Frank."

He laughed and pulled her tight against him. "Deluded, Charlie, utterly deluded." His arms went suddenly taut around her. "We didn't talk about consequences. Do you—"

"Want children?" She lifted her head and smiled at him again. "I did once. And then I didn't, because they'd be Daniel's grandchildren. But now—they'd be ours, wouldn't they? Daniel need have nothing to do with it."

"Yes." His hands drifted through her hair. "Yes."

After that they were silent for a long interval. She listened to the beat of his heart beneath her ear and felt the solid warmth of his arms around her. She felt secure in a way she hadn't since her girlhood. It was a delusion, of course. Daniel was as much of a threat as ever. Tomorrow Frank would confront him and in doing so put at risk everything he had worked for. It was criminally unfair.

Something prickled at her memory. She lay in Frank's arms and sifted through her images of the past and began to feel a faint, unexpected flicker of hope. Was it possible . . . Perhaps. Just barely. She would talk to Sophie tomorrow. If anyone else remembered, Sophie would. She would say nothing to Frank as yet. There was no sense in getting his hopes up. It was, after all, the very remotest possibility.

"Charlotte?" Frank lifted his head and pressed a kiss against her forehead. "Do you want me to stay?"

Time enough to face Daniel and his retaliation tomorrow. Tonight was theirs. She threaded her hands through his own. "Yes."

Chapter 26

The air in the House of Commons chamber had its own smell, a pungent combination of cologne and shaving soap, ripe oranges, the heat of close-pressed bodies, and some undefinable excitement that crackled through the air like an electrical current. Strange, Frank thought, that he had never noticed it before. But then, tonight all his senses were keyed to a higher pitch, like a lover going to a last assignation with his mistress and committing the fragrance of her skin and the feel of her hair to memory.

Humphrey Grandison, who had a substantial investment in the proposed Lancaster and Liverpool Railway, was discoursing ponderously on the benefits of railways. Brougham shifted his position on the bench beside Frank. "You'd think he'll claim it can cure poverty and plague next."

Frank smiled. He hadn't told Brougham what he was about to do. He hadn't told anyone but the small circle who had been part of the plan to bring down Daniel de Ribard. They were all present, waiting to hear him speak. Charlotte had brought Serena as well, saying she deserved to understand.

Charlotte. He felt a deeper smile break across his face. He was lucky. Far luckier than he deserved. If he hadn't woken with her in his arms this morning, he wouldn't believe last night had been real.

Grandison finished speaking. Frank got to his feet and asked to be recognized by the Speaker. The Speaker acknowledged him. Frank let his gaze sweep the chamber he had come to know nearly as well as Vaughan House. It was his home in a way his father-in-law's house never could be.

"The honorable member has said that railways will change the face of England. In this I quite agree with him. Those who fear change"—he let his gaze drift over the government bench—"would do well to realize that steam and iron will remake our country beyond the dreams of the most radical revolutionary. But what sort of country will this new power forge? One where profit is the highest good? Where the mass of Englishmen—and women—and children toil in factories that care more for the product they produce than the humanity of those they employ? Where commerce becomes the new game of kings and the ultimate goal is the win at any price?

"I cannot speak for my colleagues, but this is not the world I want to bequeath to my daughter. Yet this is the world in which Daniel de Ribard operates. I have cause to know. I was once his secretary. I am now his son-in-law. I have seen him at work. I know that for Ribard no lengths are too great. Winning *is* the ultimate goal. How do I know this, you may ask? Because you could say I put him to the test."

He had their attention now. He cast a brief glance at where he knew Charlotte was sitting, then began to tell his story.

The corridor was thick with shouts. Charlotte tightened her arm around Serena. Some members of Parliament were flushed with excitment. Others were gray-faced. Mercifully, most did not seem to recognize her as Frank's wife or Daniel's daughter. One red-faced man lurched toward her, the smell of brandy on his breath, his eyes narrowed with fear. "See here, Mrs. Storbridge, what the devil are your father and husband playing at?"

Paul stepped in front of her. "My sister has not been on speaking terms with her father for some years. As for my brother-in-law, I think he made his motives very plain."

Paul would kill her for saying it, but he had inherited Daniel's ability to damp pretension. The red-faced man took himself off. Frank emerged from the crowd with the lightning agility that must have enabled him to shake off the masses clamoring about his speech.

Charlotte took his hands and reached up to kiss him full on the lips in front of all her family. "That was . . . splendid."

His hands tightened briefly on her shoulders. His mouth responded to the kiss more than any of the onlookers could have realized. "There's nothing like having good material to work with."

"It was a damned good speech. I wish I'd made it." Silverton joined them and slipped his arm through Céline's.

"Praise indeed." Frank smiled briefly at his former rival, then looked at Serena. "How much do you understand?"

"You did a good thing," Serena said.

"That's it in a nutshell," Sophie murmured.

Frank gripped Serena's shoulder for a moment, then looked back at Charlotte. "I need to speak to Brougham and some others—warn them of what's to come."

"You'll want to go to Brooks's. I thought as much. We'll be fine. We should get the children home."

"It's early," Serena said.

"Storbridge."

Talking among themselves in a shadowy corner of the

corridor, they hadn't seen the new arrival. Bertram. Stillness settled over the group. Bertram walked straight up to Frank. "I wanted to hear the speech. It was good. I—" He swallowed. He was looking at Frank, but Charlotte could tell that he was keenly aware of Paul and Silverton, who had brought him home last night, and Sophie, who—Charlotte now knew—had held a basin while he was thoroughly sick in the entrance hall. "Damn it," he said at last, "I'm not going to let a blackguard like Ribard manipulate me into thinking ill of my brother-in-law. If I helped at all, Storbridge, I'm proud to have done it."

Frank clasped Bertram's hand. "I'm glad to hear it. But don't go overboard again in your view of me, Bertram. There'll be a reaction."

The jostling around them grew greater. Frank took himself off to find Brougham. Céline and Silverton left. The remaining group grew silent. "We'll see the children home," Emma said, moving toward Caroline. She looked at Charlotte. "If you're still sure—"

Charlotte clasped her Limerick-gloved hands tightly together. "Yes."

"Sure of what?" said Bertram.

"What are you doing?" Serena asked at almost the same moment.

Charlotte squeezed Serena's shoulder. "You'll know soon enough." She flicked a brief glance at Sophie. "If it works."

The house loomed up in front of them, picked out by gaslight on the corner of Upper Brook Street. It looked just as she remembered it—pale, impenetrable, gray Portland stone, Doric columns, a fanlight that spilled a prism of yellow gold onto the portico.

Charlotte's footsteps faltered. Robert, who was walking beside her, touched her arm. She smiled at him. Sophie and Paul were just ahead of them. They had left the carriage two streets over, giving the Vaughan coachman strict instructions to await their return. There was no way to predict how long this would take.

A dark figure emerged from the shadows by the area railing and came to meet them. Adam. "Ribard went out two hours ago and hasn't come back. No one else has come or gone, except a footman who appeared to be enjoying his evening off."

"Good," Charlotte said.

Paul ran his gaze over the house. "We can't be sure how long he'll stay away."

Charlotte pulled her cloak more closely about her. The night was cloudy and there was a damp chill in the air. "I think he'll find himself rather busy tonight."

"How do you know?" her brother asked.

"I sent Ianthe de Cazes an anonymous note telling her Daniel is about to become betrothed to Annabel Howitt."

"Clever girl, Charlie."

"I learned from a master."

She turned to the house again. Funny how familiar the area railing looked. As children they'd played hide-and-seek behind the narrow iron spikes. She'd always thought they seemed like spears stuck in the ground as a defense. A singularly apt comparison now.

A breeze came up, tugging at cloaks and strands of hair, stirring the damp air. "I wish we could be sure this would work," Paul said.

"Oh, come, darling." Sophie grinned up at him, blue eyes glinting in the light of the lantern she carried. "That would take the fun out of it." She looked back at the house. "We should go around behind, by the mews. The back-parlor window can be pried open fairly easily."

"How do you know?" Paul asked.

"I slipped in and out of it more than once as a girl."

"Did you?" he said. "We must have a talk about this. When matters are a little less pressing."

The five of them turned the corner into Park Street and and made their way to the mews that ran in back of the houses. Charlotte had tread these dark cobblestones with Daniel on many mist-shrouded mornings, talking and laughing as they prepared for their morning ride. The mews had been repaved in the past five years. It used to be full of loose cobbles, so one had to be careful with the horses. A different street, a different time, a different girl. But her feelings were still there, for all they were scarred over by experience.

Paul unfastened the gate to the back garden. Charlotte led the way across the flagstones, through the shrubbery, past the herbaceous borders. The crude outlines of the garden looked the same, even in the moonlight and mist. Her favorite oak tree still stood by the garden wall. She allowed herself to spare it only the briefest glance.

"Robert?" Paul said, when they stood beneath the back-parlor window. "Can you open it?"

"Don't insult French Army Intelligence." Robert looked up at the window. "We may have lost the war, but it wasn't because we couldn't pick locks."

"If he can't do it, I can," Adam said. "In British Intelligence we always prided ourselves on our ability to be more underhanded than the French."

There was a scrape and a click, and the window slid open. Charlotte unclasped her cloak and gave it to Adam, pleased to find her fingers steady.

"Charlie—" Paul said.

"Don't quibble now, Paul."

"I was going to say, let Sophie go first. She's taller. She can help pull you through."

Thank God for sensible men. Charlotte and Sophie had

made it clear that they needed to be involved, and there had been no quibbling from the men. There was none now. Paul went into the house with them. Robert remained to keep watch in the garden. Adam went around to do the same at the front of the house. As Paul boosted her through the window, Charlotte wondered if Frank would be as sensible. She decided he would be.

Sophie helped her over the sill, and for the first time in five years she was in the house she had grown up in. One of the houses she had grown up in. In place of the shock of memory she was braced for, there was a strange emptiness. The smell, she realized. Her mother's ever-present hyacinth potpourri had always pervaded all their houses.

Sophie lifted the lantern from the window ledge where she had set it. The light fell on an expanse of white. The room was still in holland covers. Daniel must be camping out in a few rooms. No doubt he planned to put the house to rights when he married. Strange to think that Annabel Howitt, whom she had never met, might soon be mistress here.

Sophie touched her arm. There was no need to risk speech. They both knew the way. Out into the corridor, also in darkness, a single taper burning in a wall sconce, the baize door to the servants' quarters standing green and motionless. Down the corridor a dozen paces, through the gleaming mahogany door to the library.

Here the smell was the same. Ink, leather, a touch of citrus. Her father's domain and therefore hers as well.

Paul left the door ajar and remained by it to keep watch. Sophie looked at Charlotte. It was Charlotte's plan, after all. Not even a plan, really. A desperate gamble built on a half memory dredged up from the past. As a child—what had she been, seven, eight?—she had opened this same door, also at night, and slipped into the room in her nightdress looking for her father. There had been more than a single lantern to light the room then. Daniel had stood at the bookshelves, replacing a volume. He had given a start, which was unusual for her father, and then had looked down at her with a smile. "You never know what wonders are to be found in books, *chérie*," he had said.

"The *H*'s," Charlotte said.

"Yes." Sophie was holding up the lantern. "There are rather a lot of them."

Rows and rows. She'd forgotten how vast the room was. She thought for a moment. "Howitt's the sixth duke, isn't he?"

"The seventh." Sophie was already counting shelves. "Is that a ladder over there?"

There was not only a ladder, but a set of library steps. They moved both into place—thank God for the thick, muffling pile of the Axminster carpet—and set to work. Sophie held the lantern. Charlotte pulled the books out one at a time and examined them. *Herder. Herodotus. Robert Herrick.* There was a film of dust along the top of the books, though the gilded spines were clean. In some, the pages had not even been cut.

In the sixth book she found a folded paper. Her pulse quickened. Sophie drew in her breath and lifted the lantern higher. Charlotte spread open the paper. It was a bill from Stultz for three evening coats.

"Courage," Sophie murmured. "We've barely begun."

They worked on. They had to get down and move the ladder and the steps. They found another bill, from Daniel's haberdasher, and a brief, inconsequential note in her own handwriting, folded as a bookmarker. Paul soundlessly shifted his position by the door. An ominous creak made them all freeze for a nerve-jangling half minute. It proved to be only the sighing of the wind.

Charlotte reached for yet another book. Horace, the

Satires. Examining each volume had become rote by now. But this book felt different. Stiffer. Heavier. She opened the red and gold pasteboard cover, and the breath stopped in her throat.

The inside of the pages had been cut neatly away. In the empty space a smaller, plainer book had been placed.

The lantern swayed in Sophie's hand. She steadied it. Charlotte lifted the smaller book from its hiding place. The cover and spine were unadorned. The flyleaf contained merely a year: 1820. She turned it over and found herself staring at a series of dates and jottings. A journal. She had put a note in Howitt's hand in her pocket, but she didn't need to fish it out to recognize the neat, precise script.

"Don't fall off the ladder." Sophie gripped her shoulder. "We'd better look at it at home."

Charlotte nodded. Paul was watching them, wonder in his eyes. Charlotte permitted herself a smile of pure triumph, but it was folly to speak more than necessary. Fingers trembling, she put the journal in her pocket and returned the hollowed-out copy of the *Satires* to its place on the shelf.

They climbed down and returned the ladder and steps to their original positions. They were about to move to the door when Charlotte saw Paul go taut. She glanced at Sophie, and then she heard it too. Footsteps in the corridor. Approaching footsteps.

Sophie flung her skirt over the lantern. The room was plunged into darkness, the heavy drapes shutting out even the cloud-shrouded moon. The footsteps drew closer, then stopped. The door creaked, letting in an oblong of candlelight. The candle went out. There was a faint, swift stir, and a muffled *thud*.

"He's unconscious," Paul said softly. "I don't think it's Ribard, more's the pity. Bring the lantern, Sophie."

Sophie pulled the still-lit lantern from the folds of her skirt. Paul was lowering a man in green-and-black Ribard livery to the floor. What her brother could accomplish with one good hand, Charlotte thought, was truly amazing.

Sophie walked over to her husband. "You've gotten better at this. He's not permanently damaged?"

"No, but he'll stay unconscious long enough for us to get away. Let's go."

"He seems to be inordinately concerned with the weather." Charlotte peered at Howitt's diary in the light of the lamp on the library table. "*Twenty-third January. Fair night. C. S.* What do you suppose *C. S.* means?"

"I don't know, but I don't think *fair night* has anything to do with the weather." Sophie looked over Charlotte's shoulder. "Harry Palmerston keeps a similar sort of journal. Emily Cowper told me about it. Men do pick the most childish codes to record their amorous adventures."

Charlotte looked up at her cousin. *"Howitt?"*

"All the more reason for him to use a code. No one would be surprised to learn Palmerston had bedded half the women in London, but the sober Duke of Howitt? Now, there's a revelation."

"That would explain his desire to keep it secret," Caroline said from the sofa. She and Emma had joined them when they returned to Vaughan House. "Quite a fall for Howitt the Virtuous."

"And to think there's never been a whiff of scandal about him. He must have found partners who were *very* discreet." Sophie turned the page. "From the look of it, he's been as active as my first husband. Good heavens, could *E. C.* be Emily Cowper? I thought she was more discriminating. I wonder who *C. S.* is?"

"Sophie," Paul said.

"Sorry, love, it takes me back to the days when I lived for gossip. It's a pity Céline isn't here. She'd appreciate it. That is—" Sophie's face went still, as though a disconcerting thought had just occurred to her.

"No." Charlotte met her cousin's gaze. "I can't speak for Emily Cowper, but Céline *is* more discriminating."

"But would it be enough?" Emma was at the sideboard, pouring sherry for everyone. "For Ribard to have such a hold on him? Embarrassing, yes, but other men—"

"Other men don't have Howitt's spotless reputation," Robert said. "It's one thing to be thought a reprobate, but a hypocrite? He'd be a laughingstock all over the city."

"And there's a difference between being gossiped about and having all one's peccadillos written down in black ink." Caroline adjusted her rose-colored gauze scarf. "Some of the husbands may not be as complacent as Lord Cowper."

Adam moved to sit beside his wife. "We met Howitt once at a party at the embassy, remember? He struck me as the sort who couldn't bear humiliation."

"He was certainly industrious." Sophie was flipping through the journal. "Here it says *Fair night—two*. Which must mean—"

"Yes," said Paul. He turned to lean against the table, arms folded across his chest. "You're not worried you'll find your own name in there, are you?"

"Darling." Sophie opened her eyes very wide. "I'd remember. Besides, I was in Edinburgh in 1820."

Charlotte smiled at this byplay, then looked back at the diary. She wondered what Frank would make of the revelations about his onetime friend and how he would choose to proceed. The diary would give him a powerful hold over Howitt. He could turn the game to his own advantage, if he chose to play by Daniel's rules.

A few moments later the door opened, and Frank

stepped into the room. His face was drawn, but he greeted them with a smile. "I'm glad you're all here. Emma, I hope one of those sherries is for me. I could use it."

Emma carried a glass over to him. "You're a fortunate man, Frank. You have a very clever wife."

"I already knew that." Frank's eyes narrowed. He looked at Charlotte. "Charlie?"

Charlotte went to him and took his arm. "We've had rather a busy night ourselves." She looked up into the face she had learned could show such tenderness. "It looks as if you may not have to resign your seat after all, darling. Sit down and we'll tell you."

Chapter 27

"Francis." The Duke of Howitt rose from behind his desk and came forward as the footman showed Frank and Charlotte into the room. Howitt's pale, sharp-boned face showed inbred good manners, faintly masking distaste. He bowed in Charlotte's direction. "Mrs. Storbridge. I don't believe we have met."

Charlotte looked at her husband's erstwhile friend and patron—the pinched face, the dark, hunted eyes. She had come prepared to dislike him, but he was too pathetic for hatred. "We have, actually. At a rout at Lady Sefton's. My cousin Sophie brought me. You and Lady Marianne had not been long married."

"Ah." Howitt gave a strained, automatic smile. "You must forgive me. And allow me to offer you my felicitations."

"I scarcely think the situation calls for felicitations, your grace. Perhaps it will simplify matters if I say that my husband and I have no secrets from each other."

"I see." Howitt's face hardened. His uneasy gaze shifted from Charlotte to Frank. "I don't know why you've come, Storbridge. I'm sorry about this, but you've left me with no choice."

"So you say." Frank regarded Howitt, his face courteous,

his gaze ice-cold. "I've asked Ribard to join us here. I've something to say to you both."

Howitt's eyes widened in a moment of stark fear. Then he drew a breath and recovered his composure, years of ducal training reasserting themselves. "As you wish. Mrs. Storbridge, won't you sit down?" He gestured toward a bronze green settee by the fireplace. "May I ring for tea?"

"No, thank you." Charlotte seated herself, settling the chocolate velvet skirt of her pelisse with care. Frank sat beside her. Howitt returned to his desk. After an interval that could have been only a few minutes but felt interminable, the footman returned to announce the Marquis de Ribard.

Daniel strolled into the room and surveyed the three of them with polite interest. "Charlie. Howitt. Storbridge. I hope whatever you have planned will be entertaining."

"Illuminating at least." Frank got to his feet and walked toward the desk. He reached into his pocket, pulled out Howitt's diary, and threw it down on the desktop.

Daniel stared down at the journal, his expression unreadable. Howitt's pale face drained of color. Charlotte thought it was only due to all those years of ducal training that he did not give way completely. When he spoke, his voice was a dry, cracked whisper. "You've read it?"

"Enough. Christ, William." Frank leaned forward, gripping the desk. "What the hell made you think covering up your pathetic little peccadillos justified giving free rein to a man like Ribard?" He glanced at Daniel, then looked back at Howitt. "Letting him marry your sister, for the love of God."

Howitt swallowed. A pulse beat in his throat like a trapped bird hammering against a windowpane. He pushed himself to his feet. "You don't understand."

"No. I don't. Was it so important to you to appear more

moral than the rest of us that you had to sink to a depth even lower?"

For a moment the ducal veneer was stripped away, revealing the angry terror of a man who knows himself to be cornered. Charlotte thought he was going to strike Frank. She thought Frank might have welcomed the fight.

Daniel folded his arms over his chest and watched the other two men as though he was a disinterested observer.

"You must be very gratified," Howitt said to Frank in a voice so controlled it crackled. "You now have the power to persuade me to do whatever you wish."

"I'm not going to play the game that way."

Howitt stared at him. "Why not?"

"If you don't know that, you know me no better than I knew you." Frank pushed the diary across the desk. "You're free. Unless Ribard has other diaries?"

"No," Daniel said from the sidelines. "Only the one."

Howitt's hand went out as though to snatch the diary up, then fell to his side.

"Keep it," Frank said. "Burn it if you have any sense. Ask me to resign if you must. But for God's sake, stop Ribard's marriage to Annabel."

"Just a minute." Daniel moved toward the desk, where the other two men faced each other. The light from the windows fell slantwise across his face, making his expression even more difficult to read than usual. "My compliments, Storbridge. You took me by surprise when you made the speech. I can't decide whether you're very clever or a great fool."

"You misjudged me, Ribard." Frank turned from Howitt to look straight at Daniel. "You thought my ultimate stake was my seat in Parliament. But it wasn't. It was Charlotte."

The two men regarded each other in silence for a long moment. Dust motes danced in the expanse of air between them. "Yes," Daniel said. "I wonder now that I didn't see it. And yet in the end you didn't risk your seat in Parliament, did you?" He looked over his shoulder at Charlotte. "How the devil did you find the diary?"

"Who says I found it?" Charlotte gave him her blankest stare.

"It must have been you, Charlie. Even so, I'm not sure how you did it. Did Lescaut and Durward help you break into the house? I always thought it would be useful to have a couple of spies in my employ."

"I thought you did," Charlotte said.

"Perhaps. But not of their caliber."

"Howitt has the diary back." Frank's gaze flickered to where the diary lay on the polished oak desk. "It's over."

"Half true." Daniel, too, looked at the diary, but he made no move to reach for it. "Howitt has the diary back. But I wouldn't say it's over."

The words settled like a lead weight in Charlotte's brain. She pressed her hands together over her stomach. "Out with it, Daniel. You have another card to play. Play it, damn you."

"Don't lose your temper, Charlie, it can be fatal." Daniel continued to look at the diary. "Surely it occurred to you that the revelation of a few liaisons, even by a man as supposedly upright as Howitt, would hardly be enough to persuade him to turn on his friend. Or did you rate the duke's moral fiber so low?"

Frank looked at Howitt, who had gone absolutely still, then back at Daniel. "Once I knew Howitt had fallen in with your schemes, I didn't know what to make of his moral fiber."

Daniel straightened his flawless cravat. "Don't you want to say something, Howitt? Don't you want to assure your friend that it took something far more serious than the exposure of your love affairs to turn you against him?"

Howitt looked as though he were physically ill. He was gripping the edge of the desk, his fingers white. Charlotte thought that if he let go he'd collapse.

"You don't want to say it?" Daniel shrugged. "I understand your reticence. It's a great secret, of course, or I'd never have taken the precaution of removing the page from your journal."

Howitt made a strangled sound deep in his throat. Daniel drew a single sheet of paper with a jagged, torn edge out from beneath his coat. "But Storbridge isn't the sort to challenge you to a duel, you know. However great the provocation."

Charlotte saw Frank go absolutely still. "Oh, dear God," he said, in a voice so racked by disgust and rage that she scarcely recognized it.

She looked at him, not understanding.

Frank and Daniel continued to look at each other. "It's considered incest, isn't it," Daniel said, his voice soft. "Sleeping with your wife's sister."

Julia. Juliet. Howitt was Juliet's father. For a moment Charlotte thought she was going to be sick. Frank's face was drained of any emotion.

"God damn you." It wasn't Frank who spoke; it was Howitt. He lunged around the side of the desk and grabbed Daniel by the throat.

The breath whistled from Daniel's lungs. He grabbed at Howitt's arms. Howitt's grip tightened. Frank grasped Howitt from behind. "Stop it, William. That's no answer."

Frank hauled Howitt away from Daniel. Howitt struggled against Frank's hold and sent them both crashing into the desk. A chased-silver inkpot overturned, leaving a dark trail on the carpet. A crystal paperweight shattered against the leg of the desk. The heavy mass of the Howitt seal crashed to the floor amid the sparkling shards.

There was a ripping sound as a seam gave way in someone's coat. Frank's arms closed around Howitt, pinning him. Howitt stared at Daniel, hair falling lank over his forehead, face twisted with rage.

"It's all right." Daniel was breathing hard, but his voice sounded soothing, faintly amused, an indulgent father smoothing over a minor peccadillo. "I won't make the secret public in revenge. That would be a shocking waste of good information. Storbridge will withdraw the accusations he made against me—quite brilliantly, I might add—in the House. He forged my name on that paper we all signed. His little band of friends can attest to it. In recompense, he and Silverton will put their support behind the Lancaster and Liverpool Railway. If we can't get it through in this parliamentary session, we will in the next. By that time I shall be the Duke of Howitt's brother-in-law. I hope you will all be at the wedding to wish us well."

"No." Frank's voice echoed through the room like a fist slamming down on a marble table.

Daniel lifted his brows. "You won't come to the wedding? It's your own affair, but I warn you it will be the social event of the season."

"I won't withdraw the accusations," Frank said, voice and gaze steady. "The story stands."

"What?" Howitt wrenched himself out of Frank's hold and stared at him. "Francis, you can't—"

"*I* can't?" Frank looked at Julia's sister's husband. "She was eighteen years old, William."

Howitt's gaze slid to the side. "You're a fine one to preach morality."

"Perhaps." Frank looked as though he might have hit Howitt if he wasn't so disgusted. "It's done. Juliet is what matters now."

"Exactly." Howitt smoothed his hair back from his forehead. "You see why I had to do what Ribard asked. Why we both have to go along with him now."

"No. I see why we can't."

"Don't be hasty, Storbridge." Daniel's voice hardened. "I said I wouldn't use the story of your wife's affair with Howitt in revenge. I didn't say I wouldn't use it. If you cross me now, I most certainly will."

"Then do so."

The clouds must have stirred outside, because the light shifted across Daniel's face. His eyes narrowed. "Is that what you want? Lady Julia's memory tarnished, your wards distressed, young Lord Vaughan challenging Howitt to swords or pistols at dawn?" He paused a moment. "Your daughter branded a bastard."

Frank glanced at Charlotte, then looked deliberately back at Daniel. "I want my daughter to have a father she can be proud of."

For some reason those words made an impact in Daniel's eyes. He was still looking at Frank, but Charlotte could feel his attention shift to her. Silence fell over the room, echoing with the past, the present, the threat of the future.

Charlotte got to her feet. "Daniel—"

She wasn't sure what she intended. A plea, a reproach, an attempt to reach some remnant of the man she thought he had been. She had no real faith that it would work, but she had to try.

Daniel looked at her. His eyes were dark and steady. She couldn't read their expression. "Don't," she said.

"Don't what?" Daniel said in a soft voice.

"Don't do this. It won't gain you anything. Frank won't give in, no matter what."

Daniel lifted his brows. "So I should do so instead, *ma chère*?"

"If you don't, you'll inflict damage to no purpose. You'll hurt a little girl I've come to think of as my own daughter. You'll hurt me. You'll hurt my husband."

Daniel stared straight into her eyes. "The man who forced you to marry him."

Charlotte looked at Frank. His face was still and set with tension. She turned her gaze back to Daniel. "The man I love, *Papa*."

There was a sudden flare in Frank's eyes. Daniel's face was expressionless. Howitt stood to the side, forgotten and irrelevant. She and Frank and Daniel were isolated in a contest of wills. Yet she had the strange feeling that whatever the outcome, she and Frank had already won.

Daniel walked toward her and stopped, less than an arm's length away. "I'm probably a fool," he said. "I shall undoubtedly regret this. But it won't be the greatest regret in my life."

He looked into her eyes for a long moment, as though searching for something he had lost. Then he held out the page torn from the diary. "I don't believe you cared much for my wedding present, *chérie*. Perhaps this will be more to your taste."

Charlotte sat with her face turned toward the carriage window. Her profile was outlined against the green silk that lined the carriage, pale and set and unreadable. Frank reached for her hand and held it tightly in his own.

She turned her head and smiled at him. There was some sort of net veiling bunched around the brim of her bonnet, which made it difficult to read her expression. "I didn't think it would work," she said.

He lifted her hand and carried it to his lips. "Greed isn't Ribard's ultimate weakness after all. You are."

She shook her head, stirring the chocolate velvet ribbons on her bonnet. "I daresay he's calling himself seven kinds of fool right now. But for a moment something I said got through to him."

Frank watched her. He knew just how dangerous it could be to make too much of the words she had spoken in Howitt's study. Charlotte was his wife. For better or worse. They had built something on a foundation of lies and deceit, something he believed would last. And yet he knew he had no real right to her. He hadn't won her; he had taken her, using the same tricks her father employed. He would never know now if she would ever have come to him of her own free will. He wondered if that was Daniel de Ribard's last curse. "You knew just the right words to bring him round," he said at last.

She looked into his eyes. Despite the shadows cast by her bonnet, her own gaze was clear and candid. "I didn't say what I said to win Daniel over. I said it because it's true."

He stared back at her, afraid to breathe because that might break the spell of the moment.

"I love you," Charlotte said. "Surely you know that by now. And I think"—she hesitated, searching his face—"I think perhaps you love me. I've tried for weeks to understand why you've done the things you've done, and that's the only explanation that makes sense of it all." She drew a breath. Her hand trembled in his own. "Or have I got it wrong? If so you'd best say so at once, before I make a complete fool of myself."

Air and happiness and disbelief rushed into his lungs. His hand closed tight around her own. It occurred to him that he was staring at her like an idiot. He released her hand and pulled her into his arms with a woeful lack of finesse. Her net and velvet bonnet thudded to the seat behind them. Her laughter washed over him in a sweet, cleansing torrent. He breathed in her nearness and covered her mouth with his own. Her kiss was warm and urgent. He sank his fingers into her hair and pulled her closer.

"How could you get it wrong, Charlie," he said, his lips against her cheek. "You know perfectly well you always get the last word."

Chapter 28

Céline spread the pages of the *Morning Chronicle* out on her beribboned silk lap. *"The Marquis de Ribard and Henry Sunderland have abandoned plans for a railway from Lancaster to Liverpool for the present. Investors in the proposed railway will be compensated through Hawkins's Bank, in which the marquis owns a controlling share. Mr. Sunderland and his wife departed for Paris yesterday, accompanied by Mr. Sunderland's sister, the* Condesa *de Cazes."*

"Poor Ianthe." Frank settled back on the drawing-room sofa, his arm tight around Charlotte. "She's so desperate to be out of London she'll actually travel with her brother."

Céline looked up from the paper. "You'll forgive me if I find it difficult to feel a great deal of sympathy for Madame de Cazes, Francis."

"Oh, I don't know." Charlotte reached up and gripped Frank's hand where it lay on her shoulder. It was over a week since that first night they had spent together, and she still found it difficult *not* to touch him, even when they were surrounded by their friends and family. "How can one not feel sorry for a woman who was foolish enough to let Frank *and* Silver slip through her fingers?"

"Charlie!" Céline twined her arm through Silverton's. "You're beginning to sound like me."

Charlotte smiled at her sister. Silverton flushed like a schoolboy. Frank's fingers moved against Charlotte's neck in a way that was as pleasant as it was disturbing.

The others politely pretended to be deaf and blind to this byplay between the two couples. The drawing room was bright with laughter and firelight, the strains of Mozart, and children's voices. Adam, once more young and slender and clean-shaven, was at the piano playing a duet with Emma. Serena, Kirsty, Emily, and Lydia were helping the younger children build a block castle, impeded by Millamant and Knightly, who were wrestling on the hearthrug. The rest of the company were disposed about the fireplace.

Paul looked up from trying to put a dislodged wheel back on a toy carriage. "Does the paper say anything about where Ribard is?"

Céline glanced at the newspaper again. "No."

"Probably because no one knows." Sophie handed Paul a bolt. "Typical Uncle Daniel."

Bertram scowled at his tasseled Hessians. He was still brooding, Charlotte knew, because the whole affair had ended without giving him the chance to fight anyone. "Do you really think Ribard will just go away and leave us all alone?"

"That depends on what you mean by *alone*." Frank's arm hardened around Charlotte in a way that belied his cool voice. "Ribard's not going to disappear. But he's conceded this particular game. I won't swear he won't cross swords with any of us again. But I don't think he'll actively try to manipulate his children."

Charlotte looked from Céline to Paul. "And if he does, we won't let him."

Céline frowned. "It does seem terribly inconclusive."

Paul gave her the smile he reserved for those closest to him. "There'll always be men like Ribard. The trick is not giving way to them."

"And if he tries something like he did with the Foreign Secretary again?" Bertram said.

"We'll stop him," Frank said. "Again."

"Here's something more." Céline was flipping through the paper. *"The Duke and Duchess of Howitt, their children, and Lady Annabel Howitt have left London for the Howitt seat in Suffolk. They are not expected to return to London for some months."*

"Have you heard from Howitt?" Robert asked Frank.

Frank nodded. "I had a letter this morning, very formal, on crested paper. He assured me of his continued support as long as I wish to remain the member for Howitt. He didn't add that he hoped we would meet as little as possible in the future, but I caught the undercurrent."

There was a bitter edge to Frank's voice, but Charlotte thought she was the only one who heard it. No one else knew the full extent of the revelations that had been made in the duke's study. She glanced at the hearthrug, where Juliet was flopped on her stomach, giggling gleefully with Gerry. Charlotte's throat constricted with fear and love. She hoped Juliet would never learn the truth about her parentage. But if she did, Charlotte and Frank would be there to help her come to terms with it. Juliet would never doubt she was loved.

Silverton grinned at Frank. "So we'll still be facing each other across the Chamber. I expect you'll go on making my life hell, but I rather think I would have missed you."

Diana, who was sitting beside Céline and Silverton, looked down at the newspaper. "This whole thing must be beastly for Marianne. Not to mention Annabel." She looked up at her brother, a sudden smile playing about her lips. "Perhaps you ought to come to her rescue and marry her after all, Ber."

Bertram's eyes went wide with horror. "Don't you dare, Di."

"Why not?" The old playfulness was back in Diana's eyes. "You've been itching to make a chivalrous sacrifice for weeks. Marrying Annabel would be much more constructive than fighting a duel."

Serena ran up in the midst of the laughter that followed. "Who's Bertram going to marry?"

"No one," her brother told her, flashing a warning look at Diana.

"Oh." Serena straightened her crumpled blue sash. "Well, I daresay that's good news for whatever girl might have been involved." She looked around at the other adults. "Is the carriage fixed? We're building a bridge."

Paul handed her the mended carriage. Adam and Emma launched into a new song and called for singers. The company broke apart into smaller groups. Paul joined Charlotte and Frank by the fireplace. He had been smiling a few minutes before when he gave Serena the carriage, but now his face had turned serious. He gave Frank one of his level, challenging looks. "We were going to have a talk when all this was over, Storbridge. About your marriage to my sister."

"Yes." Frank returned Paul's stare. Charlotte felt him go still beside her.

Paul glanced at Charlotte, then back at Frank. A slow smile crossed his face. "Oddly enough, I don't think we need to anymore." He clapped Frank on the shoulder, grinned at Charlotte, and moved off toward the piano.

Frank followed him with his gaze. "Have I mentioned what a very magnanimous man your brother is, Charlie?"

Charlotte glanced at Paul, now standing with his arm around Sophie, then back at her husband. "Paul knows

I'm happy." She moved closer within the shelter of his arm. "Frank?"

"Yes?"

"Something odd occurred to me while Céline was reading from the paper. I don't understand Daniel. I expect I never will. But I am grateful to him for one thing."

"What?" Frank said.

She turned so she could press a kiss against his neck without being seen by the others in the room. "He brought me to you."

Historical Note

Railways were in their infancy in 1822. Plans for the Stockton and Darlington Railway—which, like Daniel de Ribard's proposed Lancaster and Liverpool Railway, was in northern industrial England and transported goods, not passengers—go back to 1818. George Stephenson, the first engineer to the Stockton and Darlington, did develop a new type of rail, of the sort manufactured by Frank's factory. Stephenson was based in Northumberland (Maurice W. Kirby, *The Origins of Railway Enterprise: The Stockton and Darlington Railway, 1821–1863*. Cambridge: Cambridge University Press, 1993).

Henry Brougham was actively involved with the emancipation movement. I have anticipated history somewhat by having Frank make his emancipation motion in February of 1823. The first parliamentary debate on the abolition of slavery actually took place on May 15th of that year. The motion was made by Thomas Fowell Buxton and was somewhat less sweeping than what Frank proposes. Canning replied on behalf of the government. Brougham also spoke in the debate. In the end, a watered-down compromise was passed, just as Frank predicts.

Also in 1823, Brougham and Canning had an argument in the House of Commons that very nearly resulted in them both being ejected. I have used this argument and its resolution as the model for Frank and Silverton's altercation. The subject of Brougham and Canning's argument was Catholic Emancipation, not emancipation of slaves, but Canning did accuse Brougham of "truckling" and Brougham took great umbrage at the word and flung it back at Canning. Later, they both laughed over the incident (Chester W. New, *The Life of Henry Brougham to 1830*. Oxford: The Clarendon Press, 1961).

Lord Castlereagh (who officially became the Marquis of Londonderry in 1821) committed suicide in August of 1822, apparently because of a mental breakdown. There were stories that he claimed he was being blackmailed over an alleged affair with another man. Whether the blackmail was real or a paranoid delusion of Castlereagh's is unclear. All evidence indicates that no such affair actually occurred. If Castlereagh was in fact being blackmailed, no one is quite clear as to the blackmailer's motives. (C. J. Bartlett, *Castlereagh*. New York: Charles Scribner's Sons, 1966.)

Lord Palmerston kept a journal recording his amorous exploits, very similar to the one I have used for the Duke of Howitt (Kenneth Bourne, *Palmerston: The Early Years 1784–1841*. New York: Macmillan Publishing Co., Inc., 1982). But Palmerston, who was quite open about his liaisons, presumably would not have fallen victim to blackmail, even if his journal had found its way into Daniel de Ribard's hands.